WILD DESIRE

"I'm learning not to be afraid of the things I want," Aimee said, looking into Zack's eyes.

"Good," Zack said softly and moved closer. Taking her hand, he pulled her against him. "Have you learned yet what it is you want?"

"I—I think so," she replied. He kissed her softly, sweetly. His hands slid over her shoulders and around her waist, pulling her tighter so her body molded against his.

"Tell me what you want," Zack whispered against her mouth. With a soft moan her small hands moved across his shoulders and clasped behind his neck. She was whirling, riding a crest that lifted her feet from the ground. She clung to him as his hands roamed her body. Wantonly, innocently, she moved against him, seeking only to still the aching need he'd aroused. . . .

GOLDEN PROMISES

GOLDEN PROMISES

Peggy Hanchar

AN ONYX BOOK

NEW AMERICAN LIBRARY

PUBLISHER'S NOTE

This book is a work of fiction. Names, characters, places, and incidents either are the product of the author's imagination or are used fictitiously, and any resemblance to actual persons, living or dead, events, or locales is entirely coincidental.

NAL BOOKS ARE AVAILABLE AT QUANTITY DISCOUNTS WHEN USED TO PROMOTE PRODUCTS OR SERVICES. FOR INFORMATION PLEASE WRITE TO PREMIUM MARKETING DIVISION, NEW AMERICAN LIBRARY, 1633 BROADWAY, NEW YORK, NEW YORK 10019.

 Onyx is a trademark of New American Library.

SIGNET, SIGNET CLASSIC, MENTOR, ONYX, PLUME, MERIDIAN and NAL BOOKS are published by NAL PENGUIN INC., 1633 Broadway, New York, New York 10019

First Printing, May, 1988

1 2 3 4 5 6 7 8 9

PRINTED IN THE UNITED STATES OF AMERICA

1

"Papa!"

The scream reverberated through the big, elegant house, echoing through hallways, careening through arches, invading quiet corners in closed rooms. The huge oak doors were no barrier for the wild cry.

An unnatural quiet followed. Everyday sounds and motions ceased, startled into stillness by the unexpected premonition that something was wrong, suspended as if waiting for a heartbeat to begin again and the taint of tragedy to pass them by.

"Papa?" She stood on the stairs, her alarmed gaze going to the double doors that led from the great hall into her father's study. "Papa?" she whimpered, and took a tentative step down the stairs. Only moments before, the study doors had closed, shutting him away from her. Hurt by his rejection, she'd crept up the stairs, only to be caught here midway, her steps faltering, her breath catching in her chest at the shattering sound of a single gunshot and the ominous silence that followed. Now sound and motion returned. Sam and Hattie came to the door of the parlor.

"What was that?" Hattie asked, her dark eyes darting from side to side. The two old servants looked at the girl on the stairs and saw the crumbling composure of her face. Wordlessly they watched the slow, tottering steps, the white hands grasping the banister, and they moved forward as if of one accord. One went to stand at the bottom of the stairs, her plump arms

5

already outstretched protectively toward the slight figure; the other went to the study doors to tend the only master he'd ever known in his life.

"Why, Miss Aimee, honey, yo' all right?" Hattie's voice was low and soothing; only her dark eyes gave away her agitation. Wide-eyed, the girl descended the stairs and halted near the black woman, but she made no word of greeting.

"Papa," she whispered brokenly.

"Oh, Lawd have mercy." Sam's cry came to them. "Mastah Hiram!" His old voice broke and then he was scuttling out of the study, his eyes rolling, his dark face shiny with perspiration. He said nothing to the two women crouched at the foot of the stairs, but half-stumbled, half-ran across the wide hall and out the front door.

"Mastah Bonham," he cried, running down the street.

"What's wrong with Papa?" Aimee screamed and now she was pushing against the massive bulk of the old woman, striving to break past her and get to the too-quiet figure that rested beyond the study doors.

"Naw, chile, naw," Hattie said as she held on to her ward's shoulders. She'd been nanny to this girl for seventeen years and the need to shield her from pain was strong within her. "Yo' cain't go in theah, chile," she whispered. "Yo'r papa's had an accident."

"An accident!" Aimee repeated, her wide gray eyes studying Hattie's for reassurance. "Is he hurt? Papa, Papa, it's me, Aimee. I'm here, Papa. I'm coming."

"Naw, Miss Aimee, yo' come with me." In spite of her years and bulk, the old woman hung on to the girl, pulling her across the hall toward the parlor.

"I want to see Papa. He's hurt; he needs me." Aimee struggled in Hattie's arms, but to no avail. She could hear the slap of leather boots on the front porch; then the door was pushed open and Carl Bonham, their neighbor and the town mayor, entered.

"Aimee, Hattie," he said, looking around. "Sam said . . ."

"In theah, suh. In the study," Hattie said, and continued to pat the slender back of the grief-stricken girl. Aimee's head had buried against the familiar old shoulder, her sobs muffled against Hattie's neck.

Carl Bonham turned toward the study. He knew his way well. Oftentimes he'd stopped by to have a drink with the banker and discuss some new town project. They'd been friends for nearly ten years.

Carl Bonham approached the figure slumped over the desk, his eyes taking in absurd details. Hiram had a bald spot, he noted in surprise, his mind grasping at inconsequentials. One hand dangled helplessly toward the floor; the other lay limp and lifeless on the desk, one finger still caught against the trigger of a small handgun.

"God Almighty," the mayor whispered. He looked at the dead face of his friend and colleague, gazed into the unseeing eyes, noted the smear of blood and matter across the cheek and temple, and turned away, leaning forward to retch into his handkerchief. When he'd recovered he went back into the hall and stood looking at the sobbing girl and the subdued servants. Squaring his shoulders in an unconscious gesture of authority, he took a deep breath.

"Sam, go get Doc Allen," he ordered, "and stop at the bank and tell Jack Martin and Charlie Wheeler to get up here double quick."

"Yas, suh," Sam said backing toward the door.

"And, Sam"—the mayor's voice halted his flight—"don't say anything about this to anyone, you hear me?"

"No, suh, I won't," Sam said, and hurried away. What did the man think he'd do, Sam thought resentfully, go gossiping about poor Master Hiram? Didn't he think Sam had any loyalty?

"Uncle Carl . . ." Aimee wiped at her face and gulped back her sobs. "Is my papa going to be all right? Is he hurt badly?"

"My dear, I'm sorry to tell you this . . ." The mayor paused.

"He's going to be all right, isn't he?" Aimee asked, her gray eyes luminous from the tears she'd shed.

Carl Bonham sighed. Why did Sam have to call on him first?

"Your father's dead, Aimee," he said reluctantly.

"No." Aimee's cry echoed around the hall once more, the pain in her eyes too devastating for the mayor to contemplate, so he turned away. Once again Hattie held the trembling figure, listening to the hoarse sobs.

"Mastah Hiram, why yo' do dis to yo'r chile?" Hattie asked quietly.

The mayor was wondering the same thing. Why the devil had Hiram killed himself? True, he hadn't been himself lately, growing moody and silent, when he was normally an exuberant, outgoing man. You could nearly always depend on him for a good story, a laugh, a slap on the back. Not that he was a flighty man. He held one of the most responsible positions in town, that of town banker, and a better one couldn't be found.

Hiram had pulled the bank out of the dangerous slump caused by the recession back in 1837. Now it was 1848 and times were good for the bank and for the town, thanks to Hiram. He'd been a highly respected man whose worst offense was in being too generous. But the banker had also been a wealthy man and could afford to be generous with his friends.

Shaking his head, the mayor looked about the elegantly appointed house. Hiram had built it a scant nine years before, shortly after he'd come to Webster with his tiny daughter. He'd chosen the site on the south end of town away from the saloons and stables. So impressive was the mansion that other town luminaries had rushed to build beside him.

The house reflected the power and wealth of its owner. The wide hall divided the front of the house, with the parlor and dining room on one side and the study and ladies' morning room on the other. The kitchen and servants' quarters were at the back. Curving stairs, the pecan banister gleaming richly, led upward to large, airy bedrooms for the banker, his family, and special guests. Marble fireplaces and crystal chandeliers graced nearly every room except the kitchen and servants' quarters. The mayor had often fancied the house for himself, although he'd never told Hiram that.

Through the parlor door, the mayor caught a glimpse of plush velvet-covered sofas and thick hand-woven rugs imported from Brussels. A finely wrought French curio cabinet stood in one corner with fine hand-crafted porcelains showing through the glass doors. Hiram Bennett had loved beautiful things and had surrounded himself with them, indulging himself in the best that a man of his position could buy.

It seemed only fitting that his daughter had been beautiful as well. She was a rare jewel, polished to fit the beautiful setting. She'd been educated at the finest girls' school. Her wardrobe, ordered from Paris, had set envious tongues wagging for weeks.

Fortune had seemed to smile on Hiram Bennett in every way. Why, then, had he taken his life like this, leaving his daughter crumpled in a heap on the velvet sofa, her exquisite face distorted by grief? The mayor shook his head and turned away.

Doc Allen arrived and Carl led him to the study. Charlie Wheeler and Jack Martin entered; the urgency they'd sensed was plain on their faces and in the quickness of their breath. Carl Bonham met them in the hallway.

"What is it, Carl? We hurried right over. From the way Sam acted, it looked serious."

"It is," the mayor said. "Gentlemen, I'm afraid there's been an . . . uh . . . accident. Hiram Bennett is dead."

"He can't be. I just talked to him a little bit ago over at the bank," Jack Martin exclaimed.

"Nevertheless, he is. Doc Allen is with him now."

"What happened?" Charlie Wheeler asked.

"Here's Doc now. I'll let him tell you himself," the mayor said, thankful not to have to be the one to impart the bad news again. The men turned toward the study and the bespectacled doctor who came to join them. No one noticed the girl as she roused herself from the sofa and moved anxiously to the parlor door.

"How is he, Doc?" Jack Martin asked.

"He's dead, gentlemen," the doctor said, rolling down his sleeves. "He died from a gunshot wound, self-administered."

"Self-administered? Are you saying he done himself in?" Charlie asked.

"Why would he do that?" Jack Martin asked disbelievingly.

"Maybe this will help explain it." The doctor handed over a sheet of bloodstained paper. The girl's face blanched when she saw it. Jack Martin glanced away. Puzzled, Charlie Wheeler took the paper and read.

"Jesus," he swore, raising his head and looking at the other two men.

"What is it?" They pressed closer, craning to read over his shoulder. "What does it say?"

"It says . . . says that he . . . took money from the bank, a lot of money, for all these years, and now he can't . . . can't pay it back."

"Why would he take money? He had his own," Carl Bonham declared in outrage.

"He's been losing money on bad investments, spending more than he had coming in," Charlie Wheeler said, reading from the paper again. "He kept thinking he'd get it back some way or another."

"I don't believe it," the mayor snapped. "Hiram Bennett was one of the most honest men I've ever known."

"I believe it," Jack Martin said flatly. "He was trying to arrange some loans last week from one of the other banks. I thought he was doing it . . . he *said* it was for one of our customers. It seemed mighty funny at the time, but I . . . trusted him."

"He stole our money," Charlie Wheeler exclaimed, looking around the house at all the things he'd ever wanted and couldn't afford. His money and the money from the other citizens of Webster had helped buy all these fine things. And he'd always looked up to the banker, admired him, envied him. His eyes darted from one piece to another, automatically tabulating its price as the anger built inside him.

"Please, Mr. Wheeler . . ." The soft, rich voice brought his gaze around to the girl. Quietly she'd moved forward into the hall and stood before him, her feet primly together, her hands clasped in front of her. Her honey-brown curls had fallen loose and tumbled on her shoulders. Her velvet gown was crushed and wrinkled. The gray eyes, fringed by sooty dark lashes, matted now by her tears, were wide and solemn, like those of a hurt, betrayed child. Her full pink lips parted slightly as she drew in a small breath.

Charlie Wheeler looked at the banker's daughter and felt an urge to place his mouth against hers and taste the forbidden sweetness of her. She seemed more real to him than before, more attainable. He could see the wet streaks on her cheeks, the light sheen of perspiration on her brow and top lip.

"Excuse me, Mr. Wheeler, sir," she repeated, her voice low, the words clear and concise as she'd been taught in school.

"Yes?" he asked as from a long way off. How old was she? Eighteen? Nineteen?

"The note, sir. Does it say anything about me? Did my father leave me a message?"

Charlie looked from the girl back at the paper he held and he was reminded of the terrible hoax Hiram Bennett had played on them all.

"There's nothing here for you, girl," he said bitterly. "Hiram Bennett left nothing for any of us." Aimee looked at the man's angry face and forlornly turned back to the empty parlor, carefully closing the doors behind her as if to close out the horror of the afternoon.

The hours that followed were all part of the nightmare for Aimee. She longed to sit in the parlor with the doors closed and pretend all was as it should be, but slowly the reality of her father's death and the shocked reactions of the townspeople penetrated her shell and she was without defense against her overwhelming despair and their rage.

Loud voices filled the street outside the mansion, yet no one came to express sympathy or to lend support. No one came to offer help with the funeral arrangements, and finally Aimee straightened her young shoulders and sent for the minister and the mortician. She'd never felt so alone. She also sent for Frank, urging him to come at once. Though they'd been betrothed for only a few months, she'd come to rely on him when her father wasn't around. She needed him now.

Reverend Thompson suggested she have her father laid out in the parlor. He didn't tell her he feared for the fate of his church if the body were displayed there. Aimee set the servants to making refreshments. Hiram Bennett had always set a handsome table. She would do no less now. The first crushing blow was the coffin.

"This is not what I ordered, Mr. Horn," she exclaimed when the wily mortician brought a plain box of roughly sawed pine.

"Uh, I'm sorry, Miss Bennett." He scuffed his muddy boot against the thick imported rug and refused to meet her eyes. "It was the best I could do under the circumstances."

"You mean you have nothing better than this?"

"No, ma'am. I mean Mayor Bonham and some of the others stopped by and told me this is the one I should bring to you. They . . . uh . . . said it was the only one you could afford."

"Of course we can afford better than this for my father," Aimee cried, making her eyes wide to hold back the tears. "Bring me another coffin immediately."

"Well, you see, ma'am . . ." The scrawny little man scratched at his whiskers and looked at the floor, embarrassed to be confronting the banker's daughter like this. "I . . . uh . . . I'd have to have the money now, miss. You understand."

Aimee drew up her shoulders and stared at him

disdainfully. "Certainly, Mr. Horn. I'll get it for you."
She went to the morning room to the desk where
money was kept for the running of the household, but
there was none.

"Hattie, where's the household money?" she demanded.

"Lawd, Miss Aimee. Ah don't know. Yo' papa,
well, he ain't been puttin' money in theah foah these
pas' few weeks. He said he kept forgittin'."

"How have you been buying food?" Aimee turned
an alarmed gaze on the old woman.

"We been eatin' out o' the storage shed, Miss Aimee,
and Mistah Parrish down at the store, he give us credit
'cause he say he know the banker be good for it, if
anyone would. Only now, Jimmy just come back from
theah and, Miss Aimee, he say no moah credit, not
foah this house."

"I see," Aimee said, the desperate realities of the
situation crashing in on her. She wanted to lash out at
someone, but it would do no good. No one else was to
blame for what had happened. If only Papa hadn't
died. If only he'd hung on somehow. They could have
faced the disgrace together. Together!

She took a deep breath and rose to her feet. Abner
Horn waited in the front hall for his money, and
somehow she must find some way to pay him. Surely
Papa had left something for them somewhere. With
faltering steps she turned toward the study. She hadn't
been in it since hearing that awful gunshot hours before.

They had moved her father. He lay stretched out on
the sofa, his vigorous body forever stilled, his boisterous laughter and ready wit forever lost to them. He
lay with the injured part of his head away from her
and for a moment she was sure he was just sleeping.
She had only to reach out and shake him, but there
was an unnatural stillness to the large body that it had
not possessed in life.

Grief overcame her and she knelt beside the sofa,
her head resting against his shoulder. Sobs came, hoarse
ugly sounds that carried beyond the doors into the

front hall where the little man waited. Nervously Abner Horn twirled his hat, uncertain of whether to go or stay. She'd said she had money. He'd stay.

Then, "Where's my baby?" the fat old nanny cried, hurrying through the hall and past the carved double doors. Her plump arms wrapped around the slender figure of this child she loved. If she could do anything at all for the weeping girl, Hattie thought, it would be to take away this pain. She would give her own life if it would bring back the banker to his daughter. But it wouldn't, and the sad truth had to be faced.

"Come on, chile," she said gently. "Yo' shouldn't be in heah, honey. It don't do Mastah Hiram no good and yo' know he was a proud man. He wouldn't want yo' to see him like this."

"Yes, Hattie, I know. He was a proud man, but oh, Hattie, why did he do it? Why? Just because he didn't have enough money? Was that a good enough reason? Why didn't he think about me?"

"Ah don't know, chile," Hattie said, stroking the bowed young head. Gently she led the girl out to the front hall, where Abner Horn leapt to his feet.

"What yo' doin' theah?" Hattie demanded of him.

"Here now, mind your tongue, yo' uppity nigger," he snapped, "or I'll have you whipped."

"Yo' cain't," Hattie said. "This still Mastah Hiram's house and ah'm Mastah Hiram's property. Yo' cain't touch me." She advanced menacingly toward the nasty little man. "Are yo' the one upsetting mah baby?"

"It's all right, Hattie." Aimee raised her tear-dampened face from the old woman's shoulder. "I'm sorry, Mr. Horn," she said brokenly. "I have no money to pay you."

"Who's going to pay me for this coffin?" he whined, indicating the rough box he'd left in the parlor. "I have to make a living too, you know."

"I understand," Aimee said, and lowered her head. Her gaze fell on the brooch she'd pinned on her bodice just that morning. How happy the world had seemed then. Her father had given her the brooch on her last birthday and it was exquisitely wrought of fine gold and semiprecious stones. Fumbling with the catch, she unfastened the brooch and handed it to the man.

"Take this," she said, extending it well away from her. "It will more than pay for your . . . coffin." Her nostrils flared with distaste for the little man and the discourtesy he was showing her father.

Greedily the mortician's hand shot out and took the piece from her. Aimee drew back and wiped her hand against the crushed-velvet folds of her skirt. Silently she watched as the man held the piece up to the light.

"I don't know," he said, turning it first one way and then the other. "This is just a trinket. By itself it won't bring much."

"It should bring a good bit," Aimee said coldly, "My father ordered it especially from a New York jeweler. The stones are flawless."

"Yes, ma'am, old Hiram always made sure to get the best, but it'll just barely pay for the coffin I brought you, not for the fancy one you wanted."

"Good day, Mr. Horn. I trust you will see to the grave."

"Yes, ma'am." The little mortician shook his head. "But you'll have to get his body there yourself. My fancy wagon's broke down."

Aimee made no reply. Both women stood looking at him, waiting for him to leave, and their censure was plain. Abner Horn tipped his hat and turned toward the door. He was feeling better and better about the banker. This pretty little bauble would bring many a good night down at Jake's place. Hurriedly, lest the old black woman open the box and they changed their minds, he jammed his hat on his head and scurried down the street.

Aimee opened the box later when she'd recovered, and what she saw was enough to start the tears flowing again. There was no padding at all within the pine coffin, no soft cushions to comfort the dead man in his final rest. Hattie stood beside Aimee, her eyes dark and angry at the low pass to which her family had been brought.

"Never mind, Hattie," Aime said at last. "We'll fix it up ourselves."

Sam and Jimmy, the stableboy, set the coffin in the parlor, balancing it on two chairs. Aimee padded it with some of the white satin set aside for her wedding gown. Frank would understand, she was sure. Thick, soft pillows filled with goosedown were laid in the bottom. More satin was draped around the outside of the rough coffin to hide its humble state, and a beribboned lacy pillow from Aimee's own bed was laid for his head.

When Doc Allen and Mayor Bonham arrived to place the body in the coffin, they were amazed at the elegance in which the banker would rest. They were amazed as well at the poise of the young woman who greeted them and thanked them for their help. Was this the child who'd wept so pitiably just that afternoon? She still wore the crumpled velvet gown, but she held herself with dignity. There was a new maturity, too harshly learned, in her somber gaze.

When the men departed, Aimee slowly climbed the stairs to her room, where she gave careful attention to her toiletry. Her father had always liked her to look her best. She owned no black gowns, but there was a gray faille travel dress. She considered it, then rejected it for its plainness. She chose instead a gown of rich brown velvet, its sloping shoulders and high yoke trimmed with bands of satin ribbon and ecru lace. It fit snugly at her tiny waist, flaring into the wide sleeves and full sweeping skirt now fashionable.

Carefully she brushed her hair into a swirl of curls on top of her head, leaving clusters of shiny chestnut ringlets around her ears and temples. It was the way her father liked her hair best.

Stepping back, she studied the effect in her mirror. What she saw was a slim, pale girl who might have been going to a party or an afternoon tea with her betrothed. Where *was* Frank? she wondered. She needed him beside her now. A spasm of grief seized her and she shook, slumping forward. Taking a deep breath, she straightened, and with a tranquil poise she'd learned in school, moved from the room and down the hall to the top of the stairs. She stood, swaying slightly, listening to the hushed silence that had fallen over the house. The sound of a gun's discharge echoed in her mind.

The doorbell rang, its cheerful greeting pealing through the quiet house incongruously. Its message belonged to a brighter day, to a world filled with life and gaiety, to happy surprises and a tall, laughing man loved by all who knew him, a man who made the world seem more exciting just because he was there.

Sam opened the door and the mayor and his wife entered. Sam led them to the parlor. Reluctantly Aimee started down the stairs. She had no stomach for this duty, but she wouldn't leave her father unattended. Like a shadow she glided across the great hall.

"Look at him, lying there like a king, instead of the common thief he is," Lydia Bonham was saying. "The effrontery of it."

Aimee paused in the doorway, gathering courage for what lay ahead. "Good evening, Aunt Lydia. It was kind of you to come."

"Kindness has nothing to do with it," Lydia snapped. "Your father doesn't deserve kindness."

"Lydia," Carl Bonham said mildly.

"He was a thief, worse than a thief," his wife insisted. "At least a thief doesn't pretend to be something he isn't. Hiram Bennett was a hypocrite as well as a thief, stealing from people while he pretended to be their friend. And all the time he was taking their money and spending it on fine things while he lorded it over people like he was better than they were. Well, let me tell you, young lady, those times are past."

On and on she went. There were no words of comfort for the daughter. In spite of the mayor's mild rebuke, his wife vented her anger. Quietly, with pale face and clenched fists hidden in her lap, Aimee listened and said nothing in return. Her nails bit into her palms, leaving little half-moons of red pain.

At last the mayor led his wife away and the house was silent again. Now Aimee found comfort in the solitude. Through the night she sat, composed and dry-eyed, by her father's coffin, while lights of onlookers flickered and danced against the window pane. Now and then she could hear the rumble of their angry voices. Some friends came to bid Hiram Bennett a final farewell. He'd helped many people during his ten years as a banker. Now in his hour of shame only a few remembered him with kindness. Lucy Thompson, the reverend's wife, came to sit with her awhile. Fervently Aimee wished Frank were there, but the hour grew late and still he hadn't come.

The crowd in the street grew restless. One of the most daring flung a stone through the front bay window. Glass tinkled in the quietness and the stone tumbled to rest beside Aimee's feet.

"Put out the lights, so they can't see you," Lucy Thompson cried in sudden fear, but Aimee would not allow it and the lamps remained brightly lighted as she kept her vigil. Finally the reverend sent for the sheriff, who dispersed the crowd and the night grew quiet.

No one else came to see Hiram Bennett. He lay in isolated splendor against his daughter's bridal satin, and when morning came, Reverend Thompson returned to say a short service. A few loyal friends came for the funeral, then left shaking their heads in pity for the bereft daughter. Carl and Lydia Bonham were conspicuously not among them. The sun had nearly reached its apex by the time Sam hitched up the supply wagon and brought it around front. Jimmy and the Bonhams' stablehand helped Sam load the coffin on the wagon. Aimee tied a bonnet over her curls, and taking the shawl Hattie held for her, climbed up on the plain board seat. Reverend Thompson chose a place on the back of the wagon.

Sam took up the reins and the wagon rolled through

the streets toward the cemetery on the other side of town. The servants followed on foot behind. The sidewalks were strangely empty, the stores closed, yet Aimee knew that behind those shutters curious eyes watched the pitiful procession. No one fell into step behind the funeral wagon. Hiram Bennett had served the town faithfully for many years, but in the end he had betrayed them.

Aimee kept her gaze fixed ahead, her head high, her back straight, pride evident in every line of her body. Pride goeth before the fall, some of the townspeople thought. She wouldn't be so high and mighty when she was looking for her next meal.

One of the idlers loafing in front of the general store shifted his chaw of tobacco from one cheek to the other and spat at the wagon as it passed. Children playing in the yard skipped rope to a new refrain: "Hiram Bennett was a thief. Stole our money but it brought him grief. Poor ole Hiram went insane, and put a bullet through his brain."

"Hush up," Hattie scolded them, but they only ignored her and repeated the refrain.

At last they were through town.

Two horsemen approached from the opposite direction. Aimee recognized the tall, lanky figures of Frank Graham and his father. Relief swept through her. He'd come at last. She wasn't alone. Gratefully she signaled Sam to stop, and waited as the men drew near. Her face lit in a smile of greeting as the polished young man approached. She could see the sun glinting in the pale gold of his hair. His thin face was turned away from her and the light eyes stared straight ahead. Aimee watched with growing apprehension as the two men rode on past the wagon as if she weren't even there.

"Frank?" she whispered, the sound barely heard over the creak of leather and the plodding thud of the horses' hooves. He didn't look back. "Frank," she called again, without shame now, as she fought against the implications of his gesture. This time he pulled his

19

horse to a halt, and hope sprang anew in Aimee's breast. Frank twisted in his saddle to gaze at her for a long measuring moment. His glance was cold, without pity or warmth or any of the burning admiration he'd shown her before.

"Frank," Salem Graham called impatiently. He gave not a glance to the girl who would have been his daughter-in-law. Without a word Frank turned back to his father and the two men disappeared around a bend in the road.

Aimee sat staring after them, the blood pounding in her ears. "Drive on, Sam," she said dully.

"Yas, ma'am." He flicked the reins on the horses' backs. Aimee forced herself not to think. She couldn't bear any more today.

"I put yo'r daddy down there," Abner Horn said, pointing toward the marshy end where the town's poorer citizens and slaves were buried. Before Aimee could object, he swung on his horse and turned toward town.

"Mr. Horn, aren't you going to help bury my father?" she called after him, but the scrawny mortician merely kicked his swayback horse in the belly and plodded away. "Mr. Horn, I paid you for this help." Helplessly she watched him go, then looked around. There was no one else around except for the silhouette of a lone horseman on the horizon.

"I guess it's up to us, Sam," she said disconsolately.

"We'll make out all right by ourselves, Miss Aimee," Hattie reassured her. "Sam, yo' drive this wagon on over theah close to that grave."

Sam did as he was bidden and got down. He stood looking at the coffin resting on the wagon bed. How would he ever get it down? he wondered. He was an old man and he had only a young boy to help him. The reverend was too old and frail to be any help. But this was Mastah Hiram and Sam had never failed him. He wouldn't start now.

"I'll help too, Sam," Aimee said softly, reading the old man's expression.

"That ain't no job for a lady," Hattie scolded.

"It must be done," Aimee replied firmly, and together they wrested the coffin from the wagon and onto the ground. Aimee thought of her father resting inside the heavy wooden box. How he would have hated the ignominy of his treatment.

They had no way of lowering the coffin into the grave. Another insult for her father when he didn't deserve it, Aimee thought. He'd tried to pay back the money. She knelt beside the rough coffin, her shoulders and head bowed as she gave way to a torrent of weeping. It was too unfair. If only they'd given him time, been a little kinder. But it had been her father who'd chosen not to try. He'd simply given up. She would never do that, she vowed. She would always fight back to the very end. At last she rose to her feet and looked at her huddled servants.

"Help me move the coffin to the grave," she begged piteously.

Throwing her apron over her head, Hattie began to weep loudly. "Miss Aimee," she cried, rocking herself. "What we comin' to?"

"It'll be all right," Aimee said stoutly, and began to tug at the coffin. Sam and Hattie came to help, motioning to Jimmy to lend his weight. Slowly they inched the coffin through the mud and dirt toward the gaping hole.

Zack Crawford butted his heels against the horse's belly and urged him onward. The roan was weary, as was the packhorse. They'd been traveling since dawn. Zack was ready for a drink and a hot meal, to be followed by a long soak in a tub of hot water. Webster had to be close. He could see the outline of a cemetery off in a field, and townfolks didn't bury their dead too far away.

Even as he watched, a wagon drew over the hill and entered the cemetery. Some poor soul had met his end. Zack brought his horses to a halt in the shade of a towering oak, and taking off his wide-brimmed hat, absently wiped his brow. His lean brown face was thoughtful as he watched the people in the cemetery.

They were a motley-looking crew if ever he saw one. There was no fancy hearse, no crowd of mourners to indicate the dead was a person of substance. The faces of the mourners were black save for an old man in a clerical collar and a woman. Probably a lady of the house attending the funeral of some faithful old retainer. His speculation was further heightened as she dropped to her knees beside the cheap wooden coffin and gave way to grief.

Her back was slender and her chestnut hair gleamed in the sunlight. She was young, whoever she was, he thought. Zack placed his hat back on his head and prodded his horse. Time to move on. He felt the need for a whiskey and maybe a woman tonight if one could be had.

He cast a final glance over his shoulder. His face registered surprise as he saw that the mourners were bent over the casket, tugging it toward the open hole. Where the devil was the grave digger? That was his job. It was none of Zack's business, though. He headed his horses toward town at a gallop.

There'd been something about the woman's figure as she'd strained to shove the casket along in the mud, an air of quiet desperation that tugged at him. With a curse Zack brought his horse to a stop and looked at the figures intent on their grisly chore. Resignedly he turned back toward the cemetery.

They didn't hear him coming until he was almost upon them. They had the box at the edge of the hole now and stood contemplating the best way to lower it. At the sound of hoofbeats, they whirled to look at him. The grizzled black face of the old man registered a mixture of fear and relief, while the stout old woman warned with a telling glance that he'd better not try to do them harm. But it was the girl who drew his attention. Her pale face would have been beautiful if not for the ravages of grief. Her gown, obviously of a rich fabric, was stained with mud at the hem, and there was a smear of dirt across one high cheekbone. The ribbons of her bonnet fluttered in the afternoon breeze, but she held her head proudly. Her gray eyes were direct and unwavering as she looked at him.

"We need you," she said. It wasn't a plea. It was a command, and yet her voice was soft and musical.

Swinging his long leg over the horn of his saddle, Zack slid to the ground and walked toward the huddled group, his dark eyes holding the girl's. He could see the tremble of her soft lips, the rise and fall of her breasts as she drew in a breath, yet not even by the flicker of an eyelash did she make a retreat.

Zack came to a stop before her. She was a small girl, barely coming to his shoulders. He caught the fragrance of her hair from where he stood. She smelled like spring flowers. Silent and still, she stood waiting for his response.

Zack glanced around the graveyard. "Where are the gravediggers?" he demanded.

"They . . . they've gone back to town," she answered, and again he was touched by the timbre of her voice. "I . . . we need your help." This time it was a flat statement and he sensed the pleading in it. Asking came hard to her, and he wondered why.

"We'll need some rope," he said to the old black man. "Look on my packhorse over there."

The old man made a motion and the young boy scampered away.

"We'll have to make a sling to lower the coffin into the grave," Zack explained as he uncoiled the rope. With the help of the old man and the boy, he worked the rope under the casket and back again and threw the two open ends to them.

"When I tell you to lift with these ropes, do it," Zack ordered, and placed the loop around his shoulders and back, anchoring his feet in the damp earth for leverage. The elderly minister stood off to one side, too weak to be of any help and wisely staying out of the way. The girl responded quickly to Zack's instructions, understanding what he had in mind. The dark-fringed eyes watched him carefully, ready for his signal. Zack could see her delicate hands tightening around the ropes even before he spoke.

"Lift," he commanded, and straightened his knees so the coffin was lifted from the ground. "Keep it taut." He maneuvered the wooden box over the grave. "Hold it tight!" he bellowed when the old man's rope slipped. From the corner of his eyes he could see the girl's slender body bracing itself in a vain attempt to steady the sling. But the other end had already dipped and the coffin slid downward.

"Release your rope," he shouted at her, and for a startled moment she stared as he was dragged toward the yawning hole. Her grip loosened, the rope slithering through her hands, tearing at the soft, delicate palms. Her grip tightened valiantly in spite of the pain; then the rope was wrenched from her hands and whipped through the air, striking Zack on the cheek just before he was carried over the edge and into the grave.

He landed on top of the coffin. The fall had torn the lid open and for a moment he was face-to-face with the dead man. Startled, he drew back, then paused to look more closely at the corpse. He knelt on the coffin, taking in the rich satin interior and the shabby, rough exterior. His quick glance took in the small wound in the side of the skull. Puzzled, he looked up at the girl, who stood at the edge staring down at him.

"He is my father," she said quietly, and Zack kept his questions to himself. Carefully he replaced the lid and with the handle of his gun drove the nails in again.

"We'd better fill in the grave then," he said, and picking up the shovel, began to throw dirt in on the coffin. It fell on the board planks with a resounding thud that tore at Aimee's heart. She remained silent as the men worked, remembering her childhood. Her father had filled her young years with laughter and security. Now he was gone.

The grave was filled in, the dirt mounded over, and the tall stranger with the kind eyes was rolling down his sleeves. Wiping tears from her cheeks, Aimee went forward and placed a bouquet of early spring flowers on the raw earth, then turned to face the man who'd helped them.

"I have no money to pay you," she said.

"None was asked," he replied. Pushing his dark hair back with a large brown hand, he settled his hat in place, then reached for the reins of his horse.

"Thank you," Aimee said simply, and held out her hand.

Zack Crawford took it, marveling at the smallness of it. Then, with a quick, agile movement he swung into the saddle. "My sympathy, ma'am," he said, looking down at her. For an insane moment Aimee had the urge to lay her flushed face against the long lean thigh for comfort. But he was a stranger and she couldn't impose her grief upon him. He'd think her mad, and well she might be. Aimee stepped away from his horse, and touching his hat brim in a final farewell, he turned toward the road.

"God bless you for your kindness, sir," the minister called after him.

She hadn't even asked his name, Aimee realized, watching him ride away, and she hadn't told him hers. He was headed toward Webster, though. He'd know soon enough. Shoulders slumping in fatigue, Aimee turned toward the wagon.

"Let's go home," she said to the servants, and they climbed up on the wagon for the trip back, respectfully making room for the little minister. The capricious spring breeze blew cold, sending a handful of dry, brittle leaves scuttling along the ground. Aimee shuddered and clasped her muddied shawl tighter. What was she to do now? she wondered. She'd lost both her father and Frank. For the duration of the long ride back from the cemetery she sat slumped miserably on the hard seat, and the townspeople observed how all remnant of pride was gone from her.

2

Zack rode into town and left his horse at the first livery stable he saw, then headed for the nearest tavern. There were miles of dust and loneliness he wanted to wash away. A longing for Caroline washed over him and he wondered what she was doing at that very moment. Better to wonder whose bed she was in, he reminded himself grimly. The memory of her, soft and yielding beneath him, came to mock him and he pushed it away. Caroline was from another lifetime.

The tavern was nothing more than a log cabin of the kind raised early in the settlement of the town. It was out of step with the bustling progress of the storefront businesses on Main Street and the fine homes on the hill at the other end of town. The floor was of splintery halved logs. The bar, stained and worn smooth by the elbows of generations of patrons, consisted of a few rough boards laid across barrels.

Zack threw down the first shot of whiskey, feeling it burn the back of his throat, and motioned for a refill. Glass in hand, he leaned back to sip leisurely and study his surroundings. Several women and young girls moved around the room, serving drinks to the men, joking and leaning over them to share intimate laughter, taking care that their posture allowed enticing glimpses of the charms they had to offer.

A pretty dark-haired girl approached Zack, her smile going from one of boredom to admiration and anticipation as her gaze moved over his long legs and broad shoulders.

"Yo' look lak' yo've been travelin' some, mister," she said with a soft slur. Her voice was husky and seductive, promising all sorts of special delights, and Zack looked her over with sudden interest. He hadn't been with a woman in months, not since that last night with Caroline. He returned her bold gaze. Her stance was relaxed yet contrived to show off her bosom in a spectacular fashion. Suggestively she let her body swing slightly to and fro, causing her skirts to swish against his boots. Zack felt the heat begin in his groin and glanced back at her face. Suddenly he remembered another face, pale with fatigue and grief, with stormy gray eyes that looked at a man with candor and innocence. The girl at the cemetery! Even now he could recall the feel of her small hand in his.

She was shorter than the girl standing before him, and slender as a reed, her young breasts but a gentle, virginal curve beneath the bodice of her gown. Why hadn't there been someone there with her? Had she no family, no friends? Who was she? he wondered, and was irritated with himself for not being able to put her out of his mind.

"Did yo' forget 'bout me, honey?" the girl asked, and moved to place an arm around his neck. Zack looked down at her pouting red mouth, felt the softness of her breasts against his side, and surprised himself.

Slowly he shook his head. "I guess I did," he said gently so the words left no sting in their wake. "I got to remembering someone else."

"Ah could help yo' forget," she said almost wistfully. "Mah name's Loretta."

"That's a pretty name, Loretta." Zack turned back to the bar, gently dislodging the girl at the same time. He took out a gold coin and tossed it on the bar in front of her. "Some other time," he said with a smile that stirred some forgotten dream.

27

"Buy yourself a drink on me," he invited. For a moment Loretta stood beside him, her face reflecting her regret. She wished she had a man like that remembering her sometime. His eyes had gone all soft and gentle. She bet he would be considerate to a woman. Once more regret washed over Loretta; then she glanced toward the man behind the bar. He was staring at her with an angry frown on his face. Quickly she picked up the gold coin and pocketed it.

"If yo' change yo'r mind . . ." Her voice trailed off and she melted away down the room, her eyes searching for someone else who was alone and might need her services. The tall dark-haired man's image was stored away in the back of her mind, to be taken out again when she was alone in her bed and her thoughts and body were hers alone and girlish fairy-tale dreams still struggled to survive.

Zack tossed off the rest of his drink and ordered a third. He seldom had more than two, but the girl at the cemetery had brought back unsettling memories of Caroline. Since he'd left Maine, his nights had been haunted by images of her golden hair spread out on the pillow beside him and blue eyes the color of violets looking at him imploringly as she pleaded with him to understand why she'd married his brother instead of waiting for him as she'd promised. She needed a man who was always there, not just when his ship was in. She wasn't meant to be a captain's wife.

It needn't matter that she'd married Eli, she'd whispered, wrapping her slender arms around his neck and pulling his head down to her bare breasts. They would have these moments together, these times when his ship was in port.

It was then that he'd known he had to leave Maine forever. He'd betrayed his own brother and he hated himself for it, yet he wasn't sure he could resist the temptation that Caroline would present to him time and again. He'd left the life he'd known and struck out overland. He would put a continent between himself and his brother's wife. Perhaps then he could forget her.

Zack swirled the whiskey in his glass. He could still remember the day he left. Eli, normally undemonstrative, had clasped him tightly, his eyes unable to meet Zack's as he mumbled his farewells. Zack could see Eli was riddled with guilt for having taken his brother's fiancée, and could say nothing to ease Eli's feelings. He himself was guilty of a far greater sin.

There had been no such guilt on Caroline's face. Primly she'd stood on the steps beside Eli, wishing Zack Godspeed on his journey, while her eyes issued a challenge not to leave, a promise that he'd be back. He wouldn't be able to stay away. For the first time Zack hadn't envied his brother. He'd ridden away from them without a backward glance. Yet for all his good intentions, Caroline had haunted him every mile he'd traveled since.

Zack ordered another drink, his fourth. He should get something to eat and see about that bath he'd wanted earlier. Once he reached Independence and joined one of the wagon trains heading for Oregon, he'd have a hard time finding a hot bath. A commotion at the other end of the bar interrupted his morose thoughts.

"I tell you I got the money," a scrawny sandy-haired man was shouting, punctuating his words by hitting against the bar with a balled fist. "I want me a bottle and a women. Loretta's the one I want." He peered around the room and saw the girl standing to one side.

"Retta, girl, I told yo' I'd be back with lots of money to spend on you," he shouted, and the girl shuffled around nervously, her eyes darting from the sandy-haired mortician to the burly man behind the counter. She sidled away until the wall blocked her escape, then stood wide-eyed and silent, her expression that of a trapped animal.

Zack's eyes narrowed as he watched her. Her skittish behavior was in direct contrast to how she'd behaved toward him earlier. Her boldness was gone and now she just looked like a very frightened girl.

"Loretta don't want to go with you, Abner," the fat bartender said. "Yo' git too rough. Yo' hurt my girls so they ain't no good for a couple of days after."

"I don't mean no harm," the little man said. "Retta'n me's friends. Retta, come on ovah here. I'm going t'buy you a drink." Expansively Abner Horn waved her over. Clasping her skirts in nervous fingers, Loretta inched her way toward the bar.

"Loretta!" the bartender shouted. The girl jumped, and looked at him. "Git ovah here and stop actin' like that."

"All right, Pa," she said dully, and scurried to stand beside Abner Horn.

Abner laughed expansively. "Jake, yo' give her a drink outta that bottle ovah there." He pointed to the bottle of watered-down whiskey. "Yessir, ole Abner promised he'd give yo' a good time, and that's what we're fixin' to do." His arm went around her shoulder. Loretta gave him a halfhearted smile and nodded, her eyes darting to her father behind the bar.

"If yo' say so," she mumbled.

"That's right." The man pushed the glass toward her. "You just drink right up now," he urged. Eagerly Loretta took the glass and drank down the fiery contents. Having a couple of drinks helped, especially when she was in for a hard night. Abner Horn laughed again, the sound cutting. His hand rubbed up and down her back and slithered down over her buttocks. Loretta shivered, trying not to think that he was the town undertaker. Hopefully she held the empty glass out, but Abner pretended not to see it. His hand had snaked back to the front of her dress and he ground his groin against her hips in an obscene gesture.

"Here, now," Jake said. "None of that here. Ah run a decent place. Yo' want to take her upstairs, yo' pay me first. Yo' owe me for six drinks."

"Six drinks!" the mortician yelped in indignation. "I only had me one."

"And yo' bought two fer Loretta here," the bartender snapped.

"That only makes three drinks," Abner shouted back at him. His sandy coloring had hinted at the temper he possessed. Loretta shrank back, wishing her father wouldn't rile him so. He would just take it out on her when he got her upstairs.

"Ah'm chargin' yo' fer the drinks yo' had the last time yo' was in here," Jake said.

Abner studied the burly man for a moment, then shrugged philosophically. If he wanted to be served here again, he had to pay up as Jake decreed. The only other tavern in town was down on Main Street, where the banker and the town mayor went. He didn't feel comfortable down there, and besides, they didn't have women like Jake did.

Thinking of the banker made Abner chuckle. Reaching into his breast pocket, he brought out the brooch Aimee Bennett had given him to pay for her father's funeral.

"There you are, my good man," he said, slapping the piece down on the bar. "This'll pay all I owe you and then some."

"Oooh!" Loretta breathed, reaching for the brooch, but Jake's beefy hand came down with a resounding smack. Swiftly she jerked her hand away, nursing it against her breast while she watched her father pick up the pin and study it.

"Where'd yo' steal this from?" Jake demanded.

"I didn't steal it," the undertaker denied. "I earned it fair and square."

"Took if off some dead soul, like as not." Jake sneered. Loretta drew back, giving a slight shiver.

"Did not," Abner hotly denied Jake's accusation. "It's my pay for buryin' the banker."

Once again Zack's glance went to the two men at the other end of the bar. Loretta, he noted, had taken advantage of her father's quarrel with the scrawny little man to fill her glass from the bottle of whiskey he

31

served his special customers. It sloshed over onto her bodice as she quickly gulped it down, her eyes darting from one face to the other. Zack grinned as he saw her stealthily reach for the bottle again. Loretta was an enterprising woman, but without even glancing in her direction, the bartender had his dirty paw there ahead of her, swooping the bottle out of her reach, while he continued to glare at the undertaker.

"Ah seen the coffin when she took him to the cemetery. She didn't pay yo' that much for a coffin like that."

"She did too," the little man flared. "Took it right off her dress and handed it to me, a-sobbin' and carryin' on like she was heartbroke. Said it come direct from New York, she did. I figure it might be worth quite a bit."

"It might," the bartender said, rubbing a thumb across one of the stone, "but Ah don't take nothin' but cash money."

"But . . . but I tell you this is worth a . . . a—"

"Cash or nothin'," Jake decreed. "Loretta, git yourself away from him and work them back tables." Bleary-eyed, Loretta drew herself up and obediently made her way to the table where hard-eyed men sat playing cards, too intent on the dealer to pay much attention to the girls who clung to them. A thick pall of smoke hung in the air above their tables.

"Come on, Jake," Abner Horn whined. "I'll give you a good deal."

"Ah ain't interested," Jake declared. "Ah don't have no need of no such doodads, and Ah ain't interested in trying to sell it. Yo' sell it, get yo'r money, and come back—then we'll do business."

The undertaker opened his mouth to argue, but the look in Jake's eyes told him it was pointless. Wiping a grimy hand across his slack mouth, he pushed away from the bar and turned toward the door.

"I'd be interested in looking at that brooch," Zack said, and at the sound of his voice, Abner Horn froze in his tracks, a scared, guilty look crossing his face. Then he remembered that he had the brooch legitimately and swaggered toward the speaker.

"Yessiree, it's a right pretty piece," he said. "It's got diamonds and them there bluish stones. It was a birthday present from the banker to his daughter, and the banker he was a generous man. That there was his undoing. He was too generous."

"How'd you come by it?" Zack asked, closely examining the delicately wrought brooch. It was well-crafted and the stones were of a superior quality.

"Like I said, she give it to me for buryin' her dead. She sent for me first thing last night after her pa done hisself in, and she ordered his coffin. She was that grateful she just handed me this brooch. 'Here, Mr. Horn,' she says, real sweet-like. 'That's 'cause you been so kind about helpin' me bury my pa.'"

"You brought her a nice coffin?" Zack asked. "Dug out the grave and filled it in afterward?"

"Well . . ." The undertaker's eyes glanced slyly from one side of the room to the other as he checked to see who was listening. Some men appeared interested, so he sank into a chair, slapping his hat on the table, and bent toward the dark-haired stranger as if to speak in confidence, although, in truth, he took care to keep his voice loud enough for others in the room to hear.

"Wal, you know the banker, he kilt hisself, 'cause everyone found out he stole from the good people of this here town and I couldn't by all rights give him a good coffin, not after what he done. I dug out a grave for him, sure, but I put him down on the swampy end where they bury the niggers and other riffraff. No sir, he won't be layin' 'longside the decent folk of this community, not while Abner Horn is on the job."

"Did they get him buried decently?" Zack asked, and the little undertaker, preoccupied with his own self-importance and the attention of the other patrons in the tavern, didn't notice the dangerous glint in the tall stranger's eyes.

"I reckon they did," he answered nonchalantly, and leaned back in his chair. He glanced around the room with an expansive smile. "After I had my niggers dig the hole, I sent 'em back home. She can have her own niggers shove the dirt back in. I done all I was goin' to."

"And she paid you for your services with this piece of jewelry?"

"Like I said, she didn't have no money." The undertaker hooked a thumb under his belt buckle and tilted his chair back, balancing on two legs, while he rocked slightly. "She was real grateful. I aim to go up there one of these nights real soon and talk to her some more. I got me an idea she's goin' to be needin' some friends."

"That's commendable of you," Zack said dryly.

"Yeah, wal, you might say that," Horn replied smugly. "The truth of it is, " he confided, "she's a real fancy piece. I'd kinda like to get my hands on her for a time or two. They's some ladies that find me real . . . uh . . . masterful."

"I noticed Loretta's eagerness," Zack said blandly.

"Oh, wal, she just likes to play hard to get. You know how these whores like to put on airs."

"How much do you want for the brooch?" Zack indicated the pieces of jewelry lying between them on the table.

"Wal, seeing as how it come all the way from New York . . ." Abner paused and scratched his stubbled chin. "I reckon it ought to be worth . . . oh, fifty dollahs."

Zack smiled. The piece was worth a great deal more than that, but he wasn't going to tell the greedy, obscene little man. "I'll pay you ten, take it or leave it," he said flatly.

"Ten?" Horn screamed. "That don't even pay me fair and square for the labor I done today." He meant to say more, but one leg of the chair jerked out from under him and he went sprawling across the floor, the tall stranger towering above him.

"You can figure the rest of it went to pay for *my* labor today," Zack said quietly. "I helped bury the banker. A lone woman and two old servants weren't able to lift that pine box you called a coffin by themselves. I did the job you were paid to do."

"I . . . I didn't ask you to do it," the downed man flared, then fell silent when he saw the anger in the other man's face. Black eyes glared down at him; flaring nostrils warned him the big man had been pushed beyond his endurance. Abner Horn lay silent and shivering, suddenly fearful of his life.

Reaching into his pocket, Zack dug out a ten-dollar gold piece and flung it onto the floor beside the man. His nostrils twitched in distaste.

"This should reimburse you for your services," he said, and snatching up the brooch, he stalked toward the door.

Cowering on the floor, the undertaker watched him go, then looked at the gold piece. There was always someone bigger and more powerful to take what was rightfully his, he thought bitterly. At least he had enough to pay for whiskey and a night with Loretta. That was something. Wearily he got to his feet. He could always go back to the girl and demand more. If he went into the house at night, he might be able to get several pieces, maybe find some money she'd overlooked. At the very least, he could have a go with the girl herself. The thought made the pain in his groin flare and he looked around the room until his glance fell on Loretta. He had need of her now more than ever. He'd take her for the whole night. She'd be cheaper that way. His hands clenched into tight fists of anticipation.

"Loretta," he yelled. Startled, the girl looked around. "Get over here," he bellowed, and slowly she made her way across the room toward him, her face closed and empty-looking.

The cold evening air felt good on Zack's face. It cleared his head and helped erase some of the anger he'd felt as he'd listened to the undertaker talking about the banker's daughter. He had little doubt that was the girl he'd met in the cemetery. Zack looked at the glittering brooch. It looked like something she would wear, elegant and dainty. He wasn't sure why he'd bought it from the undertaker except that he'd felt his rage boil up at the thought of the way she'd been treated. He hated to see the obscene little man profit from her confusion and grief. None of the towns-people had attended the banker's funeral. Surely they weren't taking out their spite on the daughter.

He was surprised that he felt so protective toward her. Forget it, he told himself. She'll have family and friends who'll come forward and help her. He glanced back at the brooch. If he had a chance, he'd take it back to her. If not, he'd at least send it to her before he left for Oregon. He shoved the pin into his pocket and made his way toward the hotel, looking for a hot bath and something to eat.

Shadows were creeping past the sheer curtains at the windows, filling the corners of Aimee's room. She lay on her bed, her mind numb as she watched the day pass into evening. Since her return from the cemetery she'd sheltered here in the close, familiar surround-ings. She should go downstairs and tell the servants what to do with all the extra food, but she hadn't the heart. Just as no one had come forth to see her father the night before or to attend the funeral, so no one had come afterward to offer condolences. It was as if the whole town had conspired in their ostracism. She and her father might never have existed.

Aimee turned over onto her stomach, burying her hot cheeks against the cool pillow while she turned her disquieting thoughts back to the careful consideration of the window. All afternoon she'd lain thinking of her childhood, remembering snatches of the happy years she'd had with her father. He'd protected her from everything unpleasant in life, shielded her from its ugliness and cruelty.

The hardest thing she'd ever had to bear was their parting when she went off to school, and even then their time apart had been softened with frequent visits and extravagant gifts. Now Hiram Bennett had brought the greatest cruelty of all. "Oh, Papa, I know it's not your fault," she whispered to the night shadows. "Someday I'll have money, lots of it, and I'll remind them of the way they treated you. I'll make them sorry, I swear I will." Her bitterness welled over and she pressed her face into her pillow, her tears spent.

"Oh, Hattie, what shall we do?" she whispered.

"Chile, don't yo' worry. Somethin'll happen. Jest yo' wait and see. Yo'r daddy's at rest now. He won't know fear and worry no more. He at peace wif hisself. Now, the livin' got to go on wif livin'.'"

"I know, I know," Aimmee said sadly. "It's just that now I'm all alone, except for you, Hattie. I have no one else. You won't leave me, will you?"

"Miss Aimee, they's not nothin' can make me leave yo'," Hattie said stoutly, but in her old heart she feared too. She was a slave and had no say-so over her life. She knew too well how the winds of fortune blew one's life, first warm and benevolent, then cold and grief-filled. Her life with Master Hiram had been kind. She loved Aimee with all her being, but something deep inside told her that their time together was drawing to an end. Still, she smoothed back the silken curls from the pale high brow and hummed an old song she'd sung countless times. It had always chased away the nightmares before; maybe it would this time.

The quiet was shattered by the sound of the doorbell below. Perhaps it was Frank, come to tell her he'd been wrong this afternoon, but now he was here to take care of her. In a swirl of dark skirts and petticoats, Aimee left the room, not taking time to brush her hair or even to throw cold water on her face. She shook out her rumpled skirt while her eager steps carried her to the stairs.

"Frank, you've come after all," she cried taking a

step downward. Then she paused, for the man standing in the hall took off his hat and the lamplight was lost in the dark strands of his hair. It was the stranger who'd helped them at the cemetery. At the sound of her voice he glanced up.

Once again she was struck by his height, even looking down on him as she was. She felt overwhelmed by the bulk of his broad shoulders and powerful figure. Silently she took in the tanned planes of his face, the dark, compelling eyes, the glossy black hair sweeping back from his temples, the long line of his nose, and the strong square chin. It was an arresting face, one of strength.

"It's the gentleman from the cemetery, Miss Aimee," Sam said. "Ah tol' him yo' wasn't receiving anyone right now."

"It's all right, Sam," Aimee said, and slowly descended the stairs. "I'm sorry I didn't think to ask for your name this afternoon," she said. Now that she had reached the entrance hall, she found that he did indeed tower over her. She tilted her head back to meet his gaze.

"I'm Zack Crawford," he introduced himself, moving across the hall to offer his hand. Aimee stifled the impulse to step up onto the bottom stair to gain some height.

"I'm pleased to meet you, Mr. Crawford. I'm Aimee Bennett, but then I expect you know that already, since you've found your way to our door."

"Yes, ma'am, I do," he said simply. Aimee took a deep breath. Now that he'd found out he'd helped bury the town banker, no doubt he was here for money or some recompense for his help in the cemetery. Maybe he meant to rob them. She glanced at his face again and instinctively knew there was no danger of that. Zack Crawford was not a thief. The rich cloth of his coat and the fine leather of his boots would have dispelled that notion, but it was something else about him, something in his eyes that reassured her. He was not a man who preyed on others' misfortunes. Why, then, had he come?

"Thank you again for your help this afternoon," she said softly. "I would like to pay you something for your troubles, but I am still without funds."

"Then perhaps you'll be happy to have this back." He held out his hand, and nestled in the broad palm was the brooch she'd given to Abner Horn.

"I don't understand," she said, looking up at him. Her long dark lashes, matted from the tears she'd shed, fluttered downward against her cheek, then swept upward as she met his gaze. On any other woman the movement might have seemed coy, but so innocent were her eyes that Zack felt helpless and protective all at once.

"I spoke to Mr. Horn and he feels badly for what happened at the burial this afternoon. He's returning your brooch." Aimee stared at him blankly. She couldn't imagine the sly little undertaker returning a fee, unless he'd been persuaded by someone else. She had a feeling Zack Crawford had done much to bring on the greedy man's uncharacteristic act of kindness.

"Take it," Zack urged, and hesitantly she did.

"Thank you," she said. "The brooch means a great deal to me. My father gave . . ." She swallowed convulsively, then pinned a wavering smile on her lips. The hall was dimly lit, but even so, her chestnut hair gleamed softly, a golden halo around her young face. She was the most beautiful, most vulnerable-looking woman he'd ever seen.

Zack tore his gaze from the luminous eyes and soft pink lips and looked around. Soon he'd be gone from this town and he'd never see her again. It was best. He had no need to get mixed up with a woman again. Caroline, with her coy innocence and smoldering passion, should have warned him away from such ladies.

"I'll be going now, ma'am," he said, backing toward the door. "I'm sorry about your father."

"Wait, Mr. Crawford." She followed him across the

hall, one hand outstretched, her eyes wide and clear as they met his. "I . . . I just wanted to . . . to say that you've been kinder than many of Papa's friends in this town. I appreciate what you've done for us." Her words were interrupted by a knock at the door. Her face registered surprise as she turned toward it. Clearly she hadn't been expecting any more callers tonight.

"Do you want me to answer it?" he asked, watching the changing expressions on her face. For a long moment she paused as if gathering courage.

"Please do," she answered finally, raising her chin and straightening her shoulders. Her soft mouth grew tight, her eyes anxious yet determined. Zack turned to the heavy carved oak door and pulled it open.

"Ah . . . uh, are you some member of the family?" A well-dressed man stood on the porch, his face troubled yet suspicious-looking as he regarded this unexpected stranger. Behind him stood two women, one younger than the other and obviously related.

"Uncle Carl," Aimee said, stepping forward. There was a note of hope in her voice.

"Aimee," the mayor said, and stepped inside. His wife and daughter swept past to the center of the great hall, where they stood looking around with calculating eyes.

"I . . . uh . . . the town council has met and we've decided that . . . uh . . ." Carl Bonham was at a loss as to what to say.

"Oh, do get on with it," his wife snapped. "The council has decided to sell Bennett Hall to pay back some of the money your father stole."

"Lydia, you don't have to be so blunt," the mayor protested. "This is the girl's home."

"Well, it won't be anymore," Lydia exclaimed. "She has to be told. Surely she understands that restitution must be made. This house and all the furniture in it, the horses and carriage, everything must be sold."

"No," Aimee cried. "You can't. Bennett Hall belongs to us."

"Come now, dear, your father bought it with money he stole from the people of Webster. You can't believe we're going to allow you to keep your ill-gotten gains."

"Papa would have paid you back if he'd been given a little bit of time. I'm sure he would have. He didn't mean to take your money."

"It's no use, Aimee, we've gone over the books. He took money from the bank that wasn't his," Carl Bonham said sadly. "I don't know what drove him to it. If he'd needed money, he could have come to me."

"He was a thief who stole money from his friends," Lydia said scathingly.

"He wasn't a thief," Aimee cried, pressing trembling fingers to her lips.

Lydia Bonham paid little attention to her grief. "And when it looked like he was going to be found out, he was too much of a coward to—"

"Lydia," the mayor interrupted.

"—too much of a coward to stay and take his punishment. He did a despicable thing," Lydia rushed on. Her voice shook with self-righteous outrage as she looked at the defenseless girl. Aimee had little doubt she was included in Lydia Bonham's ringing denouncement.

"That's quite enough," Zack Crawford spoke up. He moved forward, using his height and fierce scowl to intimidate the woman into silence.

"What's to become of me if you sell Bennett Hall," Aimee asked. "Where will I go to live?"

"Well, my dear, I don't know," the mayor's wife said sweetly. "You are quite penniless now, you know. I expect you'll have to get a job as a maid or something, and then you can live with the people for whom you work. Perhaps we can use you here at Bennett Hall. That is to say . . ." She glanced at her husband. "We're considering buying it. Rose?" She whirled to look at her daughter. "Would you want Aimee as your maid, dear?" she asked, as if Aimee were already applying for the position.

"Mama!" Rose said, not meeting Aimee's eyes.

"Ummm, yes, I suppose you're right, dear." Lydia turned back to face Aimee. "I suppose you'll find someone who'll hire you," she said.

Zack could barely contain his anger. The woman was insufferable, but the problem was Aimee Bennett's. He'd intervened for her once already. He glanced at the banker's daughter. Her eyes were snapping with barely suppressed temper, and for the first time he realized she was not the meek little lady he'd at first supposed. Beneath that cool, gracious exterior was a woman of fire and spirit. He liked her better for it.

"Of course, you'll have to give up some of your high-and-mighty ways. They won't set well with your betters," Lydia continued.

Aimee's cheeks flamed at the insult. "How would you know what my betters like," she snapped, "since you aren't one of them yourself?"

"You little wretch!" Lydia fumed. "How dare you speak to me like this? You may have fooled the people of this town with that prim, refined air, young lady, but now we know you and your father for what you really are. You'll never be received in a decent home again."

"Leave her alone." Zack Crawford's strong masculine voice cut across Lydia's tirade. "I think you've said enough for one evening. She's just buried her father today."

Aimee shot him a grateful glance. Her face was pale, but her head was still high.

"Just who are you anyway?" Lydia demanded, turning a haughty eye on Zack. Even she was forced to look up to meet the stranger's eyes and she didn't like the feel of it.

"Just call me a friend of the family," Zack said quietly.

"Humph, I'm not sure I'd admit it if I were you," Lydia sniffed.

"And risk being like you?" he returned calmly.

"Why, I never—" Lydia began before his voice cut her off.

"You probably never have. You don't look the type," Zack replied easily, and Lydia was perfectly aware that the comment was made in regard to her femininity. Her cheeks grew mottled. "I think it's time you all left," Zack continued.

"I'm afraid that's out of the question," Carl Bonham said. "The rest of the committee is due here momentarily. They want to go through the house and determine the value of some of the pieces before the auction starts tomorrow."

"Tomorrow?" Aimee cried.

"Tomorrow everything will be auctioned off to the highest bidder," Carl Bonham explained. "I'm sorry, Aimee. I couldn't persuade them to wait."

"Miss Aimee," Hattie cried, rushing forward to stand beside her mistress.

"Oh, Hattie," Aimee whispered in despair, gripping the old servant's arm, her eyes wide with shock. "Don't worry. I'll find a place for us. We'll be all right."

"The sale includes your house slaves, my dear," Lydia said, and there was no denying the note of satisfaction in her voice as the slender figure went stiff with denial.

"You can't," Aimee cried. Her tearful gaze darted from Lydia's triumphant face to the mayor's troubled expression, from Sam's grieving old eyes to the dark flare of anger in Zack Crawford's glare. The room swam around her and gratefully she slid downward into the swirling serenity of unconsciousness.

"Theah, theah, my baby goin' be all right." Aimee woke to Hattie crooning lovingly as she bathed her face. Aimee looked around. She was back in her room.

"How did I get up here?" she whispered even as her restless gaze picked out the tall shadow near the window.

"Mistah Crawford theah, he brung you up heah," Hattie said. "He tell that she-devil downstairs, yo' got the right to be heah in yo'r own house, at least for the rest of the night."

Aimee's grateful gaze went back to the silent figure at the window. Zack Crawford seemed not to notice her perusal. He was concentrating on something outside in the street.

"I . . . I want to thank you, Mr. Crawford," she said, sitting up and smoothing her hair back. It felt strange to have the presence of a man in her room, even with Hattie there.

As if sensing her unease, Zack Crawford turned from the window and fixed his dark eyes on her. The shadows cast a dangerous quality to his face.

"Where are your jewels?" he demanded.

3

"I . . . I beg your pardon?" Aimee stammered. Had she been wrong about him after all? Was he here to rob them?

"Get your jewels and any other valuables you might have. Do it now!" he ordered harshly, and cast an anxious glance out the window. "You don't have much time."

"My jewelry case is on the dressing table," Aimee said flatly. How many more people would betray her before the day was finished?

Zack crossed to the table and pawed through the padded satin box her father had given her for Christmas when she was twelve. The gold chains and small pearl ear studs were carelessly strewn over the table.

"These are a child's baubles," he said, closing the lid dismissively. "Your father must have given you better pieces, more like this brooch." So he'd been drawn here by the brooch after all, and all his kindness downstairs had merely been a ruse. Helplessly Aimee stared back at him.

"Those are all I have," she said dully.

"There have to be more." Impatiently he looked around the sumptuously furnished room. The banker had spared no expense for his daughter's comfort and pleasure. Zack was certain the doting father had also showered his daughter with something of more value than the gold chains and single pearl pieces he'd found thus far.

"My father kept the good pieces in the safe in his room," Aimee answered wearily. She felt battered and defeated by all that had occurred in the past two days. If this devious man who'd only pretended to offer them kindness wanted the jewels, let him have them. She only wanted him to be gone and leave her in peace.

"Can you open the safe?" he demanded, and when she only sat staring at him blankly, he crossed the room in swift strides to take her shoulder and shake her. "Concentrate, time's wasting," he growled.

"What yo' want to know fo'?" Hattie demanded.

Zack wrinkled his brow in surprise at her suspicious tone, then gestured back toward the window. "If she doesn't recover what she can now," he explained impatiently, "she'll not have them, ever. I'm trying to help you, if you'll let me."

Hattie held his gaze for a measure of time, then eased her bulk to the window and peered out. Away down the street she glimpsed something that made her blood run cold.

"Oh, Lawd, have mercy," she cried, and fell back away from the window. A memory from her childhood of milling men and torches lighting the night sky and her father's cry of pain made her quake in her shoes. Men who came in the night like this had no good intent in their minds.

"Hattie?" Aimee cried, and the old woman scuttled back to the bed.

"Tell 'im, chile. Let 'im help yo' if he can."

"What is it, Hattie?" Aimee asked, shaken by the slick sheen on the old woman's face.

"They's bad men out theah," she said, "bad men."

"It's a mob, Miss Bennett," Zack said, stepping forward. "They're on their way here. Downstairs is a committee of the town officials. All of them are here for the same thing, to take everything they can before someone sane comes along and takes an accounting of what your father actually owed."

"You mean they're trying to steal from me?" Aimee cried in outrage.

"They won't call it stealing. They just figure they're recovering what your father took, and if somehow they collect more than is due them, who's to stop them?"

"I will," Aimee cried. "I'll get lawyers."

"By then it'll be too late. That mob isn't going to listen any more than the people downstairs. Get together what you can and get out of here, Miss Bennett."

"But this is my home."

"Not anymore. You heard what that woman said downstairs. If you stay in this town, you'll be hounded and insulted everywhere you go. Have you any relatives who would take you in?"

"None, there was only Papa!" Fear for her future made Aimee's voice tremble.

"Any friends?"

"Only here in Webster," Aimee said, and laughed harshly at her own words. "What shall I do?" she asked in despair. The realization that for the first time in her life she was alone struck her with stunning clarity. She raised a desperate face to Zack.

"First things first," he declared. "Gather up some things you'll need. In a little while the chance will be gone." He turned and looked out the window. Aimee studied the dark planes of his face. She had to trust him.

"I can't open the safe in my father's room," she said, "but Sam might be able to. Papa trusted him with everything."

"Get him," Zack ordered Hattie. "Don't let them know what you're doing. Ask him to bring up some water to tend your mistress."

"Yas, suh," Hattie said, and hurried away.

Zack turned back to Aimee. The lamplight cast a golden glow on her curls and on her skin. Zack glanced away.

"I'm on my way to Missouri. I'm taking a wagon train to Oregon," he said. "You can ride along with me as far as St. Louis, if you want. You may be able to find a job or something to keep yourself until you . . ." His words trailed off.

"Until I what?" Aimee asked fearfully.

"Until you find a man who wants to marry you and take care of you," he said.

She had no skills. What kind of job could she hold? She'd been taught to be a lady, and suddenly she realized what a helpless and dependent life she'd been trained for. The thought made her angry. She swung her legs off the bed and stood up. She was being forced to leave her home and the only life she'd ever known, to follow a strange man away into the night. And somehow she must find a job and learn to take care of herself or look for a husband. She thought of Frank. He no longer wanted her. Would any other man? It couldn't be true that life had taken such a turn.

"I don't think the situation is as bad as you say, Mr. Crawford," she said, trying to reassure herself more than him. "People are angry, but they'll come to realize I'm not to blame for all this."

"Come here," Zack ordered, much as he had Hattie. Aimee's chin thrust upward in rebellion, but he turned to fix his gaze on her and she hurried across the room.

"Before you make up your mind about what you want to do, I suggest you take a look out this window." He held the curtain to one side while he studied the crowd in the street. It had grown since he'd last looked. He felt the girl's presence at his elbow and turned to one side to give her a better view. He could feel her breath on his cheek, warm and sweet.

"There are men down there who don't care if you're to blame or not. They want someone to be a scapegoat, not only for your father's embezzlement but also for every ill that ever befell them. When a crowd gets this big and mad, it's not reasonable."

Aimee studied the throng of people. They had gathered nearly a block away from the house, but she could hear an occasional angry shout. Their torches flickered, casting a menacing light over their faces. She was reminded of the people who'd gathered the night before. Their anger had had a chance to grow. Even the sheriff wouldn't be able to disperse them this time.

"Surely they wouldn't try to harm me," Aimee exclaimed.

"Do you want to stick around and find out?" Zack demanded. His tone was flat, his logic undeniable.

"All right, Mr. Crawford, I'll go with you to St. Louis," she whispered finally. "Thank you for the offer of your protection. Someday I'll repay you for your services."

"Let's not worry about that now," he said, pulling her away from the window. One last glimpse showed that the crowd had bunched together now and were moving down the street toward Bennett Hall.

Hattie hurried into the room, Sam close behind. He carried a pail of water. Sweat stood out on his brow and Aimee wasn't sure if it was from exertion or fear. It seemed to infect all of them except Zack Crawford.

"Can you open the safe in Mr. Bennett's bedroom?" Zack asked as the old man put down his burden.

"Yas, suh," Sam said. "Master Hiram showed me how. He say if anythin' happen to him Ah was to open it for Miss Aimee."

"Good. Do it now. We don't have much time left."

"Yas, suh." Sam hurried away.

Zack turned to the old slave woman. "Hattie, is there a small trunk or bag?"

"Yas, suh, Mistah Crawford," Hattie said, readily accepting his commands. "I got just the thing."

While Hattie hurried away to find the bag, Zack took Aimee's arm and led her to her armoire. Throwing open the doors, he looked at the rows of elegant gowns and petticoats.

"Choose something stout and serviceable," he instructed. "Take boots and a hat with a brim."

Hattie bought a large portmanteau of heavy tapestry.

Zack shoved it toward Aimee. "Fill it up with as much as you can," he ordered. "Wear what you can't get in the bag. It may be all the clothes you have for a spell."

Hattie knelt by the bag. "This heah is a special bag," she explained. "I helped Mastah Hiram pack it once and I seen him do this." Her fingers sought for and found a catch which opened the bottom to reveal a hidden compartment. Zack Crawford's eyes narrowed speculatively.

"Hurry," he urged Aimee as she stood watching them.

Distractedly she riffled through her wardrobe, discarding ball gowns of pastel silks and morning dresses of taffeta and moiré. She chose a mulberry faille, new that winter, and a flowered dimity. Those alone with the brown velvet gown she wore would have to do. Quickly she stuffed some fresh undergarments into the bag. There was no room for more petticoats or any of the ribbons and silk flowers or bonnets.

"Where all yo' goin', Miss Aimee?" Hattie asked as she helped fill the bag.

"We're going to St. Louis, Hattie, and who knows, maybe we'll even go on to Oregon. Why not?" She turned to look at the old woman. "It wouldn't be so bad. We could have a great adventure," she hastened to add when she saw the look on Hattie's face, but the old woman just shook her head sorrowfully. She'd heard about the Indians and the hardships people endured out there in the wilderness. Bad times had surely come to her family.

Voices sounded in the hallway and the people in the room froze.

Zack motioned Aimee back to the bed. Quickly she obeyed, her body stiff and alert.

"What have you got there?" Lydia Bonham's strident voice demanded of someone in the hall. "What were you doing in that room?"

"Miss Aimee sent me to her papa's room to git her some brandy. She still feelin' faint," Sam answered meekly.

"Let me see what you have," Lydia demanded, and Aimee caught her breath. Hattie ran to the door and flung it open.

"Oh, mah poor baby," she lamented. "Hurry here wif' that brandy, yo' good-fo'-nothin' niggah. My baby needs somethin' fo' the vapors."

"All right, take it to her." Lydia relinquished the bottle she held. "Her high-and-mighty ways will soon change," she warned.

Sam hurried into Aimee's room and Hattie closed the door on the suspicious mayor's wife. Hands trembling, Sam put down the bottle of brandy he'd had the foresight to bring and reached into his shirt and pulled out a bundle. Laying it on the bed, Zack unrolled the velvet cloth. All the jewels Hiram Bennett had ever bought his wife and daughter were in that bundle. It was a fortune.

"Quickly, we need a sack or something to carry them in," Zack instructed. He was surprised at the quantity and value of the stones. The banker's daughter could live quite comfortably if she were careful.

Aimee went to get a small cloth reticule with a drawstring top. Zack's large brown hands scooped up the treasure and thrust it into the bag. Was he going to take them after all? She wondered. Many a man would. There was little they could do to stop him.

Zack jerked the drawstring tight and looked at Aimee, his dark eyes alive and thoughtful. "Turn around," he ordered.

"Why?" Aimee demanded. She was tired of being ordered around by this man. A few hours ago she hadn't even known him.

"Turn around and raise your skirts," Zack commanded.

"I will not—" Aimme answered indignantly. What was he up to? She had little chance to ask, as one powerful hand settled on her shoulder and she was swung around and pushed down on the bed. The other hand clasped her full skirts and yanked them upward over her head, baring her scantily covered limbs.

"How dare you?" Aimee cried in outrage, struggling to free herself. "Hattie, help me."

"Hattie, help me." Zack's words echoed her own, but it was Zack the old woman obeyed. "Tie this bag to the waistband of her petticoats, good and secure and so it won't show beneath her skirts."

"Yas, suh," Hattie said, and moved quickly to do as he bade.

"What's happening?" Aimee's muffled voice could be heard from beneath the folds of her skirts, and she wriggled some more. Zack forgot the urgency of the moment as he contemplated the gyrations of the trim buttocks covered only by the thin lawn of her pantaloons.

"Heah now, hold still," Hattie cried, and landed a well-placed slap on the object of Zack's admiration, and the spell was broken. He turned away, willing the rising heat in his loins to abate. He should have taken advantage of the tavern girl's offer. The thought of going across country with Aimee Bennett and keeping his hands off her seemed a herculean task to him.

The bag was tied in place beneath her skirts and Aimee was able to stand aright. Angrily she shook her skirts into place and smoothed her hair, her color high, her gaze not quite meeting that of Zack Crawford. She wasn't sure who had spanked her, he realized, and stifled a grin.

Crossing back to her dresser, Zack gathered up the jewelry from her case. Springing the secret lock on the portmanteau, he stored the pieces in the hidden compartment.

"Why didn't you just put it all in there?" Aimee glared at him.

"This is just a little decoy, Miss Bennett." Zack glanced up at her. "Are you ready?"

"Hattie?" Aimee looked at her beloved servants. "Are you ready, Sam?" The two exchanged glances and looked away from her. "Hurry, we must leave," Aimee cried.

"Miss Aimee—" Hattie began.

"They can't go, Miss Bennett," Zack said. His words struck a chord of fear in Aimee's heart.

"They have to," she cried. "I won't leave without them."

"You have little choice. They're slaves, part of the property to be sold off tomorrow." Zack's expression softened as he noted her distress.

"I'll buy them," Aimee cried, "I'll use the jewels and buy them myself."

"If you show the gems here, they'll take them away from you. Then you'll have neither your servants nor your jewels."

"He's right, baby." Hattie came to grip Aimee's arms. "Yo' keep them jewels. They'll help yo' wherever yo' go. Sam and me, we too old to go off to Oregon."

"Hattie, I can't leave you behind," Aimee whispered.

"Baby, sometimes we jest got to do things that's hard to do. This is one of them." There was a sound of angry voices in the street.

"We have to go, Miss Bennett," Zack said. Frantically Aimee looked at Hattie and Sam, tears rolling down her cheeks. There were tears in their eyes as well. Was she to lose everything she loved?

"Yo' take this cloak now, chile. The nights still get cold." Hattie wrapped the warm woolen cloak around Aimee. How many times had she done that in the girl's lifetime?

"I love you, Hattie, Sam," Aimee cried, hugging both of them.

Zack urged her toward the door. To linger now would only cause her more pain.

"Miss Aimee . . ." Sam stepped forward. "Ah mos' forgot. They was two other things in the safe." He held out a smaller leather pouch, heavy with gold coins, and a letter. Her name was scrawled across the envelope in her father's hand.

"Oh, Sam," Aimee cried, clasping the envelope to her breast. Her father hadn't left her without a word, as she'd thought.

"Read it later," Zack growled, and opened the door. Sam and Hattie followed them down the stairs.

"Just a moment," Lydia's voice rang out imperiously. "Where do you think you're going?"

"She's going with me," Zack said. His hand was firm on Aimee's arm.

"And what are you taking with you?" Lydia seized the portmanteau.

"What's going on here?" Carl Bonham stepped into the hall. Other members of the town council followed.

"I caught her trying to get away with some valuables."

"I've taken only a few clothes to wear," Aimee said calmly.

"We'll take a look and see." Lydia opened the bag and began to pull out the things Aimee had packed. "You have no right to take anything from here, Aimee Bennett. Everything in this house belongs to the town."

"Lydia!" Carl Bonham's embarrassed voice broke through her words. He walked to the hall table where Aimee's pitiful collection of clothes lay in a rumpled heap. "I think we can let her have a couple of gowns," he said. "She's taken modest ones."

"Thank you," Aimee said stiffly, mindful of the irony of having to thank him for what once was hers anyway. Cheeks flaming with angry color, she repacked her case. Lydia stood close by, watching. Without a word to the woman, Aimee picked up the bag and turned toward the door.

"Just a moment, Aimee," Carl said, eyeing the bag thoughtfully. "Isn't that the case your father used when he traveled for the bank?"

"I don't know," she answered.

"Let me see it." He held out his hand, and once again Aimee gave over the bag. He placed it back on the table while Lydia and the others crowded around. Carl ran a finger around the edge of the bag and smiled as he found the hidden lock that released the secret bottom.

"Hiram showed this to me once. He was quite taken by it. He thought he was safe carrying money and valuables for the bank." The bottom gave way and the jewels Zack had placed there fell out. He'd meant them as a decoy, Aimee realized, and glanced at the tall man. His expression was bland and unrevealing.

"There. I knew she couldn't be trusted," Lydia cried.

"These are only a few pieces of jewelry my father gave me," Aimee said. "They are of little value to anyone save me."

"That's not for you to say," Lydia said, picking up the jewelry. "At any rate, it will be auctioned off tomorrow along with everything else. Are you going to put her in jail, Carl?"

"I don't think that will be necessary," the mayor said. "You are leaving town, aren't you, Aimee?"

"I'm taking her north to some family," Zack spoke up quickly. A warning hand gripped her elbow. Aimee felt strangely comforted by this presence at her side.

"I think that's a good idea," Bonham closed the secret pocket, empty now, and handed the bag to Aimee. "You are free to go."

"And good riddance," Lydia snapped. "Don't ever come back here to Webster. We don't want the likes of you here."

Zack took the bag from Aimee's nerveless fingers and turned toward the door, his firm grip still on her elbow. But Aimee wasn't ready to retreat like this without fighting back. She paused and looked at the faces of the people who'd once been her father's friends.

"I'd like to thank all of you for your kindness," she said. "I pray God will show you the same mercy you've shown me." Her eyes were clear and bright as she looked around the room, and some men looked away.

Aimee followed Zack out of the house that had been the only home she'd ever known. The future seemed frighteningly uncertain to her, but she held her head high.

They left through the side door, avoiding the angry mob at the front. Zack led her along the street to the empty town square and the livery stable beyond. A boy had been left behind to care for the animals. He rolled his eyes uncertainly when Zack rousted him out.

"Can you ride a horse?" Zack demanded. Mutely Aimee shook her head. Zack pointed out a sleek mare and the stablehand led it forward to the mounting block. In a daze Aimee settled herself on its back, one knee hooked over the horn as she'd always ridden.

"Straddle it," Zack ordered, and without demur Aimee complied, although she'd never ridden that way before. Ladies didn't straddle their mounts, but what others thought no longer seemed to matter. Everything was changing so swiftly.

Zack mounted his own horse and motioned her to follow as he headed out of town at a full gallop. They quickly left the familiar streets and buildings behind. They traveled north for nearly an hour, neither of them saying anything. Then they cut across the countryside. Zack's progress became stealthy and he halted often to listen for the sound of pursuing hoofbeats. Finally they left the cover of bushes and trees and regained a roadway. The moon rode low behind her, so Aimee guessed they were heading west.

Because she was unaccustomed to riding astride, Aimee's muscles soon began to protest, but she made no complaint. Resolutely she clung to the saddle horn, grateful that the mare was docile enough to follow Zack's mount. The moon rose higher in the sky, the hour grew later, and still they moved down the silvery ribbon of road. Aimee rode silently, slumped in her saddle, emotional fatigue laying claim to her remaining strength. It was only when she'd sagged too far forward and nearly toppled from her horse that she cried out. Zack reined in his horse and turned to look at her. Her face was a pale oval in the moonlight, her eyes weary shadows. Her slim shoulders drooped.

"I'm sorry," she whispered. "I'm all right now."

"You're ready to fall out of that saddle," he observed. Catching the mare's bridle, he led the way past trees and brush deep into the woods. When he'd found a clearing near a small stream, he dismounted and came around to help Aimee. Her limbs felt boneless. Unresisting, she slid down into his arms and leaned against the hard strength of his body. This day, with all its sorrow and hateful revelations, had been too much for her. She'd not had enough sleep and even less nourishment. Her head felt giddy.

Zack led her to a seat on a fallen log, then went to gather up twigs and dry leaves to start a fire. She should help him, Aimee thought numbly, and sat on where she was, watching him with a feeling of detachment. None of this was real, not her father's death or the embezzlement of bank funds or their flight through the night. The darkness pressed in around her and it seemed to represent all the unknown terrors of her future. She'd been gently bred and was ill-prepared for what lay in store for her. Bowing her head and covering her face with her hands, she gave way to a torrent of weeping. Before, her tears had been for her father. Now they were for herself.

"It won't do you any good to cry," Zack admonished, and his voice was brusque. "It won't change things back to the way they were."

"I know that." Aimee wiped at her tears, resolving not to cry anymore.

"You'd better gather some more firewood," Zack said, and she saw that he already had a small fire going. While she'd been indulging in self-pity, he'd been busy seeing to their comfort.

"All right," she said quietly.

"Don't venture too far away from the fire," Zack called, and hunkered down to nurse the flickering flame.

Soon he had a briskly burning fire and banked the coals to heat a coffee pot. The horses were hobbled and their saddles thrown on the ground between the log and the fire. Bedrolls were already spread open and Aimee thought no feather bed had ever looked more inviting. She dropped her load of dried branches near the fire and went to sit on the log and stare into the leaping, crackling flames. There was something soothing about a fire. She thought of all the nights she and her father had sat in the parlor with a roaring fire in the elegant fireplace.

Remembering her father's letter, she took it out and sat staring at the familiar bold scrawl. How like Hiram Bennett was that flamboyant slope of line and curve, the energy and impatience of the letters that followed. What message would her father have left for her? What could he have said in the end that would excuse what he'd done to her?

"You won't know what's in there unless you open and read it," Zack said, and Aimee broke the seal and took out the heavy sheet of paper.

My dearest Aimee,

If you have received this letter, then you'll already know the worst. I have one last hope that may save me yet. If nothing can be done, then I pray that you will forgive me. I have tried to give you the best in life, and you should demand no less for yourself in the years ahead. None of this is your fault and you mustn't believe it is. I have no regrets, Aimee, only that I won't see you married. I have no excuses. Bad judgment on some investments. Now I'm about to be found out. I thought I could keep it quiet until I made things right, but there's no time. Everything I've built may soon be brought down. Kingdoms are often lost for the want of a few more dollars.

God bless you, my Aimee. May the fates deal more kindly with you than they have with me. Don't think too harshly of me.

Your loving Papa

Aimee crushed the letter to her chest, unseeing eyes raised to the dark sky as she rocked back and forth in her grief. Hoarse sobs escaped her throat. Suddenly, strong arms were there pulling her gently against a broad chest.

"Why did he steal the money?" she sobbed. "Why? Papa wasn't a thief. He wasn't."

"Shh! Don't think about it now. It's over and there's nothing you can do about it." She was wrapped in a cocoon of strength and warmth, the way she'd always been with Papa. She buried her head against Zack's chest, nuzzling into the warm hollow at the tanned throat, taking in the manly smell of him that was like Papa's and yet different.

Her sobs quieted and she lay against Zack Crawford, comforted by his nearness. He held her long after her body had trembled with its last sob, long after her breathing had evened out and slowed. She felt good in his arms, small and dainty and womanly. His cheek was against hers, stuck there by the plaster of her tears and a slight hint of perspiration. Her emotional outburst had raised her body heat, enchancing the fragrance of her skin. It inflamed his senses and caused a quickening in his loins. The heat of her body penetrated his own and awakened fires long dampered. Fires he'd thought only Caroline could rouse again.

Zack raised his head and looked down at her. She lay still and wary in his arms. Her eyes were wide and luminous, the pupils dark as if she too had felt the change between them. Her cheeks were flushed and hot, tendrils of chestnut hair clinging to her temples. Zack put up a hand to brush them away. His fingertips trailed across the soft curve of her cheek and he was lost. Gently he gripped her chin in his big hand and his mouth swooped down to claim hers, tasting the sweetness he'd known would be there. She was startled and made no resistance. His tongue traced along the fullness of her lips, but in her innocence her mouth remained closed to him. His hand dropped, grazing lightly against the soft mound of her breast as he gripped her waist and pulled her tighter.

The fire crackled at their feet, shooting out sparks, but it offered no danger to her, not with this man holding her, boldly claiming her lips. Instinctively she wound her arms around his neck. She felt as if the leaping fire had reached out and was consuming her in its hungry flames.

With a cry she wrenched herself free. "Is this your way of helping a lady in distress, sir?" she cried, her eyes wide and accusing in the firelight. He still gripped her arms and she could see him working to bring his own emotions under control. His eyes, dark-shadowed and unreadable in the firelight, studied her with a mingling of surprise and regret. Slowly he released her and stood up.

"I'm sorry, Miss Bennett," he said. "I forgot myself. Reassure yourself, this won't happen again. I'll take you safely to St. Louis as promised."

Aimee hung her head, remembering her own response to him. Perhaps she was partly to blame. "I'm sorry too," she muttered, and didn't look at him.

Zack studied her bent head and a grin played across his lips. He'd never had a woman apologize before. "We'd better have a bite and get some rest," he said, kneeling beside the campfire. "I want to get an early start at daybreak." He dished up some beans onto a plate and handed it to Aimee. Gratefully she accepted the food, but after the first bite was unable to eat any more. Zack handed her a cup of strong hot coffee and settled himself on the ground with his own plate and cup.

Aimee sipped at the hot liquid, feeling its warmth settle her jangled nerves. She felt strangely restless, and time and again her gaze darted to the man who sat silhouetted in the fire's glow. The flames cast his profile, and from beneath her lashes she studied him. All day he'd offered her his help. What did he expect to gain from it? He could have knocked her down and taken the jewels he'd helped her smuggle away from the town council, but he hadn't. Zack glanced up and caught her perusal. Embarrassed, Aimee looked away.

"Where are you from, Mr. Crawford?" she asked idly.

"Maine is my home," he answered. Setting aside his

plate, he leaned back against the log, his long fingers wrapped around the tin cup of coffee as if for warmth.

"Have you family back there?" Aimee asked more for politeness than a need to know.

"A brother." He didn't volunteer more.

"What did you do in Maine?" she asked, and knew she was being too inquisitive, but the dark night pressed around her and a loneliness seeped into her very soul. Besides, she felt a stirring of interest in this compelling dark-eyed stranger.

Zack crossed one long, lean leg over the other. At first she thought he meant not to answer. "My family owned a shipping business," he said finally. "We brought back goods from Europe and sold them in our own stores."

"It sounds profitable," she ventured.

"It was."

"What made you leave Maine? It couldn't have been easy to leave your family behind."

"It wasn't," he said flatly. "I had little choice." Aimee longed to ask him more, but knew instinctively he'd told her all he would about his past.

"Why did you choose to go to Oregon?" she asked just to keep him talking. It seemed to hold the darkness at bay.

"Why not? Everyone's going there. It seemed as good a place as any to strike out for."

"Can anyone go?"

"If they've got the money for a wagon, a team of oxen, and enough supplies to last them for three or four months."

"What if I decided to go to Oregon, how would I go about getting those things?" Aimee asked.

Startled, Zack looked at her. "You can't be serious," he said, and she could hear the barely repressed irritation in his voice.

"I've been thinking—"

"Then stop thinking," Zack said, laying his empty cup aside. "The trip is hard and dangerous for even the hardiest. It would be suicidal for someone like you."

"I'm stronger than I look," Aimee flared. "I wouldn't be any trouble to you."

Zack looked at her in consternation. "To me!" he exclaimed. "You aren't expecting to go to Oregon with me, are you?"

"Why not?"

"Why not?" Zack muttered under his breath. His gaze swung back to meet hers. "I offered to take you as far as St. Louis, Miss Bennett, and no farther."

"I wouldn't expect you to do it without remuneration. I would pay you with some of the jewels."

"I don't want your jewels."

"I'll pay for the wagon and team of horses and the supplies."

"Oxen," Zack said.

"I beg your pardon?"

"Oxen." He raised his voice in exasperation. "They use oxen because a horse can't pull a wagon and survive the rigors of the trip. You can't either."

"I am not a horse, Mr. Crawford, and I would survive it. I come from good, sturdy stock." She leapt to her feet and stood staring down at him, squaring her shoulders in an effort to look large and more substantial. If he weren't so angry with her he might have laughed.

"The answer is no, Miss Bennett. I won't wet-nurse a pampered, helpless female two thousand miles across country in a covered wagon. I don't want your death on my conscience."

"I see." Aimee sat down again. "What will I do in St. Louis?"

"What will you do in Oregon?" he countered.

"The same thing I would do in St. Louis."

Zack sighed. "That's not true, Miss Bennett. In St. Louis there are shops and schools and theaters, all the things you're used to. In Oregon there aren't even any houses. The Indians are hostile. They murdered some missionaries a few years back. Even if you made it across the moutains and deserts, you'd find the hardships in Oregon not to your liking. You're best to stay in St. Louis and look for a husband."

"And what if I have no desire for a husband? I was engaged to be married back in Webster, but when he heard of my father's . . . bad business judgment he . . . he . . ." She bowed her head, unable to go on and tell him of Frank's behavior toward her. It had been too humiliating.

"Regardless of what happened to you back in Webster," Zack said, and his voice was not unkind, "Oregon is not the answer for you. It's too rugged. You'd better get some sleep now. We ride at dawn."

Defeated, Aimee settled herself into one of the bedrolls. What was she to do with herself? she wondered bleakly. She heard a rustling in the underbrush and her worries for the future were put aside as new fears assailed her. Their fire seemed a small comfort in so vast an unknown darkness. She'd never been outdoors after dark. The prospect of sleeping here in the open with only this stranger to protect her was frightening.

She lay thinking of her room back at Bennett Hall, with its rich, heavy curtains to hold out the night and the deep, soft pillows and Hattie there to bring her a cup of hot cocoa and croon away her fears. What was happening back at Bennett Hall this very minute? Were the members of the town council still there, greedily assessing the riches they'd found? Would someone kind take Hattie and Sam and love them as she and her father had? Fervently she prayed so. Her thoughts turned to Frank. Would he be sorry she'd left? Would he think of her and wish he'd done something to help her?

A cry rent the night and Aimee sat up, her eyes growing enormous in her fright. On the other side of the fire, Zack Crawford glanced up, amusement plain on his face.

"It's nothing," he said, "just a bobcat. He won't

come by the fire. He'd just as afraid of us as we are of him.''

"Are you sure?" Aimee asked, looking around distrustfully. "How do you know he won't come creeping up on us while we're sleeping?"

"I'll stay awake and keep watch for a while," Zack reassured her, although he feared a different kind of predator. They still weren't far enough away from Webster for him to feel completely safe. If those old servants of hers talked, someone from that mob might come after her. She'd taken a fortune with her in jewels. Some men killed for less.

Unaware of Zack's concerns, Aimee was reassured. She lay back against the saddle and this time her lashes dropped down against her cheeks, then flashed up, only to droop again. Her last image was of Zack sitting back against the log, his long legs stretched out toward the fire, his hat pulled low over his forehead. A tin cup of coffee was nestled in his large brown hands.

She awoke with a gasp and lay still, her body tense, her gaze moving wildly around the campsite. The fire had burned down to a few glowing coals and Zack was nowhere in sight. He'd left her, abandoned her here in the wilderness. She was about to cry out when she caught the stealthy movement of a shadow. Someone was out there. She pulled in a long, shaky breath and held it.

Was it a bear or some other wild animal? She lay rigid, suppressing the shiver of fear and apprehension that threatened to shake her out of her bedroll. Her chest grew tight as she held her breath, waiting in the still, menacing darkness.

Suddenly there was a crashing sound in the brush; a horse neighed and danced around warily. A woman screamed. Had it been she? Two figures merged and struggled with each other, the smaller one quickly subdued by the larger one. Aimee sat up, straining to see into the blackness. Zack Crawford walked toward the fire, pushing someone in front of him.

"We have a caller," he said when he saw Aimee was awake.

"Let go a' me," a woman's voice cried, and she shrugged her shoulder, trying to break his grip on her.

"Let's see who we have here." Zack pulled the figure around to face him. Aimee drew back against the log as she took in the wild appearance of the intruder. The woman flung her dark hair away from her face and glowered at her captor.

"Who 're yo' expectin'?" she demanded.

"Loretta," Zack said in surprise, releasing her arm. "Why the devil have you been following us? You nearly got yourself killed."

Defiantly Loretta glared at Zack, rubbing absently at her wrist. "Ah ain't followin' yo'. Can Ah help it if we're going in the same direction?" Her gaze went to the banked fire and coffeepot. "Ah could do with somethin' to eat, if yo' can spare it," she said.

"I'll heat something up for you," Zack offered, and motioned her to sit on the log. Aimee stayed where she was, the blanket gripped around her shoulders while she studied the newcomer. The girl wasn't much older than she, but she didn't look or act anything like the girls with whom Aimee had gone to school. Although she was pretty enough, she wasn't a lady. There was a hardness to her expression and a toughness to her voice. Dark, tangled hair fell forward to shadow her face.

"You haven't told me what you're doing here," Zack reminded her as he threw wood on the fire and set the coffeepot and pan of leftover beans back over the flames.

"Ah saw yo' leavin' town. Ah was leavin' myself and wasn't sure where to go."

"So you followed us."

"Ah didn't exactly mean to be followin' you. Ah just had to get away and Ah was kind of afraid to light out on my own."

Zack glanced back over his shoulder toward the road. All he needed now was to have Jake and some of his friends come looking for Loretta. "So you're running away from your father. Why?"

"Ah can't stay there," Loretta said with such complete despair that Aimee looked at her curiously. What could have happened to make a daughter want to leave her father? Loretta answered her unspoken question by flinging her hair back and holding her face to the firelight.

"Who did that? Your father?" Zack asked, and Aimee stared at the bruised and battered face in disbelief. A father wouldn't do that to his daughter. She couldn't remember Hiram Bennett ever raising his hand to her.

"No, it was Abner Horn," the girl said bitterly, and letting the curtain of hair fall forward, sat staring into the fire. "He always gets crazy when he's had a little whiskey. After yo' bought that brooch from him, he had the money to pay for me for the night and to buy all the whiskey he needed. He drank hisself into a stupor and Ah scooted outta there. Ah figure Ah got till dawn afore they discover Ah'm gone and come after me."

"Didn't Jake try to stop him?" Zack ask sympathetically.

"He never stops a customer if he pays cash money. Ah ain't ever goin' back. Yo' can't make me."

"I won't try," Zack said mildly. He poured her a cup of coffee and dished up a plate of beans. His problems were growing by the minute. He should have bypassed Webster. But he had little choice. Both women needed help. He couldn't turn his back on Loretta any more than he could have failed to help the banker's daughter. "We're on our way to St. Louis. You can join us if you want."

"Ah'd be obliged," Loretta said gratefully. "What're yo' goin to do in St. Louis?"

"I'm heading out to Oregon." Zack poured her another cup of coffee.

"Oregon." Loretta repeated the name like it was the promised land. "Ah heard some men talkin' 'bout it," she said wistfully. "It sounds like a real pretty place."

"I wouldn't trust everything I hear," Zack said, and began cleaning up the pans. "They aren't telling about the hardships it takes to get there, and I hear it's not much better once you reach Oregon. It's not a venture to take on lightly." Impatiently he got to his feet. "Where's your horse?"

"Ah tied him to a bush out yonder a ways," Loretta said, pointing back toward the road.

"I'll go get him," Zack said. "You crawl into that bedroll and get some rest. We leave at daybreak."

Loretta rose and turned toward the makeshift beds. She glanced at Aimee, who had remained silent throughout the conversation with Zack.

"Who're yo'?" the tavern girl asked suspiciously. She'd been aware of the girl in the sleeping bag, but she hadn't seemed to matter with Zack there.

"I'm Aimee Bennett."

"The banker's daughter," Loretta said with some surprise, and began taking off her boots. "Did your daddy really steal all that money?"

Aimee drew in her breath, unused to such bluntness. In her world it would have been rude, but then, she was no longer welcome in her world.

"So they say," she answered stiffly, and turned her back on the other girl. Loretta seemed not to notice the rebuff.

"Did yo' get any of it?" she asked tactlessly.

"Not a penny!" Aimee snapped, but Loretta misread her anger.

"That's too bad," she sympathized. "Ah'd a been ashy over it too."

"What?" Aimee asked.

Loretta threw aside her boot and studied the other girl. Was she making fun of her? Loretta wondered.

"Ashy," Loretta repeated. "Mad like and all."

"I didn't get mad over not getting any money," Aimee said flatly.

"What do yo' reckon yo'r pa done with all that

money he took?" Loretta speculated. "He musta had a woman somewhere."

"It's really none of your business," Aimee snapped, pushed beyond reasonable endurance by this rude creature.

"That's the truth," Loretta said good-naturedly. "Ah didn't have any money in yo'r daddy's bank. Reckon bein' poor has some recompense."

"I don't care to discuss this anymore," Aimee said in frosty tones that Loretta couldn't help but discern.

"If yo' say so," she answered, her good humor gone. She was used to being snubbed by the gentility of Webster.

"How did you know Zack?" Aimee asked the question that had been bothering her ever since he had so readily identified their company.

"He come into the tavern early on tonight. He was real polite-like." Loretta's voice took on a soft, wistful tone and Aimee felt herself growing angry toward the girl.

"Do you work at Jake's place?" she asked, and couldn't keep the disdain from her voice. Loretta heard it and her lips tightened in anger.

"Jake is my pa," she said simply.

Aimee couldn't hide her surprise. Suddenly all the conversation she'd heard between Zack and Loretta made sense. She was sorry for the other girl. "Why didn't you tell him you didn't want to work there anymore?" she asked curiously.

Loretta glanced at the fair-haired girl and realized that Aimee Bennett had no idea of what life was like outside the elegant halls of that big mansion she'd lived in.

"It's none of yo'r business. Ah don't want to talk 'bout it no more," Loretta said, glad for the opportunity to give the banker's daughter back a bit of her own, but even more, a deep sense of shame made her want to hide the sordidness of her existence from this prim-and-proper girl. She's probably still a virgin, Loretta thought derisively, and stretched out on the pallet and was soon asleep.

Aimee lay staring up at the stars, bright white in the crisp, cold night air. She was still smarting over Loretta's questions. It seemed even the lowliest had heard of how the mightiest had fallen. Had they all secretly hated and envied Hiram Bennett for his wealth and position? Better to be despised for having it than victimized for not having it, she thought bitterly. Without money, one was helpless, at the mercy of others.

She could hear Zack Crawford hobbling Loretta's horse with the others. What was she doing in the middle of the wilderness with a strange man she'd never met before today and a runaway whore from Jake's bar? What was going to happen to her when she reached St. Louis? The cold stars blinked down on her without offering an answer, and finally Aimee closed her eyes and slept.

4

She was awakened by a soft cry. She lay wide-eyed and still beneath the blankets while she gazed around, striving to penetrate the darkness. The fire had been allowed to burn down and was a bed of glowing, winking coals. What sound had awakened her?

By the waning light of the moon she could make out the silhouette of Zack Crawford leaning against the log. His legs were stretched out before him, his rifle rested near at hand, but his head slumped wearily on his chest. He'd fallen asleep guarding them, Aimee thought gratefully. Even as she watched him, he stirred in his sleep and moaned.

"Caroline, Caroline!" he cried out again, and jerked awake. Bolting upright, he sat looking around guiltily, angry with himself for giving in to fatigue. He wiped his hand across his face as if wiping away the remnants of a bad dream and rolled a cigarette. Aimee glimpsed his face as he leaned toward the fire and brought forth a burning twig to light it. His expressions was troubled; then the light was gone and only the glowing tip of his cigarette remained. Somewhere deeper in the forest an owl called out a lonely, melancholy sound. Aimee snuggled back into her bedroll and closed her eyes, but she couldn't forget what she'd seen and heard. Who was Caroline, she wondered, and why did she haunt Zack Crawford's dreams so?

It was still dark when she was awakened again, this time by the nudge of Zack's boot against her foot.

"It's time to go." He was a dark shadow towering over her. Aimee sat up and looked around.

"It's still night," she said sleepily.

"It will soon be daylight," he answered. Aimee could see Loretta pulling on her boots. The fire had been built up and the coffeepot put to heat. A pan of salted fat back was sizzling over the coals.

Aimee pushed ineffectually at her tumbled hair. Her body ached from sleeping on the hard ground. She felt irritable and grumpy. Morning was never her best time, and Hattie seldom woke her before nine o'clock.

"We can't ride out in this darkness," she protested. "Why don't we at least wait until the sun rises?"

"At the rate you're moving, the sun'll be up before you," Zack teased with disgusting good cheer. "We have to get an early start if we want to make St. Louis by tomorrow. The *Missouri Queen* is due to sail the next day and I plan to be on it." Aimee's ears perked up.

"Where will the *Missouri Queen* take you?" she asked, snuggling beneath the blankets. The predawn was colder than the night had been.

"Independence," Zack replied, and glanced at her. "There's a basin of water over there, if you want to wash up." He pointed to the end of the log.

She wasn't going to be allowed to linger, Aimee thought with growing irritation, and stood up. Loretta had already begun to roll up her blankets and now she carried the bedroll to the packhorse, where Zack tied it on. Aimee could hear the murmur of their voices and soft laughter. Feeling even more disgruntled, she shook our her skirts and pulled on her boots, then crossed to the basin of water. He could at least have set it on the fire to warm, she thought irritably, and remembered the warm, scented baths that had been readied for her every morning after she'd finished her breakfast tray. She plunged her hands into the water and splashed it on her face, shuddering at its coldness. Hurriedly she dried her face and hands on the hem of

71

her petticoats and turned toward the fire. Loretta and Zack had returned and Loretta sat with a cup of hot coffee cradled in her hands while she gazed up at Zack with an adoring expression. Obviously the girl was moonstruck by him, Aimee thought, and seated herself on the log.

"I'm ready for my coffee now," she said regally. Zack glanced over his shoulder, then silently poured a cup of coffee and brought it to her.

"As soon as you've eaten, you'd best get your gear together so I can pack it," he said, glancing at the bedroll she used.

"I have no gear," Aimee retorted, still feeling out of sorts at the early hour and the camaraderie she sensed between Zack and the tavern girl. Again Zack said nothing, returning to the fire to fork up the meat he'd cooked.

"It'll be mighty hard sleeping on the ground tonight, if you don't have bed gear," he said mildly, but his meaning was all too clear. She wouldn't be pampered on this journey. Well, she had no intention of being treated special. Aimee sniffed and might have folded the bedroll, except that Loretta chose that moment to giggle conspiratorially. Aimee's back stiffened. She was being laughed at! She longed to throw the cup of scalding coffee at the tavern's girl's face, but Zack was there again and this time he held a tin plate of fried meat.

"Here, have something to eat. You'll feel better," he said not unkindly. Aimee looked at the fat congealing around the edges of the fried pork and turned away. She was used to eating lightly toasted muffins and marmalade and herb tea served from a tray with a rose fresh from the garden while she was still in bed. She couldn't possibly eat anything so heavy this early in the morning.

"I'm not hungry," she murmured disdainfully.

Zack's lips tightened, but he still held the plate out for her. "We won't be eating again until nightfall," he said. "You'll get mighty hungry before then."

Aimee looked at the plate again and shook her head. "No, thank you," she said primly, and finally Zack took away the plate, and hunkering down by the fire, ate the food himself. Across from him, Loretta ate heartily, her eyes gleaming with laughter as she looked from Zack to Aimee and back again. Aimee sipped at the hot coffee, grateful for its warmth on her queasy stomach. She felt isolated and lonely.

Without another word, Zack folded her bedroll and put it on the packhorse, then saddled the rest of the horses and kicked sand over the fire.

"Time to go," he said, and without a backward glance mounted and turned his horse back toward the road.

They were well on their way by the time the sun was streaking the eastern horizon. Numbly Aimee clung to her saddle, willing herself to stay awake and not fall off her horse. They traveled for hours. Aimee's bottom grew numb and she grew hot and thirsty as the April sun climbed higher. Zack rode on ahead as he had most of the morning, his packhorse trotting along behind. It was up to Aimee and Loretta to urge their reluctant mounts forward and keep up. Aimee longed to stop and take a rest, but was determined not to be the first to complain. Finally a pressing need to relieve herself broke her resolve.

"We must stop for a while," she called out. She could see Zack's horse come to a halt and he swiveled in his saddle to look back at her.

"Is there a problem?" he asked, and Aimee felt a blush rise on her cheeks as she sought a reason for her request.

"Ah got me a need to find a bush," Loretta said. "Mah teeth's fair ready to float away." Aimee was aghast at the tavern girl's bluntness and grateful at the same time that she'd spoken up. Zack looked from one of them to the other and finally nodded his head.

"All right, we'll take a break," he said, and led them off the road and to a small clear running stream. Gratefully Aimee climbed down and walked around, trying to work the blood back into her limbs. Loretta disappeared into the bushes. At first, Aimee felt too embarrassed to go into the woods and thus reveal her own need, but Zack gave her a devilish grin.

"M'lady," he said, and bowed mockingly. Color high, Aimee swished her skirts with displeasure and stalked away. What had happened to change the mood between Zack and her? she wondered. He'd been so kind the day before. Now he seemed not to think highly of her at all. In fact, he seemed to prefer the company of the tavern girl to hers. At least with Loretta he laughed and talked.

Aimee returned to the stream to find Loretta was already there seated on a stump. Zack stood nearby, leaning over her. The sun shone on his dark hair and broad shoulders. He seemed to belong in this setting of newly budded trees, tumbling stream, and pungent smells of dried leaves and fresh, moist earth.

"It's a hard journey," Zack was saying as Aimee approached, "but they say Oregon is worth the risks."

"Ah heard the men in Pa's saloon talk about it. They called it the promised land just like in the Bible," Loretta said wistfully. "Do you reckon a woman like me would be welcome if she was to go out there?"

"I think a woman like you would be a real asset to getting the country settled," Zack said warmly, and turned as he heard the rustle of Aimee's skirts against the dead leaves. He saw the anger in her face, but could think of no reason for it. He'd stopped as she'd requested, although they could ill afford the time. Wearily he shook his head. Miss Aimee Bennett was having a hard time of it, and no doubt about it, but he feared more hard times were ahead for her.

"Time to mount up again," he said, and turned back toward his horse. Now Aimee deliberately rode apart, angry that Zack had so warmly encouraged Loretta about Oregon when he'd been against her going. At least she'd offered to pay for the trip. It was obvious that Loretta had no means to pay. Why, then, would Zack prefer her company? The answer was all too clear.

Once again, Zack set a fast pace for them to follow and soon Aimee grew accustomed to the jog of the horse beneath her and began to take an interest in the countryside. It had been a long time since she'd gone to St. Louis with her father, and then she'd ridden in their carriage with Sam driving. It had been a wonderful adventure and Aimee could still remember the excitement of staying in the stately Hotel Royale. They'd dined in the best restaurants and marveled over the new botanical gardens. They'd shopped in the stores that lined Grand Boulevard, where one proprietor had catered to her doting father. Hiram had bought her more petticoats and gowns than a young girl could ever use before they were outgrown.

Aimee frowned. She couldn't stay in St. Louis. Her father wouldn't be with her this time and the memories of their last trip there would be too painful to bear. Besides, she hadn't the money to stay in the Hotel Royale and she had no idea of what other hotels were suitable. No, St. Louis was out, she decided. But where would she go and what would she do? She felt very frightened again. Silently she rode along, her mind racing.

"Shore is pretty country, ain't it?" Loretta said, bringing her horse alongside Aimee's. Tall oaks and maples towered on either side of the dirt road, their branches forming a green canopy overhead.

Aimee barely glanced at them. "I suppose it is, if you like the country," she answered absently. Time was running out. She had to come to some decision. Ignoring Loretta's attempt to be friendly, Aimee kicked her horse and hurried up to ride alongside Zack.

"I've been thinking," she said excitedly.

"What about?" Zack grunted and cast a glance over his shoulder. He'd been doing that a lot today, although he tried to reassure himself that no one would be coming after them. Still, he prodded his horse's belly and the two women had to hurry to keep up.

"I've been thinking that I might as well go on to Independence with you," Aimee said. "I don't know anyone in St. Louis."

"You won't know anyone in Independence either," Zack said.

"That's true," Aimee replied, untroubled. She'd thought this all through very carefully. "I remember someone at school telling how her aunt had traveled out west to Missouri to teach school. Perhaps you didn't know they have a shortage of teachers out there."

"And you think you're qualified to teach school, Miss Bennett?" Zack asked.

"And why not?" Aimee flared at his tone. "I'm as well-qualified as most women who go into teaching."

"No doubt you are," he agreed, "if you were to try teaching back east."

"East or west, what difference does it make?"

"What would you teach your students?" Zack asked, seeming to ignore her question.

"I don't know. I suppose I would teach deportment and fine needlework and I could teach the pianoforte and writing of verse." Aimee's enthusiasm grew.

"I'm sure those would be of infinite benefit to young ladies in a log cabin out on the plains," Zack replied, and there was humor in the line of his mouth, although he didn't look at Aimee.

"I'm sure they would," Aimee said with a sweetness she didn't feel. "Just because women live in the wilderness is no reason to forget the social graces. I'm sure they'd be grateful to have someone teach their daughters these things."

"They'd be even more grateful if you could teach their daughters how to read and figure their numbers a little," Zack returned acidly.

"That goes without saying," Aimee snapped. "I would teach them literature and mathematics." This last was said with less conviction, since Aimee wasn't as good with figures as she wished herself to be. She could add and subtract as quickly as Hiram Bennett himself, and she was especially good with fractions, but she'd never cared much for toting a column of figures or determining the angle of a curve. She'd been grateful those things were not required of young ladies of breeding but had been left for men to learn.

"I'm sure I would have some practical knowledge to impart to them as well," she said now, as much to reassure herself as Zack. Why did he seem so intent on discouraging her efforts?

"I wondered if I might prevail upon your generosity, Mr. Crawford, and at least continue to Independence with you?" She hated to ask his help again when he'd refused her request to go to Oregon, but she feared traveling on to Independence unescorted. Besides, once they were in Independence, he might change his mind about taking her on to Oregon. But Zack was remaining stubbornly uncooperative.

"No," he said abruptly. "My generosity ends in St. Louis."

Aimee bit her lip. "I'm willing to pay you for your trouble," she hastened to reassure him.

"We've had this conversation once, Miss Bennett. My answer hasn't changed."

"But this time I only want to go to Independence, and I'm willing to pay you in gold coin. That's certainly more than Loretta is able to do." Zack cast her a dark slanting look and she sensed she'd said the wrong thing.

"Contrary to what you may have learned as a child, Miss Bennett," he said coldly, "money doesn't buy everything you want."

"You're right, Mr. Crawford," she answered tightly, her cheeks blazing with anger at his reprimand. "Some people deal in commodities other than money to get what they want."

Zack gave her a level stare that had her looking away first. "You'd best save your money, Miss Bennett. You'll have need of it before you're through." His words were like an indictment falling on her ears. "Now, if you'll excuse me, I'll ride ahead and see if there's a bridge to cross that creek up ahead."

Of course there was. Any fool could see this road was well-traveled by farmers carrying their wares to be shipped along the Mississippi and by travelers on their way to free land in the west. Aimee knew Zack had used the excuse so he wouldn't have to ride beside her. Well, it didn't matter to her. She wasn't the one all moonstruck over him like a common tavern girl.

"Yo're figuring on going on to Independence then," Loretta said, bringing her horse alongside Aimee's again.

"Yes," Aimee said shortly, and refrained from asking of what concern it was to her.

"That's kinda what Ah had in mind too," Loretta said. "Except Ah ain't like yo'. Ah ain't traveled 'round enough to know how to get there."

"I believe there are steamboats that take people and their goods up the Missouri River," Aimee replied. "Papa and I went to the docks to watch the last time we came here."

"Thar, yo' see what Ah mean," Loretta said. "Yo' been around some and Ah ain't. Yo're right smart and know how to do things. Ah don't."

Aimee's mood toward the girl was softened some by her words. "It's true, I have traveled with my father quite a bit," she said.

"Ah was thinkin' that if Mr. Crawford don't want to take us along with him after we get to St. Louis, maybe yo' and me could go t'gether."

Aimee glanced at Loretta in astonishment. How could she possibly think Aimee would be willing to travel with the likes of her? Still, Aimee didn't want to be unkind and say so. Instead she cleared her throat and glanced at the broad figure ahead. Zack had reached the stream and was waving them on. Obviously there had been a bridge.

"I'm sorry," Aimee said with mock regret, "but I'm sure Mr. Crawford will change his mind about our traveling together. He's been most kind in assisting me."

"Ah don't hardly blame him," Loretta said, "yo'

being so purty and ladylike." She sighed wistfully. "That ain't somethin' Ah figure Ah could ever be."

"You could have been," Aimee said, touched by her sincerity. "It's just a matter of learning."

"Ah heard yo' telling how yo' could teach the daughters of some of them ladies out west how to be genteel and proper. Do yo' suppose somebody like me could learn?"

"Certainly," Aimee replied. "I could teach you myself if we had the time." She felt safe in making such a statement. Soon she would never see the tavern girl again.

"Could yo'?" Loretta cried disbelievingly.

"If there were time, but we'll be in St. Louis tomorrow," Aimee said, "and this is not the place to try teaching a girl proper deportment."

"Could yo' try?" Loretta insisted. "Any little bit would help me." Once again Aimee was touched by the girl's eagerness to better herself.

"All right," she said slowly, not really sure where to begin.

Loretta looked at her with a beaming, expectant face.

"Let me give it some thought, Loretta," Aimee said, stalling for time.

"That's all right. Ah ain't in a hurry. Ah waited this long to be a lady, Ah figure Ah can wait a little longer." Loretta grinned.

"One thing you can practice is eliminating the word 'ain't' from your vocabulary," Aimee said. "You should say 'I'm in no hurry,' instead of 'I' – well, instead of the way you said it."

"Ah'm in no hurry," Loretta repeated painstakingly and slowly, trying to copy the same soft tones Aimee had used. For the rest of the afternoon she trailed behind, muttering under her breath as she practiced.

Zack pushed them hard, stopping only once to fill canteens from a swiftly flowing creek. Dusk fell around them and Aimee's body felt cramped and sore from the long hours of riding. She was also ravenous. Now she longed for a bite of the salt pork she'd refused that morning.

"Are we going to ride all night, Mr. Crawford, or will we be stopping soon?" she asked finally, carefully keeping her tone pleasant. Perhaps if she humored him, he would see she would be no trouble and agree to let her travel on to Independence with him. At first she thought he meant not to answer; then he reined his horse to one side of the road and peered through the woods.

"This looks as good a spot as any," he said, and led them deep into the trees. Aimee bent low in her saddle as she observed Loretta and Zack doing, and still the branches tore at her hair and clothes.

"Why don't we stop and make camp here?" she called in protest, but this time Zack made no answer. Temper growing, Aimee followed for what seemed miles through the forest and at last he stopped.

"We'll camp here," he said, and wearily dismounted.

"This spot doesn't look any better than any number of places back there closer to the road."

"That's just what's wrong with them," Zack explained while he began unloading his saddle horse. He glanced up at her. "They were all too close to the road. There are men who make it a habit to prey on travelers along this route. The harder it is for them to find us, the better chance we have not to be robbed or killed in our sleep."

"Oh, I didn't know," Aimee said lamely.

"There's a lot you don't know about things out away from the towns and the law, Miss Bennett. That's why you'll be better off if you take one of the steamboats heading dead east. It's your best bet. One of those places'll have a school looking for a teacher with your qualifications or a man looking for a wife."

"You seem in a great hurry to marry me off to someone, Mr. Crawford," Aimee observed. "Is there some reason for it?"

"None whatsoever, Miss Bennett," Zack answered, and continued unsaddling the horses. "Except that it seems to me that's what ladies like you are trained for, to marry some man who's well-established and can provide a good home for him."

"Well, it is what I was trained for," Aimee said, "and I'm quite capable of doing just that."

"I have no doubt of it." Zack had bent to gather twigs and start a fire. Loretta was already gathering wood.

"Why do I have the feeling you don't hold such accomplishments in very high regard, Mr. Crawford?"

"But I do, Miss Bennett." He repeated her name with such grave formality that she knew he was laughing at her. "Women like you have a place in the scheme of things, but your place is not out west somewhere. You'd be a burden to some poor man out there."

"Is that why you refuse to take me on to Independence or to Oregon?" Aimee demanded. "You think I'll be a burden."

"Partly," Zack said, and so he wouldn't have to fend off questions for which he had no satisfactory answers, he bent to blow against the smoldering leaves. He'd spoken the truth to her. He was sure she couldn't survive in the tough western town of Independence. But there was another reason he didn't want her to continue the journey with him. Ever since he'd held her in his arms and kissed her the night before, he'd been unable to think of anything else. He was running from one woman. He didn't need to get tangled up with another.

"Go gather some firewood," he ordered, and outraged at his peremptory tone, Aimee clamped her lips together and stamped off, unable to understand how such a courteous, helpful man could have turned so surly and uncooperative in one short day.

Her second night of sleeping outdoors was much easier for Aimee. She was growing used to the vision of bright stars over her head and the rustling of small animals skittering through the undergrowth. She would never get used to rising before daylight to crawl into a saddle. At dawn they made their way back to the road and by midday had reached the outskirts of St. Louis. It had grown in the short time since she and her father had been there. They rode past large two-story frame houses with gardens in the small front yards and stables at the back.

"Have you reconsidered your decision about my traveling with you to Independence?" Aimee asked as they cantered through the quiet cobblestone streets. She was certain he hadn't, but it was worth a try.

"I thought I'd made myself clear about this," Zack replied. "You don't belong out west, Miss Bennett. I won't help you make a mistake that could only hurt you."

"That's only your opinion," Aimee snapped.

"Yes, it is, but one I feel so strongly about that I've come up with an alternative for you."

"Oh?" Aimee tried not to be curious, but she was.

"I have a brother back in Maine. You'd like it there. It's along the coast. Eli would be happy to have you as a guest for as long as you need to get back on your feet. Caroline would introduce you around. You'd get to know the folks in town. They're all good people and you'd be welcome there. I'd even pay your travel expenses."

It was a generous offer and Aimee knew she should be considering it with thanksgiving, but something else had caught her attention.

"Caroline?" She repeated the name, remembering it was the name he'd cried out in his sleep that first night on the road.

"Yes, Caroline," Zack said, and his voice was different when he said her name. "She's my brother's wife."

Aimee stared at him for a moment, thinking she'd just discovered something about Zack Crawford that he wouldn't have wanted her or anyone else to know. "It's a kind offer," she said. "Why would you do that for me? I'm a stranger to you."

"My conscience won't let me just walk away from

someone so ill-prepared to take care of herself," Zack said, and he sounded angry.

"You think me pretty useless, don't you?" she demanded.

"I didn't say that." Zack glanced away so she wouldn't see the truth in his eyes.

"You've said everything but that. Well, I'm not as helpless and useless as I look and I no longer want your protection. I'll travel to Independence on my own."

"You'd be a fool to try it," Zack said without thinking.

"Not such a fool as you might suppose, and I have no intention of going to Maine to live with *your* Caroline." In her anger she blurted out the words, not meaning to hurt him. Zack's head jerked around in surprise, his dark gaze catching hers, and Aimee looked guilt-stricken.

She knew about Caroline and him, Zack thought in dismay. How had she found out? How had he betrayed himself? Fury twisted through him. "Madam, we are now in St. Louis. I will take my leave of you," he said, raising his hat in a stiff, angry salute. While they had talked they had crossed into the central portion of the city. Now Zack waved a hand down a street. "This is Jefferson Avenue," he said. "You'll be able to find a reasonably priced hotel suitable for a lady of your position." He pulled sharply at his horse's reins and galloped away toward the docks.

Loretta and Aimee sat looking after him, feeling abandoned and uncertain. His strong presence had been reassuring to them both. What had she done? Aimee thought miserably. She'd managed to anger him so badly that he couldn't get away from her fast enough. Forcing a cheerful smile, she turned to Loretta. "Well, it looks like you and I will be traveling together," she said.

Loretta turned from her study of the busy street down which Zack had disappeared. Surprise was still evident in her eyes. "Ah'd better get busy and find some work then," she said, "if'n Ah want to have the money for mah steamboat ticket."

"Work?" Aimee asked in surprise. "How can you get a job and earn enough money in time?"

"Shoot, it won't take long, especially since Ah won't have to give Pa a share," Loretta said. She'd gotten off her horse and was digging in her bedding. She pulled out a rumpled red dress and shook it out. Looking around, she spied some bushes near an empty lot and headed toward them. Aimee followed close behind.

"What are you going to do?" Aimee asked.

Using the horse as a shield, Loretta slipped off the bedraggled skirt and blouse she wore and pulled on the wrinkled satin gown. It fit over her hips tightly and barely covered her breasts. Using her fingers, Loretta tried to bring some order to her tumbled black hair. She smiled up at Aimee.

"Ah'm goin' down to the docks and find a tavern. Thar's always a man or two lookin' for a little company."

"I thought you ran away from Jake's place to get away from all that," Aimee said, aghast at what Loretta was about to do.

"Ah did," Loretta said, "but it ain't the same thing now. Ah got to do this to git the money Ah need to go on to Independence and then on to Oregon." She shrugged her shoulders. "Ah don't know no other way."

Aimee stared at her a moment more, unable to comprehend that Loretta would deliberately offer herself in exchange for money, no matter how badly she needed it.

"Loretta, wait," she cried. "I'll buy your passage to Independence."

"Ah can't let yo' do that," Loretta protested.

"Why not?" Aimee demanded. "You're willing to take money from men."

"Thet's different. Ah earn that money," Loretta said.

"Then you can earn your money with me," Aimee cried. "You can be my maid."

"Yo're maid!" Loretta exclaimed, and for a moment Aimee feared she'd offended the other girl. "Ah don't know much about being a maid," Loretta said doubtfully.

"There's nothing to it. You can do it if you want to."

"Do yo' think Ah could?" Loretta asked eagerly.

"It's one of the things I'll teach you," Aimee said, feeling good that she could offer help to someone less fortunate than she. "Come on."

Loretta slithered out of the gown and back into her traveling clothes, then climbed back on her horse. She gave Aimee a grateful grin and together the two girls headed down Jefferson Avenue to the hotel Zack had pointed out. She would have to do something about their clothes, Aimee thought, and felt happier than she had in days. She and Loretta were setting out on a great adventure together.

Grandly Aimee signed the register and paid for a night's lodging, ignoring the clerk's raised eyebrows at their disheveled appearance. Surely he'd seen travelers before. Then she caught a glimpse of herself in the mirror and ordered a hot bath brought up immediately.

"I've never seen anything so grand," Loretta exclaimed when they were shown into their rooms.

"It's not as elegant as the Hotel Royale," Aimee said, but she was pleased enough. The room was spacious and light, the linen clean, and hot water was quickly brought for their baths.

Aimee went first. She couldn't abide the thought of bathing behind the saloon girl. When all the aches and pains had been soaked from her body and her long hair was shimmery clean, she stepped from the tub and let Loretta have a turn.

"Mmmm, Ah never knew soap could smell so good," Loretta exclaimed as she carefully lathered her skin. Aimee smiled. She was grateful to have someone share the trip with her. It would have been unbearably lonely, otherwise. She tried not to wonder about Zack and what he was doing now.

Loretta was so appreciative of each new experience that she made Aimee feel worldly. When they had finished their toilette Aimee lent Loretta one of her gowns and the two girls set out for the shops along Grande Avenue. Their steps were jaunty and they talked and laughed easily. People turned to look at two pretty young women enjoying themselves in the bright, sunny afternoon. For the first time since her father's death, Aimee felt eager for what the future might bring.

The afternoon passed happily as the two girls tried on gowns and bonnets. Aimee bought with a generous hand, taking a special enjoyment from Loretta's delighted surprise. They bought new gowns and petticoats and bonnets trimmed with feathers and ribbons. When the sales clerk brought Loretta a plain, drab gown more suitable for a maid, Aimee waved it away and chose a pretty pastel dimity instead. Loretta's smile was beatific. So grateful was she that Aimee found herself feeling ashamed of all the advantages she'd enjoyed and taken for granted. Freely she dipped into her bag of gold coins, urging Loretta to choose the petticoats and gowns she liked.

"Ah don't hardly know how to thank yo'," Loretta said at one point. "Ain't . . . Hadn't nobody ever bought me pretty things like this before. Yo' won't be sorry. Ah'll pay yo' back, though. Ah promise, Ah'll work my fingers to the bone for yo'. Ah'll be the best maid yo' ever had."

Her gaze was so fervent and admiring that Aimee didn't know how to answer her. They gathered up their packages and carried them back to the hotel, then paused for tea in the hotel dining room. Loretta's eyes grew round as she gawked at the chandeliers hanging from the great domed ceiling, and she giggled uncontrollably at the waiters in their black tails. Her good humor was so infectious that soon Aimee was giggling with her. It felt good to laugh again, to remember she was light hearted and young.

After tea the two girls went to the steamship company to book passage on the *Missouri Queen*. The ticket office was in a disreputable-looking area down by the docks, and once again Aimee was glad to have Loretta at her side. When it was time to pay for her tickets, Aimee withdrew the sadly dwindled pouch of gold and found she didn't have enough for both tickets.

"Yo' don't have to pay for mine," Loretta offered. "It ain't too late for me to go out and earn me some money."

"Don't be silly," Aimee said. "I have something else." She glanced around the large dingy room. It was empty save for a dark little man loitering near the door. Drawing Loretta to one side and using her as a shield, Aimee reached beneath her petticoats and drew a brooch from the bag of jewels.

"Yo' can't sell yo'r pretty pin," Loretta cried when Aimee turned back to the ticket seller.

"I have more," Aimee declared. "Besides"—she rubbed one gloved thumb over the bright gems—"it was never one of my favorite pieces." Loretta was struck silent by Aimee's careless dismissal of such a beautiful piece. She couldn't imagine owning just one such treasures, and she was sure she'd never give it up if ever she did.

Aimee carried the brooch to the ticket window and held it out to the man. "Would you be willing to take this brooch in exchange for the tickets?" she asked hesitantly.

The man took the pin, and keeping his expression carefully guarded, held it to the light.

"Are these stones real?" he asked suspiciously, turning the piece so the light caught in the ruby and emerald stones.

"I believe they are," Aimee answered, and waited with pounding heart. What would they do if the man wouldn't give them the tickets?

There was little danger of that. The ticket master

often took keepsakes in exchange for tickets. Emigrants arrived here with their hopes high and their pockets light. Gold watches and wedding rings had often been slid reluctantly across this counter, only the first of many of the sacrifices the emigrants would be called upon to make during their journey. Carefully he studied the brooch wondering about the girl and how she'd come to have such a magnificent piece. Finally he lowered his gaze to the anxious young face and nodded his head.

"It'll do," he said, and handed forth the tickets. Jubilantly the two girls took their prize, pushing them safely into their reticules, then quickly, lest the ticket master change his mind, they left the office and hurried down the street. Their spirits were high and they didn't notice the dark little man following them.

The attack was swift, taking them unawares. Aimee felt hard fingers bite cruelly into her arm and she was pushed toward the gloomy shadows deep in a side alley. She was too shocked to call out at first. Fear knotted in her throat. Loretta recovered first and launched herself on their attacker, kicking and scratching at him so vigorously he lost his grip on Aimee.

"Run," Loretta cried to Aimee as she struggled with the dark-clad figure, but Aimee couldn't leave Loretta. She began pounding on the man's chest and shoulder with her reticule. Her blows fell too soft to harm him, but they drew his attention long enough for Loretta to land a sharp blow to his head. The thug staggered away from them, his hand clutched to his ear.

"Run, Aimee," Loretta screamed again, and this time both girls picked up their skirts and made for the street. Her petticoats caught around Aimee's legs and she fell sprawling in the dirty alleyway, her head banging painfully against the stones. A wave of blackness washed over her and then receded as she tried to struggle back to her feet.

"Come on, Aimee, hurry." Loretta was there beside her, urging her on, but Aimee's head was reeling and she felt as if she might be sick. She pushed herself upright.

"Go on without me," she urged Loretta, but the other girl only shook her head.

"Ah cain't leave you," she cried. "Stand up, Aimee. We can still get away." She glanced over her shoulder at their assailant, who had recovered now and with a snarl was running toward them.

"Get away while you can," Aimee cried, and pushed herself to her feet, leaning against the wall to still the ringing in her head. The man was nearly upon them. Loretta whirled to meet his attack, but this time he was prepared for her and his wiry strength soon overcame hers. Painfully he twisted her arm behind her and placed the sharp point of a knife against her throat. All the fight went out of Loretta and she stood whimpering, her eyes rolling in fear.

"Give me your jewels," the little man rasped, "or I'll slit her throat quicker than you can call out." His gaze darted from one girl to the other.

"No," Aimee cried, forcing herself to stand aright. "Don't hurt her." Loretta stood mute, her eyes fearful and pleading with the little man. For a moment Aimee thought of her as she'd been that afternoon, laughing and happy. "Here's my bag." Aimee held it out. "There's gold in it. There's no reason to hurt her."

The little man dashed the reticule to the ground. "That ain't what I had in mind," he growled. "I want what you got hid beneath your petticoats."

"Don't give it to him, Aimee." Loretta had found her voice and her courage. "Run while you can." The man pressed the point of his knife against her throat and blood welled, thick and red. Once again fear leapt in Loretta's eyes and she fell silent.

"Don't hurt her," Aimee beseeched the man, and with fumbling fingers drew the bag of jewels from beneath her petticoats and held it out. Darting a quick glance around as if he expected a trick, the man licked his lips warily. As if making up his mind about something, he snatched up the bag, and giving Loretta a heave so that she landed on Aimee, he sped down the alley to the street. Aimee and Loretta lay in a heap listening to his fading footsteps, and fell into each other's arms weeping.

"Are you all right?" Aimee asked when they'd calmed themselves enough to assess the damage.

Gulping back the last of her tears, Loretta nodded, then lifted her tearful gaze to Aimee's. "You shouldn't have given him your jewels," she said softly.

"I had no choice," Aimee replied. "He would have killed you if I hadn't."

"Why should you care what happened to me?" Loretta asked disbelievingly.

Aimee paused for a moment, considering all they'd been through. "Because you're my friend," she answered simply, and realized it was true.

5

"Do you mean that?" Loretta asked breathlessly. "Yo' consider the likes of me a friend?"

Aimee looked at the tavern girl and realized they'd shared a lot of plans and dreams in the past few days. Slowly she shook her head. "Yes, we're friends," she said, and tried not to think of the fortune in jewels she'd just lost. Instead she thought of Loretta fighting their attacker instead of running away to safety as she might have done. Still, Loretta had had no jewels to lose. Aimee pushed away the thought. It was done now and couldn't be undone, but what was she to do? She scrubbed at her wet cheeks and tried not to break into tears of self-pity.

"Look, he forgot to take your money bag," Loretta cried, lifting the dirty bag and holding it out to Aimee. "You still have some money left." Her eyes were bright and Aimee knew a moment of elation before she felt the weight of the bag in her hands and knew there were precious few gold coins left. Slowly she opened the drawstring, letting the few coins spill into her lap. They were all she had in the world, those and the new gowns and bonnets they'd bought that afternoon and the two steamship tickets to Independence. Anger coursed through Aimee. They had to get the jewels back, they had to. She got to her feet and tried to brush the dirt from her skirts; then, retying the ribbons of her bonnet, she set out down the alley.

"Come on, Loretta," she said briskly.

"Where we goin'?" Loretta asked, running to catch up.

"We're going to the police and demand they recover our jewels," Aimee declared. They'd regained the street and Aimee set off determinedly, although she hadn't the slightest notion where the police station was.

"We cain't do that," Loretta said, running to catch at her arm.

"Why not?" Aimee demanded.

"Yo' cain't jest go to the police," Loretta declared. "They won't help you and you might git into trouble yo'rself."

"That's nonsense," Aimee scoffed. "We've been robbed. We can't let the culprit get away with it. Just let me handle this."

"If yo' say so," Loretta said with a shrug, and reluctantly followed Aimee down the street. Asking for directions, Aimee soon found the way to the constable's office. Now that she was here, she felt less sure of herself. She could sense Loretta hanging back. Determinedly Aimee raised her chin and stepped inside. The sheriff was seated at his desk, his chair tilted back against the wall, his dusty boots resting on the battered desk. He was engrossed in conversation with a man who sat with his back to the door. Aimee cleared her throat and the constable glanced up at her and slowly lowered his feet back to the floor.

"What can I do for you, little lady?" he asked. The man seated at the side of the desk never turned around. The light from the window reflected on his graying blond hair and the slim shoulders in their richly tailored suit.

"I've come to report a robbery," Aimee said, and stepped forward.

"Who was robbed?" the sheriff asked.

"I was," Aimee said. "H-he knocked us down and threatened us with a knife."

"He held it right to my neck and Ah thought he was goin' ta slit my throat like Ah was a pig at slaughterin'

92

time. He brought blood, see?" Loretta pointed to the cut on her throat.

"He-he said he'd kill her if I didn't give him my j-jewels," Aimee stuttered. Together the two girls gasped out the details of their attack.

"All right, all right," the sheriff said finally. He wasn't used to dealing with crying women. He was better suited to knocking the heads of rough-and-tumble characters who drank too much and tried to shoot up the town or broke a few windows. "What did he take from you, a locket with your mother's hair, a birthstone ring?"

"N-no, sir." Aimee sniffed and wiped at her eyes with a lacy handkerchief. "There were diamonds and emeralds and rubies and . . . oh, I don't know what all. There were rings and necklaces that my father gave my mother."

"What were you doing walking around with a fortune in jewels, and in that part of the city, unchaperoned?" the sheriff demanded.

"I . . . I had gone there to buy passage on the next riverboat. My . . . my father died recently and I'm . . . we're on our way to live with an aunt. This is my maid."

"Where're you from?" the sheriff demanded, casting a quick glance at his companion, and for the first time Aimee gave some thought to the other man, who had still not turned so she could see his face.

"I'm . . I'm from Natchez," she stammered, and knew from the look in the sheriff's eyes that he didn't believe her.

"You're not by any chance running away, are you?" he demanded.

"N-no, I told you, I'm on my way to an aunt in . . . in Cincinnati."

"Why did you get off the boat here?" The sheriff's small eyes were definitely suspicious now as they studied her face. "If you came up from Natchez, you shoulda just stayed on the boat."

"Uh, yes, I . . . I know." Aimee began to back

93

toward the door. She could feel Loretta gripping her skirts tightly. "I . . uh . . . my maid got boat-sick and we had to get off for a while."

"That's right," Loretta said. "My innards was jest a-roilin' and Ah couldn't stay on thet boat. Miss Aimee was right kind to let me git off for a time."

"What boat did you come in on?" the sheriff demanded. He'd gotten to his feet now and he seemed enormous to the two girls. Loretta kept sidling toward the door, never once loosening her grip on Aimee's skirts.

"Uh, I can't remember . . ." Aimee's voice died away. Her eyes were enormous as she looked at the sheriff.

"It's all right, Sheriff. I know this young lady." The man lounging on the corner of the desk looked at the girls. There was a smile on his thin, elegant face. His pale blue eyes studied the two girls. "How are you, Aimee?"

"Mr. Benjamin!" Relief flooded through her. Why hadn't she thought of him sooner? He was one of her father's associates.

"I was sorry to hear about Hiram's untimely death," he said kindly.

"It was quite unexpected," Aimee answered, and waited, uncertain of what to do now. Apprehensively she glanced back at the sheriff. Arlo Benjamin got to his feet and smiled placatingly. "Jeb, I can vouch for Miss Bennett's credentials. I expect you'd better spend your time trying to recover the jewels."

"If you say so, Mr. Benjamin. I'll get right on it." The sheriff reached for his hat and with a final nod at the slim blond man he left the office.

Benjamin turned his pale eyes to Aimee again. She could feel Loretta's grip tighten on her skirts and the tavern girl drew back as if to lose herself in the late-afternoon shadows of the room.

"Well, Aimee, you've grown into quite a young lady since I last saw you. How old are you now, eighteen?"

"My next birthday," she answered, feeling uneasy. She was still reacting to the scare the sheriff had caused, she thought. She was grateful that Arlo Benjamin had been here to vouch for her. She forced herself to relax and smile at him. "I remember meeting you the last time I was here five years ago with my father."

"Ah yes, five years ago." Arlo nodded as if remembering something very pleasant, then rose briskly to his feet. "You should have told me you were in town. I could have helped you with your travel arrangements and accommodations. Are you staying at one of the hotels?"

"Yes, we're at the— Ouch!" A sharp kick cut short what she was about to say. She cast an angry glare at Loretta, who only shook her head warningly. Aimee sighed. She was getting tired of Loretta's misconceptions and suspicions. She'd lived in a world of low characters and trouble with the law, but Aimee was used to turning to figures of authority for help. Still, she remembered the sheriff's reaction before Arlo Benjamin had spoken up for her.

"We haven't found a hotel yet," she said lamely.

"I see. How long are you staying in St. Louis?" Arlo persisted with his questions.

Loretta's tug on her skirt sent another warning, and without really wanting to, Aimee heeded it. "I . . . I don't know. As I told the sheriff, I'd intended to book passage to Cincinnati, but now that my jewels have been taken . . ." Aimee let her voice dwindle off.

"The man took everything from you?"

"Everything," Aimee said, and prayed he wouldn't ask to see her reticule.

"Then you'll need a place to stay while you're here. You will, of course, come home with me."

"Oh, no. We'll find a hotel."

"But, my dear, you'll have no money to pay for your room." Arlo Benjamin smiled sympathetically. "I insist that you stay at my home until the sheriff has recovered your jewels and you can be on your way."

"Do you think he'll be able to find them?"

"I shouldn't be surprised if he does. He probably has a good idea of where to look for the culprit. You're not to worry about anything now. You're welcome to stay with me as long as need be."

"That's very kind of you." Aimee ignored Loretta's yank on her skirts.

"Good. I'll take you there now and notify the sheriff later as to where you are."

"The sheriff?" Aimee asked.

"Yes, so he'll know where to deliver your jewels when he finds them."

"Yes, of course," Aimee said, and hoped the relief wasn't evident in her voice.

"My carriage is just outside." Arlo held his arm for her and escorted her to a smart spring buggy with two sorrels hitched to it. With the utmost courtesy he handed her up before turning back toward Loretta. The tavern girl sidled away.

"Ah'll jest go back to the boat and git our clothes," she said.

"There's no need for you to do that," Arlo Benjamin said with an engaging smile. "I'll have my man go around and collect your things."

"Oh, no, sir, Ah couldn't let you do that. Miss Aimee is very particular about her things and she don't wan' nobody to te'ch 'em 'cept me." Loretta rolled her gaze to Aimee, and in spite of her impatience with the other girl's behavior, she felt compelled to support her in her fib.

"That's true, I am," she said. "Loretta can collect my bags and hire a hansom to bring them to your house."

"If you insist," Arlo said reluctantly. "Just tell him my name and he'll know where to bring you."

"Yes, sir," Loretta said, and with a last glance at Aimee, she was off, speeding away down the street in the opposite direction of the hotel. Aimee watched her go, wondering what had gotten into the tavern girl. Had the incident with the thug affected her judgment?

Arlo climbed up into the buggy, and with a warm, intimate smile that left Aimee feeling apprehensive, he picked up the reins and urged the horses forward.

Aimee remembered the Benjamin mansion. She remembered the turrets rising dark and menacing against the sky, the great entrance hall where her footsteps echoed forlornly, the curving stairs that led up to the second floor and the narrow, darker stair that led up to the third floor and the nursery. She'd been taken there to have tea and cakes while her father and Arlo Benjamin had closeted themselves in the study with cigars and brandy and a few hour's talk of commerce and banking. Aimee had hated the large dark room that had seemed empty in spite of the expensive toys lining the walls and shelves. She'd wandered around looking at each and every thing, taking care not to touch, for instinctively she'd known she wasn't welcome to do so. This room was not like the nursery she'd grown up in at home.

She'd been startled at the sudden appearance of a young man several years older than she who had been watching her for she knew not how long. In spite of her polite greeting, he had continued to regard her with hostile silence until she'd fled back to the schoolroom bench, where she'd sat for hours in excruciating apprehension and boredom until the maid had come to say her father was ready to leave. She'd learned later that the dark, brooding boy was Arlo's son.

Now, as she entered the great hall, she thought of that visit so long ago and wished she hadn't accepted Arlo Benjamin's offer. Still, if he could provide some help, she must put aside her pride and doubts. After all, he had been a friend of Papa's.

"My maid will take you to your room to refresh yourself," Arlo was saying. "Perhaps afterward you would join me in the study for a sherry or some tea?"

"Thank you. I should be most happy to do so," Aimee said graciously. Following the maid up the curving stairs, she stared at the elegant chandeliers and wall coverings and thought of home. Had Carl and Lydia moved in now? Where were Hattie and Sam? Were they still there, serving new masters now?

"This will be your room, ma'am," the maid said,

opening a door onto a richly furnished feminine bedroom. It was so different from the cold, gloomy third-
floor nursery that a sigh of relief escaped Aimee's lips.

"It's lovely. Thank you," she said gratefully.

"There's fresh warm water in the pitcher, ma'am,
and I'll be just outside the door should you be needin'
anything else," the maid said, and with a final bob of
her head left the room. For the first time in hours,
Aimee relaxed a little. It was true she had little or no
money and her jewels had been stolen, but Mr. Benjamin seemed to feel she would soon have them back.
Things were definitely looking up. Who needed Zack
Crawford's help anyway? She was not without friends.

Aimee set about repairing the ravages of the attack in
the alley, splashing cool scented water over her face and
smoothing her bedraggled curls. She brushed at her
muddied skirts, but it made little difference. The maid
showed her the way to the parlor.

"Come in," Benjamin said when she presented herself at the door of the elegant room. Aimee entered, her
eyes growing wide as she looked around. Hiram Bennett had been a man of exquisite taste, indulging his
fancy for the beautiful and exotic no matter what the
cost, but now Bennett Hall seemed modest compared
with the grandeur of this parlor and its furnishings.

"Was your room satisfactory?" Arlo asked, crossing
to a richly carved cabinet and pouring himself a tum-
bler of whiskey.

"Yes, thank you, it's lovely." Aimee forced her
attention back to her host, smiling timidly. Somehow,
being here like this, she felt as if she were twelve again,
as she'd been when she'd first visited. Arlo made her
feel protected and cared for the way Papa always had.

"You still look a little pale from your ordeal." Arlo
picked up an ornately cut glass bottle and poured some
of its contents into a stemmed glass. "I think a little
sherry will put some color back into those cheeks," he
said, offering it to her.

Aimee sipped at it tentatively. She'd never taken spirits before, but she knew many of Papa's lady friends

had a glass of sherry before dinner. That Arlo Benjamin had brought her a glass made her feel grown-up. Aimee smiled up at him and took another sip. Arlo's eyes narrowed speculatively as he watched the soft pink lips settle briefly on the rim of the glass, then move away again. A drop of moisture trembled on her lower lip. His expression tightened.

"Tell me everything that has happened to you since your father died," he said, strolling to the fireplace. A flame burned cheerfully on the grate. There was about the whole room such a sense of comfort and beauty that Aimee felt herself relax.

"I hardly know where to begin," she said softly, and Arlo saw a spasm of pain darken her eyes.

"Come and sit by the fire and begin wherever you wish," he invited, and soon had her seated comfortably with her feet resting on a footstool and her glass refilled. Aimee sank back against the thickly padded settee and took a deep breath. It felt good to have someone fuss over her again and to concern himself with her comfort. It seemed perfectly natural when Arlo Benjamin seated himself beside her. Papa and she had often sat thus when she was troubled and needed to talk.

Slowly Aimee began her story, and Arlo listened as she told him of the way the town had treated Hiram Bennett at his death. Now and then Arlo asked a question, skillfully drawing from Aimee an account of the help Zack Crawford had given her, and he laughed outright at the way they had whisked the jewels from under the very noses of Lydia Bonham and the town council. Even Aimee was able to laugh about it all now that she was safe and warm with someone who cared about what happened to her. She had little doubt that Arlo Benjamin would help her. Their faces were still bright with shared laughter as Arlo took her hand in his and gazed into her eyes. Then his face sobered and Aimee looked at him inquisitively.

"What is it?" she asked.

"I was just wondering about this man who helped you. Do you know anything about him?"

"Only what he told me," Aimee replied. "He's from the east and he's planning to join a wagon train going to Oregon." Aimee was surprised at the pang of regret she felt at the thought that Zack Crawford was even now preparing to leave St. Louis and begin his journey west. She would never see him again.

"Have you thought that he might be the one who took your jewels?"

"The man who attacked us was nothing like him," she exclaimed.

"Perhaps it was someone he hired."

"I don't believe so," Aimee replied softly, but she felt confused. "He had ample opportunity to take them from me on the trail, but he didn't."

"Did you travel alone with him?"

"There was Loretta, my maid."

"Ah, yes, your maid," Arlo mused. "So then he couldn't rob you without having a witness, so he waited until he got to St. Louis and hired a waterfront thug to do the job for him. He was probably waiting around the corner for the man to bring the jewels to him."

"Why, I can hardly believe it," Aimee cried.

"Didn't you suspect him?" Arlo asked.

"At first I did," Aimee said, feeling foolish that she'd trusted so easily, "but he seemed so harmless and he did help me away from Webster and the townspeople. "

"He was helping you because of the jewels."

"But he gave them to me to carry. He had my maid tie them under my petticoats."

"If you'd been caught, he would have claimed no knowledge of them and he would have walked away clear. No, my dear, this unscrupulous man used you to smuggle the jewels away. How else would the thug have known you had the jewels hidden under your petticoats?"

It all made sense now. Aimee felt her anger rise. All his talk of sending her to his brother, all his pretense of being concerned about her well-being had been but a ruse to relax her guard. He'd played her well. Angrily Aimee downed the last of her sherry while she thought of all manner of torture for the devious Zack Crawford. What a fool she'd been.

"What of this girl you claim is your maid?" Arlo asked. "Could she be in on it?"

Aimee's eyes grew enormous at this new thought. It couldn't be that Loretta had betrayed her as well, but where was she now? She still had not arrived from the hotel with their clothes. Even now the tavern girl was probably hurrying to meet Zack, taking all of Aimee's new gowns as well. She'd been tricked and betrayed by them both. Her face grew pale with anger at their duplicity.

"There, there, my dear." Arlo put an arm around her trembling shoulders. "We'll find them and get your jewels back."

"I . . . I trusted them. I th-thought they were my . . . my friends," Aimee said, and was comforted by his arm around her. He smelled of wool and tobacco just like Papa used to.

"Do you have any idea where they might have gone?" Arlo asked, stroking her back in a gentle, sensuous motion that was soothing.

"They have passage on the *Missouri Queen* going to Independence, or at least they told me that's where they wanted to go," she said bitterly. Arlo murmured words of empathy and pulled her against him.

It felt wonderful to be petted as Papa had once done. She lay against his chest and felt his hot breath on her brow. His hand stroked and stroked her back.

"Don't give them another thought," he said soothingly. "I'll send some men around to find them and we'll soon have your jewels back."

"You're very kind," Aimee sighed.

"I want to take care of you, sweet Aimee," Arlo whispered huskily, and pressed his lips against her brow. "You're not to worry about anything else. You're with me now." His stroking hand had moved to her shoulder and stroked downward across the rounded softness of her breast. A shiver of alarm raced through her and she tried to push away.

"No, stay, sweet little Aimee," he crooned. "I'll take care of you. I'll buy you nice presents and pretty clothes. You'll stay here with me. I'm all alone now and you can keep me company. We'll be good for each other, very good." His hand stroked down to her breast again, and this time it stayed, cupping and caressing the softness. Through the thin dimity of her gown, Aimee could feel the heat of his palm against her skin, and panic was born within her. She'd never been touched like this by a man, not even Frank Graham, whom she'd thought to marry.

"Please don't," she cried, pushing against his chest.

"Don't fight me, Aimee. I won't hurt you," Arlo said huskily, and his mouth settled on hers, his thin lips cold and slippery on hers, his tongue probing obscenely against her tightly clenched mouth. "Be nice to me, Aimee, and I won't turn you in to the sheriff. You took those jewels when you knew they belonged to the town."

"They belonged to me. My father gave them to me," Aimee cried.

"They needed to be sold to pay back your father's theft. You knew that and you took the jewels anyway. You could be arrested and put in jail. But I won't let it happen to you. All you have to do is give a kind old friend a little pleasure. This will be beneficial to both of us." He lowered his head to kiss her again.

Aimee struggled against him, pitting the strength of her slim young body against his larger wiry one. His hands caught her wrists in a grip that bit cruelly into her skin, and Aimee gasped back a cry of pain.

"There's no sense in your fighting me about this, Aimee. I'm only offering you a business deal. I'm a businessman, remember. I give you something, you give me something. That's the way it's done."

"I don't want anything from you," Aimee cried, flailing her arms in an attempt to free them.

"Don't be a fool. You need me and I need you. I'm a lonely man, Aimee. My wife is dead and my son has left me. You could make my life worth living again. I could give you a good life. We could tell everyone you're my niece come to stay and keep house for me. We could work it out."

As he gasped out these enticements, Arlo continued to push her down on the sofa, overpowering her with his superior strength. Aimee could feel herself tiring.

"There's nothing to be afraid of, Aimee. You'll see. I'll be good to you. I won't hurt you. You're a virgin, aren't you, Aimee?" The thought seemed to fire his lust even more.

"Please, Mr. Benjamin, let me go," Aimee cried. "You're my father's friend."

"Friend?" he cried, his bony fingers still gripping her wrist. His chest heaved from his exertions, but he had her neatly pinned beneath him. "He wasn't a friend. He was a fool, a stupid man who lost his nerve. For years I tried to convince him there were ways to take money from the bank, but he was too honest. Every man has his price and Hiram's was no different. He fancied himself a philanthropist, always doing something for that little town, schools, churches. He even wanted a hospital." Arlo's eyes glittered with contempt. "He gave me bank funds to invest, then lost his nerve and wanted them back." Arlo laughed. "He always was a fool. He deserved to die. If he hadn't taken his own life, I would have shot him myself."

Aimee's eyes grew wide and dark with fear as she listened to him talk.

"A man has to take what he wants regardless of who gets hurt." His gaze rested on her. "Right now, I want you and I mean to have you."

Tears were coursing down Aimee's cheeks. This evil man had caused her father to kill himself. "You brought my father to ruin," she accused.

"Your father brought himself to ruin by his own weakness."

Her father hadn't deliberately set out to steal from the bank. He'd just been desperate and hadn't known what else to do. Sobs built within Aimee's breast, and her body trembled with them. A light flared in Arlo Benjamin's eyes as he looked down at her.

"You're an evil man," she cried.

"I prefer to think I'm resourceful."

"You won't get away with it. I'm going back to Webster and tell everyone the truth."

"The truth is the same, Aimee. Your father stole the town's money."

"But not for himself."

"See if they believe you." Arlo laughed, his thin lips opening just enough for the brittle sound to emerge. "You can never go back there. The good people of Webster have a wanted poster out for you. If not for me, the sheriff would have locked you up today."

"You're lying," Aimee cried. "How did they know about the jewels?" She was certain Hattie and Sam hadn't told. Lydia! Aimee remembered the mayor's wife commenting once how lucky she was to be inheriting such valuable gems.

Arlo shrugged. "Enough talking. Hiram had himself a beauty of a daughter. I'll teach you things your father never could. You'll learn how to get money from some of the richest men here in St. Louis. You're beautiful, a lady of breeding. You could be an asset to any plan."

Aimee lay still and silent beneath him, listening to his ramblings, sickened by his plans for her. And she'd thought he would help and protect her. She had to get away from him.

"I'll make you rich, Aimee," Arlo was saying. "You'd like that, wouldn't you? You grew up knowing a certain way of living and you want to keep that, don't you, girl? Stick with me and I'll give that back to you."

"You'd make me rich?" Aimee asked, making her voice eager.

"You'd have all the money you need to buy pretty clothes and any doodads you wanted."

"Would I live here in this house with you?" she asked, looking around the room.

"Yes, yes," Arlo said eagerly. "All you have to do is be nice to me, Aimee, just please me a little."

Aimee brought her gaze back to the pale blue eyes and forced a smile to her face. "I like money," she said softly, keeping her voice low and teasing.

"Ah, I knew we could come to terms," Arlo said, smiling down at her. He released her arms and Aimee was unable to avoid another slobbering kiss from him. When he forced his tongue between her lips, she cringed inwardly, forcing herself to hold still. She could feel his bony fingers creeping down her sides and fastening themselves on her breasts. He squeezed painfully and Aimee pressed herself to him, trying to loosen his hold on her. Mistaking her intent, he drew back and laughed shakily.

"That's more like it," he said, and raised himself to his knees while he fumbled with the fastenings on his breeches. Aimee drew up a knee and lashed out, kicking at him as hard as she could. Her foot thudded against him and she heard his yell of pain as he fell to the floor, his hands clutching at himself, his face distorted as if in agony. Surprise held Aimee still for a moment. Had she really hurt him so badly? Should she get help for him? Then the realization of what he'd tried to do to her galvanized her to action. She sprang to her feet and fled across the room and out into the hall.

"Come back here, you little fool," Arlo gasped hoarsely. "I'll have the sheriff after you." But Aimee kept going, swinging open the door and running into the street. She was without her bonnet and shawl. The cool evening air raised gooseflesh on her arms, but she had no intention of going back into that house. Luckily she'd tied her reticule with its pitifully few coins and the steamboat tickets at her waist and it banged against her legs as she ran. She clasped the small cloth bag in her hands protectively and slowed her footsteps to a fast walk. There was no need to call attention to herself by running. Arlo Benjamin's words rang in her head. She could be arrested and sent to jail for taking the jewels, and she no longer had them. Zack Crawford and Loretta had tricked her out of them. Even now they must be laughing at her stupidity.

Aimee walked for what seemed like hours, uncertain of what to do next or where to go. Darkness was drifting into the streets of St. Louis. The night crowds were more boisterous. Men, already drunk in spite of the early hour, spilled from the doorway of one tavern and lurched down the street to another. Finally, not knowing where else to go, Aimee turned her footsteps back to the hotel, grateful to see the welcoming lights.

"Psst." The sound came from the dark shadows at the side of the hotel. Aimee halted and peered through the blackness, unable to make out the form lurking there and afraid to go closer and investigate. Tentatively she took a step toward the brightly lit door of the hotel.

"Psssst!" The sound was more insistent, and once again Aimee paused.

"Don't go in there," a whispered voice admonished her. "Sheriff's in there lookin' for you."

Aimee drew back from the door. "Loretta?" she asked cautiously.

"Yeah, it's me," came the voice. "Ah been waitin' here for yo'. Ah knowed you'd come back heah sooner or later."

"Why are you hiding here in the shadows?" Aimee asked softly.

"Like Ah said, the sheriff and thet feller that was with him are settin' in there lookin' for you. Quick, hide. They're comin'." Aimee scurried into the shadows with Loretta. Breathlessly they waited as Arlo Benjamin and the sheriff opened the door and stepped out onto the sidewalk. For a while they stood looking around.

"I don't believe she's coming back here," the sheriff said.

"We'll wait," Arlo said grimly. "Sooner or later, she'll show up." The two of them disappeared back inside the hotel.

"How did they know where we were?" Aimee wondered out loud.

"Ah musta been follered," Loretta grunted.

Aimee drew a trembling breath and peered through the darkness at Loretta. "Why are you still here?" she asked. "I thought you and Zack Crawford would be long gone by now."

"Me and Mr. Crawford?" Loretta repeated in surprise. "He don't want to travel with the likes of me."

"You mean you weren't part of his plans to steal my jewels?" Aimee demanded.

"Ah ain't a thief," Loretta cried huffily. "Besides, Ah never even knew you had the jewels until you pulled the bag out in the ticket station."

"Zack knew they were there and he could have told you," Aimee accused her.

"If Ah took your jewels, why would Ah still be here takin' a chance on being caught by the sheriff?" Loretta demanded, arms akimbo as she glared indignantly at Aimee. Suddenly Aimee believed her to be innocent, and a wave of relief washed over her.

"I'm sorry, Loretta," she whispered. "It's just that Mr. Benjamin said that you and Zack must have been in this together."

"Mr. Benjamin don't look to me lak' a man to trust," Loretta replied.

"He wasn't, but how did you know?"

"In mah business, you git so's you kin tell," Loretta replied. "Now, we'd better git away from here or thet sheriff'll have us yet. Ah already got our clothes out of the room and sneaked out the back way, so they think Ah'm still up theah waitin' for you. Won't take 'em long to git wise and check up on us, so we'd best git away while we can."

"But where will we go?" Aimee asked, picking up one of the bags and following Loretta down the back street.

"Ah figure we kin go to the boat and stay overnight there. Once the boat sails, they cain't git us as easily."

Aimee followed Loretta's lead, grateful to have her

friend beside her. Loretta moved through the back streets with an ease and confidence that amazed Aimee, since the tavern girl had never been there before today.

"I have a good sense of direction," Loretta said over her shoulder when Aimee commented on it. The tavern girl led them safely past the riverside taverns and bawdy houses and soon they were at the dock where the *Missouri Queen* was tied up.

"Wait!" Loretta cautioned when Aimee would have run forward, and the two girls stood in the shadows for a while watching. Soon Loretta pointed out a man who lounged near the gangplank talking to some of the boatmen. "He don't belong down here. The sheriff must've sent him," she said finally, "but how did he know where to look?"

"It's my fault. I told Arlo Benjamin everything. Where we were going, everything."

"Why'd yo' do thet?" Loretta demanded in disbelief.

"I trusted him," Aimee said bleakly. "What are we going to do? How are we going to get on the boat?" Loretta stood looking around. Some men came out of a tavern nearby and headed toward the *Missouri Queen*. Some of them staggered, and laughed, then with arms slung over their companions' shoulders, stumbled back to the steamboat.

"Ah got an idea!" Loretta cried, and began digging through her bag until she found the rumpled satin dress.

"I thought you threw that away," Aimee said.

"Ah ain't never had me many dresses. Ah ain't about to throw any away. You never know when they come in handy." She began to undress, and slid the red satin dress over her head.

"What are you going to do?" Aimee asked.

"Ah'm goin' ta make a stir, and when thet sheriff's deputy comes to see what's wrong, you take the bags and git on board."

"But how will you get on board?"

"Ah'll figure out something," Loretta said. "Are you ready?"

"Will you be all right?" Aimee asked.

Loretta smiled. "Jest fine!" Aimee watched as she walked toward a group of men who had left the tavern.

"Out of mah way," she said, pushing one of the drunken men so he toppled and fell to the ground.

"Here now," he bawled, flopping over to peer up at her. "You got no call to do that."

"Ah got a right, you drunken bum. While Ah'm workin', yo're down here drinkin' away my money. Yo're no good." She landed a kick and the man rolled away over the muddy cobblestones.

"Hey, Les, yo' sure got yo'r woman riled."

"She ain't mah woman," the man bellowed, and rolled to his feet.

"Now yo' denyin' yo' know me?" Loretta shrieked, and landed a punch on the man's jaw.

"Thet's sure some woman yo' got there, Les," one of his companions called, and the other men cheered and hooted.

"Ah done tol' you, she ain't mah woman," he bellowed, and danced aside drunkenly as Loretta took another swing at him. Laughter bubbled up within Aimee, mingled with concern for her friend, and she forced her attention back to the man at the gangplank of the *Missouri Queen*. He'd stopped talking and was watching the ruckus Loretta had created, but he didn't move.

"Go on," Aimee urged him under her breath.

"Ah suppose yo' goin' to tell me yo' don't have a coupla kids, either," Loretta was shrieking, her fist flailing at the poor bewildered man. "Yo' always was a low-down, no-good drifter. Ah took yo' in and give yo' a bed to sleep in and wash yo' clothes and give yo' money and yo' won't even admit yo' know me or yo'r own kids. Yo're a mean man, Amos Hicks, a mean man." She landed another blow.

"Now, yo' cut thet out or Ah'll give yo' a taste a my own fist, woman," Amos cried, and Loretta let out a scream that made Aimee jump. Was she injured? Should Aimee go to her aid? But once again Loretta's arm flailed through the air and her fist connected with the man's jaw.

The man at the gangplank had moved toward the din now, and the way was clear. Quickly Aimee carried the bags, and dodging from one pile of cargo to another, made her way to the riverboat. With her heart thundering in her ears, she ran across the gangplank and dropped behind some cargo stored on the lower deck. Cautiously she peered out at Loretta and the men onshore.

"Ah'm not Amos," the man was bellowing now, and took a wild swing at Loretta. Nimbly she ducked aside and the punch landed on the ear of one of the onlookers.

"Wat'd yo' hit me fer?" the man yelled, and balled up his fist and swung. Suddenly the whole group seemed embroiled in a mass of swinging fists. Even the sheriff's deputy was caught up in it. Aimee watched as Loretta ran across the dock and up the gangplank.

"Loretta, I'm here," Aimee called softly and in a moment the tavern girl was beside her. "Are you all right?" Aimee asked anxiously.

"Right as rain," Loretta said, and grinned. Suddenly the two girls were giggling, crouching behind the cargo while they gave way to their mirth. They were aboard ship, and if they could just avoid detection before the ship sailed, they'd be safe.

"What do we do now?" Aimee asked, looking around. "If we go to our rooms, they may find us."

"We could sleep down here till the boat sails," Loretta suggested.

"Here?" Aimee looked around her. The lower deck of the packet was cluttered with rigging and cargo, and down at the stern end came the sounds and smells of animals. She glanced back at the wharf. The fight had broken up now and the sheriff's deputy was returning to his post near the boat ramp. "I guess this is better than some places I could have spent the night," Aimee whispered, and crouching lest the deputy see them, they made their way among the cargo, searching for a place to sleep.

"Come over here," a voice called softly. Warily the two girls looked at each other and then at the tall, gangly figure that loomed up near them. "Ya'll be safer sleepin' up near the bow with the rest of the folks," he said. "The roust 'bouts and stokers sleep back here and they might bother ya'll durin' the night."

"Who're you?" Aimee demanded fearfully.

"Billy Parsons," the friendly young voice said. "Ah'm from Tennessee and Ah'm headed for Oregon. They's other folks'n their wagons up here in the front."

Aimee looked at Loretta. "Can we trust him?" she whispered.

"We have to," Loretta whispered back. "Besides, he sounds nice and friendly." They followed the skinny figure toward the bow until he came to a small protected space closed off by stacks of cargo.

"The wagons are parked jest ovah there," he said, pointing ahead. "This'll give ya'll some privacy and if you need help I'll jest be on the other side of that stack o' cargo." He paused and looked at the girls. "Did ya'll bring some blankets?" Dumbly the girls shook their heads. "Ah'll git ya'll some. The nights kin git dampish here on the river." He turned and disappeared behind some crates. Uneasily the girls looked around.

"Do you suppose we'll be safe here?" Aimee asked. "Can we trust him?"

"He won't hurt us," Loretta said, and there was so much conviction in her voice that Aimee glanced at her.

"How do you know?" she asked. "He might just be acting friendly and helpful to lower our guard and then rob us or worse."

"Ah just know he won't," Loretta said. "Ah could tell by his voice." Busily she began placing their bags for pillows.

"This should keep ya'll warm fer the night." Billy

was back and he held two rough wool blankets in his hands.

"Thank yo'," Loretta said, taking them from him. "We're much obliged."

"Yo're welcome," Billy mumbled, shuffling his feet a little. The pale light from the ship's lanterns shone on his red hair. Aimee was sure he had freckles. Something about him was reassuring. Loretta seemed to have known that instinctively, just as she'd known that Arlo Benjamin was not to be trusted.

"Ah don't believe Ah got yo're names," he said now, and Loretta made the introduction.

"Ah'm right glad t' make yo'r acquaintance." Billy stood staring down at Loretta. "What are two pretty girls lak' yo' runnin' from the law for?"

Aimee glanced up from her place on the makeshift pallet and was surprised to see the way Loretta's lips pouted prettily and one hip jutted out, swaying provocatively. Loretta, Aimee observed, was a bit of a tease when it came to men.

"We ain't really runnin' from the law," Loretta said softly, and her voice sounded all breathless like she'd been running for hours. She hadn't been breathing that hard when she'd run from the men on the wharf, Aimee thought, and sat watching her with wide eyes. "We're trying to git away from some bad men who wanted us to . . . to do things a . . . a lady wouldn't do." Loretta hung her head as if too shamed even to speak of it. "Yo' won't tell them where we are, will yo'?"

"Yo're safe here with me. Ah'll watch out for yo'. Yo' just rest now. Won't nobody bother yo' while Billy Parsons is on the job."

"Thet's right kindly of yo', sir," Loretta said, and Aimee could nearly see the young man's thin chest swell with manly pride.

"If'n yo' need anythin' durin' the night, yo' jest call out to me," Billy admonished, and then was gone, his expression flustered every time he looked at Loretta.

"How do you manage to do that?" Aimee asked

when the two girls were settled under the warm blankets, their heads pillowed on their travel bags as they studied the starry sky above them.

"Do what?" Loretta asked.

"Oh, sway your hips and make your voice all soft and . . . and mysterious-sounding. You had that boy practically eating out of your hand."

"Ah fairly did, didn't Ah?" Loretta said smugly, then giggled. "It jest sorta comes to me thet's the way men want me to act, so Ah jest do it. Seems to me yo'd have to fo'get yo're a lady to do it. Ah don't think yo' could ever act lak' thet, 'cause yo're ever' inch a lady."

"I'm not so sure that's something to be desired," Aimee said wearily.

"Yo' cain't change it now," Loretta said. "Yo' was born a lady. It ain't something thet'll leave yo'." The wistful note was back in her voice.

"I wish I could be a little more like you," Aimee said softly.

"Yo' do?"

"Yes, you were very brave and quick-witted back there on the wharf. You know how to take care of yourself. Not like me. I've handled things very badly so far."

"Yo' ain't had much chance t' learn how t' take care a yo'self," Loretta consoled her. "Yo're bound to make mistakes in the beginnin'."

"I understand now what Zack was trying to say," Aimee went on. "You'll be an asset in Oregon."

"Ah aim to be," Loretta said with such determination that Aimee suspected she wasn't sure what an asset was. She'd have to explain tomorrow, she thought sleepily. Suddenly she began to laugh.

"What's so funny now?" Loretta asked.

"Here I am sleeping under the stars for another night," Aimee said. "Life takes some strange turns."

"Ain't that the truth," Loretta said, and yawned. "Aimee?"

"Umm?"

"Ah don't hardly believe what thet Mr. Benjamin tol' you 'bout Zack Crawford. Ah don't believe he took yo'r jewels. Mah innards tell me he's not a thievin' man."

Aimee lay considering her words studying the star-studded night sky, and listening to the slap of water against the hull of the boat. For the first time she accepted that her old life was forever gone. She must learn to be more like Loretta. She must learn to trust her innards—and like Loretta's, Aimee's innards told her that Zack Crawford was not a thieving man. Another thought occurred to her.

"Loretta," she whispered urgently, "if by chance we see Zack again, don't tell him about the jewels being stolen."

"If that's what yo' want," Loretta mumbled.

Aimee lay back against her makeshift pillow and looked at the sky. She'd see Zack again. They'd be traveling to Independence together after all. Smiling, she closed her eyes and was soon asleep.

6

❧

The whistle was loud and piercing, startling them
from their sleep. Both girls sat up and looked at each
other, then grinned and brushed the sleep from their
eyes. Roustabouts had finished the rest of the cargo
and the gawky sternwheeler was preparing to pull
away from the wharf. The decks vibrated with the
churn of her motors, and the gangplank had been
drawn in. Quickly the two girls shook out their skirts
and brushed their hair; then, certain they looked pre-
sentable, they ambled forth in search of their staterooms.

Aimee had purchased first-class passage for them.
Their rooms were on the upper deck and opened off
the long narrow cabin which served the dual purpose
of a dining and sitting room.

Loretta's mouth fell open at the elegance of the
wood paneling and the ornate mirrors. "It's a floatin'
castle," she exclaimed, and Aimee chuckled, thinking
she might well think that, what with the pristine white
pillars and beams with their ornate carving and embel-
lishments. Even the smokestacks towered over all,
majestic and graceful.

They left their bags in their rooms and at last felt
safe enough to stand at the rail with the other passengers and watch the squat boat maneuver away from
the dock. The muddy Missouri water swirled around
the boat's hull.

A disturbance onshore drew their attention. A lone
man was being chased by several others. They caught

115

him and two of them held his arms while the others took turns landing blows on his unprotected head and face. Valiantly the man struggled to free himself and by sheer strength jerked one arm free. He landed a blow on his other captor and for a moment it seemed he might free himself yet, but more men rushed forward and he was overcome by their sheer number. Silently the people at the rail watched the brave man's struggle.

"It's shameful," a woman cried. "Where are the law-enforcement officers?"

"There's the sheriff over there. He's just watching them," a man exclaimed.

"He's with Arlo Benjamin," a man beside Aimee replied. "He doesn't do anything unless Benjamin tells him to."

"But they're killing that poor man," the woman cried, and Aimee turned her attention back to the struggling figure. With a growing sense of dread she studied the tall dark-haired man, remembering how she'd told Arlo Benjamin about Zack Crawford. It couldn't be, she thought anxiously, but Loretta stirred beside her and cried out.

"It's Zack!" Even as the girls watched, the battered man braced himself against his two captors and swung his knees up, kicking out against the others who were intent on their attack of him. His feet landed neatly in the chest of one man and the ruffian fell backward, carrying two other men with him as they sprawled across the dock. With a mighty heave, Zack jerked the two men who held his arms forward so they lost their grip. One quick blow and he was free, sprinting across the dock toward the *Missouri Queen*, but she'd already moved away from the boat landing and was entering the deeper channel of the river.

"Don't let him get away, you fools," Arlo Benjamin roared, and with howls of rage the men were after him. Without pausing, Zack leapt into the muddy river and came up with his arms cutting through the water in clean, powerful strokes.

"Come on, you can make it!" The people on board the *Missouri Queen* called encouragement, and men ran to haul out the long pikes that were used to snag floating cargo or logs from the river. Aimee's heart seemed to stop as she watched Zack swim after the riverboat. He'd never make it and if he got too close to the stern he'd be sucked into the paddle wheels. Her hands were white from gripping the railing until she saw Zack grab hold of a hooked pole. Quickly he was pulled to safety.

"Come on," Loretta shouted, and led the way down the gangway to the stern deck, where people had gathered around the exhausted man.

"Mr. Crawford, I thought you came aboard last night," the captain said.

"I did," Zack gasped, wiping at the runnels of muddy water coursing down his face. "I went ashore this morning to look for someone. These men attacked me when I left the hotel."

Had he gone back looking for her? Aimee wondered. No, he'd made it plain he wouldn't concern himself about her any further.

"Did you find who you was lookin' for?" the captain asked, and Zack shook his head.

"They must have gone on to Cincinnati and points east, as I advised." He stopped wiping at his hair and stared back at the receding wharf. "I hope so, anyway," he murmured.

Aimee's heart leapt. He *had* gone back looking for her. He hadn't been able just to walk away from her. The thought was reassuring.

People began to drift away. When Loretta would have gone forward to talk to Zack, Aimee caught her arm and motioned to her to wait. With a nod of understanding, Loretta turned and made her way back along the deck. At last Zack stood alone at the rail, gazing back at the docks and warehouses of St. Louis. There was about him an air of regret that emboldened Aimee to step forward.

117

"Zack," she said softly, and smiled as he whirled and looked at her in astonishment.

"Aimee," he cried, and she saw relief in his eyes at seeing her again, but then he pulled his expression into stern lines and glared at her. "What are you doing on this boat?" he demanded. "I thought you headed east."

"I didn"t want to go east," she said softly. "I'm going out to Independence and teach school."

"That's a fool thing to do."

"Perhaps, but I won't know that unless I try. What was the trouble on the dock?"

"Just some men trying to rob me. I'm not quite sure what they wanted."

"Did they take anything from you?"

Slowly Zack shook his head. "They didn't even take my wallet. They kept saying something about jewels." His gaze swung to Aimee. "Your jewels are all right, aren't they?" he asked, and in that moment, if any lingering doubt of Zack's innocence had remained, it would have died there, so filled with concern was the look in his eyes.

"I'm fine," she said, trying to restrain the surge of happiness she felt. "You've been hurt. You should have those cuts tended."

"I suppose I'd better," he said, gingerly touching one cheekbone. He glanced at her. "I'll see you later, won't I?"

Aimee nodded. "I'll be here," she said softly. Zack returned her smile and limped away, his boots squishing with every step. Aimee looked at the large wet boot prints he'd left on the deck and on impulse placed her own smaller foot in one. His stride was so much longer than hers, she had difficulty in stepping into the others. Suddenly, afraid someone had observed her moment of foolery, she swished her skirts and headed for the promenade deck to look for Loretta, but she was nowhere to be found. Forlornly Aimee walked along, staring at the wooded shoreline crowding the narrow river. Her thoughts were in turmoil.

There was no reason for her to make such a fool of herself over Zack Crawford. He'd made it plain he wanted no part of her, and the fact he'd gone back to the hotel to check on her meant next to nothing. He'd meant only to ease his guilty conscience for having abandoned her so abruptly. No, she must be very careful from here on. She'd trusted her father and he'd failed her, and she'd trusted Arlo Benjamin and he'd meant to use her in the worst way possible. Zack was no different. She must keep her guard up against him.

Sedately she paced, her resolve hardening against Zack and his dark, roguish charm. She'd been the fool too much lately, and it had cost her dearly. She must learn how to survive on her own. She must be wary. Reaching this conclusion, she felt stronger and surer of herself. Standing at the rail, she watched the landscape pass by. She was going to a new life, and the old one was sliding away from her as surely as the muddy Missouri waters swirling away on either side. The riverboat's whistle sounded and it seemed to Aimee a clarion call to the bright promise of what lay ahead.

Loretta came to stand beside her. "They's sure a lot of people on this boat," she declared, "and nearly every one of 'em goin' on to Oregon." Her words cast a pall over Aimee's newfound sense of purpose.

"Are you so set on Oregon?" she asked. "Have you ever considered just settling in Independence?"

"Nah, Ah been wantin' to see Oregon for a long time." Loretta gazed out at the river as if she were looking at the fertile green valleys and mountains of Oregon already. "Ah want to start all over fresh and new. Ah figure Ah can make me a new life out there, where it don't matter what Ah been."

"It's just that I'll miss you so," Aimee sighed.

"Ah won't be goin' right away," Loretta said with a laugh. "Ah got to earn me enough money to pay for my way there. Ah been listenin' to them people down there with their wagons and such."

Aimee looked over the railing to the lower deck,

where flatbed wagons had been stored for the trip upriver. Some of them bore curved bows of wood over which white drill cloth would be stretched later.

"It seems to me a strange way to travel," Aimee observed.

Loretta just laughed. "It seems downright excitin' to me," she declared, and suddenly Aimee's future as a teacher in Independence seemed lackluster.

"Loretta, I would hardly have recognized you," a voice said behind them, and both girls whirled to find Zack standing nearby. He'd bathed and changed clothes and looked considerably better. Although the muddy river water was gone, the bruises and cuts from his beating were not. Aimee felt an urge to gently touch his bruised chin and place a small kiss near his scraped cheekbone, as she had Papa's injuries when she was younger. Quickly she quelled the feeling.

"Mr. Crawford," she said primly, "I see you are looking somewhat better for your ordeal."

"Thank you, Miss Bennett," he said, mocking her gently for her sudden formality. What had happened to the warmth and concern he'd seen in her eyes earlier?

"Seeing you lovely ladies makes me feel better." The sun glinted on his dark hair and there was a devil's light in his dark eyes. Aimee felt her breath catch.

"Them men was shore poundin' on yo'," Loretta observed. "Ah was mighty happy to see yo' git away from 'em. We had to step right sharp to git away from 'em ourselves."

"You had some trouble?" Zack said, looking at Aimee. "You didn't tell me that."

"It was nothing." Aimee cast a warning glare at Loretta. "They were just some ruffians. We got away from them easily enough and came to the boat last night to make sure we didn't miss it."

"That was wise of you." Zack gazed at Aimee speculatively. "Tell me, did you see your father's friend Arlo Benjamin? He was looking for you. He asked if I'd seen you recently."

"I'm sorry to have missed him," Aimee said with feigned regret. Once again she sent Loretta a warning glance. The girl was fairly bursting to speak her piece. Zack glanced from one girl to the other as if trying to assess what they were saying and what they were holding back. Smiling encouragingly, he tried another tack.

"I'm pleased to see you were able to travel on to Independence at this time." He turned his devilish charms on Loretta. "You seemed to feel it would take you some time to raise the money for the trip."

"Miss Aimee bought me my ticket," Loretta said proudly.

Zack glanced at Aimee in surprise. "That's most generous of you," he said, and his dark eyes were warm with approval. Aimee felt herself flush under his gaze.

"An' thet's not all," Loretta gushed on. "She bought me this gown and petticoats and bonnet. Ah never owned me a bonnet before, and Ah got me two more gowns and petticoats in mah bag."

"You surprise me, Miss Bennett," Zack said.

"I don't see why," Aimee declared. Didn't he think she was capable of generosity?

"An' what's more, Miss Aimee is teachin' me how to be a lady an' she's lettin' me be her maid." Loretta fairly beamed at him.

"Loretta!" A young man stood on the lower deck waving up at her.

"There's Billy. Ah have to go. Ah'll talk to yo' later," Loretta cried, and in a swirl of petticoats was gone.

"Well, you're quite the benefactress, Miss Bennett," Zack said wryly, and the warm approval in his eyes was replaced by cynicism.

"Well, the job I offered her was much better than the one she had in mind," Aimee snapped.

"Was it?"

"How dare you question my good intentions, sir? I haven't seen you offer her any help. In fact, you ran away and left us both back in St. Louis."

"That's true, I did," Zack answered. "I have no excuses to offer for my behavior."

"It's only what I expected from a man of your caliber," Aimee sniffed, too angry to be fair. Her pride had been stung by his critical conclusions about her. Wouldn't he ever think well of her? And why should she care anyway?

"I fear you're becoming somewhat cynical about men, Miss Bennett. That's a pity for one of your tender age."

"I'm not so young. I'm almost eighteen and I'm not so innocent about men and their duplicity and underhandedness or about their . . . their lustful ways."

"Lustful ways?" Zack grinned and his eyes sparkled with good humor. He had, she observed, a dimple in one cheek when he smiled.

"Lustful ways!" Aimee repeated indignantly. "Why, beneath that superior smile you're probably no better than Arlo Benjamin."

"I thought you hadn't seen Benjamin. What a little liar you've become," he teased.

Aimee's face reddened at being caught. "Well, I . . . I wish I hadn't," she stuttered.

"What is he to you?"

"Nothing. He was my father's . . . friend and associate. He's a truly hateful man who . . . who . . ."

"Exposed you to some of his lustful ways," Zack said grimly. The laughter was gone from his eyes.

"Yes, well, he tried. He tricked me into going to his house and then he tried to press his attentions upon me. I . . . I made it clear they were most unwelcome."

The laughter was back. "And how did you do that, my oh-so-proper Miss Bennett?" he inquired. Aimee's chin flew up and she met his eyes squarely.

"I kicked him and then I ran away."

"I'm most impressed," Zack said, and his eyes fairly danced with humor, although he strove to keep his expression serious. It was true he was impressed by this dainty bit of fluff who stood before him so defiantly. She had more steel to her than he'd given her credit for. The boat trip to Independence was long and boring; perhaps he would put aside his earlier resolve to stay clear of Miss Aimee Bennett. But part of him knew he could never treat her so lightly. She'd been reared a lady and was struggling now to cope with situations beyond her experience. That she did so with such spirit touched him.

"I am not impressed by any of the gentlemen I've thus far met," Aimee said. Her tone was scathing and she looked Zack up and down as if he were a poor specimen indeed. "You are all devious and self-serving. How dare you question my motives when your own are so . . . so dastardly."

Had she read his mind? Zack wondered. "Such flattery, Miss Bennett! Are you working your wicked womanly wiles on me?" he inquired, and couldn't hold back a chuckle at the look of outrage that crossed her face.

"Why, I've never," she gasped.

"But you have, Miss Bennett, ever since I presented myself to you back in Webster and offered my help."

"I assure you, Mr. Crawford, my thoughts were only of my father. That you could suggest I entertained any other emotion but grief is most unkind." But Zack would not let her become morose. Her father's death was behind her.

"Your thoughts were not of your father when you kissed me," he said, "or later when you tried to persuade me to take you on to Independence."

"You took advantage of my grief, as I should have guessed you would," Aimee snapped. "It . . . it was most distasteful to me."

Zack let out a hoot of laughter. "It was not distaste I saw in your eyes, Miss Bennett. You enjoyed the kiss as much as I, and if the truth be told, you'd probably like another. Well, it will do you no good to try your wiles on me. I'm immune to them."

"You may rest assured, sir, that my . . . my wiles will never be turned in your direction, not if you were the last man alive and I sorely in need of your help. You are no gentleman, so you don't know how to treat a lady. Now, if you will excuse me, I will continue my walk." With a snap of silk, she unfurled her parasol and turned a stiff, slim back to him.

Still chuckling, Zack watched her go, his eyes taking in the slight sway of slim hips beneath the voluminous skirts. She had fire, all right. One broad brown hand came up to touch the cheekbone that still ached, and suddenly he felt better than he had in months. "Whooee," he called out, grinning and shaking his head. The slim womanly figure paused and he thought she might turn and look at him again, but with a swish of her skirts she walked on and soon disappeared around the corner of the cabins.

He was a maddening man, Aimee thought, and she would spend no more thought on him. She stood in the bow of the boat, taking deep breaths to calm herself. The pounding of her heart was from the insults she'd endured from Zack Crawford and had nothing at all to do with the fiery lights in his dark eyes. She stood watching the sunlight sparkle off the brown water and concentrated on the farms and small towns they passed. Nearly everyone stopped what he was doing and hurried to the riverbank to wave to the passengers. At either side of the bow were stationed lookouts to keep a sharp eye out for sand bars and snags that could rip the bottom out of the boat. Now and then the boat pulled up to one of the landings to take on cargo or drop off supplies, but it was soon under way again. Its main destination was Independence, where many of its passengers would begin the next leg of their westward journey.

Aimee could see Loretta off talking to Billy Parsons. He was a tall, gangly youth with broad shoulders and a shock of red hair. He seemed a lighthearted soul, for he often threw his head back and his laughter rolled freely through the warm afternoon air. Loretta hung on his every word, her own laughter mingling with his.

Feeling abandoned, Aimee wandered along the lower deck, observing the wagons wedged into every available spot. At the stern end of the boat, the livestock and oxen had been quartered and their lowing could be heard occasionally above the slap of the paddle wheel. Women called to their children, who ran nimbly in and about the wagons. This was a great adventure to them. Men sat in bunches talking about their westward trek. Many of them were farmers, looking for new and fertile land that wasn't worn out.

"Ah hear flour and beans are goin' purty dear in Independence," one commented.

"Ah don't have to worry none 'bout thet," another said. "Ah brung mah own from home."

"How much 'id you figure for the trip?" another asked anxiously

"Just like this here book said," a farmer replied, fingering a worn copy of the *Emigrant's Guide to Oregon and California*. "Ah figured them fellers've been out there onc't already. They know what's needed. Ah got me two hunnert pounds a flour, a hunnert'n fifty a bacon, ten pounds a coffee, twenty a sugar and ten a salt," he recited proudly as if to reassure himself he had enough. "We got us a coupla cows to give milk for the young 'uns. Ah figure we're in good shape."

"What happens when the wolves git yo'r cows, 'n' the Indians steal the rest of yo'r food?" a wiry little man asked. He wasn't nearly as well-supplied and he felt apprehensive. He hated the smugness of the other farmer.

"Won't no wolves or Injuins get my young 'uns' vittles," the farmer answered, slapping his hand against the worn stock of his rifle.

Aimee moved on.

"Ah heard them Conestoga wagons ain't the best kind fer a trip like this," a man was saying. "Heard it was too big and heavy fer out there. Ah had me this one special-built." He slapped the seasoned hardwood side of his wagon proprietorily. "Cost me a good bit too, but Ah want it to last me a few yeas after Ah git out there to Oregon.''

Aimee walked on, listening to the excited emigrants. They were at once eager and apprehensive about this trip, wondering what they'd find on the other end of their long journey. For most of them, there was no turning back. Their courses had been set and their lives would be whatever awaited them in the vast unknown of the Oregon territory. As she listened, Aimee's curiosity about this great land on the other side of the continent grew. What must it be like to just pack up and go, she wondered, leaving behind all the failures and disillusionments of the past? She sighed and wondered about her own destination. Would Independence be kind to her? She had little money left. She'd have to find a job quickly. She pushed aside her worry. It would all work out somehow, she thought.

The midday meal was served in the long elegant central cabin set aside for the ladies. Loretta never arrived and Aimee ate alone. Afterward she wandered to the library for something appropriate to read. In spite of the warmth of the afternoon, a fire burned in the small potbellied stove and the room was stuffy and dark. Other ladies and their maids were already seated in the comfortable padded velvet chairs, exchanging confidences over their needlework. Their subdued dress and refined air noted them as ladies of breeding. It was the sort of company to which Aimee was accustomed.

Choosing a place for herself, she smoothed her full skirts and opened her book. But she was too restless to read. She glanced around the room, wishing Loretta were there to talk to her. The low, genteel voices of the women set an atmosphere of rest and serenity that was stultifying. Loretta would surely liven up things if she were here, Aimee thought and restrained a giggle at the picture of the ladies' horrified faces as the tavern girl let loose with some of her homespun wit. Suddenly she couldn't bear to stay in the cabin. Unladylike as it might seem, she was going to stroll along the deck once more. Hastily she put aside her book and left the cabin, feeling the censorious gazes of the other ladies upon her back.

The promenade was empty, and though Aimee kept a sharp lookout, she caught no glimpse of Loretta. Zack Crawford was standing on the main deck talking with the pilot. Not that she was looking for him, she reminded herself furiously. Finally, feeling neglected and depressed, she returned to her cabin and napped. She woke just as the gong sounded for dinner. Loretta stood in front of the mirror fussing with her hair.

"Where have you been?" Aimee asked sleepily.

"Visitin'," Loretta said mysteriously. "There're so many interestin' people on this boat and Ah been talkin' to 'em about Oregon."

"Oh, I see," Aimee said dully. The long, boring afternoon had made her realize just how much she would miss Loretta once they parted company. She preferred not to think of Zack at all. They completed their toilette and hurried to the dining room.

"Ah ain't never seen so much food at one time," Loretta said, trying to decide between a black-cherry torte and a pecan pie.

"Do you always allow your maid to sit at table with you?" a matron asked, eyeing Loretta disapprovingly.

"Always," Aimee said with an innocent smile.

"Oooh, they got fifteen kinds a dessert," Loretta said, quickly finishing the torte on her plate and signaling the waiter to return with more.

Much later the tavern girl pushed aside her plate and placed a hand on her stomach. "Ah'm fair to bust," she declared. "Whew, Ah ain't ever seen that much food in mah life. Ah reckon Ah need a walk around the deck to settle mah vittles some." Surreptitiously she stuffed a napkin into her bag and rose. Aimee was sure she'd taken some tidbits for Billy. The passengers on the lower deck must provide their own meals and were not allowed to partake of the vast array of food in the first-class section.

"Good night, y'all." Loretta bobbed her head and hurried away.

"My dear, I think you'd be better advised to let your servant dine with the others downstairs for the rest of her meals," the matronly woman said.

Aimee bit back her angry retort and smiled sweetly. "Oh, she's not my maid, ma'am," she replied.

"But you said she was."

"No Ma'am," Aimee's eyes danced with humor. "I said I always let my maid sit at table with me. And I would if I had a maid. The truth is I'm her companion. She asked me to come along on this trip and keep her company. She's just inherited a great deal of money and property and is on her way to Independence to check on her holdings."

"Really?" The woman's jowls shook with consternation. "But . . . but her manners," she exclaimed. "You must admit they leave a little to be desired."

"I suppose that's true," Aimee sighed, "but you see, it's hardly her fault. It was the way she was brought up. She lived in Africa, you know, when she was a child."

"Africa?" The woman's eyebrows raised.

"Yes, that's when her father was searching for his diamond mine. They nearly starved there. They were living with a tribe of cannibals, and you know what they eat." Aimee's eyes were wide as she looked around the table. "She told me it's only been recently that she has a taste for any other kind of meat." The matron gasped and clasped her napkin to her mouth.

"Well, if you'll excuse me, ladies, I'd best go check on her. I believe the moon is full tonight and it's always a dangerous time." The woman's face blanched and she looked around the table at her companions. Barely able to suppress her mirth, Aimee left the dining room, stopping at her room only long enough to take up a shawl. Once again she walked along the promenade, enjoying the serene beauty of the moon on the river and the dark silhouettes of trees along the shore. The muddy river shone white in the moonlight.

"Mark three!" called a leadsman taking soundings in a shallow stretch of the river. Aimee paused to watch and listen. The man moved nimbly about on the fore-deck, casting out his marker again. "Quarter-less-three," he called up to the pilot in the wheelhouse on the top deck. Aimee strolled slowly along the deserted prome-nade, finding the solitude soothing after the bustle of the dining salon. Her soft-soled slippers made but a whisper of sound on the waxed boards of the deck.

The tranquillity of the night was in direct contrast to the anxiety she felt. What was she to do about her future? Would Arlo Benjamin send men after her? He knew where she was heading. Foolishly she'd told him. Was it true that the people of Webster had sent out posters to have her arrested? What did Indepen-dence hold for her? She should have listened to Zack and taken up his offer to go east. She could have been on her way to a safe home with his brother and Caroline. What did it matter to her what was between Zack and his brother's wife?

Her thoughts turned to Zack. Her afternoon en-counter with him had been disquieting. She'd tried her best to remain aloof, but their repartee had left her feeling depressed. Obviously he didn't find her as ad-mirable a figure as he did Loretta, and Aimee could hardly blame him. Loretta was so alive and unafraid. She could take care of herself instead of being a cling-ing vine. In her self-condemnation, Aimee gave little thought to the decisions she'd made the past week or the courage they had required.

Restlessly she quickened her steps and rounded the corner of the cabins, nearly bumping into two men who were talking.

"Murrell don't want no slipups on this one," one man was saying. "Do what yer supposed to and ye'll be in the brotherhood." He held out his hand and clasped the other man's in a way Aimee had never seen before.

"Excuse me," Aimee said, and would have stepped

around the two except that the big man moved forward, blocking her path.

"Who're ye and what're ye doin' standin' there spyin' on us?" he demanded. The moonlight fell full across his face and Aimee could make out the sinister features and hooded eyes. A scar ran down one cheek from his eye to the corner of his mouth.

"I . . . I wasn't spying," she stammered.

"What do yo' want me to do?" the other man asked, and now Aimee noticed that he was small and wiry with a stubble on his skinny chin. The moon glanced off his bald head.

Aimee fought back the panic. "I'm sorry if I disturbed you. I just came out for an evening stroll around the deck."

"An evening stroll, eh?" the tall man said. "Are you alone?"

"Yes . . . well, no. I . . . uh . . . I'm waiting for someone." Aimee began to edge backward.

"Yeah, like who? Your maid?"

"Actually, uh . . ."

"Did I keep you waiting?" Zack was there, his hand at her elbow, his dark eyes smiling down at her. He bent his head and dropped a light kiss on her lips. His teeth were already flashing in a smile when he raised his head and looked at the men. The tall man had already faded back into the shadows, only the white of his shirtfront showing. There was something unnatural in his stillness, as if he were a snake coiling to strike.

"Is there a problem?" Zack asked, and although he kept his manner light and friendly, Aimee could sense the tautness in him.

"No, not now," the little man was saying. "I was jest tellin' the young lady there that she shouldn't be walkin' these decks at night unchaperoned. I can see she's in good hands now."

"Yes, she is," Zack said, and his tone was made of steel.

"Well, I'll just be on my way then," the little man said. Donning his cap, he scurried away up the deck.

Aimee glanced back at the shadows. The tall man had disappeared, slipping away silently. There was something ominous about that.

"Who were those men?" Zack asked.

"I don't know," Aimee replied. "I just came upon them. They seemed somewhat upset that I'd disturbed them."

"He was right about one thing," Zack said absentmindedly. "It's best if you don't walk alone at night on these decks. There's nothing to stop some member of the crew or one of the deck passengers from coming up here. They're all a pretty hard lot."

"Some aren't," Aimee said without thinking, and at Zack's look of surprise hurried on. "Loretta met one of them, a Billy Parsons, and he seems very nice."

"Loretta knows what she's doing, Aimee," he said. "She's used to being around them. She knows whom to watch out for and who's all right. Don't take the chances she does. You'd end up in trouble."

"You've made it very clear just how helpless you think me," Aimee said crisply.

"Not helpless, just naïve and trusting and . . . helpless in some ways. But it's not your fault and I don't hold it against you."

"That's truly generous of you," Aimee said sarcastically.

Zack took her arm and walked her to the rail, looking out over the river. "Let's not fight anymore," he urged. "We're going to be together on this boat until it docks in Independence. Let's call a truce until then." His voice was so sincere, Aimee couldn't deny him.

"All right," she agreed.

"Half-twain," the leadsman called out, his voice rising forlornly through the misty darkness. Somewhere on the main deck someone strummed a guitar.

"Why are they testing the water depth so often?" Aimee asked.

"The river gets pretty shallow along here. The pilot's not taking any chances. These boats don't draw a lot of water to stay afloat, but the bottoms can be ripped out by a sandbar."

"If it's so dangerous, why doesn't he pull over for the night?" Aimee asked, suddenly feeling apprehensive.

"He might yet," Zack explained, "but it's easier to see the snags on this river at night than in the daytime. It's a toss-up as to which danger he wants to risk."

Aimee shivered. "I didn't realize riverboat travel was so dangerous," she replied.

"You're cold," he said, and placed his arm around her shoulder, sheltering her against his chest. It felt good to be held thus.

"I'm quite all right," she said stiffly, but she didn't pull away. Zack ignored her protests and hugged her closer. "Those are only a few of the dangers on a riverboat," Zack went on pleasantly. "There's always a chance the boilers might blow, or a fire start in the furnace room or the kitchens, or then, some thief could scuttle her in order to rob her."

Aimee blanched. "Do you mean someone would sink the boat and cause all these people to drown just in order to rob it?" Solemnly he shook his head. "I don't believe you," she cried. "No one would be that cruel. You're just trying to scare me."

"Perhaps I am," Zack said with a sigh. "Would you rather I treat you like a dainty, helpless lady and not tell you the truth? I would be protecting you from the big bad world, but I wouldn't be helping you learn to take care of yourself in it."

Aimee considered his words. "You're painting it worse than it really is," she accused.

"I wish I were," Zack said, and his voice sounded sad. "There's duplicity and greed in all of us."

"Are you saying no one is to be trusted, then?" Aimee asked.

"I'm saying: as soon as we reach Independence, get back on the boat and go back east."

"We've been over this before," Aimee said. "Besides, the people out west won't be any worse than the people in the east."

"Some of them won't be. Some of them are hard-working, decent folks looking for a better way of life for themselves and their families, but there are many who've come west to escape the law."

Aimee sighed impatiently. "Why is it, Mr. Crawford, that every time we're together you lecture me?"

His features twisted into a smile. "You're right, Miss Bennett. It's not the thing to do when a man has a beautiful young woman alone in the moonlight."

The moon had etched his face in its pale light, and glinted off his dark hair. The soft darkness, the soothing motion of the boat, and the thrum of the guitar cast an aura of intimacy between them.

"You're very beautiful in the moonlight," he said with a strange new note in his voice.

"You are too," Aimee blurted, and sensed there was no laughter in him at her words. For a long moment they looked into each other's eyes, striving to pierce the enigma cast on each by the deepening shadows. He was going to kiss her, she realized, and turned away first, spurred by a restless energy within that she could not name or control. Her disquieted gaze fell on the flatbed wagons below.

"So many people going to Oregon," she murmured. "Will they really find a better life there?"

"They think so," Zack replied, and his voice sounded hollow and faraway to her ears. Was he sorry he was here beside her with his arm around her shoulders? Did he feel impatient with her for acting the fool? Now she longed to have him kiss her as he had that night in camp, but she couldn't tell him so without looking the bigger fool.

"Why are you going there? You seem to have had a good life back east with your own business and your own ships."

"True, I did," Zack replied, and removed his arm from around her shoulder. Aimee missed the warmth and weight of it. Taking a thin cigar from a case, he hesitated. "Do you mind?"

"Not at all," Aimee replied, and watched as he bit off the tip and lit the cheroot.

"Why did you choose to travel overland?" she persisted, wanting to understand Zack Crawford better. "You could have sailed one of your ships around the Horn as so many do."

"I could have," he replied, and drew on the cheroot. The fragrance of it filled the air. "All my life I've perched on the shore of this continent and looked to the sea to make my profit. I've often sailed to England and France and know the southern isles better than I know my own hand. But except for a few eastern cities and the lands bordering the great northern lakes, I know very little about this country. I thought it time I learned."

"I see," Aimee said. "That's a most commendable attitude. But what will you do when you reach Oregon, become a farmer?"

"I'm not sure yet. The Hudson Bay Company has been out there for years trading furs and supplies with the trappers and Indians, but there's going to be a need for additional supplies with all these emigrants settling there. Maybe I'll get a ship and start a business on that side of the continent as well."

"I wish you well with your plans," Aimee said forlornly, remembering that once the *Missouri Queen* docked in Independence she would never see him again. Zack heard the wistful note in her voice.

"Are you still planning to teach, once you get to Independence?" he asked.

"As you've pointed out, it's about the only thing for which I'm suited," she admitted. "But I'm planning to teach practical things, and if I don't know how to do something, I'll find out and then pass it along to my students." She paused. "I think I can be a good teacher," she ended lamely.

Zack nodded. "I believe you will be. I'm sorry if I seemed to criticize you too much. It's just that I've felt some responsibility for you, having whisked you away from Webster."

"You did what was best," Aimee said, thinking of what Arlo Benjamin had said. The town council had a wanted poster out for her. "I never thanked you properly for your help."

"None needed," Zack answered.

She'd expected him to say that. He was that kind of man.

"I'm sorry for bringing up Caroline," she said timidly, not wanting to anger him further, yet wanting to mend the rift between them.

"Caroline is part of the past," he said, and his tone was cool, warning her not to pursue the subject. He must have loved her very much to still be so bothered by the sound of her name. Some of the magic was gone from the evening. She shivered and rubbed her arms.

"It's getting cooler. I'd better look for Loretta," she said, disappointed that their discussion must end on such a cool note.

Zack seemed to feel that way too, for he took her arm. "I'll walk along with you," he said. "There are other scoundrels on this boat besides me, and it's best you don't wander around after dark alone." There was laughter in his voice again, and Aimee flashed him a smile, grateful for his company a while longer.

"I'll keep that in mind, sir," she answered lightly.

They found Loretta on the lower deck with Billy, who was looking at her with adoring eyes.

"Theah yo' are," Loretta cried when she saw Zack. "Ah been wantin' to meet up with yo'. Ah want yo' to meet Billy Parsons. He's from Tennessee an' he's on his way to Oregon."

"Ah'm glad to meet you, sir," Billy said, snatching his hat off and bobbing his head.

"Are you traveling alone, Billy?" Zack asked.

"Yes, sir, Ah am." Billy worked the hat in his hands. "Mah ma and pa died last winter of the cholera, 'n' a neighbor took in mah little sister until Ah kin git settled out yonder in Oregon and send for her. Ah figure Ah kin kinda work my way across by scoutin' and huntin' for game. Ah'm real handy with a gun."

"I'll bet you are," Zack agreed.

"How 'bout you, sir? Are yo' travelin' by yo'rself?"

Zack glanced at Aimee and shook his head. "Yes, I am," he said emphatically.

"Have yo' got yo'r own wagon?" Billy asked.

"No. I'll pick up my provisions, including a wagon, in Independence. I hear there are people who get that far and have to turn back."

"So Ah've heard, sir. Do yo' reckon the trail's as dangerous as they say?"

"I believe it's even worse, Billy. Only the toughest and the strongest are going to make it."

"Yes, sir, that's kinda what Ah figured too."

"Well, ladies, I'll bid you good night." Zack touched the brim of his hat and turned away.

"Good night," Aimee called softly, and he carried the sound of her voice with him to his cabin, where he cursed himself soundly for his conscience. For a moment there, standing by the railing, he'd known he could kiss her and once kissed, he was sure he could have brought her back to his cabin. What had stopped him? Her innocence, he thought wryly. Miss Aimee Bennett had a great deal to learn about life and its disillusionments and about men and their lustful ways. As tempting as he found her, he had no wish to be the one to teach her those hard lessons. Soon they would reach Independence and he would never see her again. The thought should have pleased him, but didn't.

7

Sometime during the night, the pilot did pull the riverboat in to shore. Gratefully the stokers found a place to stretch their weary bodies. Mindless of the hardness of the deck or the itchy soot that covered their faces and mighty forearms, they quickly fell asleep. Before the first light of dawn had tipped the eastern horizon, orders were given, furnaces were stoked, and the *Missouri Queen* edged away from shore and headed north along the winding, treacherous river.

Aimee and Loretta slept late and went to breakfast long after the other ladies had eaten. Later, as they strolled the decks, it seemed to Aimee that the female passengers contrived to stay well away from them.

"They look lak' they think Ah'm going' ta eat 'em," Loretta snapped when a woman had scurried to one side to let them pass. Aimee felt a moment of regret at her fib the night before.

"Does it bother you a great deal?" she asked hesitantly. She'd have to explain and make it right.

"It surely don't," Loretta said. "Ah don't hold much with women who sit around sewing little flowers on a piece of cloth."

"But that's what ladies are supposed to do," Aimee reminded her.

"Seems lak' a pretty useless way to spend yo'r time," Loretta observed, and once again Aimee felt like chuckling.

"You're right," she agreed.

"Ain't thar . . . I mean, *Aren't* thar any other way fer me to be a lady?"

"We'll work on it," Aimee promised. A commotion at one end of the deck drew them. A crowd had gathered around the captain and some of his men. Aimee glimpsed Zack standing in the crowd and thought he'd never looked handsomer. He wore a jacket and leggings of deerhide and a broad-brimmed hat over his dark hair. He stood head and shoulders above most of the other men, Aimee noticed, and hoped he'd look her way so she could wave or something. But his eyes were narrowed speculatively as he studied the little man being held captive.

"I found him on the main deck, sir," the deckhand was saying. "He was ready to chop in the hull with this ax." A murmur of dismay ran around the crowd.

"What's the meaning of this?" the captain demanded.

"He's lyin'. I tell you, I wasn't goin' ta do any such thin'." The man's voice sounded familiar, so Aimee pressed closer to get a better look at him.

"I know all about your kind," the captain growled. "You're one of the riverboat pirates who sink ships, and while the crew's scrambling to save the passengers, you steal everything you can. Well, I'll not have it on the *Missouri Queen*. I've fought off Indians and every other kind of varmint runnin' this river, and ain't some polecat like you goin' to sink my ship. Who's your partner?"

"I . . . I don't have a partner," the man stammered. "I tell you, I wasn't doin' nothin' wrong. I'm jest ridin' up to Independence is all."

"You ain't goin' ta make it ta Independence unless you tell me who else is in on this with you," the captain growled. "We're goin' to hang you from the boiler deck so's you dangle over the stern wheel. That paddle wheel'll beat you to death. It's a slow, painful way to die."

"I ain't done nothing wrong, I tell you. I ain't got

no partner," the little man whined. His eyes darted nervously around the throng of people, looking for some way out of this situation.

"String 'im up," one of the deckhands growled, and men jostled him one way and then the other. In the scuffle his cap fell off and Aimee could see his bald head. It was the little man she'd bumped into the night before on deck.

"Tell us your partner's name," the men shouted at the little man, and buffeted him with their fists.

"Get a rope," someone cried, and Aimee could see the little man's face crumple with fear.

"Wait, wait," he cried out. "All right, I'll confess. I was supposed to sink the ship. I—" A shot rang out and the little man slumped.

Zack caught the man and lowered him to the deck. "He's dead," he said, feeling for a pulse.

"Who fired that shot?" the captain roared, and people looked at each other in perplexity.

"It came from that direction," someone said, and all eyes looked to where he pointed. There was no one there.

"Don't anyone move, don't leave the deck," the captain ordered, and everyone waited while his men searched the deck, salon, and even the staterooms. They found no sign of the assassin.

"It has to be someone here then," the captain bellowed, and the passengers eyed each other uneasily. Zack moved across the deck until he was standing protectively behind Aimee. She was grateful for his presence. A movement at one end of the deck drew her attention and for a moment she was gazing into the dark face of the man she'd seen talking to the dead man. His fierce gaze warned her to silence; then he ducked his head furtively and sidled away. Aimee had seen enough.

"That's him," she gasped, and turned instinctively to Zack, more grateful than ever now that he was there. The captain had come to talk to him, but he turned to Aimee when she gripped his sleeve urgently. "He's here. I just saw him," she cried.

"Who?" Zack demanded, and took hold of her hands. They were icy cold and her eyes were wide and frightened-looking.

"The man you're looking for," she blurted. "The dead man's partner."

"Where is he?" Zack looked around.

"He's right there." Aimee pointed, but the place where the man had stood was empty. He'd disappeared as if into thin air. "He's gone now, but I know he's the one you want."

"Are you sure? How do you know that?" Zack demanded.

"They were talking together on deck last night," Aimee answered. "He was telling the little man he'd better not fail, and something about a brotherhood."

"John Murrell's men," the captain said grimly. "They belong to something called a Mystic Brotherhood. They're the meanest lot of scum on the river."

"Are you sure, Aimee?"

"I came around the corner and bumped into them. The tall man was very angry. He . . . he frightened me. Then you came and he just sort of disappeared into the shadows."

"Do you think it's your man, Captain?" Zack asked.

"Aye, I do. I'll have my men search the whole boat for him. They're a bad lot. We're not safe with one of 'em on board." The captain turned aside and ordered his men to begin the search.

"I think you'd better go to your cabin and stay there until he can be found," Zack said to Aimee. When she tried to protest, he took hold of her shoulders, peering into her eyes urgently. "You may be the only one who can identify him. Your life could be in danger. Stay with her, Loretta. I don't want her to be alone."

"Yas, sir," Loretta said.

"And lock the door. Don't open it for anyone except me."

"We won't," Loretta agreed. A shiver of fear passed

over Aimee, and without a word of protest she turned back to her cabin. Loretta trailed along behind her. Neither girl relished sitting in the cabin while all the excitement went on around them.

"Seems lak' to me we'd be safer if we stayed out here where all the people are," Loretta observed.

"I was just thinking the same thing," Aimee replied. "Let's find a quiet corner where we can watch things. It should be safe enough if we stick together."

"Ah know jest the spot," Loretta replied, and led the way to a secluded spot where deck chairs and barrels of food supplies for the kitchens had been set out of the way. "Billy'n me found it last night," Loretta continued with a secretive grin.

It was a well-protected place. No one would notice them there, but they'd be able to see most of the activity along the deck. They hid themselves and peered out at the deckhands and male passengers hurrying around looking for the riverboat pirate. The men looked tense and worried. Were there more than two? They cast quick nervous glances over their shoulders as if expecting to see a riverboat pirate looming behind them. Lookouts were posted on either side of the boat to keep a sharp eye out for signs of other outlaws prowling the shoreline waiting to board the boat at one of the bends.

Breathlessly the girls waited and watched. A tall dark-haired man walked along the deck. Although she couldn't see his face, something about him made Aimee feel uneasy. He wasn't searching as the other men had been, nor did he glance over his shoulders nervously.

"Loretta, it's him," Aimee whispered frantically. The man paused and looked around as if he'd heard her.

"Where?" Loretta asked, and raised up to get a better look.

"Get down." Aimee grabbed hold of her skirts and yanked her down. Together they crouched behind the barrels.

"Are yo' sure it was him?" Loretta whispered.

"Yes, I'm sure." They waited.

"Do you think he's gone yet?" Loretta whispered impatiently.

"I don't know. I don't hear anything," Aimee whispered.

"Let's take a look."

"Be careful."

Together they stood up and peered from behind the barrels—right into the dark, menacing face of the river pirate.

"Run," Aimee cried, and sprang away, while Loretta sprinted down the deck in the other direction. The man grabbed for Aimee and she heard the tear of cloth as she scrambled away. She ran down the promenade and could hear the thud of heavy boots behind her. Why hadn't she heeded Zack's advice and gone to her cabin? Where was he now?

"Zack!" she screamed, and ran faster, holding her skirts high above her knees. "Help, Zack."

Rough hands grabbed her from behind and she felt herself lifted off her feet.

"Now, you little bitch, yo're goin' for a swim," the man grunted, and hauled her to the rail, lifting her high.

"No!" Aimee screamed and fought him, kicking out with her feet, but he had her over the railing and she could see the water churning beneath her. Wildly Aimee grasped the man's jacket as he released her. Her own weight pulled her down, and she dangled.

"Let go," he shouted, and sought to loosen her grip on him. He got one hand free and she could feel the cloth of his jacket slipping from her other hand. Frantically she flailed out with her free hand and grasped the railing, just as he broke her hold on his jacket. She swung out from the boat, nearly losing her grip on the rail, then fell back against the painted wood, her feet already scrambling for a toehold on the ornate trim. Her arm felt as if it had been wrenched from its socket, but she forced herself not to think about it, struggling to grab hold of the railing with her other hand.

Suddenly there was an excruciating pain in her knuckles and she looked up. The pirate stood above her with his pistol butt raised, and even as she cried out, he brought it crashing down against her fingers again. Aimee screamed and willed herself not to let go. If she fell into the water, she'd be drawn under the hull and back into the paddles. It would be a sure death for her. Tears coursed down her cheeks and she screamed again as she felt the steel of his gun crashing against her fingers yet again.

"Stop that, you bastard," a voice roared, and before the pirate could reverse his gun to shoot at his pursuer, Zack was there, knocking his gun aside and landing a punch on his chin. The pirate fell back against the deck.

"Zack!" Aimee screamed, fearing he might not know she dangled there helplessly.

"Hang on, Aimee," he called. "I've got you." His strong hands gripped her wrist, pulling her up. Now that she knew she was safe, Aimee couldn't hold back the sobs. Gratefully she looked up at Zack and saw the dark shadow of the pirate.

"Zack, look out," she screamed, and saw the flash of a knife. Zack's hold on her was broken as he tried to fend off his attacker. Aimee clung to the railing, her eyes level with the deck where the two men struggled for the knife. Zack's fist arced through the air and the man's hold was loosened. The knife went skittering across the deck, slid off the side, and fell into the river.

"Good God A'mighty," someone shouted on the deck below as he observed the dainty boots and lacy petticoats dangling in the air. Hands reached out to grab Aimee's ankles. With a scream she looked down. Men were peering up at her. "We got you, girly," they cried. "We'll have you down in a jiffy."

Aimee glanced back at Zack and the pirate fighting on the upper deck. Zack knocked the pirate down and with a cunning born of fear the man picked up a strut knocked loose in their struggle and with a quick, desperate motion swung it at Zack, who collapsed on the deck.

"Zack," Aimee cried, and struggled to climb up to him. The pirate hovered nearby menacingly.

"There he is," some men at the end of the deck cried, and ran toward the cornered pirate. With a last desperate glance around, the man leapt over the side of the boat, his dive taking him clear of any danger from the stern wheel.

Aimee saw no more, for the men on the deck below had hold of her legs. "Let go, lady," they called to her, and Aimee released her hold on the railing and slid down into their waiting arms. When they had set her aright on the deck, she turned toward the stairs.

"Zack Crawford's hurt," she cried. "He tried to stop the pirate." The men followed after her as she raced up to the second deck. He was already on his feet, and shaking his head, stumbled to the railing.

"Aimee," he called hoarsely when he saw she was no longer there.

"The pirate got away, man," someone told him, but he only pushed the man aside and staggered down the deck toward the stern, straining to see back along the river.

"It's not the pirate I care about," he shouted. "There was a girl . . . a young woman clinging to the side of the boat. Aimee," he shouted.

"I'm here," she cried, and hurried along the deck toward him. At the sound of her voice he whirled and stared at her disbelievingly.

"Aimee," he said, and his voice was husky with relief. "Are you all right?"

Tears trembled in her eyes as she shook her head. "I was so scared," she whispered. "Were you hurt?"

Zack shook his head, his eyes not leaving her face. His eyes were bright with joy at seeing her safe again; then joy turned to anger. "Why didn't you go to your cabin as I told you?" he shouted, and his eyes flashed with barely repressed fury. Even his eyebrows arched in sharp V's and his mouth was grim.

"I'm sorry," she stammered.

"Sorry! " His tone was scathing. "You could have been killed for your foolishness, and so could I, and all you can say is you're sorry."

"What else do you expect from me?" Aimee said. "I had no idea this would happen."

"You are by far the most stubborn, unthinking young woman I've ever met. You don't have the common sense God gave a mule and you never listen to any advice I give you," he stormed. "Well, I won't worry about you again. You are on your own and if you end up at the bottom of this river, I won't blink an eye, because you probably will have brought it on yourself by your own bullheadedness."

"Bullheadedness," Aimee cried, stung that he should talk to her in such a manner in front of all these people. "I didn't ask you to worry about me, Zack Crawford, and you haven't the right to tell me anything at all. Now, you can stay here on deck and brawl all you wish, I am going to my cabin to rest a bit. It is my sincere wish that we won't meet again on this journey."

"I'll do everything in my power to grant you that wish, Miss Bennett," he answered, and stalked away.

Aimee glanced around at the other men, who shuffled their feet and hurried off. They had no wish to tangle with the fiery temper of this slight girl. She was a spunky thing, though. Few of them felt the inclination to square off against the likes of Zack Crawford the way she had.

"Yo're hurt," Loretta cried, seeing Aimee's bruised and bleeding hands.

Dazedly Aimee looked at her hands. In all the excitement and her worry over Zack, she'd hardly noticed the pain. Now it washed over her and she blinked back the tears. Her knees felt as if they would no longer support her.

"We're much obliged for your help in finding this man," the captain said. "He would've sunk the boat and cost a lot of people their lives."

"It was nothing," Aimee said wearily.

"All the same, we're much obliged. Did you get a good look at the man? I want to give a description to the authorities in the towns along here. They can watch out for him."

"Yes, I can describe him," Aimee said, and sank to the floor in a dead faint. She never knew that it was Zack Crawford who shouldered his way through the other men and knelt beside her, or that it was his strong arms that carried her to her cabin. It was Zack who tenderly cleaned her bloody hands and bound them so they could heal, and it was Zack who sat outside her cabin long after she'd fallen asleep, cursing himself for having spoken to her so after all she'd gone through. He'd turned back to apologize to her and had seen her fall to the deck, and he'd felt the blood drain from his head, leaving him light-headed.

The cabin door opened and Loretta stepped out. "She's sleepin' lak' a babe," she said. "Why don't yo' go tend to that cut on yo'r face."

"I'm all right," Zack said, shrugging aside her concern.

"She's not goin' to wake up for some time, so tend that cut," Loretta urged him. Zack met her knowing gaze and glanced away, angry that she saw more than he himself wanted to see.

"She's one of the most helpless females I've ever seen," he declared roughly.

"She's shore innocent about some thangs," Loretta agreed, "but Ah'm to blame for this. We was goin' to the cabin but we wanted to see some of the excitement."

"It isn't just this, Loretta. It's her, the way she is."

"She cain't help thet none. Ah guess it was the way she was raised, to be all kind of helpless like a kitten and soft and dainty. She cain't change thet now."

"No," Zack sighed, "I guess she can't." He stood up. "Would you keep an eye on her?"

"Ain't Ah been?" the girl demanded.

"Yeah, I guess you have," Zack said with a tired smile, and made his way down the deck toward his own cabin. Loretta stood where she was, watching him leave. Slowly she shook her head. Zack might not know it yet, but he cared a great deal more for this helpless girl than he meant to. She might have minded, Loretta thought, but now there was Billy. Humming a little tune, she crossed to the rail and stood watching the muddy river churning away beneath them.

Zack was as good as his word. Aimee never saw him again during the rest of the boat trip, which was just what she wanted, she told herself. But when she walked along the promenade, she found herself looking around for him. She missed his teasing and his presence. Lo retta was once again spending her time with Billy Parsons on the main deck. The trip had lost its charm for Aimee and she was grateful when the bell sounded and the announcement made that they were approaching Independence. All over the boat, people were gathering their belongings. Although the riverboat would continue to the upper Missouri river as far as Minnesota, where it delivered supplies and hauled back cargoes of crops and furs, few passengers would be journeying so far.

The boat landing bustled with activity as teams of oxen were harnessed to the wagons. Amid much whistling and shouting the wagons were rolled down the gangplank and through the streets to the campground on the other side of town. Storekeepers and townspeople waved to the newcomers. Business would be brisk in the next few days.

Aimee caught a glimpse of Zack's tall, broad-shouldered figure as he made his way down the gangplank and disappeared into the crowd. She would likely never see him again, she thought morosely, and busied herself with her bags. Loretta looked woebegone as well. She and Billy had made their farewells. He would sign onto the first wagon train heading west and Loretta would stay behind in Independence to work and earn passage for the next portion of the journey. Fervently they'd vowed to look for each other in Oregon, although both knew the territory would be so vast they would have little chance of meeting again.

Independence was a roistering, energetic town, far larger than Aimee had anticipated. The thousands of travelers who thronged her streets and shops buying provisions made it seem even larger. Once it had been a supply depot for fur traders, a last touch of civilization perched on the edge of a vast wilderness. Now its rough log cabins had given way to fine two-story homes and steepled churches and a brick courthouse.

Aimee and Loretta walked from the wharf to the hotel, gawking in the windows of the stores. These shops were piled high with parts of wagons, guns, sunbonnets, dry goods, harnesses, and just about any other practical item needed by the overlanders. In addition there were barbershops, wheelwrights, blacksmiths, and taverns.

"We should be able to find work here," Aimee said optimistically.

The rooms at the hotel cost more than she'd anticipated and she paid for only one night, carefully hoarding her remaining coins. She hoped she'd be able to get a job soon. Resolutely she smiled at Loretta and picked up her bag.

"Ah cain't stay here with you," Loretta said. "Ah'll just go find myself someplace else to stay."

"Why would you do that?" Aimee cried in panic. Loretta couldn't leave her now.

"Ah cain't have yo' spendin' yo'r money on me. Yo' don't have thet much left."

"It doesn't cost any more for two to sleep in that room that it does for one. At least stay with me for tonight. We can go out and look for jobs right away, today. We're bound to find something."

"Do yo' think so?" Loretta asked doubtfully.

"Of course we will," Aimee said. "This is a big town. They need schoolteachers and maids."

Loretta brightened. "That's right," she exclaimed, "Ah'm a maid now."

The two girls went upstairs together, their minds

busy with plans for their futures. They refreshed themselves and set out, agreeing to meet back at the hotel in time for supper. Aimee hurried off to the mayor's office, her confidence high. By late afternoon she'd arrived back at the hotel, her feet tired and aching, her confidence flagging. There was no need for a teacher or even for store clerks. Too many women, newly made widows, had been turned back on the trail. They swarmed the city looking for any job they could find to feed their children and get enough money for passage home.

Panic had set in by the time Loretta returned. Her story was the same. Few women needed maids and those who did already had them, often genteel ladies of breeding in reduced circumstances. They had no need of a backwoods girl of questionable origin.

"What are we to do?" Aimee asked dismally.

"Ah suppose Ah could always go back to the taverns," Loretta said hesitantly.

"No, there's got to be some other way," Aimee exclaimed. "Don't give up yet. Tomorrow will be better. We'll find something tomorrow."

Listlessly they ate a spare supper, suddenly conscious of its cost, and went up to bed. Who knew if they could afford the hotel by tomorrow night?

"We could go to Zack for help," Loretta suggested as they lay bleakly staring into the dark.

"Never," Aimee snapped. "I'd sooner ask the devil. Besides, he's probably already gone off to Oregon."

"No, he hasn't. Ah saw him today. He was buying provisions at the general store." She paused. "He's got a wagon. He's going with the next wagon train. They leave next week."

"I wish him well," Aimee said sarcastically to hide the sudden pain she felt. "Did you see Billy as well?"

Loretta was silent for a moment, and when she spoke her voice was suspiciously unsteady. "He's traveling with Zack."

"I'm sorry," Aimee said, and didn't know how else to comfort her friend. Would it help if she said she felt the same disconsolate loss? But of course she didn't. Zack had been kind to her in the beginning, and for that reason she hated to see him go. That was all.

They fell into an uneasy sleep and the next day once again made the rounds looking for work. Again Aimee was the first to return to the hotel, where she sat counting her pitiful supply of coins. One more night at the hotel was all she could afford. She fingered the brooch that Zack had brought back to her the night her father had been buried. It was all she had left and she hated to sell it now, but she might have to.

She sat thinking of all that had befallen her since that fateful afternoon of her father's death. She'd been so frightened afterward, not sure of where to go, but she'd at least had Zack there helping her and she'd had her mother's jewels. Now she was without either, alone except for Loretta. Somehow Aimee felt responsible for the other girl. She mustn't let Loretta return to the life she'd known before. But how could she help Loretta when she couldn't even help herself?

Loretta provided the solution. She arrived at the hotel flushed and smiling.

"Aimee, Ah found a way for us to go to Oregon," she called out triumphantly.

"Oregon?" Aimee exclaimed. "I don't want to go to Oregon."

"Ah thought you did," Loretta said, crestfallen. "Ah overheard you tell Mr. Crawford you'd pay him some of your jewels if he'd take you."

"It was just a whim," Aimee admitted. "He convinced me that Oregon is not the place for me." The truth was that the further west they'd traveled, the more she realized the truth of Zack's warnings. She should have taken his offer and gone east, but her stubborn pride had held her back.

"Ah found jobs for us on the wagon train," Loretta was saying. "We could work our way out to Oregon."

"What are you saying?" Aimee cried in disbelief, staring at the other girl as if she were demented.

"They was one family what needed a maid, so Ah

tol' them Ah'd come. The wife is crippled and needs someone with a strong back to lift her. Ah figured my back is strong enough for thet. An' another family needed a teacher fo' their children. We can live with the families in their wagons and travel with them and eat with them and ever'thin'," Loretta finished on a triumphant note. Aimee looked at her flushed face, considering all she'd heard. She had little choice, she realized. She couldn't stay here in Independence. She would starve and she couldn't return to St. Louis. Arlo Benjamin's threat of arrest was there.

"Oh, Loretta, do you think we should?" she whispered. "Zack said the trail is so dangerous."

"Other women and children are traveling over it," Loretta said blithely. "If they can make it, Ah guess we can too." Aimee looked into her eager eyes and felt a flutter of anticipation.

"I guess we could at that," she agreed, and forbore to ask if this were the same wagon train Billy and Zack would be traveling with. Somehow, she knew it was.

"We're goin' to Oregon," Loretta cried, laughing and clapping her hands with glee.

"Oregon or bust!" Aimee repeated a phrase she'd overheard one of the emigrants make. Arms around each other, the two girls danced around the room, then paused, staring into each other's eyes in consternation. They were going to Oregon and the future loomed dark and uncertain before them.

Zack wasn't as jubilant about their new plans.

"You never stop being the fool, do you?" he demanded. He sat his horse, glaring down at her.

"And you never stop telling me about it, do you?" Aimee whirled from her task to meet his angry gaze. He wore the same fringed leather jacket and leggings he'd worn on the boat, and his broad-brimmed hat was pulled low over scowling eyes. She hadn't seen him since he'd walked away from the *Missouri Queen*.

Aimee pushed at the windblown tendrils of hair trailing across her cheek and glanced around at the other covered wagons. She was painfully aware of how she must look. She'd spent the last three days helping Agnes Stuart prepare for the journey. Despite the dour woman's bossiness, Aimee was sure she knew little more about it than Aimee did herself. If not for the children, Aimee might have changed her mind about going with the Stuarts. Ulcie Stuart was a vague, disorganized man whose pale eyes seemed to view the world with a helpless resignation. His wife was a bitter, unhappy woman who felt she'd married beneath her and that somehow her husband had failed her abysmally. It was not a happy household.

There were five children and Aimee strongly suspected another was on its way, although Agnes had yet to confide such to her. The young ones—Sally, age four, and Tad, a chubby cherub of three who meticulously mimicked everything his older sister did—had already endeared themselves by wrapping their arms around Aimee's neck and giving her sloppy kisses. Eight-year-old Hannah and six-year-old Jamie had been more reserved, but had come around. Aimee felt confident. Only Wakefield, who was twelve and trying manfully to be like his father, had snubbed her.

"So you think you're going to Oregon now." Zack all but sneered, and Aimee raised her chin and met his gaze defiantly.

"I *am* going," she said. "It's all arranged. You can't do anything to stop me, so why don't you just go about your own business?"

"What do you hope to gain by going to Oregon?" he demanded. "It's a wilderness there, not at all what you're used to."

"What does anyone hope to gain? Have you gone around asking the rest of these people what they're looking for in Oregon? Have you tried to dissuade them as you have me? Leave me alone, Zack. Don't concern yourself with my welfare."

"I wish to God it were that easy," he grunted. "I feel responsible for you. I'm the one who dragged you away from your hometown."

"You helped me escape. I appreciate that. Your obligation is ended."

"Tarnation, woman," he exploded. "I've never seen anyone more stubborn or bullheaded than you."

"So you've said, many times," Aimee said coolly. "Now, if you'll excuse me, Mr. Crawford, I have a great deal of work to do before the wagon train pulls out." Aimee went back to her work. Lifting a box of smoked bacon onto the tailgate of the wagon, she began storing slabs of it in the barrel of flour, which would insulate it from the heat. She worked quickly, using the energy of her own anger to carry the task along. White flour splattered on her skirt and when she lifted a hand to brush away a tendril of hair, a dusting was left on one cheek. Zack dismounted and stood watching her. Aimee glanced over her shoulder in mock surprise.

"Are you still here?" she asked innocently. "Don't tell me you're all prepared for the trip."

"Listen, you little fool." Zack caught her arm and spun her around. "This is no game. You're making a decision that could cost you your life."

"Am I?" Aimee glanced around at the other wagons, sitting still and serene in the afternoon sun. Their heavy canvas coverings, stretched over hickory bow frames, gave them a festive air, as if great white birds had nested in the meadows. Children darted in and around the wagon tongues, calling to each other in their games of hide-and-seek.

"If this trip is so dangerous, why are people taking children and pregnant women?" she demanded.

"God only knows what spurs these men," Zack replied. "What family are you with?"

"The Stuarts. I'm to teach their children while we're on the trail."

"Ulcie Stuart?" Zack asked abruptly, his dark eyebrows drawing down.

"Do you know him?"

"Yes, I know him," he said, then glared at Aimee. "I might have known."

"What do you mean?" Aimee asked in alarm.

"Look around you," Zack demanded. "He's the most ill-prepared for this trip of anyone here, and he has the most dependent on him. He has five children and his wife is expecting. He barely has enough supplies to feed his family, let alone an extra mouth." Alarm grew within Aimee at his words, but Zack wasn't finished.

"Look at this wagon! It's too worn-out to make the whole trip across those plains and mountains, and he has few spare parts. He isn't going to make it, Aimee. His wife and children have no choice but to follow him. You have."

"Have I?" Aimee asked.

"Don't play games with me, Aimee. Heed what I tell you."

"And if I don't?" she challenged. Zack pulled her toward him, his hands biting into the tender flesh of her arms. He held her so closely she could feel the heat of his body, and for a moment her thoughts were so scattered she paid little attention to his words.

"I could shake you until some common sense rattled into that beautiful head of yours," he growled, and for a moment she thought he meant to kiss her. "There's nothing for you in Oregon, but there's death and disease waiting every step of the way there. Why would you want to go and risk your life like this?" His words were almost a plea, and for once Aimee put aside her flippancy and answered him.

"I'm looking for a home, a place where I can live without shame," she answered softly.

"You could have done that back east. Webster was the only place that knew about your father."

"That's not true." Aimee bit back the rest of what she'd meant to say.

"Who else?" Zack demanded.

"Arlo Benjamin knew. He knew about the jewels as well, and . . ." She paused.

"Go on." Zack shook her slightly.

"They had posters out for me," she whispered, for

the first time giving in to the misery that thought had caused her. "If I go back, he'll have me arrested. You see, I have little choice. I must either stay here in Independence and eventually be found or I must go on to Oregon."

Zack studied her face, then with a sigh wrapped his arms around her. "My poor Aimee," he whispered, cradling her as if she were some precious object. Her head lay against his shoulder and she took in the manly smell of him, felt the strength of his arms, and she never wanted it to end. But he set her aside, his expression irritated that once again he'd been trapped by her helplessness.

"I'll see what I can do," he said, and striding to his horse, leapt into his saddle and galloped away. Aimee watched him go. She should have felt despair over all he'd told her, but somehow she didn't. For the first time since she'd decided to join this wagon train, she felt confident. Zack would be on it too. Nothing bad could happen with him nearby.

"I'll not have you entertaining men friends," Agnes Stuart said, coming around the side of the wagon. "I am a Christian, God-fearing woman, and I'll not have my children exposed to wanton or lewd behavior."

"No, of course not," Aimee replied. "We were just talking."

"Humph, I saw you and it was more than talking you were doing. If it happens once more, you'll be out, is that understood?"

"Yes, I'm sorry. He's just a good friend. It won't happen again."

"It had better not." Agnes turned away and looked around the campsite, her thin mouth pinched and bitter-looking. "Is Mr. Stuart back yet?"

"No, he—" A steely glance from Agnes Stuart's pale blue eyes made Aimee pause. "No, ma'am, he's not back yet," she said primly, and turned back to her task of storing the bacon. Zack's words came back to her and now she noted the food supplies. They did seem meager for the months ahead, when there would be little chance to replenish them at the scattered forts. Carefully Aimee tapped the flour down around the pork. It seemed more important than ever that it not spoil.

By evening Aimee's back was aching. After she'd finished the flour barrels, she'd been required to help with the preparing of the evening meal. Since she knew nothing of cooking, she was relegated to toting and carrying and stirring the stew.

"Should I add more vegetables to it?" she asked hopefully, remembering the skimpy fare the night before.

"There's more than enough," Agnes Stuart answered. "Waste not, want not." Aimee thought of the five young Stuarts, all of them as thin as their parents except for the chubby Tad. Was Agnes really as stingy as Aimee had first supposed, or was she of necessity rationing their supplies? The thought was chilling. The journey had not yet begun. What would it be like when they were weeks out into the prairies?

After supper, Aimee helped wash the metal plates and forks and prepared the children for bed. Beds for the younger children were made in the back of the wagon. Aimee and Wakefield slept in bedrolls under the wagon along with Ulcie and Agnes. It wasn't the best of accommodations but Aimee was growing used to sleeping out-of-doors. Besides, by leaving the hotel and sleeping in the Stuart campsite, she could save her last few coins.

Now Aimee pulled the coverlets under the chins of the youngest Stuarts and prepared to tell them a story. It was their favorite time of the day and they listened so attentively, with their eyes rounded in delight that Aimee tried to outdo herself. The sound of approaching horses interrupted the storytime. Aimee peeked out the drawstring opening. Ben Thompson, the wagon master, and some other men had ridden up to the campsite. Zack Crawford was with them.

"Stuart, we been lookin' over everybody's outfits and yours don't hardly look like it'll make it," Thompson began without preamble. "What provisions have you made for breakdowns?"

"Why, uh, none," Ulcie said slowly. "I guess I just figured not to have any breakdowns."

"Them mules you got don't look too good either," another man observed.

"I traded my horses for them back in St. Louis," Ulcie said hesitantly. "He told me horses wouldn't stand the trip."

"He told you true. Mules are good when they ain't been run to death, but these aren't going to make it, not pulling your wagon."

Helplessly Ulcie looked at the men. "I guess I'll just have to start out with what I got and trust in the good Lord to pull me through."

"They's many a skeleton out there on the plains, Stuart, men who thought just like you."

"There's a man over at the livery stable," Zack said. "He's got a couple of yoke of oxen he'll trade you for that team of mules."

"Well, I don't know," Ulcie vacillated. "I don't know if oxen are as good as mules."

"They're not as fast, but they're a little more reliable and a durn sight cheaper to feed," Thompson advised. He seemed to have hit on the right argument.

Ulcie nodded. "I'm much obliged to you."

Thompson turned his attention to the wagon. "You'd best get that wheel off and take it down to the blacksmith to fix." He nodded toward a wobbly wheel where the wood had shrunk away from the iron ring. "Ask if he's got a spare you can take with you."

"Yes, all right, I will," Ulcie promised, grateful now for the advice he was getting.

"Some of the men'll come around tomorrow and take a look at that axle and the underpinnings," Zack said.

"Yes, all right. Thank you."

"No trouble, Stuart. We don't want a lot of problems once we get out on the trail." Thompson signaled to the other men. They doffed their hats and headed their horses out of camp.

"You see, Aggie," Ulcie said jubilantly. "We're going to be all right. We've got good people who'll help us."

"What do they want in return?" Agnes asked sourly, and the smile faded from Ulcie's face. His shoulders slumped in defeat.

"I don't know," he said wearily. "I just don't know anymore." He sat down by the fire and stared into the flames as if he were a million miles away from this Missouri campsite.

In the days that followed, Zack and the other men dropped by the campsite often to give Ulcie Stuart tips on how to prepare his wagon for the long, torturous trip. A grease bucket was acquired and filled with animal fat and tar and hung from the rear axle. It would be used to coat the wheel hubs.

The mules were traded for the oxen, great lumbering creatures that swayed from side to side as they walked. Gleefully the children named them and soon seemed to feel a great deal of affection for the dumb beasts that would pull them across a continent. Their names were scratched into the great wooden yokes that hung around their necks. The axles were checked and found to be sturdy, but another pair was made and lashed beneath the wagon. If an axle broke, an overlander was out of luck unless he had a spare.

Likewise the women stopped by to visit and offer advice. Under their directions, eggs were stored in barrels of cornmeal, and a goodly supply of coffee was laid by for all to drink. Aimee and Agnes learned that sometimes the water was too laden with alkali to be drinkable; coffee made it palatable.

Aimee began to know the other travelers. Royce Sawyer and his crippled wife, Helen, were the family with whom Loretta would travel. They were a middle-aged couple with kindly faces and a gentle manner. Aimee envied Loretta her lot.

Prudy Bigelow was no older than Aimee, but she

was already married and carrying her first baby. Her broad, plain face still flushed with pleasure every time she looked at Adam Bigelow.

Gladys Brewer was a sharp-tongued woman with a love of gossip.

There were others, but Aimee's favorite was Biddy Potts. Biddy never seemed to get annoyed with anyone, even her noisy brood of six children. She came often to help Agnes and Aimee, offering her advice on a number of things that would make life on the trail easier for them. She taught Aimee the proper medicines to pack, snakemaster for snakebites and laudanum for everything from headaches to cholera. She persuaded Agnes to purchase some shirts, mirrors, and beads for trading with the Indians for extra food. Aimee began to feel better prepared for the trip ahead and knew Zack had had a hand in all the assistance offered. The day of departure drew near, and excitement was at a fever pitch.

8

"Yo' look tired," Loretta observed. "Seems lak' yo' got the worst of this arrangement." They were strolling along the outer perimeter of the encampment. The lights of Independence glowed forlornly in the distance. All was quiet and peaceful now in the gathering twilight. Suppers were over and the campfires burned down to glowing coals. The children had been put to bed, worn out from their day of play and discovery. Their parents sat chatting in low tones to their neighbors, speculating on what tomorrow would bring.

Before dawn the wagon train would be pulling out to begin its journey westward. The animals were rested, repairs had been made and provisions bought. There was no need to stay longer. The sooner they got on the trail, the better it would be for them at the other end. They would have to keep to a tight schedule to make it to Oregon before the snows trapped them in the mountains.

Already other wagons were arriving and setting up camp while they bought supplies and checked last-minute repairs. Other wagon trains would be forming and leaving almost daily from now until mid-May.

"If those little monsters give you too hard a time," Loretta said, "you just give 'em a bop on the head. Thet'll settle 'em down fast enough."

Aimee smiled. "It isn't the children. I get along well enough with Sally and Tad. Hannah and Jamie are just mischievous, and Wakefield ignores me. I'm just tired from all the packing. Agnes hasn't been feeling well."

"Ah thought she jest wanted you to teach her children."

"Well, she does, but I have to share some of the chores, and there's extra work with the packing. How are things with the Sawyers?" Aimee sought to change the subject. She didn't want to to complain. Loretta had already helped enough, coming by in her free time to give Aimee a hand with the Stuart children. Even with this help, Aimee never seemed to be caught up on her work and she was always tired. There was barely time or energy left to teach the children.

"Helen Sawyer is very kind to me," Loretta said, and Aimee was surprised to see she looked troubled.

"Is that bad?" she asked with a grin. Loretta had seemed moody lately.

"No. Ah ain't had many people be kind to me. Yo're one of 'em, now Mrs. Sawyer. Ah don't know how to repay her."

"You are repaying her just by being there to help her in and out of the wagon and with all those hundreds of things a woman needs done that are too personal to ask a man's help, even your own husband."

"Ah suppose yo're right," Loretta said, and fell silent. Aimee glanced at her friend, thinking how much Loretta had changed in the weeks she'd known her. The lustrous black hair was clean and shiny, held back from her face with a pink ribbon that matched her gown. She'd filled out a little, so there was a softness to the rawboned lines of her face and arms. It became her. She was always dressed neatly now, her gown fresh and unsoiled. She bathed daily, as did Aimee, in spite of primitive conditions. Even her speech had begun to change. She worked with Aimee daily to improve, consciously eliminating "ain't" and other words from her vocabulary.

"Billy don't much care if Ah'm a lady," she said one day, "but Ah want to talk proper and learn to read and write." So Aimee had worked with her on these things and Loretta was learning quickly. But the sparkle was gone. Even when Aimee mentioned Billy, Loretta glanced away and didn't bubble over with funny stories or open declarations of her feelings as she once had.

"Is something wrong, Loretta?" Aimee asked finally, hating to see her friend so troubled. Loretta glanced up as if startled to find Aimee still there beside her. "Can I help with anything?"

"Nah." Loretta shook her head and the black waves swished across her shoulders. "Ever'thin's jest fine."

"How's Billy?" Aimee asked, thinking to provide her friend with an opportunity to talk if she wished.

"Ah reckon he's jest fine too," Loretta said, and Aimee knew she'd wouldn't say more. They'd come to the outer edge of the encampment. Beyond stretched the endless miles of prairies and mountains through which the Oregon Trail cut.

"It's kind of scary, isn't it?" Aimee asked, hugging her arms to herself. "It's so vast. We could get lost out there and no one would ever find us. Do you feel frightened sometimes?"

"There's other things thet scare me worse," Loretta said, and as if making up her mind, turned to Aimee. "If someone had been kind to yo' and yo' done somethin' that yo' knew would make thet person sad if they found out, would yo' keep it a secret?"

"I'm not sure," Aimee said, puzzled by Loretta's words. Was she trying to tell Aimee something and hadn't the courage, fearful of how Aimee would react? "If this person is a good friend, she'll probably understand."

"D' yo' think she would?" Loretta cried. "D' yo' think she'd know Ah didn't have no choice?" Aimee's heart warmed to the other girl. She'd come to know and understand Loretta's sense of honor. Loretta could never be disloyal to a friend.

"If you were to tell her so, I think she'd understand."

"Maybe," Loretta said doubtfully, and began to walk again, her head down, her steps short and jerky.

"On th' other hand, maybe she wouldn't." She paused abruptly. "But if she found out, then she'd be even more fussed at me."

"I don't understand what you're talking about, Loretta," Aimee said, hurrying to catch up. "If you tell me what's troubling you, we can work it out."

"Nothing," Loretta mumbled. Silently Aimee walked beside her friend, concern furrowing her brow. She'd never seen Loretta like this before. Suddenly Loretta whirled to face her.

"Once we're out on the prairie, cain't nobody send me back, kin they?" she demanded, her gaze almost fierce as she looked at Aimee.

"I've heard they don't turn back for anyone," Aimee replied, "but why would someone want to send you back?"

"It don't matter now," Loretta declared, and some of the old sparkle was back. "Ah jest got to worryin' about Billy knowin', and Ah'll never tell him, never." Her tense body fairly shook and she hooted with laughter. "It's goin' t' be all right," she declared. "Ah'm still me. Ah ain't . . . ah'm not the old Loretta."

"I like the old Loretta too," Aimee replied, thinking this was more like the old Loretta than the pale, silent creature she'd been earlier.

"Yo' been the best friend a person could have," Loretta declared, and gave Aimee a quick hug. "Ah got to go find Billy. Ah been treatin' him somethin' terrible lately," she called over her shoulder, and Aimee was left standing alone in the dark, her mouth hanging open as she thought back over the conversation that hadn't made a bit of sense to her, but obviously had to Loretta. Bemused, Aimee strolled back through the encampment toward the Stuart wagon.

"Good evening, Miss Bennett," a husky masculine voice called. Zack Crawford stepped out of the shadows. Smoke from the cigarette he held drifted upward in the cool evening air.

"Good evening, Mr. Crawford," Aimee said, feeling unaccountably shy with him. One hand came up unbidden to smooth back her hair.

"Mind if I walk along with you?" he asked pleasantly, and fell into step beside her.

Nervously Aimee sought some topic of conversation. "I haven't thanked you for the help you gave the Stuarts," she said.

"Stuart's thanked me enough already," Zack replied wryly. "In fact, if he expended as much energy on his rig as he does in thanking me, he'd be in a lot better shape."

"Still, I'm very grateful. I know you did it to help me out too. Someday I'll find a way to repay you for your time and trouble."

"I haven't asked it."

"I know, but if there's anything I can do for you, please don't hesitate to tell me."

Zack glanced at her sharply, wondering if she had any idea at all of what was running through his mind, and decided she hadn't. Her eyes were clear and innocent as they met his. "I'll keep that in mind," he answered. "There is one thing."

"What?" The expression on her face was eager.

Zack gazed at her for a long moment, letting his eyes give her the answer. Slowly her expression changed and he saw the awareness of him as a man grow on her. Then, and only then, did he step forward and pull her toward him. He'd thought of little else but the way she'd felt in his arms that day he'd come to the Stuart wagon. Now he wanted to hold her again and try to understand why this small woman haunted him so.

He lowered his mouth to hers, lightly brushing her lips in a tingling sensuous movement that made her catch her breath. Her eyes were tightly closed, her lips moist and full. Her slender young arms had twined around his waist and she stood waiting for his kiss. Zack lowered his head once more and this time his lips were warm and demanding on hers, his tongue rasping across the soft fullness of her lips, seeking entrance to the sweetness beyond. She moaned and swayed against him, her young body unendurably sweet, her kiss chaste and untried.

Zack paused, gazing down at her pale face, illuminated by the moonlight. She was so beautiful and untouched. Her innocence caught at him and he puzzled at it. This was no Caroline, with her pretty wiles and schemes. This wasn't the kind of woman he usually sought out. Why, then, did she continue to draw him? Sighing, Zack set her away from him. Aimee looked at him in breathless confusion. The kiss had shaken her to the soles of her feet and she feared she might not to able to stand alone.

"Didn't I do it right?" she asked timidly, and Zack smiled at this further sign of her innocence.

"Too well, I'm afraid," he said, "but tomorrow we must be up early. Your wagon is just over here." He took her elbow and guided her toward the pale shadow of one of the wagons. "There'll be a lot of confusion tomorrow. For your own safety, try to stay near the wagon and keep the children with you."

"Yes, I will. Thank you for your concern."

"Good night, Aimee."

"Good night, Zack." They gazed at each other for an awkward moment and she longed to have him take her into his arms again, but he merely touched the brim of his hat and turned away. Aimee stood watching him go, her body trembling with unnamed desires.

"Was that Zack Crawford?" Agnes Stuart asked from her place beneath the wagon.

"Yes, he . . . Loretta had to leave and he walked me back to the wagon," Aimee stammered, remembering Agnes' admonitions the first time Zack had come.

"That was kind of him," Agnes observed in her thin, whiny voice. "In fact he's been overly helpful to Mr. Stuart and me since you joined us. People don't do things like he has unless there's something in it for them."

"There's nothing between Mr. Crawford and me," Aimee exclaimed. "He's just a friend. He . . . he knew my father." It wasn't exactly a lie, Aimee thought. Zack had certainly been there at the end. She began to prepare for bed.

"Perhaps you should continue to be . . . pleasant to Mr. Crawford," Agnes advised. "We're bound to need his help before this trip is over."

"Yes, ma'am," Aimee said sullenly, and in that moment began to heartily dislike her benefactress. She'd tried hard to make allowances for Agnes Stuart because of her pregnancy and reduced circumstances, but there seemed little excuse for such mean-mindedness. Aimee crawled into her bedroll and settled herself for sleep. She was tired. The days had been long and demanding, and tomorrow the trip began in earnest. Tomorrow they would be on their way to Oregon.

"Turn out, turn out!" The cry rang over the encampment. The wagon master took off his hat and waved the first wagon forward. Men standing beside their teams slapped the reins against the broad backs of their oxen and the clumsy beasts leaned into their yokes. The great iron-rimmed wheels began to roll and slowly the wagons moved forward. Their journey had begun.

"Oregon or bust," someone cried out, and soon the cheer was taken up by all. It rang around the encampment as other wagons pulled into line. Some men pointed their guns at the sky and fired. There was an air of celebration. Aimee felt a great welling of excitement. What had Loretta said once about being a part of history? Aimee had never thought of it that way before. Her concern had been only for herself and her circumstances, but now she thought of all the men and women who walked beside the slow-moving wagons, their faces hopeful as they turned them toward the west. What dreams they all carried with them. She was no different, Aimee realized, and for the first time felt a kinship with the other emigrants. She felt lighthearted and eager. Gaily she waved at the new arrivals

166

who stood watching the wagon train's departure. They would be leaving themselves in a few days.

Out onto the broad green prairie the lead wagon rolled, and the rest followed. They stretched along the trail for nearly three-quarters of a mile, with the spare milk cows and oxen trailing behind. Nearly everyone walked to make the load easier on the draft animals. No one seemed to mind. The sun shone brightly on their heads and the spring breeze was warm on their faces. The prairie was fragrant with spring flowers. It seemed they were on a picnic or a spring outing. Everyone's spirits were high.

Outriders raced ahead of the column, although there was little reason for their services now. The path lay clear and unchallenged before them. Back along the caravan someone started a song, and soon others had joined in so that all up and down the procession could be heard singing. Laughter rang out easily. For the moment their fears and anxiety had been put to rest. They had begun their journey to a new life, and the way seemed paved with sunshine and green meadows and goodwill.

They angled northwest, traveling easily through the prairie. Zack rode alongside his wagon while Billy drove. Far ahead, Aimee could catch a glimpse of Loretta as she walked beside the Sawyers' wagon. She was chatting amiably with Helen Sawyer and seemed her old self this morning. Aimee longed to run up through the wild prairie grass and share this moment with her friend, but Zack had admonished her to keep a sharp eye on the children, and she was learning to accept his advice. As if summoned by her thoughts, Zack broke out of line and rode back to greet her.

"Good morning, Miss Bennett," he called, tipping his hat to her. "How are you holding up?"

"In good form, Mr. Crawford," she called gaily.

"I quite agree," he replied, and there was no doubt to his meaning or the admiring look on his face. It made Aimee want to laugh, but she kept her expression prim. "But don't be too optimistic," Zack admonished. "The trip is just beginning."

"I'll still be here at its end, Mr. Crawford," Aimee assured him, tugging her long skirt free of the prickly grasses that caught at the hem.

"Your skirt will last longer if you tuck it up a bit," he advised. "You won't feel as tired at the pull of it on you all day."

"It's fine as it is," she answered. "Don't worry about me."

"All right, I won't," he called, and with a cheery wave galloped back to his own wagon. Aimee watched him go, wishing he'd stayed awhile longer.

Although they were one of the earlier wagon trains, they were not the first to cross over the trail and it was well-marked by previous travelers. The morning passed and the emigrants settled into a comfortable gait. By midday they were grateful for a break and a chance to rest. The first leg of the journey would be taken in easy stages until their bodies had become accustomed to the pace.

"Lawdy, Ah'm tired," Loretta said as she and Aimee sat in the shade of a wagon nibbling at the cold victuals prepared the night before.

"I may never move again." Aimee set her plate aside. She was too tired to eat. Her feet were sore and her legs ached. Throwing off her calico bonnet, she lay back in the fragrant green grass and gazed up at the vast blueness above. "Can you imagine all that sky?" she sighed. "It goes on for miles and miles without even a cloud." She sighed again and didn't recognize the contentment it conveyed. Closing her eyes, she lay listening to the sounds around her and half-dozed, dreaming of Zack Crawford and the kiss they'd shared the night before. That kiss had awakened feelings she couldn't put aside. She wished he were here to kiss her again. Perhaps this time she'd do it better and he wouldn't stop so abruptly.

"Hello, ladies. Care if we join you?" a voice asked, and Aimee opened her eyes. Zack stood above her, plate in hand, grinning down at her with daredevil lights in his eyes. His gaze freely roamed over her as she lay stretched out on the grass.

"'Course not," Loretta said, and twitched her skirts to one side, so Billy could sit beside her. Aimee sat up and straightened her skirts decorously, her eyes downcast, her cheeks pink. Somehow Zack made her feel all flustered and bothered. She longed to be poised and restrained in his presence, but he always caught her off-guard.

"Heard we're on the lookout for Indians already," Billy said, quickly forking down his food. His eyes were on Loretta, so he didn't see Zack's warning nod.

"Indians?" Aimee asked in dismay.

Loretta's eyes were wide with fear as well. "Nobody told me nothin' 'bout Indians," she exclaimed. She clasped her arms around herself and peered around anxiously.

"I don't believe they're much to worry about now," Zack said reassuringly. "The Indians in this area will be the Kanza tribe. They'll be more interested in trading with you than in harming you."

"All the same, Ah'm takin' my rifle with me this afternoon," Billy declared.

"Yo' won't be in danger, will yo'?" Loretta asked in alarm. "Ah couldn't bear it if anythin' happened to yo'."

"Ah'll be right careful," Billy reassured her, "but it's up to us menfolk to protect the rest o' ya'll."

"Yo' will be careful, won't yo'?" Loretta cried, and threw her arms around him. Billy patted her shoulder, his face reddening at her display in front of others. Zack and Aimee glanced at each other and smiled.

"You're not eating?" he asked, motioning toward her untouched plate.

"I'm not very hungry."

"Try," he urged. "It will be a long time before we stop this evening." His tone was gentle, his glance warm, and to please him Aimee picked up her food and nibbled at it.

"How far yo' reckon we come so far?" Loretta asked, smiling at Billy. Her feelings for the thin Tennessean were all too obvious.

"Ah figure 'bout ten mile," Billy answered. "What d' yo' think, Mr. Crawford?"

"That's what I figure," Zack said, putting aside his empty plate. He leaned back and stretched out his long legs, and unconsciously Aimee measured her own against his, marveling at his length. "We'll probably make another ten before we camp for the night." He turned to Aimee. "Are you up to it?"

Aimee's spirits sank at the thought of walking another ten miles that day, but she nodded and smiled gamely. "I'll make it."

Zack's brown eyes studied her warmly. "You surprise me at every turn." He leaned forward and began to pick the burrs from the hem of her skirt.

"Maybe that's because you underestimate me at every turn," she answered, and once again her gaze was captured by his.

"Not always," he said softly, and she knew they were no longer speaking of the journey but of the kiss they'd exchanged the night before. Aimee felt her heart leap. The kiss had moved him as much as it had her. She drew a trembling breath, unable to look away from his dark eyes.

"How many miles did they say we have to go to reach Oregon?" Loretta asked.

"They estimate it's over two thousand miles," Billy said.

"Two thousand miles. Ah'll surely never make it," Loretta exclaimed. Looking into Zack's eyes, Aimee knew she could make it. She could do anything, be anything to please him.

"Turn out," the cry sounded, and the peacefulness of the nooning was broken. People hurried to store their belongings. Dishes were packed away dirty and would be washed at the evening stop. Men hurried to rehitch the animals to the wagons.

"We're on our way again," Zack said, getting to his

feet. He reached down to Aimee, extending a square brown hand. His eyes smiled into hers. Aimee placed her hand in his and felt herself being pulled to her feet.

"Are you rested enough?" he asked, and she shook her head.

"You're underestimating me again," she teased, and wasn't aware that the impish laughter in her eyes made him want to crush her to him and taste again the sweet honey of her lips.

"Until tonight, then," he said instead. No matter how tired she felt, she'd make it without a whimper. He let go of her hand and strode away to his horse, and without looking back, rode off, joining the other outriders. Aimee watched them go, noting they were more heavily armed than they'd been that morning. A tremor of fear coursed through her, then she remembered Zack's words. If he said the Indians meant them no harm, then she believed him.

"Aimee, mama said you're to come at once." Four-year-old Sally tugged at her hand, and retrieving her hat, Aimee waved good-bye to Loretta and turned back to the Stuart wagon.

By mid afternoon, most of the travelers had begun to tire, but pushed on uncomplainingly, determined not to be the first to lag behind. The younger children had long since grown tired of the novelty of walking through the tall grass plains and were sprawled atop the loads inside the wagons, some of them lulled to sleep by the sway of the slow-moving wagons and the warm rays of the sun beating down on the canvas coverings.

Aimee had long ago reached the limit of her endurance and yearned to crawl up on the back of the wagon for a nap herself. Removing the broad-brimmed bonnet, she wiped at her damp forehead before clamping it back on again. As unattractive as the homemade affair was, it shielded her fair skin from the burning prairie sun. She was grateful to Biddy for giving it to her.

Relentlessly the caravan moved on. The rolling green plains seemed to go on endlessly, broken occasionally by a stand of woods or a sparkling stream. The sun moved lower in the sky, the air cooled. The children awoke refreshed and once again ran up and down the column, clambering in and out of the moving wagons in spite of their mothers' shrill warnings.

The outriders returned with news of a suitable campsite ahead and the pace quickened. Everyone was eager for a rest. They halted in a shallow green valley rimmed by a small woods with a swift clear stream nearby. Waving his hat and whistling, the scout directed the wagons into a circle so they formed a corral about a hundred feet wide. The wagon tongues were interlocked, each one extending under the wheels of the wagon in front. A heavy chain was run from one wagon to the next all around the corral until they were safely locked together. Although the outriders had found no evidence of the Kanza Indians, the men decided the animals would be driven into the corral after supper. In the meantime they were turned loose to feed on the tall prairie grass and lookouts were posted. Ben Thompson was an experienced trail leader and he left nothing to chance.

Campfires were lit and kettles of food hung on tripods to cook. Children hurried to the woods to collect dry wood to feed the fires. Others hurried toward the stream with wooden buckets swinging between them. Everyone fell to the chores with alacrity, for there was a promise of fiddle-playing and dancing later on. Tired as they were now, the prospect of a social hour was appealing.

"Aimee, you'll have to tend to supper tonight," Agnes said peremptorily. "I'm not feeling well. The day's journey has been too hard on me. I must lie down."

"Yes, ma'am," Aimee answered with a sinking heart. She was tired too and she hadn't had the benefit of riding in the wagon all day as Agnes had. Still, the woman was pregnant. In dismay Aimee looked at the empty kettle and the wide eyes of the Stuart children. Other than the assistance she'd given Agnes the last few days, she'd never cooked a meal. Sighing, she picked up a bucket.

"Wakefield, you and Jamie gather firewood. Hannah and Sally, you take this bucket down to the stream and bring back water."

"What can I do?" Tad asked, one chubby hand shaking her skirts.

Aimee smiled in spite of her fatigue. "You can gather twigs for the fire," she said, "but stay near the wagon."

"You can gather your own firewood," Wakefield growled petulantly. "I ain't doin' it."

"I'm not doing it," Aimee corrected automatically. "Someone will have to do it if we want to eat."

"Not me," Wakefield said sullenly. "That ain't man's work."

Aimee bit back tears of vexation. "You'll have to do it, Wakefield," she half-pleaded. "Your father isn't here and your mother's ill. There's no one else."

"You do it," he snapped with a curl of his lips. "That's what you're along for."

Aimee's temper flared. "I am not a servant," she snapped. "I am a teacher and I was hired to conduct school for you on this trip. Now, I insist that you go get some wood, so I can begin supper."

"No, I won't," he shouted, and Agnes put her head out of the covered wagon.

"What on earth is going on here?" she demanded.

Gratefully Aimee turned to her. "I've asked Wakefield to get wood for the fire, and he refuses." She was certain Agnes would instruct him to do so at once.

"I don't blame him. You can't expect the children to do your chores for you, Aimee. Now, hurry or supper will be late for Mr. Stuart. Children, run and play." With a swish the canvas covering was closed again. With triumphant glances the Stuart children ran off toward the stream. Speechless at the unfairness of it, Aimee watched them go; then, taking deep breaths to calm her anger, she picked up the bucket. She would have to gather firewood and tote the water as well as make supper. Her slim shoulders sagged with discouragement.

The beans in the stew were hard and undercooked and the coffee too strong. Everyone complained, even Agnes, who'd recovered enough to come to the fire and eat with her family. Her good health stayed with her after supper as well, for she walked with her husband to the circle of dancers at the other side of the corral. Aimee was left to clean up the supper dishes alone. Tears of anger at the injustice stung her eyes, and she worked furiously, scrubbing the pot with sand from the creek Now and then a sob of self-pity escaped her lips and she wiped at her cheeks with the back of her hand.

She always seemed to land in one undesirable circumstance after another, she thought miserably. Why couldn't she have traveled with a family like the Sawyers? Helen Sawyer seemed a kind lady whose plain face shone with gentle humor in spite of her handicap. Royce Sawyer doted on his wife, and now that Loretta was with them, they treated her like a daughter. It was too unfair, Aimee thought bitterly. What had she done to deserve all that had happened to her? She flung the rags over one of the wheels to dry and threw away the cold dishwater with extra vehemence.

"Whoa," Zack Crawford said, jumping backward to save his boots from the dirty water. "I thought you'd be over at the dance."

"I'm sorry, Mr. Crawford," Aimee said crisply, returning the dishpan to the wagon with a bang. "I have no time for such frivolities. I've been busy with my chores. First, I've gathered firewood and then carried the water and prepared the supper, which no one liked, and finally I've straightened the campsite, and all of this after walking twenty miles." She paused to get a breath and regain control of the sobs that threatened to spill forth.

"No one said it would be easy," Zack said gently.

Aimee whirled and flounced away from him. She was hot and tired and she could feel the grime on her face. She longed for a bath. Seating herself on a makeshift camp stool, she wiped at her cheeks with the hem of her dress.

"I suppose you're here to tell me you told me so," she said sarcastically.

"I hadn't planned to." Zack squatted down beside her. "I came to ask you for a dance." Aimee stopped scrubbing at her face and smoothed back her hair, conscious suddenly of how she must look to Zack. He had taken the time to wash away the day's grime and his hair was combed neatly in place. He sat on his haunches grinning at her invitingly. The fiddle music called to Aimee, and suddenly her feet forgot the miles they'd walked that day and would again tomorrow, and began to tap a rhythm. Zack's grin widened.

"Come on," he cried, leaping to his feet and holding out his hand. Aimee took it and they were speeding across the corral to the light, where other figures moved to the vigorous strains of the fiddle. Those who could not or chose not to dance, stood watching, their hands clapping in rhythm. Even the children had formed their own dance circle nearby, mimicking the steps and glee of their elders as they enjoyed this carefree moment.

"Yo' made it," Loretta cried as she sailed past in Billy's arms, and her laughter floated back to them. Zack swung Aimee around the clearing, his strong arms holding her securely, while her skirts flew out behind her. It seemed to Aimee that her feet barely touched the ground. Faces of the onlookers became a blur. She grew breathless as they danced one jig after another. At last the fiddler took pity on the gasping, sweating dancers and played a slow dance. Zack held her as close as propriety allowed, his dark gaze capturing hers, and for Aimee the other dancers ceased to exist. She and Zack danced alone in a world of their own. The plaintive strains of the fiddle came to an end and they stood staring into each other's eyes.

"Aimee," Zack whispered, his eyes filled with a fire that kindled something deep inside her. His grip tightened on her elbows, urgent and compelling. "Aimee—"

"Aimee. Mama says you better come put us to bed now," a little voice piped, and Sally stood at her side. Her wide eyes stared up at them. "How come he's lookin' at you that way?" she asked, and Aimee's face reddened. Quickly she stepped back, and taking the child's thin shoulder in one hand, turned her back toward the wagon.

"We'd better go now, Sally," she said, and pushed the child ahead of her.

"Good night, Mr. Crawford," Sally called back.

"Good night, Sally. Good night, Miss Bennett." His voice was gently mocking, the laughter as evident to her as if she'd turned back to see it in his eyes. Aimee made no answer as she herded the children back to the wagon, but later, when covers had been tucked in and bedtime stories told and all was quiet, Aimee lay on her own pallet thinking of the dance and the feel of Zack's strong arms around her. As she gazed up at the stars, Webster seemed very far away, and somehow it didn't matter anymore. Contentedly, Aimee turned on her pillow and fell asleep.

A gunshot broke her sleep. All around her, dark shapes were rising from their beds or clambering down from their wagons to begin a new day. Even as Aimee watched, cookfires were being stirred to readiness and iron pots set over them. The men were already gathering up the yokes for the oxen and harnessing the mules.

Groaning, Aimee lay back. She couldn't get up now. She was too weary. If she tried to stand, she'd surely fall down. The wagon rustled and creaked above her as Ulcie clambered out. Little Tad cried out sleepily and Agnes soothed him back to sleep.

"Aimee, it's time to get up," Agnes called sharply, and Aimee clamped her teeth tightly and crawled out of her bedroll. Stoically she set about building up the fire and putting the coffee to boil. The spider was set over the coals and Aimee cut slices of bacon and put them to frying. She was learning, she congratulated herself. Was it only a few weeks ago that she'd turned up her nose at Zack's offering of fried pork? Now she not only ate it, she cooked it! There was a strange kind of satisfaction at the thought. She'd have to tell Zack she was not as useless as he had supposed.

Breakfast was a quick affair, eaten on the run, and once again the dirty dishes were stored for washing later. Belongings were swiftly stowed, and before the sun showed on the eastern horizon, the overlanders were ready to move on.

"Turn out," the wagon master shouted, and once again the wagons pulled into line. Another day had begun on the trail.

9

At first Aimee was sure she couldn't make it. Her feet were sore, her cramped muscles protested, but as she continued to put one foot in front of the other, her muscles stretched and the trek became easier. Zack and some of the other men had set out on a hunting trip. They would try to supplement their food supply with as much fresh game as they could get. The sun rose, offering its warmth and light as compensation to the toiling travelers. Children called out to one another, their voices as piercing and sweet as the morning song of the field sparrows hidden in the grass. The prairie chickens boomed out their hollow mating call. A slope bloomed with the pale pink of May flowers.

"Shooting stars," Biddy Potts called as Aimee paused to pick a bouquet. They were aptly named, Aimee thought, looking at their swept-back petals.

The wagons wove through fields of grass that grew belly-deep to the oxen and cattle. Walking became more difficult as the stubborn stalks caught at the travelers' feet. Once again small children clambered into the wagons, and those who must continue on foot walked behind, striving to stay in the wheel ruts, where the grass had been crushed down.

At first the prairie seemed monotonous, stretching away for endless miles, but as the hours passed and she grew bored, Aimee began to notice the subtle differences in the land through which they passed. The tall stalks of grass were not all the same. There seemed to be several varieties, and when she gazed off across the plains, she could see the darker shadings where the land dipped and rose again. She began to listen closely to the sounds of the prairie, noting the monotonous drone of the insects, distinguishing the differences in the bird calls, although she didn't know their names.

They stopped for the noon meal and Aimee hurried to feed the children so she could sit awhile and talk to Loretta while she ate. But Loretta seemed pensive and disinclined to talk. Aimee thought it was because the men hadn't returned from their hunting trip and tried to cheer up her friend. Anyone could see Loretta was in love with the redheaded Billy.

"You had a good time last night," Aimee remarked, giving Loretta the opportunity to chatter about Billy if she wished.

"Ah did," Loretta said shortly.

"I didn't know you could dance so well," Aimee tried again.

"Ain't nothin' much to it," Loretta said, and so morose was her mood that Aimee refrained from correcting her English. They sat in silence, eating their cold leftovers from the night before.

"You're very lucky to be with the Sawyers. They're such nice people." Aimee tried a different subject.

Loretta stiffened a moment; then her shoulders sagged. "Ah reckon they are," she said without enthusiasm.

"I wish I were with someone like the Sawyers instead of working for Agnes Stuart," Aimee blurted out, thinking of the way most of the chores had fallen to her now that the wagon train had left Independence.

"Yo' don't know what yo're talkin' 'bout," Loretta cried. "Life ain't always fair. Yo' got to take what comes to yo' and make the best of it."

"That's easy for you to say," Aimee flared at her friend's lack of sympathy. "All you have to do is take care of one person and I notice Mr. Sawyer gathers wood for you and carries the water and builds the fire.

Ulcie Stuart doesn't do any of that and Agnes won't make the children help." Her list of complaints was cut short as Loretta leapt to her feet.

"Yo' don't know nothing 'bout the way things really is," the girl said angrily. "For ever'thin' good that happens to yo', yo' got to pay a price, and it don't do no good to complain or try to get outta it. Yo're the lucky one, Aimee, an' yo' don't even know it." With a swirl of her skirts, Loretta stalked away, the set of her head stubborn and rigid, her shoulders squared.

What on earth was the matter with her? Aimee wondered, staring after Loretta's stiff figure.

The afternoon was much like the morning. Aimee grew tired, but she seemed to be holding up better than she had the day before. She spent the monotonous hours thinking of Zack, wondering if the men had found game yet, certain that if they had, his was the shot that had brought it down. The scout led them to a campsite and the wagons pulled into the corral with little direction needed. Even before the chains had been wound around the corral, campfires were going. There was no sign of the hunters and Aimee found herself glancing over her shoulder often as she worked. Some of the women whose husbands had gone were doing the same; still, nothing was said. No one seemed in the mood for a dance that night. Everyone remained near his own campfire, quietly talking, the women mending.

"There ain't nothin' to worry 'bout, folks." Ben Thompson went around to the campfires reassuring everyone. "I've seen hunting parties stay out two or three days."

"Do you reckon the Indians mighta got 'em? Maybe they need some help," Prudy Bigelow said anxiously. She was newly married, and although she wasn't showing yet, everyone on the wagon train knew she was expecting her first child.

"Now, Missus Bigelow, don't you worry none. Your Adam is one of the best men I know with a gun. Like as not, they got us some game an' are havin' to tote it back to us."

"Ah hope so," Prudy said, twisting her hands nervously. "Ah don't know what Ah'd do if somethin' happened to Ben."

"Don't you be thinkin' that way," Biddy Potts scolded her. "You just come on over to my campfire and visit with my family. No sense you sittin' over here scaring yourself with what-ifs." The plump woman put an arm around the slender waist and hurried Prudy off. Aimee watched them go and wished someone would take her mind off the missing men. She crawled into her bedroll early and lay thinking about Zack Crawford. He was a strong, self-reliant man. He could take care of himself, she reassured herself, but memory of the tales she'd heard back in Independence about the savage Indians that roamed these plains made her close her eyes tightly and say a little prayer for his safe return. The camp grew quiet and Aimee wondered how everyone could sleep when the men were still missing.

Suddenly there was the sound of hoofbeats and the emigrants roused themselves so quickly that Aimee knew none of them had been sleepy after all. Torches were lit and held high in an effort to see the approaching horsemen. Were they the returning hunters or were they Indians come to pour their wrath down on the hapless emigrants? Some distance out, a voice hailed the camp and the lookouts called back. Visibly everyone relaxed. It was the missing hunters. They rode into camp wearily, and strapped to the back of a packhorse was the carcass of an animal that looked like a large deer.

"Elk," someone called. "They make good eating." There was a babble of voices as everyone examined the prize and asked questions about the kill. While the others regaled the gathering with tales of the day's events, Zack slid down from his horse and headed for one of the campfires where a pot of coffee had been kept warm for them.

"Zack," Aimee called, and ran barefoot across the grass, the hem of her voluminous nightgown held high above the dampness of the dew. her hair hung loose around her shoulders and down her back. The weight of it seemed almost too much for her slender neck. The light from the campfire cast a red-gold halo around her head and Zack had a sudden urge to twist his fingers in the silken strands.

"Are you all right?" she asked, coming to a stop near him. Her eyes were wide with worry, her voice breathless from hurrying to him.

"I'm fine," he said softly. "You mustn't worry about me so." One hand went unbidden to touch her cheek and caress a sleek strand of hair.

"I . . . I tried not to," she stammered, "but we were all worried. We were afraid the Indians had attacked you."

"They didn't, and we're back safe and sound," Zack said lightly. Aimee longed to throw her arms around his slender waist and rest her head against his chest, just until the fearful pounding of her heart had stilled.

"Zack," someone called. "Come tell us about those Indian tracks you found." With a last glance at Aimee, he walked toward the crowd. Aimee hung back, listening to the excited talk for a while before returning to her bed. Now that the men had returned, she felt utterly exhausted. Crawling back into her bedroll, she lay listening to the low drone of talk around the campfire. They were talking about Indians, and Aimee should have been apprehensive, but with Zack safely back, she felt sure nothing bad would happen to the wagon train. Like a trusting child, she fell asleep.

The next few days were like the first two. The emigrants grew less anxious about Indians when they didn't appear. It was a big prairie and the Indians might not even be aware they were there, some told themselves. Others knew the Indians were only biding their time before they came to trade with the wagon train. The weather held. The evenings were cool, the days warm and dry. The lumbering wagons made good time and soon they were too far away from Independence for anyone who might have considered it to turn back.

The first night after the hunters returned, the camp dined on roast elk meat, and although it took some getting used to, Aimee soon found she preferred it to the fatty pork they'd brought. Once again evenings were given over to games for the children and dancing for their elders. The emigrants were a lively bunch, and despite the wide disparity of their backgrounds, were forming into a cohesive group. One and all participated in the fandangos and reels that were danced. A sense of freedom from the rigid social mores of home allowed them to join wholeheartedly in the fun. One night some of the men formed a cotillion, and egged on by their laughing wives, danced until it seemed the prairie might shake beneath their feet. All fell into bed that night exhausted and relaxed. A few hours' sleep and they were up to set the wagons rolling again.

Soft muscles hardened, legs grew strong as the sturdy, determined emigrants pushed on toward their rendezvous with the Platte River. The hunters went out again, but came back with only a few prairie rabbits, and their meals became monotonous affairs of beans and pork and panbread tasting of ashes.

At the end of their second week, as they drew near the crossing of the Big Blue, the Indians showed themselves, a straggly line on the horizon. Anxiously the emigrants continued toward the river as if nothing untoward were happening, but mothers shooed their children into the wagons and men rode with their thumbs on the hammers of their rifles. They were the Kanza tribe, word came back along the line, and believed to be friendly. Don't fire on them, the men were admonished, but stay alert.

"Hail, white man," the Indians called as they drew near and held up their hands, palms out to show they came in peace.

Ben Thompson waved the train onward while he and some of the men turned aside to meet with the Indians. Zack was with them, and Aimee felt a moment of apprehension for him.

Smiling and gesturing, the Indians indicated they

wished to trade, holding up strings of fresh-caught fish and freshly killed rabbits. The carcass of a deer was thrown across an Indian pony. Warily the emigrants eyed the newcomers, taking in their scanty attire, leather breeches and the feathers and bones adorning their hair and chests. They weren't as fierce-looking as Aimee had expected.

"Are they gonna scalp us, Aimee?" Jamie called from the wagon.

"I don't think so," she replied honestly. "They just want to exchange food for some of the things we have."

"They don't look very dangerous," Hannah observed.

"No, they don't," Aimee agreed. There was something pathetic about the Indians. They were dirty, their blankets tattered, and they seemed as uncertain as the emigrants themselves. At Ben Thompson's nod the Indians broke into smiles and rode back along the moving wagons, holding high their wares. Hesitantly the women dug through their supplies, pulling out bits of calico and shirts and beads to trade for fresh meat for their families. Long after the trading had finished, the Indians rode along beside the wagons, calling out to the emigrants in friendly voices, sometimes begging for an extra string of beads or whiskey. The wagon master had forbidden the trading of spirits to the Indians, and most travelers carried only enough whiskey for medicinal purposes. They turned a deaf ear to the Indians' blandishments.

In late afternoon they came to the crossing of the Big Blue. On the other side the trail led them to the Platte River, and at last they would turn westward. Ben Thompson stood on the bank studying the water.

"Some of the men think we ought to rest here tonight and cross in the morning when we're fresh," Harry Potts said.

The wagon master shook his head. "Ah don't agree," he said, pointing to the sky. "You see that cloud head up there? It's going to rain tonight. If we wait till mornin' we may not get across. These rivers can flood over their banks in one night. I want to be on the other side."

"You know best," Potts yielded, and headed back up the slopes toward the wagons.

"Head 'em down here," Thompson shouted, waving the first wagon forward. Cautiously the man urged his team forward.

"Can we just wade across?" Jamie asked doubtfully as they waited for their wagon to negotiate the sluggish waters.

"Looks like it," Aimee said cheerfully. "Don't worry. The men won't have us do anything that's dangerous."

"Are you sure, Aimee?" Hannah asked.

"Mr. Crawford wouldn't, I'm sure of that," Aimee replied, watching Zack as he accompanied a wagon into the river. The water reached halfway up the sides of the wagon. It rolled to a stop.

"Hiah," Zack cried, slapping at the oxen with his hat. Reluctantly they waded further into the river, until the water nearly covered their backs. Their eyes rolled wildly. Zack rode his horse in front of the frightened animals, and despite their fear, they pushed on across the river.

Everyone cheered when the wagon lumbered out on the other side, water running in rivulets from the wooden bed. Their anxieties laid to rest, the emigrants hurried to get the rest of the wagons across.

"Climb up in the wagon, Aimee," Zack directed when it was the Stuarts' turn to cross, and she complied. Perched on the back load, with the children clinging to her on both sides, Aimee watched the swirling water climb higher. Whimpering, Agnes Stuart cowered in the front, her fear infectious, so the children were soon crying in fright as well. Aimee longed to admonish her, but Agnes' temper had become so unpredictable that she kept silent, soothing the youngsters as best she could.

"There now, we're safe and we've crossed the river," Aimee said as the wagon bumped and jolted up the riverbank. The children opened their eyes and peered around distrustfully; then, seeing she'd spoken the truth, they leapt down and ran to explore this new terrain.

"I thought surely this was the reckoning day," Agnes cried from the front. "My heart is beating like a drum. I was so fearful, I'm light-headed." The woman swooned back against the covers and looked at Aimee. "You'll have to take care of things, Aimee," she said limply, and closed her eyes with a weary sigh. When had she *not* taken care of things on this trip? Aimee thought angrily, and climbed out of the wagon. All around her, people were hauling their belongings out of the wagons.

"What's everyone doing?" Aimee asked Biddy.

"All the bedding has to be spread out to dry," Biddy answered without pausing what she was doing. "It got wet in the crossing."

"Do you think ours did too?" Aimee asked helplessly.

"I expect so," Biddy said. "Here, let's take a look." She bustled over to the Stuart wagon and felt around inside. "Yep, feels like it just come out o' the washtub. You'll have to haul out everything and spread it out on trees and bushes. The men are building fires now to help some with the drying."

Agnes Stuart looked at her askance. "You mean I'll have to get out of the wagon?" she asked in dismay. "I can't. I'm a sick woman. I can't get up."

"Yo'r things'll sour on you if you don't," Biddy said implacably.

"I can't haul and lift things, Aimee, not in my condition. You'll have to do it." Aimee's heart sank. Biddy looked at her and her face was full of sympathy.

"That's a pretty big job for the girl to do alone," she said. "Where's your husband?"

"Mr. Stuart's with the other men, helping the wagons to cross. He can't be everywhere and do everything. We'll just have to do our share, Aimee."

"Where's them kids o' yours," Biddy exclaimed. "They oughta be here helpin'."

"My children are off playing, as children should do.

Aimee knew when she took on this position what was expected of her. Now, I must ask you to go back to your own business and leave us to ours," Agnes said regally, and there was nothing else for Biddy to do. With a last sympathetic nod of her head she walked away, muttering under her breath. Aimee began to take the things out of the wagon, spreading them as she saw the other women doing. Agnes took a pillow and sat against a tree, her head thrown back wearily, her mouth drawn down.

Aimee worked quickly. The children had come back at times to report on their discoveries and had mentioned a stream. Aimee wanted a bath, and the promise of one made all the drudgery bearable. Her back was aching by the time she had the last of the bedding spread to dry and the food barrels and the rest of the Stuarts' belongings set out. She stood looking at everything and thinking somehow she must find a way to fit it all back into the wagon once it had dried out. Sighing, she brushed aside the loose red-gold strands that fell against her cheek. Now she had to gather wood and get some water from the stream and prepare supper. The evening chores stretched ahead of her endlessly.

Suddenly Aimee sat on the ground well away from Agnes, laid her head upon her bent knees, and gave way to tears of fatigue. She was so tired and lonely, and Agnes had grown increasingly dependent on her. Aimee felt like wailing out her frustration; instead she cried quietly, somehow ashamed of her weakness. At last the crying was done and she reached for the hem of her petticoats to mop her eyes. A large brown hand was there holding a clean white handkerchief. Aimee glanced up into Zack's face.

"How long have you been there?" she demanded, embarrassed that he'd caught her weeping.

"Not long. Feel better?" he asked kindly, and she felt like bawling again.

"Uh-huh." She nodded, and taking his handkerchief, dabbed at her eyes and blew her nose. "Oh," she said when she realized what she'd done. "I'll launder it for you." He only smiled and with one finger caught a lingering tear from her eyelash.

"Can I help?" he asked.

Aimee shook her head, determined to prove to him that she was not helpless. Why couldn't he have come around when she had everything under control? "No, I was just . . . just feeling lonesome." She struggled to her feet.

"And tired," Zack said, his eyes studying the dark circles under her eyes. He'd seen how she carried the brunt of the work for the campsite. Ulcie Stuart wasn't much account, in Zack's estimation. Although he was on hand when work needed to be done, he usually stood to one side watching others do it. Obviously he was willing to let a mere girl carry a bigger load than she should.

"Why didn't you have Wakefield and the other children help you with some of the unloading?"

"Agnes doesn't want them to—she wants them to just be children and not be burdened with unnecessary work," Aimee said lamely. "Besides, I can do it. I've learned to do a lot of things I couldn't do before."

"You don't have to do it all by yourself just to prove anything to me," he said, his dark eyes regarding her fiercely.

"I'm not," she denied, but he had observed how Agnes used her condition to excuse herself from work. The unfairness of it rankled with him.

Zack looked at the girl closely. The lines of her face were too finely drawn and she'd lost weight. "Are you getting enough to eat?" he demanded.

"Yes. Agnes portions out the food, but there's enough. I think she's worried it won't last until we get to Oregon." Tiredly she looked around. Cookfires were already going in other campsites. As usual, she was behind. "I'd better get started with supper," she said, and her voice shook with fatigue. Zack's lips tightened as he spied Agnes asleep under a tree.

"I'll gather some wood for you," he said, noticing

there was none in the campsite. Gratefully Aimee nodded in acceptance. She was too tired to refuse anyone's help right now. Picking up the water pail, she made her way toward the stream. Her thoughts were on Zack, so she was startled when Wakefield appeared at her side.

"I come to tote some water for you," he said sullenly. Wordlessly Aimee let him take the bucket. Back in camp, she was surprised to see a pile of wood neatly stacked, and Jamie and Hannah were bringing more. Zack knelt nearby, coaxing a fire to life.

"Come here, son," he said to Wakefield. "I'll show you how to start a proper fire."

"I already know how," Wakefield said defiantly.

Zack glanced at him, his dark eyes boring into the boy. "Then I expect you'll be building the fires from here on out," he replied.

"That's woman's work."

"Are you calling me a woman?" Zack demanded with mock anger.

"No, sir," Wakefield said quickly. "It's just that I don't see my pa building fires."

"Maybe your pa was expecting you to do it," Zack said slyly. "Could be you've been disappointing him all this time and he was too kind to tell you." Wakefield considered his words. "It takes a big man to survive on the trail and to take care of his family. I guess there's no worse kind of man than one who'll let his women do work that's not suited to them. Somehow, I got the idea you weren't that kind of man."

"No, sir, I'm not," Wakefield replied.

"I didn't think so," Zack said kindly, and stood up. The fire was blazing hotly now. "There're a lot of things a man has to do in life that he might not like doing, but he does them anyway, because he knows it's his job." Zack settled a hand on the boy's thin shoulders. "Your pa's lucky to have a son like you to help take care of the family."

"Yes, sir," Wakefield said, and his chest swelled with pride. He'd seen how Zack Crawford handled himself and how the other men looked up to him. Praise from the big man meant a lot to Wakefield. "I guess I'd better go get some more water," he said, backing away.

"That's a good idea, son." Zack nodded, then turned to the other children. "You'd better mind your brother. He'll tell you what your chores are."

"Yes, sir," they chorused.

"Go get some more wood for Aimee," Wakefield ordered, and the younger children fled. Zack watched them go, then turned to Aimee with a smile.

"Thank you," she said softly. Her fatigue had lifted. "They're really nice children."

"Things should go a little better for you now. If you have any more trouble, let me know."

"I will," Aimee said. "Will you stay to eat? Agnes traded for a rabbit for supper."

"One rabbit for the eight of you?" Zack asked.

"I'm going to make a stew. There will be plenty."

"Some other time," Zack said, although he would have liked to stay and watch Aimee as she moved around the campsite, the firelight gleaming in her hair and on her face.

"Mr. Crawford . . ." Agnes' strident tone sounded, and guiltily Aimee moved away from him.

Zack saw the look on her face and swore under his breath. What was the woman doing to the girl? "Mrs. Stuart," he said, tipping his hat. "How are you this evening?"

"Not well," Agnes whined. "I fear I should never have begun this journey. My health is far too delicate, but Mr. Stuart was so set on going. He felt the opportunities for him would be greater in a new land."

Zack listened to her talk, his own thoughts held in check. Ulcie Stuart was another one of those men who hadn't been able to make a success of anything he'd tried and so he'd headed west, hoping for something better, never recognizing that likely as not, he'd fail there as well. Only now, he'd involved his family's safety and well-being. Ulcie was a lazy man looking for easy answers and was perfectly content to let others carry his burdens for him.

Agnes' litany of complaints had come to an end, and before she could begin anew, Zack once again tipped his hat and bade her good evening. Aimee watched him leave and turned back to stir the pot of stew.

"I overheard you ask him to stay for supper," Agnes said scathingly. "You had no right to do so."

"I thought it would do no harm," Aimee replied. "He'd been kind and helpful. I wanted to repay his kindness."

"You'll have to find some other way," Agnes snapped. "I'll not feed your men friends. It's enough that we've agreed to take on one extra mouth." She stalked away. Aimee watched her go, anger seething through her. She was used to the hospitality her father had shown people. His table had always been generously laid, and any and everyone welcome to partake. Those days were gone, Aimee thought, and shut her memories away.

After supper, Aimee cleared away the dishes and hurried to repack the wagon. Some of the bedding was still damp, but she dared not leave it out with the threat of rain. At last the children were settled and she was free. Gathering up a clean gown and petticoat, she hurried down to the spring to bathe. The water gleamed still and cold beneath the moonlight. She stripped away her dirty gown and petticoats, leaving on her chemise and pantalets, then plunged into the cold water. Once the shock of it had worn off, she turned on her back and swam from one side of the pool to the other. Her arms and legs churned in the clear water, and she grew warm and comfortable. When she'd scrubbed her long hair and skin with the bar of rough soap, she climbed out on the bank and reached for her clothes.

"A mermaid rising from the sea," a husky voice said, and Aimee froze where she was, her pulse hammering in her ears. She knew it was Zack. He stepped forward into the moonlight. She should run away from his gaze, she thought. Her chemise was wet and clung to her body, the dark areolae of her nipples clearly visible through the thin wet cloth.

"Don't you know it's dangerous to swim alone after dark?" he asked softly.

"I don't care," Aimee replied. "I'm clean again. It was worth any danger I risked." Bending, she picked up a petticoat and wiped at her arms and shoulders. Zack laughed, the sound rich and intimate coming to her through the darkness.

"Do you always feel that way about the things you want?" he asked softly. Aimee paused, considering his words. There was a world of meaning in them.

"I'm learning not to be afraid of the things I want," she answered finally.

"Good," Zack said softly, and moved closer. Taking her hand, he pulled her against him. "Have you learned yet what it is you want?"

"I . . . I think so," she replied. He kissed her softly, sweetly. His hands slid over her shoulders and around her waist, pulling her tighter so her body molded against his. "You'll get wet," she whispered. The protest was kissed away, his lips sliding across hers in silken strokes.

"Tell me what you want, Aimee," Zack whispered against her mouth, and with a soft moan her small hands moved across his shoulders and clasped behind his neck. Her lips were soft and yielding beneath his. Her young body pressed against his with a wild yearning that set a fire burning in him. His tongue brushed across her lips, felt the sleek hardness of her small teeth, and tasted the sweet, moist fruit beyond.

Aimee was whirling, riding a crest that lifted her feet from the ground. She clung to him, afraid to let go, not even wanting to. Her hands tugged his head down to hers and once again he tasted her sweetness. His hands roamed her body, brushing against the full sides of her breasts and settling on the sweet plumpness of her buttocks as he pulled her closer. Aimee

192

could feel the hard ridge of his desire and it ignited a flame within her. Wantonly, innocently, she moved against him, seeking only to still the aching need he'd aroused.

Zack's hands caressed the slim body, settling on the softness of her breasts. Impatiently he brushed aside the damp, clinging material, and his mouth, hot and demanding, moved across her cool, silken flesh until it found the sweet, tight bud it sought. Aimee gasped and arched her back, baring herself to him, delighting in the tantalizing feelings his touch evoked.

"Oh, Zack," she moaned softly. He raised his eyes to hers and saw the trusting light there and felt the cold light of reason drain away his desire. He could claim her now if he so desired, but the thought of all the responsibility that went with such a claim made him draw back.

"What's wrong?" she asked, bewildered by his withdrawal. Had she failed him in some way? She reached out for him again, but he caught her hands and held them against his chest.

"I'm sorry, Aimee," he said. "I should never have started this. You deserve better."

"What do you mean?" she asked, puzzled.

"I mean I have no right to take advantage of you like this."

"But you're not," Aimee cried. "You asked me what I want. This is what I want, Zack, you and me, together." Her face was luminous in the moonlight.

"You don't understand, Aimee," he said. "It wouldn't be you and me together, at least not for long. You need a man to marry you, to be there all the time to take care of you. I'm not that man."

She looked at him blankly, taking in his words. "What are you saying?"

"I don't want to be tied down, Aimee. I want to be free to come and go when I want, without some woman depending on me. Likewise, I don't want to be depending on a woman to be waiting for me."

"It's Caroline, isn't it?" Aimee asked miserably. "You're still in love with her."

Zack took a deep breath. He hadn't given Caroline much thought at all these past few weeks. "Yeah, it's still Caroline for me," he lied. He could barely look into her face. All her pain and shame were visible for him to see. He drew in a shaken breath, ready to deny his words. But it was best for her in the long run, he thought, and remained silent. "I'm sorry, Aimee," he said softly.

"Sorry?" she cried. "If you still loved Caroline, why did you come down here and let me make a fool out of myself?" She paused, horrified as she thought of how wantonly she'd responded to his caress.

"I thought I could . . ." He paused, and his meaning was all too clear. He'd come intending to make love to her, knowing he could walk away from her when it suited him. "I found I cared too much for you to let that happen," he said. Her hand flashed through the air and landed on his lean cheek in a stinging slap that hurt her as much as she'd intended it to hurt him.

"I hate you," she cried. "Agnes was right about you and the kindness you showed me. It was all part of the seduction."

"It wasn't, Aimee. Please believe me," he pleaded, but she was busy gathering up her clothes, bitter tears scalding her cheeks.

"I'll never believe anything you ever say to me again," she cried, and shouldered her way past him, running down the path to the campsite. Halfway there she stopped and finished dressing, then continued at a sedate pace back to the Stuart wagon, where she buried her head in her covers and wept long into the night.

10

Now, when Aimee and Loretta met, there were two long faces. The rain had held off for the night, and a weak sun filtered through the clouds. The wagon master decreed a day of rest. Gratefully the women hauled out their damp bedding and spread it on the grass, then, taking up their dirty clothes, headed for the spring.

Aimee and Loretta knelt side by side to scrub clothes in the icy water. At last they had everything spread on bushes to dry, and sat dangling their feet in the spring, each girl preoccupied with her own thoughts. Aimee frowned and glanced at Loretta just as she looked at Aimee. Their faces were a mirror of each other, and suddenly they saw the humor in their behavior. Bursting into giggles, they hugged, relishing the sense of kinship they felt.

"I'll tell you my problems if you'll tell me yours," Aimee offered, and waited. Something had been bothering Loretta for a long time, ever since they'd left Independence, but she'd refused to talk about it.

"Maybe Ah should tell somebody," Loretta said. "Maybe yo' kin give me some advice."

"I'll try. What is it?"

Loretta took a deep breath. "Yo' first."

"All right." Aimee shrugged nonchalantly. "It's Zack Crawford."

"Ah thought it might be." Dimples flashed as Loretta grinned.

"Don't laugh at me. He's really outdone himself. He's . . . he's led me on and then . . . then he . . ." Aimee sputtered to a stop, remembering her behavior here at the spring the night before. In order to express her anger at Zack, she'd have to reveal her own wantonness.

"He made advances toward yo'," Loretta said elegantly, her eyebrows raised mockingly.

"No . . . yes, he did," Aimee said, and took a deep breath, "and he didn't." Her mouth set in a pout.

"Oh." Loretta sat thinking about what Aimee had said, or rather hadn't said.

"He played me for a fool," Aimee cried. "He made me . . . made me kiss him back and then he pulled away and said he wasn't the marrying kind and all sorts of hateful things. I tell you, Loretta, he's bossy and deceitful and calculating and—"

"And scarified," Loretta said wisely.

"Scared?" Aimee cried. "Why, I don't think Zack is scared of any man."

"But a woman might scarify him," Loretta observed.

Aimee stared at her in disbelief; then, at the memory of Zack's experienced lovemaking, she burst into laughter. "Zack is not a stammering, blushing boy with women," she said knowingly. At Loretta's grin, she blushed furiously. "I mean . . . I don't expect he is."

"Ah didn't expect he was either," Loretta teased, "but Ah don't reckon he considers yo' just any woman."

"You're wrong," Aimee muttered, and laid her chin on her bent knee and stared pensively into the bright water. "He's in love with someone else back east."

"Are yo' sure?"

"He told me so last night." Aimee picked up a pebble and flung it into the clear spring.

"If'n a girl's smart enough, that won't make much difference," Loretta suggested casually.

Aimee glanced at her. "What do you mean?"

"She's back east and yo're here. Yo' kin make him forget 'bout her."

Aimee felt a gleam of hope stir within her breast, then turned away. "Yes, I could," she said casually, "if I wanted him to, but I'm not so sure I do. Zack isn't the only man on this wagon train." It was true that other young men had passed by the Stuart wagon with more regularity than absolutely necessary, and each time they made a point of tipping their hats to her.

"Then Ah guess you don't have a problem after all," Loretta said, and Aimee looked sheepish.

"It's your turn," she said. "What's been bothering you all this time?"

The teasing lights in Loretta's eyes died and she twisted her hands in her lap. For a long time she remained silent, and Aimee thought she'd decided not to talk after all.

"It's Mr. Sawyer," she half-whispered, and refused to meet Aimee's eyes.

"What about Mr. Sawyer? Does he treat you badly?" Loretta shook her head that he hadn't. "Doesn't he like you?"

Loretta shook her head the other way. "Too much," she mumbled.

"What are you saying?" Aimee demanded gently. "Has he tried to take advantage of you?"

"It wasn't 'xactly like that," Loretta said quickly. "He ain't the sort to take advantage of anybody. He tries to do right by people. It's just that he . . . he was so sad." Loretta's eyebrows drew down in concentration as she tried to make Aimee understand. "Helen's been crippled a long time and he needed someone."

Slowly, comprehension crept over Aimee. "Oh, Loretta, you didn't," she exclaimed. "He must have forced you to it. He's a horrid man," Aimee cried. "His poor wife is ill and crippled and he's given in to his baser desires."

"Oh, Aimee, some times yo' fair have the simples," Loretta answered crossly, and Aimee was uncertain of what to say next. Loretta had never spoken to her in such a manner before. They sat silently studying the water for a time, and finally Loretta stirred and spoke again.

"Ah'm right sorry Ah said that."

"I understand," Aimee said quickly, determined not to fail her friend again. "You must be distraught by the shame this man has inflicted on you. You must inform someone of this, so Mr. Sawyer can be punished."

Loretta sighed. "Ah cain't fault him for what's happened. He's a good man. He loves his wife."

"Loves her?" Aimee hooted.

"He does. If'n yo' saw him with her, how gentle and all he is, yo'd know what I say is true. He ain't the kind to tarryhoot around, for all his wife is sick." Aimee was surprised at Loretta's staunch support of Royce Sawyer.

"He jest needed to be with a woman," Loretta said dully. "Ah couldn't nay-say him." She looked at Aimee appealingly. "Ah was hopin' yo' wouldn't fault me for it."

Aimee looked up, startled. "I don't blame you," she cried. "You had no choice."

"Yas, Ah did," Loretta said firmly, and once again Aimee fell silent, uncertain of how to deal with this.

"What about Billy?" Loretta's eyes turned bleak.

"Ah don't know what he'd do if he found out. Ah'm scarified he might." She looked ready to cry.

"It will be all right," Aimee said, putting an arm around Loretta and patting her on the shoulder.

"Ah'm fearful Helen already knows," Loretta went on miserably.

"Oh, Loretta, she'll make you leave their wagon. What will you do?"

Loretta flung her hair back from her face in a gesture that reminded Aimee of the first time they'd met. "Ah ain't goin' t' tell Billy. Ah ain't goin' t' tell anybody. Not yet, leastways. Ah don't want t' bring shame t' Mr. Sawyer. He treats me better'n mah own pa did. An' Miz Sawyer tells me how Ah'm like a daughter to her. Ah don't want her t' be sorry for havin' me with 'em." Aimee listened to the misery in her friend's voice and knew there was little she could offer to help. She'd never had to handle situations like this and she had no right to feel self-righteous.

"Yo' don't think porely of me for this, do yo'?" Loretta asked, and Aimee shook her head. "Ah tried real hard t' act lak' I thought you would've, but Ah failed."

"No, you didn't," Aimee said, taking her hand. "You've acted with a great deal more generosity than I would have shown. Royce and Helen Sawyer are lucky to have you with them and they know that. But, Loretta, no matter how hard you try, you can't make everyone happy. You have to think of yourself and what you want."

"Ah got what Ah want. Ah got Billy," Loretta said softly, and in spite of all she'd heard, Aimee envied her friend. Then the thought of having to be kissed and fondled by Royce Sawyer, who was old and somewhat portly, made her recoil in disgust. How could Loretta bear it? How could she let one man make love to her while she loved another?

"Yo' won't tell anyone about this, will yo'?" Loretta asked, and Aimee hugged her friend.

"I won't say a word," she promised. "And, Loretta, if something's bothering you, you can always come and talk to me about it. I may not be able to help, but I can listen."

Loretta squeezed her hand gratefully. "Looks lak' hit's goin' to pour down," she said, wiping at her eyes and nodding toward the low gray clouds that seemed too heavy to stay in their proper place in the sky. They'd slipped closer to earth. All around, women were hurrying to gather up their still-damp clothes. Aimee and Loretta scrambled after their own, snatching them up as they ran from bush to bush. The first fat raindrops were already plunking against the ground, sending up litle sprays of dust. The girls ran back to the wagons and stored the clean, damp clothes under the canvas covering.

"What can we do now?" Aimee stood beside Loretta

in the rain. Neither had any idea of where to go to wait out the rain. The younger Stuart children were sprawled over every available space in the wagon. The two girls looked at each other. Their hair hung in heavy wet strands down their backs and their bodices were already wet through.

"We could go back to the Sawyer wagon. There's room for us there," Loretta offered, but Aimee shook her head, shying away from the possibility of meeting Royce Sawyer. After what Loretta had told her, she wasn't sure she could be civil to the man.

"Don't feel that way about him," Loretta said, reading Aimee's mind.

Aimee flushed. "I'm sorry." Still she made no move toward the Sawyer wagon. They stood shivering and chilled in the downpour and Agnes poked her head out.

"Have you seen Jamie and Hannah?" she called above the roar of the rain beating on the canvas.

"They weren't down by the spring," Aimee answered.

"Go down to the wagon of that Biddy Potts woman and see if they're there," Agnes instructed, and withdrew her head into the dryness of the covered wagon. Aimee and Loretta glanced at each other.

"That woman's just made of hard-up meanness," Loretta snapped, and stalked away.

"Wait, don't leave. Go to Biddy Potts's with me."

Loretta barely took time to consider. "All righ'. We can visit with her a spell. She'll make room for us."

The two girls made their way along the line of wagons. The rain was coming down so hard they could barely see the woods a few feet away. Thunder, loud and insistent, filled the air, followed by a shaft of blue lightning. Aimee jumped and cried out. Even Loretta looked unsettled by the storm, her wide eyes rolling from side to side as the lightning continued to light up the soggy gray landscape. The ground seemed to tremble under the pounding rain and sharp claps of thun-

der. The girls ran the rest of the way to Biddy's
wagon.

The Pottses had set up a makeshift canvas roof with
two corners fastened to the hickory bows of their
wagon and the other two tied to the stout limbs of
trees. It gave them a larger protected area from the
rain. Biddy had had her fire pit built at one end of the
protected area and now a kettle whistled cheerily.

"Law, come in out'n the rain," Biddy cried when
she saw the drenched girls. Handing them a clean rag,
she hustled them to a seat on an upended log near the
fire. "Yo' set here and warm up," she instructed.
"Ah'm jest makin' mah young 'uns some kettle tea.
Yo'll stay and have a cup, won't you?"

As if she needed to ask, Aimee thought gratefully.
She was chilled to the bone. A cup of tea sounded
wonderful and brought back memories of cold, damp
evenings when Hattie had bundled her near the fire
and fed her hot tea for her cold.

"We're looking for Jamie and Hannah," Aimee said,
remembering why they'd come.

"Them young 'uns're here, safe and sound in the
wagon there. Yo' didn't need to worry 'bout them.
They's company for mah kids." The wagon rocked
with movement and laughter as the children frolicked.
Aimee was sure that with her six, Biddy didn't need
extras, yet there the big woman was, making steaming
cups of kettle tea, lacing the hot water liberally with
milk and her precious supply of sugar. When the children had been served, Biddy brought cups to Loretta
and Aimee and settled herself on a stump.

"Travelin' ain't goin' t' be easy now," she said,
staring out at the rain, "but Ah reckon a body'll
manage it somehow."

"I hope it stops soon," Aimee said. "I don't know
how I'll be able to cook supper in this."

Biddy cast her a sympathetic look. "Mebbe Agnes
can stir herself 'nough to hold an umbrelly while yo'
cook."

201

"Perhaps," Aimee said doubtfully. "She hasn't been feeling well lately."

"She's the poorest hippoed woman Ah ever seen," Biddy said. "There ain't nothin' wrong with Miz Stuart that a little walkin' and movin' round wouldn't help. A body ain't meant t' sit still allus lak' she does."

"She's in a delicate condition," Aimee said lamely. It was hard for her to be loyal to Agnes Stuart, but she felt she must make the effort. She was painfully aware that Jamie and Hannah were within hearing inside the wagon.

"So's Prudy Bigelow and Amelia Parks. They still manage to take keer of they fam'lies, 'steada pushin' it off on someone else's shoulders. Yo're carryin' the load real well, Aimee," Biddy said kindly. "Ah ain' nevah seen a better worker."

Aimee stayed silent and sipped at her tea. It wasn't really tea, just water and milk and sugar, but it was hot and it had been served with kindness and companionship. Tears pricked the back of her eyes. She'd worked very hard the past few weeks, doing more than she should have, feeling she had to prove her own worth, and there had been not one word of acknowledgment or praise. Now that she heard the words from someone else, they were nearly her undoing. Biddy saw how Aimee was moved by her words, and her lips tightened in anger.

Everyone already knew how stingy Agnes Stuart was. She had to be to get by with a no-account man like Ulcie Stuart, but it didn't cost a body anything to say a kind word or two, especially when they were working the poor girl to death and underfeeding her. The trail had been easy so far. How would Aimee survive later on when the trail got hard and the strength of every hand was needed to preserve body and soul and move the wagons along? Biddy shook her head. How would any of them fare?

"Good thang we crossed yest'rdy. Thet river's goin' t' swell up sump'n turrible come mornin'," she observed. "This ain't goin' t' let up fastly. Hit's goin' t' be hard travelin' here on." They sat listening to the pounding of the rain on the canvas. In the distance, the roar of the Big Blue swelled angrily.

Biddy's predictions held true. The rain fell day after day in a steady deluge that turned the ground to mud and mired the wheels. Grimly the emigrants struggled on, making sometimes as little as five or six miles a day before they were forced to set up camp and let the exhausted animals rest.

They traveled northward until they hit the Platte River and then turned west, following along its south bank. Eventually they would have to cross the swollen river, but for now they eyed its turbulent waters warily for signs of flooding.

The land had changed now. The tall grasses of the prairies were gone, replaced by short grass and treeless flat plains. Only a few scruffy trees clung stubbornly to the sandy soil of the riverbanks, their fate doomed by the fickle river's numerous floods. During the day, the emigrants trudged through mud, sometimes knee-deep, and at night huddled under the flimsy shelter of oiled cotton drill that couldn't keep out the deluge. They ate their food half raw, for the rains never ceased long enough for them to get a good fire going.

Biddy's lean-to was set up over a central fire and the emigrants took turns cooking their meals there. To add to their woes, firewood became scarce and the women and children were set to gathering buffalo chips to burn, but in the rain they'd grown soggy and often crumbled in the hand. Many of the travelers grew sickly and feverish. Still, the wagon train pushed on, its people driven by the fear they would be trapped in the mountains by fall blizzards if they fell behind now.

Each day, Aimee sloshed through the mud, her fastidiousness long since discarded, and at night she huddled beneath the shelter of the wagon bed, her oilcloth no longer protection enough from the dampness that seeped from the ground into her bedding.

She was content simply to lay her head down. As she sloshed along at the back of the wagon, she no longer made an attempt to avoid the mud puddles. There were too many. Nor did she brush at the mud that coated the hem of her skirts. The rain would soon wash some of it away, and what did it matter after all?

Up ahead, Ulcie Stuart cracked the whip over the backs of his oxen and pulled his coat collar around his throat. In the past few days he'd developed a racking cough that shook his spare frame. Caught up in her own misery, Agnes seemed not to notice. More and more often the Stuart children went to Biddy Potts's wagon for food and sympathy, and Aimee began to take their day's ration of food to add to Biddy's pot. After the children had eaten, she would take bowls of food back for Ulcie and Agnes. Aimee knew it was an unequal distribution, for Agnes never gave her enough to feed everyone, but Biddy never said anything, only adding more from her own supplies.

As they traveled westward along the trail, the terrain changed yet again. Now the flat plains were broken by sandstone cliffs. Despite the rain, the men were able to hunt and now their game was different from what the emigrants were used to. An antelope was brought in, and when the rain let up briefly, with hoots of glee, the bedraggled emigrants corralled their wagons and built a hot fire in a pit and set the antelope to roasting. What wasn't eaten that night was carefully cut into strips and dried, as best the weather would allow, for the times when they wouldn't be able to build a fire. Those times were numerous, for the rains began again and the tired, cold emigrants struggled on.

Ulcie Stuart grew worse. His bony shoulders hunched in his damp jacket as chills shook his thin frame. The oxen, given little direction, lumbered along on their own, automatically following the wagon ahead as they had for weeks. One day they veered a bit, pulling the wagon off the trail enough that one wheel slewed into a mudhole, and the wagon shuddered to a stop.

Inside the wagon, Agnes screamed. "What have you done, you fool?" she cried, sticking her head out the drawstring opening. Ulcie roused himself and looked around, taking in this new problem with a sense of dread. Dully he stared at the stuck wagon, wondering what to do, while behind them teams were pulled to a halt on the narrow trail.

"What's the holdup?" someone called.

"Wagon stuck," the answer was shouted back, and sent up and down the line. Men sloshed back through the rain and mud and put their shoulders to the wheel.

"Hiah, get that team moving," Zack Crawford yelled. It was the first time Aimee had seen him close up since their talk by the spring. She tried not to look at him, but the sight of his tanned lean face and broad shoulders drew her gaze. Automatically he took control, and the other men looked to him for directions. Taking off his wide brimmed hat and leather jacket, he handed them to Aimee, his dark eyes meeting hers in a long, measuring look. Aimee held his jacket out of the mud, trying not to notice the warmth of the man still clinging to it.

Zack put his shoulder to the tailgate of the wagon and gave a quick command, and all together the men heaved while in the front the oxen braced themselves on their short powerful legs. Slowly, with a low, sucking protest, the mud gave up its hold on the wheel and the wagon rolled free. The men headed back to their own wagons, while Ulcie laid the whip across the backs of his oxen and plodded off.

Aimee handed Zack's coat and hat to him. "Thank you for the help," she muttered, and turned to follow the wagon. Zack fell into step beside her, studying her from beneath his hat brim. With her hair wet and plastered to her head, she looked even younger and more vulnerable.

"How are you doing?" he asked, noting her pale face.

"My health couldn't be better, Mr. Crawford, thank you for inquiring."

"There's no reason to be so bitter," he said.

"You're right, of course," Aimee said with mock sweetness. "After all, this is only a temporary setback. Actually I'm having tea later on with Mrs. Ulcie Stuart and the ladies of her literary guild, and for supper I've been invited to dine with Mr. and Mrs. Harry Potts at their gracious tent and covered wagon. If the weather holds, we're going to have fireworks on the lawn. I plan to wear my new white silk slippers. I do hope she has some of those delicate little cakes I like so much and that her cook doesn't overdo the vegetables. We're having asparagus from her garden, as well as strawberries. I plan to be home early, as I'm rather tired and want to retire early. Hattie will have the pillows plumped and the sheets turned back on my bed. They'll smell of lavender and I'll tell her to put a warming pan at the bottom for my cold feet." Her voice broke.

"Don't, Aimee," Zack admonished. "You're just torturing yourself with such dreams."

"It's not my dreams that torture me," she cried, turning to face him in the middle of the muddy trail. The rain pounded against her face, causing her to squint her eyes. "This is the torture. All this rain and the mud." Aimee held her arms out. "It's not being able to be dry or warm, not being able to eat your food without the grit of mud and ashes between your teeth. I'm tired and I want to go home. I want to sleep in my own bed and have Hattie sing to me. I want Papa." She stopped talking, too weary to go on with her tirade.

"I know what you're thinking," she finally went on, turning away from the sympathy she read in his eyes. "That everything you predicted about me is true. I'm weak and helpless and I won't make it. Well, you're wrong, Zack Crawford. I'm going to get through this. I can stand on my own two feet. I don't need anyone, least of all you." Grandly she turned and trudged up the hill. Her feet slid on the muddy slope and she went down, sprawling in the mud. Zack sprang forward to help, but she was already getting to her feet, her hands out to ward him off.

"I can do it myself," she shouted angrily, and glared at him. Mud coated her hair and one cheek, but she stood before him haughtily, her bearing as regal as a queen's, and he was reminded of the first day he'd seen her in the cemetery trying to bury her father alone. He lowered his hand.

"If you need me, Aimee, I'll be there to help," he said.

Without answering, she turned and slogged after the wagon. Zack watched her go, saw her put an arm around one of the Stuart children and bend low to say something comforting, but she never looked back at him. Sighing, he mounted his horse and carefully made his way back along the line.

As the muddy trail worsened, the burden on the oxen became more apparent. Up and down the line, heavy pieces of furniture, heirlooms from a bygone day, were hauled out of the wagons and left sitting forlornly at the side of the trail. The rain would soon swell the wooden joints and the sun would splinter the veneer. Tearfully the women gave up their treasures and turned their hopeful eyes to the trail ahead.

Then the rain stopped. They awoke one morning to the twitter of birds stirring in the dripping leaves. The overlanders crawled out of their beds and looked at the cloudless blue sky and the first streaks of the rising sun. They smiled at each other, then laughed outright and clamped each other on the shoulders. At last, a surcease of the interminable rain. With lighter hearts they loaded their wagons and headed down the trail. The ground was still muddy underfoot but the sun would soon dry it out, and tonight they'd set up camp early and dry out their belongings again.

Their happy mood stayed with them throughout the day as they wound through the prairies, making better time than they had in days. Aimee felt her own spirits lift. They'd been through the worst misery she'd ever known.

"I can survive anything now," she confided to Loretta at the nooning stop. "Nothing could be as bad as all that rain."

"Don't be countin' yo'r chickens too soon," Loretta warned. "They's still a lotta trail left."

"Loretta, Aimee," Billy called to them. "Zack sent me to fetch you."

"Zack Crawford?" Aimee exclaimed as if she'd never heard of him. "Humph, I'm not someone to be fetched. If he wants to talk to me, he can come here."

"He's got sump'n t' show yo'," Billy said. "Yo' ain't never seen anythin' lak' it afore and yo' ain't lak'ly to again."

"What is it?" Loretta cried, getting to her feet.

"Come take a look," Billy urged, taking her hand. Loretta cast a quick look back at Aimee, not wanting to leave her friend and not wanting to miss out on any excitement either.

"Oh, all right, I'll come," Aimee relented. Together they hurried over the prairie toward a rise. Other people from the train were already hurrying toward the ridge where Zack and Ben crouched.

"'Now, Mr. Crawford, what did you wish to show us?" Aimee asked haughtily.

"Shhh, be quiet and get down," Zack said, and before she had a chance to voice her outrage at his manner, he took her arm and pulled her down beside him. "Look out there," he said, pointing over the rim of the hill. As far as the eye could see, there were mounds of earth beside small holes, and thousands of large rodentlike creatures scurried about busily.

"Don't that beat all," Loretta said.

"What are they?" Aimee asked.

"Prairie dogs. That village of theirs must take up a good square mile or more."

"Wish Ah had my gun with me," Billy said. "I could git a mess of 'em fer supper. How d' yo' reckon they'd taste?"

"I don't know," Zack said, "but I'd have to be

mighty hungry to try one. Thompson said we should be running into buffalo soon."

"Ah hope so," Billy replied. "That antelope was a long time ago and Ah got me a hunger fer sump'n else 'sides fatback."

"Turn out," Ben Thompson called, and the passengers straggled back to their wagons.

True to his promise, the wagon master called an early halt in the afternoon, so the women could wash and dry their dirty bedding. They paused in a flat, sandy basin where the muddy Platte River wound gently through the land.

"This water's so muddy, don't hardly do much good to wash yo' clothes in it," Prudy Bigelow complained, and the other women shook their heads in agreement, gathering up only what had to be washed. The rest was hung to dry and air.

"It's too thick to drink," Biddy said, looking up and down the broad, shallow stretch of water. Although they'd traveled beside the river for nearly a week, this was their first real chance to look at it up close. Its meandering path had been obscured by the deluge most of the time.

"Far's Ah kin see, this ain't much of a river," Gladys Brewer said scathingly. "It's too near the top a the ground to suit me."

"It's jest flowin' bottom-side-up is all," Biddy commented wryly, and the women laughed, happy to be standing in the sunshine.

The afternoon passed leisurely for the women and their children, who ran freely around the riverbanks searching for frogs and garter snakes. They were all relieved to be out of the confines of the wagons. Some of the men had ridden off in search of fresh meat, while others saw to repairs on their wagons. Their idyll was interrupted when a group of Indians rode over a rise and into camp, catching everyone off-guard. Men reached for their guns while women and children ran for their wagons, which were strewn out in a line along the riverbank, rope lines laden with bright quilts and clothing linking them. They hadn't felt it necessary to corral in the middle of the afternoon.

Anxiously they waited, watching as the Indians pulled their ponies to a halt.

"Friend," one of the Indians said, holding up his hand, palm-out, as the Kanza Indians had done weeks before. Each man sat his horse with a grace and confidence seldom seen in the white men, and they carried shields and bows. Some had rifles slung across their saddles. Their dark hair was plaited with brightly colored feathers and their muscular chests were bare. The men readied their guns and the women shielded their children behind their full skirts. The Indians stared around at the group of emigrants, their dark eyes unreadable. No one knew what to do next. One Indian lifted a pair of fat brown birds into the air and uttered something.

"Ah believe they want to trade," Biddy said, coming forward. "How much d' yo' want fer thet hen?" she asked, and held out the pair of socks she'd been scrubbing. The Indian shook his head and pointed to one of the bright calico shirts hanging on the line nearby.

"We got us a trade," Biddy called, getting the shirt for him. Proudly she took the prairie chickens and held them aloft.

"They want to trade some fresh game." The word went up and down the line and women hurried to their wagons for something to barter. The Indians had more prairie hens, some rabbits, and thick chunks of buffalo meat. The women traded away their husbands' shirts and socks and occasionally a bright quilt.

That evening when the hunters returned tired and empty-handed, they were greeted by the odor of fresh meat roasting over the fires. Later, as they sat around the campfires, their bellies replete, smoking their pipes, they good-naturedly endured the ribbing of their womenfolk. It had been a good day, all agreed, and they looked forward to tomorrow. Someone started fiddling and soon the younger, more energetic of the party started a dance. Across the campfire, Zack caught

Aimee's eye and she thought he might ask her to dance, but Ben Thompson came to hunker down beside him and talk. After a while the two men rose and left the campfire. Aimee bit back her disappointment. There'd come a time, she vowed, when Zack Crawford would want her attentions and she'd be too busy to notice him. With a gracious smile to a young man who stood blushing and waiting for her hand, she rose and danced until the fiddle stopped playing and everyone headed for his bedroll.

The days that followed were fairly easy for the travelers, and once again their confidence and enthusiasm grew. Many of them felt they'd weathered the worst of the trail. Wiser heads knew they hadn't. There were weeks and months of trail ahead of them, and they'd lost time during the week of rain. Ben Thompson pushed forward, memory of the Donner tragedy urgent in his mind. If they didn't make better time, they too might be caught in the mountain passes for the winter with no food.

Aimee felt stronger and happier now that the awful, chilling rain was behind them. She could endure anything, she thought, as long as the sun was shining. Even the tasks of feeding and caring for the Stuarts seemed less a burden, and sometimes during the noon rest periods she was able to try teaching the Stuart children their sums and letters. The children were coming to accept her, indeed to look to her for the nourishment and care they weren't getting from their mother. Aimee felt sorry for them. If not for her own efforts and Biddy's help, the young Stuarts might have truly suffered. Instead they were healthy and lively children and Aimee found herself growing more fond of them every day. Agnes still babied chubby three-year-old Tad, taking him into the wagon with her to cradle him in her arms, even when his sturdy, writhing little body struggled to be free and out with his brothers and sisters.

Hannah had grown to be Aimee's favorite. Eight years old and self-contained as she viewed the antics of her brothers and sisters, Hannah seemed to Aimee the most vulnerable, the most in need of love and understanding. Gently she wooed Hannah until the girl came to trust her.

As the wagon train wended its way long the trail, Aimee was aware of Zack's constant presence, almost as if he were making a special point to watch out for her. Several times a day he rode by the Stuart wagon, and occasionally he would stop and raise his hat to her.

"How are you doing, Aimee?" he would ask, studying her closely, and in spite of herself she would blush under his dark gaze.

"Very well, Mr. Crawford," she would answer coolly, and busy herself with some task, ever aware that he still sat astride his mount staring down at her, and she would wonder if her hair was tucked neatly in place or if her cheeks were smudged, while all the time she pretended he was no longer there.

One morning as she was on her way to Biddy's wagon, she rounded a tailgate and came up short. Standing under a lone pine tree, Zack was engaged in washing himself. His shirt was laid aside and his pants were unfastened and hung at his hips. His bare chest and shoulders gleamed in the yellow morning light. Scooping up handfuls of water from a pail balanced on a stump, he flung them against his face and chest. Droplets caught in the thick mat of hair that grew across his chest and plunged downward across his hard, flat stomach. Aimee felt a tightening in her own stomach and tried to look away, but there was a mesmerizing kind of beauty and grace in his strong, muscular body. She stayed where she was, her gaze shamelessly riveted on the tall, lean man.

Unaware he was being watched, Zack picked up the bucket and poured the remains of the cold water over his head, calling out in sheer exuberance as it washed down over him. Shaking his head from side to side like a great bear, he shook the water from him. It flew out in gleaming silvery drops and fell to the dry earth. Zack's laughter rang out and Aimee felt her own mood lightening, sharing his joy in the soft, warm morning and the exhilaration of a bath, no matter how makeshift. Picking up a linen towel, Zack rubbed at his hair briskly and turned suddenly. The laughter died in his eyes as he caught sight of Aimee watching him.

With a gasp, Aimee took a step backward, but there was no place to go. She'd been caught and there was no hiding it. She stayed where she was, her gaze captured by his, and felt the heat of something between them, something that had started at the spring and been left unresolved. Slowly her gaze wandered back down across his chest, noting the thick, hard muscles, the trim waist, the graceful sinuous curve of his hip where his pants hung precariously. His strong fingers gripped the towel too tightly and his eyes were dark and a little bit angry that she'd caught him unprepared. He was unable to hide the flare of desire in his own eyes.

In the distance someone called and the spell was broken. Aimee turned away, her head high, her cheeks flaming, her body clamoring for something, she knew not what. Behind her, Zack swore and jerked his pants taut and fastened them. His heart was hammering too hard and his breath came in quick, short spurts.

"Damn," he muttered under his breath. "Damn Aimee Bennett. Damn all women." Mindless of his wet skin, he jerked on his shirt and stalked toward the corral. He never rode near the Stuart wagon that day or the one that followed, not allowing himself even a thought for Aimee's welfare, but by the next day the need to see her face was too strong. He rode by quickly, barely doffing his hat, contenting himself with a single quick glimpse of a newly freckled nose and cheeks pinkened by the sun.

"She knows," Loretta said. They'd had several sunny days now and Loretta had come to walk behind the Stuart wagon while she visited with Aimee.

"Who knows what?" Aimee asked guiltily, thinking someone must have seen her spying on Zack as he bathed.

"Helen knows about Royce and me," Loretta said morosely. She looked ready to cry.

"Oh, Loretta, did she say so?"

"No, but she knows."

"What did she say?" Aimee asked. "Will she make you leave her wagon? Maybe Biddy will take you in."

"She ain't mad at me. She understands," Loretta said as if she still couldn't believe the things Helen Sawyer had said.

"I don't understand," Aimee said disbelievingly. "She doesn't care that her husband is being unfaithful to her?"

Numbly Loretta shook her head. "She said she ain't been a proper wife in years and that it was too much to ask of a man. She said she felt better knowing he'd found someone to make him happy for a little while."

"She doesn't know it's you," Aimee exclaimed.

"She knows. She's known all along," Loretta said. "She's just too much a lady to name me. She . . ." Loretta paused and for a moment Aimee thought she was trying to swallow back her tears. "She said she was worried 'bout me. She wanted me to be happy and not feel Ah had to do anything Ah didn't want to. She . . . said she loved me." Loretta fell silent and the two girls walked along for a while.

"Ah tol' Royce Ah couldn't be with him no more," Loretta said finally.

"What did he say?" Aimee asked. Loretta was silent for so long that Aimee thought she meant not to answer.

"He cried," she said finally, and her voice was low and sad. "He never meant to hurt his wife. He . . . he begged me to forgive 'im. Ah ain't never had no man be sorry for what he done t' me."

"He should have been sorry," Aimee said stoutly. "He took unfair advantage of you, just as Agnes does of me. We have little choice on this journey. As single women we can't travel on this wagon train without being with a family, and both families have used us in the worst way possible."

"That ain't true 'bout the Sawyers," Loretta said. "They been good t' me. Even Royce. He never makes me do any of the heavy work."

"He used you nonetheless. He knows you're dependent on him and can't refuse him. He's an evil man."

"He ain't like that, Aimee. He'd jest a human being caught up in something he cain't control. He ain't t' blame 'cause his wife is crippled. He cain't help any of it. He's crippled too. He's been kind to me."

"You don't have to pay for kindness, Loretta," Aimee snapped.

Loretta looked at her in exasperation. "You're changing, Aimee. Yo' ain't the same as when we started on this trip."

"Maybe I am," Aimee answered, suddenly angry herself. "I'm learning to stand on my own two feet, and that means knowing what's right for me."

"Without thinkin' about somebody else?"

"Yes," Aimee said firmly.

"That seems hard to me," Loretta chided her.

"We're going to Oregon, expecting a better life for ourselves. People like Royce Sawyer and Agnes Stuart hold us to something we don't want to be." What Aimee said was true, Loretta admitted, and felt more confused.

"I'm going to survive this trip to Oregon, and when I get there, I won't be anyone's servant again," Aimee declared. Loretta studied her friend. The rose-hued skin was tanned from the days in the sun and the sleek roundness of cheeks and limbs had given way to a thinness that bordered on gauntness. The trip was being made harder than need be by Agnes and her stinginess and selfish cruelty.

Loretta sighed, wondering for the first time if her dream of going to Oregon was worth the price they were having to pay. With a small wave she fell back and headed for the Sawyer wagon, her thoughts in turmoil. There were no easy answers to her dilemma. She had come to love Helen as the mother she'd never had. She had no wish to hurt her. Yet to see a strong, good man like Royce Sawyer humbled and shamed roused her sympathy too. Over it all was another fear. If Helen knew, might not others have guessed as well, and if so, how long would it be before word got back to Billy? She couldn't let him hear it from someone else. She'd have to tell him herself.

Stoically Loretta fell into step beside the Sawyer wagon, fiercely avoiding the gentle, forgiving gaze of the woman seated in the wagon or the sight of Royce Sawyer's broad, thick body and bowed head. Somehow, she'd brought shame to the Sawyers and to herself, when she'd meant only to return their love and kindness. The sun beat down on their heads, birds called from the prairie grass, and the sound of insects crying out against the injustice of the wagon train's passage filled the air, but Loretta wasn't listening. She was sunk too deeply in her own despair.

11

"Look out yonder," a man called, and some of the travelers shook themselves from their reverie and lifted their gazes to the far horizon. Dark clouds loomed menacing and threatening. A flashing band of silver and crystal obliterated the line where sky met earth. The apparition seemed to hang suspended over the flat plains. Teams were pulled to a stop as men stood pondering the sight.

"It's the coming," one of the women cried out, and a shard of fear stabbed through the hearts of others. Some men fell to their knees as they discerned that the black-and-silver vision was moving toward the wagon train.

"Hailstorm!" Ben Thompson rode his horse pell-mell along the line of wagons. "Get to cover. Hailstorm!" His words seemed to galvanize the overlanders to action. Quickly mothers gathered in their children, urging them into the safety of the wagons, while men hurried to unharness the teams. There was no shelter for them on the wide-open plains and the men couldn't risk the crazed animals running away, dragging the wagons behind them. Now there was a roaring of faraway wind as it swooped toward them, and it seemed as if the dark clouds had boiled up from the pits of hell itself.

"Aimee!" Agnes screamed. "Hannah and Jamie are missing. Find them . . . oh, bring my babies to me."

"I'll check at Biddy's wagon," Aimee said. "They're bound to be there. They always are."

"Hurry, Aimee, hurry," Agnes cried. "Bring my babies back here to me."

With Agnes' plaintive cry ringing in her ears, Aimee hurried away. All around her, people were scurrying, fear etched on their faces as they tried to secure their belongings before the storm hit. The menacing storm line had crept closer.

"Get under the wagons," Ben Thompson yelled, and people scurried for cover. In the distance, Aimee could see the group of outriders riding hard for the wagons, scant yards in front of the storm. The sun had been obscured now by the black clouds, the starkness of the sky intensifying the sense of impending doom.

"Get to cover, climb under the wagons," voices shouted, and still Aimee hurried on toward Biddy's wagon.

"Aimee!" Zack's voice was hoarse and urgent. He brought his horse to a sliding stop. "Where are you going? Don't you see that line of hail? Get to cover." His horse stamped the ground impatiently, its nostrils flaring, eyes rolling wildly.

"I have to find Hannah and Jamie and take them back to their mother."

"They're at Biddy's wagon. She'll take care of them. There's no time to get them back to their mother. Find some cover," Zack shouted, and Aimee's temper riled.

"There's no need for you to shout at me," she cried. "I'm perfectly capable of taking care of myself. Just go along and find someone else to bully." Flouncing around, she marched back toward the Stuart wagon. She could hear Zack's horse as it wheeled and galloped away.

Lightning struck nearby, the nearness of it raising the hair on her nape. With a loud scream of fear, a horse broke away and galloped off across the plains. Others followed in its wake. Suddenly fearful, Aimee stopped and looked around. The earth nearby was smoking as if newly scorched, and the loud roar of ice pellets pounding against the ground filled the air. Aimee felt the first sting of them raining down on her head with a force that stunned her. Putting up a hand to ward off the stinging ice, she looked around frantically for cover. She'd never expected it to be like this. A large piece of ice struck her cheek and another her temple. Aimee staggered and fell, her hands outflung to catch her fall. She could feel ice balls beneath her, already covering the ground, and fear seized her as she realized how foolhardy she'd been. She could be pummeled to death here within sight of the wagons, and no one could help her.

"Zack!" The name was torn from her throat, and miraculously he was there, his strong arms lifting her, cradling her against his chest as he carried her toward a wagon.

"Crawl under there," he shouted above the sound of the falling hail, and Aimee slithered under. Zack followed and turned to face her, his gaze seeking her own in the dark shadows. Aimee tried to remain calm, tried to hold in the terror that had seized her at the first blow from the falling hail. Zack was there with his lean hard body protecting her even now from the hailstones that bounced against the ground and under the wagon. His arms were strong and reassuring.

"Aimee," he said gently, and her composure crumbled. Her mouth twisted as she began to cry. "It's all right now, baby," he crooned softly, and cradled her head in the hollow of his throat, pulling her body closer to his.

"I . . . I'm always cr-crying," she hiccuped, "and you're always telling me it w-will be all right."

"It *will* be. Trust me," Zack said, brushing the silken hair away from her cheeks. Lightly he kissed her temple and cheek and then her eyes—those eyes that were luminous even in the dark shadows and were now staring at him the way she had the day she watched him bathe.

Beyond the edge of the wagon the hail continued to fall, closing them into a separate world by its very density and noise. Zack gazed into her eyes, his breathing ragged against her cheek. Aimee stared back at him, feeling the heat rising in her body, feeling a need she'd never known existed before she met this man.

"Aimee," Zack whispered hoarsely, and his hands gripped her waist, pulling her closer. His lips claimed hers, his tongue, hot and urgent, thrust against hers. He moved over her, his lean body resting the full length of her, and she welcomed his weight, welcomed the aching, surging sweetness of the contact. His hands caressed her, smoothing back her hair, brushing across her round cheek, lingering on the soft pulsing warmth of her throat, and plunging downward to the curving mound of her breasts.

She felt the scrape of his bearded chin against the softness of her throat, the roughness of his thumbs brushing against her sensitive nipples, the shivery smoothness of his teeth as they nipped and suckled, and she thought surely she must die for the aching beauty of it. His knowing hands moved yet again, putting aside unwanted clothing, grazing along smooth, untouched flesh until he found the center of her, hot and moist and ready for him. He moved against her, his shaft hard and certain in its path to her. Aimee felt the first thrust of pain and arched away from it. He cradled her, waiting until the pain was gone, willing himself to remember she was a virgin. He felt the yielding warmth of her, the clasping, clinging sweetness of her, and he moved, slowly and carefully at first, then with increasing fervor. His kisses were fierce and compelling on her mouth, his teeth scraping gently, urgently against the yielding softness of her lips.

The pounding hailstorm had lost its terror; it was part of them now, part of the passion that gripped them. She could sense it building to a crescendo and she willed it never to stop.

Gasping in air, they lay still connected, yet suddenly apart as they hadn't been only moments before. Each reclaimed himself and finally turned to face the other. Only the sound of their breathing filled the air beneath the wagon. The fury of the storm had passed on and now a shout went up from one of the other wagons. Zack rolled away from her and adjusted his clothing, then turned to help her. He spoke no words, but his eyes were on her, waiting for her reaction. Aimee kept her gaze averted. What had she done? This was madness.

"Aimee," Zack whispered. "I'm sorry." His words wounded when they'd meant to soothe.

"Don't talk," she answered. "Don't say any more."

Zack looked as if he were about to speak again, then nodded and crawled to the edge of the wagon. "Wait until I leave before coming out," he said, and was gone. Aimee lay watching as he mounted and rode away.

"Whooe, would you look at the size of this hail," someone shouted, and voices began to chatter excitedly as people came from their shelter and looked around. Aimee clambered out from under the wagon. Zack was nowhere in sight.

They seemed to be surrounded in a sea of ice balls. Gleefully the children ran around gathering up the hailstones and flinging them at each other until parents called out a warning. Men hurried to assess the damage to their wagons. Some of the canvases had been ripped by the force of the hail falling against them.

Oxen and cattle had fled across the plains, trying to escape the painful onslaught. Men with horses were already engaged in rounding up the scattered teams. It would take them the rest of the afternoon to round up the lost cattle and horses.

The women dug out pails and kettles and began gathering up hailstones. They would wash them and serve iced tea for supper. Others gathered the hail for the making of ice cream. Given a new task, the children fell to helping, the thought of ice cream all the reason they needed.

By evening the men had most of the teams of oxen back and the wagons corralled for the night. A couple of milk cows had not been found and there was speculation the Indians had stolen them. After supper the children gathered in the center of the corral to take their turns at the makeshift cranks on the buckets of ice. Milk and sugar had been mixed for ice cream. One or two of the women had rolled out pie crusts on the seats of their wagons and filled them with wild berries the children had gathered before the storm hit. Carefully they'd baked the pies over the hot stones and now small portions of berry pie and ice cream were handed around to all.

There was a festive air to the gathering, as people remembered ice-cream socials back home. After the desserts had been savored, someone brought out a fiddle and the overlanders formed a circle of dancers. Aimee stood to one side watching, for once not willing to join in the merrymaking. All afternoon, since Zack had left her, she'd been in turmoil. What had possessed her to give herself to him in such a wanton manner? She could never again fault Loretta for her behavior, when she'd behaved far worse. She thought of talking to Loretta, but something held her back. What had occurred was between Zack and her, and she didn't want to share it.

Aimee wandered along the perimeter of the corralled wagons, thinking of that moment during the storm. Even in his passion, Zack had been gentle with her. She had been the eager one, answering his kisses with a wild ardor of her own. It was the storm! She'd been frightened and Zack had been there and she'd merely reacted out of her need to be comforted and reassured. She hadn't acted badly. Zack had. He'd taken advantage of her fear.

But Aimee knew it wasn't so. Ever since that night by the spring, she'd thought of little else but Zack and the feel of his arms around her. And what of Zack? How did he feel? Was he sorry it had happened? He'd said he was. She remembered his rejection by the spring. Did he feel trapped now? He'd said he didn't want to be responsible for anyone. He'd also said he loved Caroline, but there had been no hesitation, no thought of the woman he'd left behind. How could he love Caroline and make love to Aimee as he had? Had he been thinking of Caroline all the time? She refused to believe he had.

Confused, Aimee hiked along the path to the little stream. She knew it was unwise to leave the wagon train alone after dark, but she couldn't bear to stay and listen to everyone's merriment and risk running into Zack. She needed to think.

She arrived at the clear running stream and sat in a patch of grass beside it, listening to the water as it chuckled over rocks and grass roots. After the storm, the clouds had cleared away and now the prairie moon glowed in the velvety darkness of the sky. Aimee took a deep breath and leaned back, her head cradled in her hands as she gazed dreamily at the twinkling stars. Her thoughts went back to that moment under the wagon.

Funny, she'd always thought the taking of her virginity would come on her wedding night in a sumptuously appointed room with lace and candles and flowers and a man who would whisper pretty words in her ear. Instead it had occurred in the mud under a wagon. There had been no words, only a searing need and groping hands, and she hadn't been afraid as she'd thought she would be. Aimee lay pondering the mysteries of men and women and their mating, and wondering why there was such a fuss connected with it. It was wonderful, not scary. She didn't feel ashamed, she decided, and she would go with Zack anytime he wanted. Surely he would realize he no longer loved Caroline, that it was Aimee he needed and wanted. She could imagine him now as he stood before her, his hat in his hands, his eyes earnest and appealing as he spoke to her of his love and pledged his undying devotion.

"I love you, Aimee," he would say. "I was wrong to speak to you as I did by the spring that day. You are brave and courageous and I want you for my wife."

"I love you too, Zack," Aimee whispered to the

prairie moon, "and I forgive you for all your unkindness. I will marry you, but only if you promise never to speak to me that way again. You may kiss my hand now."

She laughed prettily and raised her hand to her imaginary lover. Her arms looked pale and slender in the moonlight. Everything about her seemed more beautiful tonight. She dropped her hands to her chest, cupping her breasts as Zack had done, and was surprised at the tingling surge of desire the gesture awakened in her. She should move her hands away, she thought lazily, but kept them there on the soft mounds, remembering the feel of Zack's hands caressing her just so.

"Aimee." It was Zack's voice, low and urgent. Aimee snatched her hands from her breasts and sat up.

"I'm here," she cried. He'd come to her again, she thought, and felt a wild, sweet singing inside herself. Zack stepped out of the shadows and walked toward her.

"It isn't safe to wander off like this alone," he said, pausing some feet from her.

"I know. I just wanted to be alone tonight."

"Would you like to talk about it?"

"About what?" Aimee asked, although she well knew.

"About this afternoon," Zack persisted.

"Must we? There's little to say. It happened and now it's over."

"Dammit, Aimee, it's not over. I feel guilty as hell."

"There's no need to."

Zack glanced at her, puzzled by her words. Aimee glanced down at her hands in her lap. This wasn't what she'd expected to hear from Zack. She'd been lying here dreaming of a lover's kisses and whispered love words.

"Well, I do." Zack paced along the grassy bank and whirled to look at her. "Are you all right?" he asked. "I didn't hurt you, did I?"

"No, I'm fine," Aimee answered in a low voice.

Her head was bowed, so he couldn't see her face in the moonlight, but he imagined the shame she must be feeling. Damn fool, he berated himself. She's an innocent girl and she's had enough done to her. You should have kept your hands to yourself. You should never have touched her. But he had, and that first touch had led to another, and then another, until there was no turning back. Even now, watching her in the spill of golden light, he felt an overwhelming urge to raise her face and shower it with kisses while he reassured her there was no reason to feel shame. What had happened between them hadn't been wrong. Only it *had* been wrong. He didn't want to make a commitment to her, and to take a woman like Aimee meant a lifetime responsibility.

"Look, I'm sorry," he said now, stalking restlessly across the bank to stand before her. Aimee raised her head and tilted it back so she could look up at him. The moonlight burnished the graceful, curving line of her slender neck and Zack caught his breath.

"I'm not," she answered deliberately, and he felt as if the breath had been knocked from him.

"Don't play games with me, Aimee," he snapped. "We both know you were a virgin."

"Yes, I was," she replied calmly.

"And you've been brought up a certain way."

"Oh?"

"You know what I mean. You weren't brought up like some women are, women like Loretta."

"Are you being snobbish and judgmental, Mr. Crawford?" she asked. "Please be careful what you say. Loretta is my best friend."

"Why are you making this so difficult?" he demanded.

"I'm not making it difficult, you are," Aimee replied, and got to her feet to face him. "I don't understand why you're here, Zack."

"Because . . . I want to make it up to you about this afternoon."

"There's no need to. We're both adults. I made no demur. I was a full partner in what transpired between us. I beg of you, don't give it another thought. I shan't. Now, if you'll excuse me, I'd best get back to the wagon."

"Dammit, Aimee, I don't know why you're acting like this," he repeated lamely, and stood watching her walk back to the wagons. Shaking his head in perplexity, he lay down on the ground. It was still warm where Aimee had been. He snatched off his broad-brimmed hat and sat staring out across the prairie, a feeling of helpless frustration seizing him. He'd called himself every kind of fool since leaving Aimee under the wagon. He'd give anything to call back his deed, but it couldn't be done. The feel and taste of her had stayed with him all during his chores, until he was nearly driven crazy with the desire to go back and crush her to him again. But he wouldn't give in again to his desires. He didn't need a woman like Aimee Bennett in his life.

Zack skipped a stone at the tumbling water, muttering under his breath. He'd come down here to the creek to give her the opportunity to rail at him, and, through her anger, be exonerated for his deed. He'd hoped she would scream at him and tell him how much she hated him. Instead she had been calm and accepting of what had occurred, almost as if she'd been glad. No, he was wrong about that. Aimee wasn't that kind of woman. She'd expect a man to take care of her and pledge himself to her. Well, he wasn't that kind of man. He wouldn't do it, no matter how much she begged him. But then, she hadn't begged him, had she? He tossed his hat away from him angrily and sat staring back at the wagon train. The music had stopped now and the campfires had died down. Aimee was nowhere in sight.

What was she up to? he wondered. Why hadn't she been angry? Any other woman would have been outraged, would have demanded he marry her. Any other woman, but not Aimee. The trouble with her was, she never did quite what you expected of her. Just when Zack thought he had her figured out, she surprised him. Look at the way she'd taken over the Stuart children and cared for them. Everyone on the wagon train knew that if it weren't for Aimee the Stuarts would have had to turn back, or worse, would have become a burden on other families. Zack sat chewing a thumbnail while he thought about her. Damn her, he thought, and leapt to his feet as if he would flee the image of her. He couldn't. She was like a light inside him.

They'd been on the trail nearly a month. Muscles were trail-hardened and the overlanders moved through each day's routine with calm acceptance. Meals were cooked, dishes washed, children bathed, pains and scrapes tended, teams harnessed and unharnessed, bridles and wheels mended, and every other chore performed that went with moving a wagon train farther along the trail.

Zack never came around now. Sometimes Aimee could see him in the distance riding out with the other scouts or helping to herd up the teams and cattle. He seemed always to be there helping other people, but he never took time for Aimee. She never sought him out, but as the days passed into a week and then a second, she found herself reassessing what had happened between Zack and her. Obviously it had meant nothing to him. He'd forgotten all about her already. Well, it had meant little to her as well, she decided. She'd give Zack Crawford no more thought. It was easier said than done, for she found herself looking for his tall, lean figure among the other men.

In her preoccupation, Aimee didn't notice the desperate quiet that had settled over Loretta. More and more, Loretta kept to herself, either sitting beside Helen Sawyer for hours on end, reading, or walking off by herself. One day during the nooning, Aimee noticed Loretta going off for one of her solitary walks.

"Wait, Loretta. I'll join you," she called, but the other girl just kept walking without looking back. Troubled, Aimee turned back to the Stuart wagon.

Agnes had become even more of an invalid now, seldom leaving the wagon except for the most necessary needs. Ulcie had grown quiet and morose, often sitting in the shade of the wagon instead of unharnessing his team and tending to his chores. The other emigrants shook their heads in disgust at the lazy man, but for once Aimee felt a tinge of pity for him. The chest cold he'd caught during the weeks of rain had hung on. Aimee often heard his racking cough in the night. Ulcie had become pale and weak and he looked tired and thin. Sometimes Aimee and Wakefield lifted the heavy yoke off the oxen while Ulcie stood nearby, chest heaving as he struggled to breathe.

The women of the train engaged in trade with the Indians easily now, so accustomed had they become to the strangely garbed and feathered red men. Another fear had settled over them as they traveled past the scantily marked graves of previous travelers. Most of the victims had succumbed to one of the virulent fevers that often overtook the wagon trains, sometimes killing off whole families before they ran their course. Cholera seemed to be the worst, and gathered around their cooking fires, the women spoke of it in dread, each one praying it would not claim some loved one of her family. Aimee looked at Ulcie Stuart's wasting body and knew that if cholera were to touch their wagon train he would be among the first to go. Sometimes Aimee longed to shake Agnes out of her self-absorption and point out the dangers to her family, but she remained silent, doing the best she could each day. In some strange way, the Stuarts, with all their weaknesses, had become her family.

The train was nearly five hundred miles out from Missouri, someone reckoned, and the emigrants looked at each other in pride at how far they'd come. Some gave thought to the nearly two thousand miles left to travel and were doubtful. Most were confident. They'd come this far. One-fifth of the trip was behind them.

One day as they veered toward the north fork of the Platte River, they came upon a stranded wagon.

"Keep the wagons moving," Ben Thompson ordered, and he and some of the men rode ahead to investigate. In no time at all they were back.

"We need to leave some food for these folks," Ben called, riding up and down the line. The women dug into their meager supplies, all save Agnes.

As the train rumbled past the stranded travelers, a man ran forward.

"Wait for us," he called. "My missus and me'll join you. Wait, I tell you." He ran alongside the moving wagons, his long thin legs pumping disjointedly.

"Wolves got my mules. My missus needs to ride with someone. Have you got room for her?" He ran from one wagon to another. The overlanders looked away, ashamed they couldn't offer him help. To do so might mean death for them and their families. The desperate man came to the Stuart wagon.

"Won't you make room for her? She's feeling poorly and can't walk."

Tad Stuart sat at the back of the wagon, his wide blue eyes staring at the troubled man. Wanting to soothe the man's unhappiness as others did his, he reached out a hand and patted the stranger's cheek. The man took Tad's baby-fat fingers in his.

"Leave my baby alone," Agnes shrieked, slapping the man's hands aside. Snatching Tad out of reach, she turned and beat at the intruder's head until he fell back from the wagon. The man sank to his knees beside the trail. Burying his face in his hands, he began to weep. The wagons moved on, but the sound of his sobs haunted the overlanders for days after.

Since the trail followed the northern tributary of the Platte, they would have to cross the treacherous south fork, with its swirling water and hidden beds of quicksand. The wagons paused for a day while the men rode out to find a herd of buffalo the outriders had spotted. Their hides were needed nearly as badly as their meat. The hides were tacked around the wagon boxes. With wheels removed, the wagons became waterproof rafts and could be floated across.

Once the overlanders had negotiated the river crossing, they found themselves in territory completely different from the flat valley they'd traveled before. Now
the trail rose sharply, carrying them to a high, waterless tableland; then it dropped steeply into a valley.
The men labored with ropes and chains to lower the
wagons down the steep incline. In spite of their efforts, one wagon broke loose and went careening down
the steep trail to land in a broken heap at the bottom.
No lives were lost, and the emigrants counted themselves fortunate but the wagon and much of their
supplies were damaged and useless. Zack offered the
use of his wagon to the now homeless family, and
other emigrants hurried to gather up what food and
goods they could spare.

A feeling of sharing prevailed. The trail had welded
them into a close-knit group, and what happened to
one, happened to them all. Their kindness seemed to
draw the goodwill of the gods, for at the bottom of the
long and difficult descent was a woodsy glen. It was
the first shade the emigrants had seen in weeks. Nearby
was a spring of cold, clear water. Gratefully the emigrants rested in this idyllic setting.

Pleased with the opportunity to wash, the women
gathered up their clothes and bedding and hurried
down to the stream. Aimee did the same, casting a
look about for Loretta. It would be good to sit in the
sun with her friend and share impressions of all that
had happened so far. But Loretta was nowhere to be
seen. Aimee worked alone, and when her washing was
completed and hung to dry, she fluffed out her skirts
and went in search of her friend.

"I don't know where she's gone," Helen Sawyer
said when Aimee stopped at their wagon to inquire.
"Something's bothering the girl. I wish I could help
her." Aimee saw real concern mirrored in the crippled
woman's eyes and refrained from railing at her for her
passivity over her husband's infidelity. Sighing, Aimee
walked away, taking great pains to skirt Royce Sawyer
where he sat mending his team's harnesses and yokes.

No matter what Loretta said, Aimee could never look at the quiet man without thinking of him as evil.

She hiked along the twining creek, following it deep into the woods, until she saw Loretta sitting alone on a fallen log, her chin propped against one knee as she gazed with sad, unseeing eyes into the woods.

"Loretta?" Aimee said hesitantly. Now that she was here, she wasn't sure her presence was welcomed. Loretta raised her head and looked at Aimee "Do you want me to go?"

"Nah." Loretta nodded. "Ain't no good me settin' here by m'self. Ain't goin' t' solve nothin'."

"Is anything wrong?" Aimee asked.

"Nah, not really, just me, Ah guess. Ah made ever'thin' wrong fo' ever'body."

"Loretta, you never would," Aimee cried in quick defense of her friend.

"Ah tried t' be somethin' Ah'm not," Loretta said, "an' it don' work. Billy said it right. He said Ah was a whore an' that Ah couldn't ever change that." She shrugged her shoulders and smiled, but it never reached her eyes. "Ah reckon he was right."

"He knows what happened with Mr. Sawyer?"

Loretta bobbed her head. "He knows ever'thin'. Ah kinda figured he had the right t' know 'bout me, if'n he was fixin' to marry me. Ah couldn't take the chance he'd hear it from someone else."

"Oh, Loretta, I'm so sorry," Aimee said, throwing her arms around Loretta's heaving shoulders. Disappointment at the redheaded Tennessean swept through her. "Don't you listen to what Billy said. He doesn't know how good you are, Loretta. He doesn't deserve you. He isn't good enough for you." Comfortingly she patted the other girl's back.

"Don't put him down lak' that, Aimee." Loretta raised her tearstained face. "Billy was brought up in a proper, God-fearing home. He don't know how it is with folks lak' me. He don't see that all Ah have to give anybody is m'self. Ah owed Royce Sawyer. He took me in and treated me lak' a daughter. He was like a papa t' me."

"Papas don't do those things to their daughters," Aimee said, and was shocked at the look of surprise and disbelief on Loretta's face.

"They don't?" Loretta asked uncertainly, and Aimee knew a little more of the awful abuse Loretta had borne and taken for granted. Her anger at Billy grew even more.

"If Billy's upbringing was so proper and God-fearing, he should have had compassion for you," she snapped. "Where is he? I'm going to talk to him."

"No, Aimee. It ain't no good. Yo' cain't force someone to love yo' if'n it goes against their grain. Besides, Billy ain't been around much. He's been goin' with the outriders as much as possible. Some of 'em been figurin' t' go on ahead and catch up with the next wagon train." Her voice fell to a whisper.

"Not if I talk to him first," Aimee declared, leaping to her feet.

"Let it be," Loretta pleaded, and Aimee sat down again, although she made no promise. The first chance she got, she intended to give Billy Parson a piece of her mind.

But no such opportunity presented itself before they were on the trail again. Aimee put her own troubled thoughts of Zack away as she pondered how to help Loretta mend the misunderstanding with Billy. There had to be a way. Now she understood what had motivated Loretta to give in to Royce Sawyer, and although the tavern girl was misguided in her reasoning, her gesture had been generous. She had given what she had to give. Aimee felt like crying, but determined to do something concrete to help her friend.

"Zack," she called one day as he rode by. She hadn't spoken to him in several days. Surprise was evident on his face as he reined his horse to a halt and turned in his saddle. So she'd given up on the silent treatment and was ready to give him a piece of her mind. He reminded himself he deserved it.

He waited as she ran to him across the sparse grass. The wind caught a honey-colored strand of hair and whipped it about her cheek. Zack controlled the urge to reach out a hand and tuck it behind her ear again. She stood gazing up into his face, and in spite of himself his hungry gaze lingered on the rounded swell of her bodice, then shifted away while the heat crept into his loins. He concentrated instead on the smattering of freckles across her small nose.

"Have you seen Billy?" Aimee asked, and Zack was startled at her query. He hadn't expected it.

He nodded out at the open prairie. "He's out there somewhere with the other riders. They're keeping a closer watch out for Indians now."

"Is there any danger?" Aimee asked, momentarily diverted.

"Not really. We just don't want to take a chance."

"I see." She stood back from the horse, suddenly aware of Zack's gaze on her.

"Why did you want to see him?" Zack asked.

"I need to talk with him," Aimee answered. "When you see him again, ask him to stop by the Stuart wagon the next time he's in camp."

"All right, I will." Zack sat waiting for her to go on, but she took another step backward.

"Thank you. I'm much obliged." She whirled and ran to catch up with the Stuart wagon, while behind her Zack sat watching her go, cursing her for her indifference to him and cursing himself for caring. He spurred his horse and galloped away.

The outriders came in that night and told of spotting some Indians north of the trail. These were a different tribe from those the overlanders had dealt with so far.

"The Blackfeet," Ben Thompson said. "They're a wily lot. They'll come right in and steal our teams if we aren't careful. We'll set out extra patrols tonight."

Aimee had no chance to talk to Billy as she hurried to clear up supper things and get the children ready for bed. The next morning the camp broke early and the wagon train was on the move again. Ben Thompson was pushing them hard, but no one complained. They'd caught his unease. They were only a few days' journey from Fort Laramie and still not halfway to Oregon.

They'd covered nearly fifteen miles by the time they stopped for the nooning. Men unhitched their oxen and put them to graze on what scanty grass could be found. Weary travelers looked for bits of shade beside the wagons while they ate their cold meals and sipped at the tepid water. It tasted of wood from the barrels where it was stored.

Some of the men crawled under the wagons to take a short nap. As had become his practice Ulcie left his tired oxen standing in their yokes, still hitched to the wagon. He slumped against the wheel, drawing in great gulps of air, his thin chest heaving, his lips gray. A coughing spasm shook his thin shoulders and he pressed a handkerchief to his mouth and shivered. Was he coming down with a fever? Aimee wondered, and thrust the idea away from her. What would they do if fever struck the family now? As ineffectual as he was, Ulcie was still the only mainstay of the family.

Royce Sawyer had taken his wife out of the jolting wagon and placed her on the ground in the shade of the canvas covering. She sat twisting her hand in the tendrils of grass while she looked around. Aimee watched as Royce brought her a drink of water and patiently tended to his wife's needs. Where was Loretta? she wondered idly, and saw her walking off toward some of the strange rock formations they'd begun to pass. Soon they'd be passing Chimney Rock, Ben Thompson had told them that morning. Aimee watched Loretta go and knew by the slump of her shoulders that she and Billy hadn't patched up their differences yet.

Sighing, Aimee found a patch of shade and lay down. In the distance thunder rumbled. There was going to be a storm. Maybe it would cool things down a little.

"Aimee, can I lay down with you?" Tad asked, and crawled up beside her.

"Come here," she said, and pillowed his small head on her arm. He settled himself and looked up at her with a disarming smile.

"I saw a butterfly today," he whispered.

"That's nice, Tad," she said, and closed her eyes, hoping he'd take the hint and nap himself. But rest evaded her. Her thoughts turned to Loretta. She'd tried to help, but it had come to nothing. She only hoped somehow they would work things out.

In the meantime, what was she to do about Zack? It was obvious he had been avoiding her ever since the day of the hailstorm. He'd made it very clear he wanted no serious ties to her and he was scared to death she'd make a claim on him now, after what had happened between them. Well, she'd tried to make it equally clear she had no designs on him. She was happy on her own. She'd remained as aloof as she could under the circumstances. She longed to have him come around so she could snub him, or better yet, have him see how the other young men vied for her company. But he was always riding out with the scouts. She'd show him one day.

Aimee closed her eyes again. They'd traveled hard and fast and she was tired. A lethargy settled over her. She might never move again. The thunder seemed louder now. Aimee opened her eyes and looked at the sky. No cloud marred its surface.

The earth trembled beneath her and a roar seemed to fill the air. Horses screamed and even the cattle bawled in fright. Startled, Aimee sat up and looked around. Men were shouting and running, while women with terror-stricken eyes staggered to their feet. There was a pounding of horse hooves as one of the scouts rode up to the line of wagons.

"Buffalo," he cried, and Aimee sprang to her feet and looked in the direction people were pointing. What she saw filled her with terror. A weaving, crawling line of black and brown bodies thundered across the prairie, their hooves raising a cloud of dust behind them. The nostrils of the lead cows seemed to breathe fire and their racing hooves struck sparks against the ground.

"Oh, Lord, have mercy," a woman cried, and collapsed on her knees in the dirt, her face raised in supplication to the sky. Memory of the hailstorm and the initial fear it had sparked came to Aimee and she looked around for some help. They had survived the hailstorm; they would survive this. They mustn't give way to panic. But this was worse, much worse. Even as Aimee stood watching, the undulating line of stampeding buffalo veered and headed toward the strung-out wagons.

The outriders were already heading toward the lead bulls, waving their hats and shooting their guns into the air, but it had little effect on the great beasts' headlong charge. Some of the riders turned back to help the wagons and people move out of the path of the stampede. Some of the men who had been resting under their wagons were hurrying to harness up their teams in an effort to pull their wagons to safety. Others simply abandoned their wagons, and grabbing up their children, made a dash for a rocky slope nearby.

"Ulcie," Agnes Stuart screamed from the wagon, but her husband was already flicking his whip across the backs of his oxen. For once his sloth had worked for him. The oxen moved forward and Aimee swung Tad into the wagon beside his mother. "Where are the other children?" Agnes called, but already the young Stuarts were racing toward their wagon, fully aware of the danger they faced.

"Run for those boulders," Zack called as he rode by. "Stuart, head your wagon up that incline."

Ulcie nodded his head and flicked the whip again. Aimee and Wakefield herded the younger children in front of them as they scurried for the safety of the large rock formations Zack had pointed out. In a vain attempt to protect them, Ulcie turned the wagon so he was between the stampeding herd and his children. They could no longer see the approaching herd, but they could hear the roar of their hooves louder and more fearsome than any roll of thunder. The sound would stay in her heart forever, Aimee thought. Fearfully Agnes knelt in the back of the wagon, gripping the edge of canvas as she watched the approaching buffalo.

"Hurry, Ulcie, hurry," she cried, but he seemed to need no prodding. With an efficiency that surprised Aimee, he drove the wagon up the rocky incline and among the boulders. Other wagons were right behind them. Ulcie looked back at the stranded wagons sitting helpless while their owners struggled with frightened teams.

"Wakefield, take the team," Ulcie called to his son. "Stay here with your mother."

"Pa, where're you goin'?" Wakefield called, but Ulcie took no time to answer. He ran back down the incline toward the other wagons. Aimee could see Helen Sawyer sitting in the grass where her husband had placed her earlier, her useless legs spread out before her. Royce Sawyer had managed to harness his team of mules to the wagon, but they were frightened by the noise and smells of danger and shied in their traces. Suddenly the lead mule broke and the whole team ran with him.

"Whoa!" Aimee could hear Royce's voice above the noise of hoofbeats, but as if of one body the team gathered speed and raced away, pulling the wagon and Royce with them. Aimee could see him brace himself, trying to bring the mules to a stop, but they pulled him through the dirt as if he were nothing. His feet caught on the rocks and grass and were dragged from under him.

"Let go, man. They'll drag you to death," someone shouted, but Royce had wrapped the reins around his arm and now they tightened and held fast while his team dragged him across the rocky ground. At any moment he could be flung under the wheels of his wagon. Zack spurred his horse and galloped after the runaway wagon.

"Ulcie," Agnes screamed from the back of the wagon, and Aimee looked back in the valley. Ulcie Stuart was running toward Helen Sawyer, left abandoned and forgotten on the ground. The herd was nearly on them now. Mesmerized, the emigrants watched as the thin man bent to gather the invalid woman up in his arms. Her deadweight was greater than he'd expected and he staggered under his load, then began to run back toward the rocks. Aimee could see the effort it cost him, the baring of teeth, the bulging eyes. He would have trouble breathing after this exertion, she thought numbly.

"Miss Helen," Loretta cried out. She'd been pulled back from her walk in the rocks by the commotion, and now she was stunned by what she saw. She slung her legs over a rocky ledge and leapt down, heading toward Ulcie and Helen.

"Loretta, you can't go down there," Aimee cried, and caught her around the waist, hanging on for dear life.

"Let me go," Loretta cried, beating at Aimee's hands, but Aimee wouldn't loosen her grip. Even as they struggled, the stampeding herd caught the fleeing figures. One moment they were there in plain sight, two people struggling toward safety, and then they were gone, trampled under the hooves of a thousand crazed bison. Loretta slumped in Aimee's arms. Stinging, choking dust rose, obscuring the vision of those who had made it to safety, but the thunderous rush of bodies was awesome. Stunned, Aimee stood staring down at the undulating backs of the herd, while behind her Agnes Stuart's scream sounded over and over again.

"Mommy, Mommy," Tad cried, clinging to his mother, but Agnes was too immersed in grief and shock to give him comfort. Aimee went to the wagon and took the youngster into her arms while she turned to face the other Stuart children. Hannah had an arm around Sally and Jamie, comforting them through her own sobs, while Wakefield stood white-faced and shocked. There was nothing Aimee could say to ease his pain. Hadn't she been there herself? Didn't she know that in those first moments, no one could help? She patted Tad comfortingly, juggling him against her to let him know someone was still there for him.

Then the sound passed beyond them, the dust settled. The rumble of the passing herd faded in the distance. The emigrants looked at each other. No one said a word. No one knew what to say. The silence seemed deafening after all the noise. Only the quiet sobbing of Agnes and her children could be heard. Slowly the emigrants looked around, seeking familiar faces and feeling relief when they were accounted for. Occasionally a mother called out the name of a child, and when he appeared, swooped him into her arms. The sound of approaching horses broke through the overlanders' shock. Zack rode up, leading Royce Sawyer's team and wagon. Royce sat on the front of the wagon, his face grimacing in pain, one arm held against his side. His clothes were filthy and ripped in a hundred places. He was skinned and bruised and bloody, but alive.

"Where's my wife?" he called out before the wagon had rolled to a stop. No one answered. People shuffled their feet and looked away. Royce's gaze fell on Loretta. "Loretta," he shouted, "where's my wife?"

Loretta took a trembling step forward and gripped the edge of the wagon. "She's out there," she said, nodding toward the trampled ground where the buffalo had passed. There was no sign of life or even of bodies on the raw earth. They had been trampled into the ground.

"What d' y' mean, she's out there?" Royce bellowed, looking from the place Loretta had indicated back to her. His face was mottled, his eyes accusing.

"Ah'm sorry," Loretta cried. "Ah shoulda been with her. Ah shoulda helped her. It's all my fault." She slid to her knees beside the wagon wheel, her face wet with tears and anguish.

"You let her die!" Royce said flatly.

"Ah didn't know she needed me, and when Ah did, it was too late." Loretta buried her face in her hands and slumped in misery. "Ah loved her too. Ah never woulda let her get hurt. She was good to me." Aimee saw the accusations building in the faces around her. They'd stood in safety and watched as a man struggled to save the invalid woman. They felt uncomfortable and ashamed that they hadn't lent a hand, although they all knew it would have made no difference. Still, this girl knelt before them taking the blame, and gratefully they accepted her as their scapegoat.

"It's all my fault," Loretta sobbed over and over, and several people nodded in agreement.

"It's *not* her fault!" Aimee cried. "Loretta was already in the rocks when the stampede started. I saw her walking here when we first stopped for the noon rest. She had no way of knowing there was danger. She tried to go down and I wouldn't let her. Ulcie died trying to save your wife, and he couldn't. What good would it have done for Loretta to die too?"

Royce turned his red-rimmed eyes back toward Loretta. "I ain't blamin' you, girl," he said roughly. "I'm more to blame than anybody. I shoulda put her into the wagon before I hitched up the team. I was just afraid I'd lose my mules." He put his head in his hands and started to cry. Embarrassed, the other emigrants turned away. None of them faulted Sawyer for his actions. Wouldn't they have acted the same way? To lose a team on the trail was a danger every man guarded against. Without a team, there was no way to go on, or even to turn back.

Slowly the people made their way back down the incline to the place where once they'd sat resting themselves. Of the wagons left behind, there were only splintered boards and broken wheels. Nothing could be salvaged. Little could be found of the two people caught beneath the trampling hooves. A burial detail formed and dug a grave for the pitiful remains. Ulcie Stuart and Helen Sawyer, strangers in life, would be buried together.

Agnes Stuart was beside herself with grief. The other women of the wagon train did their best to comfort her. One of the men pulled out a bottle of whiskey he'd carefully hoarded and handed it to Royce Sawyer, then graciously passed it around to all the other men before carefully capping it and putting it away again.

Ben Thompson said prayers over the grave and the emigrants huddled around, their hands tightly clasping the hands of their loved ones as they bleakly considered the journey ahead. They'd been lucky so far, they realized. This was the first catastrophe that had cost them lives, and now they saw how quickly the trail exacted its toll.

"It could have been worse," Ben Thompson reminded them as he stood over the grave. "There could have been more of us trampled to death, but due to the quick warning of our scouts and the action of all of you, we were saved. I think we need to give thought today to the bravery of the man who gave his own life trying to save a helpless invalid woman. Most of us knew Ulcie Stuart, knew he was a man with faults as we all are. But in that moment of need, he did not fail his family, leading them to safety and then rushing back to save another soul. His children can always stand proud and tall when they talk about their papa."

Agnes Stuart sobbed piteously, but Wakefield's expression didn't seem as stricken as before. Manfully he stepped forward and took a handful of dirt and sprinkled it on the canvas that held his father's remains, then urged Hannah forward, then Jamie and Sally, and finally little Tad. Those who had not been impressed by the father were by the son. Gravely they stepped forward to shake his hand and kiss the tear-stained cheeks of the younger children.

What would these poor orphaned children do now, they wondered, with a mother prostrate with grief and only a young girl to help them out? From here on, they'd heard, the trail got rougher. They went away shaking their heads and discussed the fate of the Stuart widow and her children among themselves. The obvious solution was to leave them at Fort Laramie. They could return to Missouri with the first supply train heading east. Their adventure on the Oregon trail was finished.

Loretta and Royce Sawyer stood at one side, united in their mutual grief for the gentle invalid. Loretta wept quietly as the yellow prairie dirt was thrown on the canvas-covered bodies. Royce bit back his own harsh sobs and put an arm around the girl's shoulder and pulled her head against his chest. Clumsily he patted her head while the tears poured down his cheeks. They stood thus wrapped in their grief, unaware of others who glanced at them with sympathy and curious speculation.

Aimee turned away from the grave site and saw Billy standing rigidly at one side, his eyes riveted on Loretta and Royce, his face suffused with ugly color. She could read all the anger and condemnation in his stance and she hurried over to touch his arm. He jumped at the contact and glared at her.

"Billy, don't think the worst of her until you've given her a chance to explain," she pleaded. "You don't know everything."

"Ah know enough," he snapped, and rudely jerked away from her hand.

"Billy," Aimee called, but he stalked to the remuda and saddled his horse and galloped out of camp. Helplessly Aimee watched him.

Zack came to stand beside her. "Trouble?" he asked, and Aimee shook her head.

"He doesn't understand and he's so angry. Why can't he put aside his own pride and see that Loretta needs him now?"

Zack glanced back at the girl still huddled in Royce Sawyer's arms. "She seems to be doing all right," he observed.

"Not you too," Aimee snapped. "Are all of you the same, full of male pride and totally blind?"

"Only when we're in love," Zack said in a low voice.

"Is that how you were with Caroline?"

"Caroline?" Zack gazed at her in surprise, as if he'd never heard the name; then, pursing his lips, he made an odd little whistling sound. "I guess I was," he admitted. "Blind about a lot of things and full of— what did you call it?—male pride."

Aimee felt irritation sweep through her. "Then you're all dolts," she declared, "and you deserve everything that happens to you."

Zack stood considering her words. "I guess you're right," he answered; then, placing his hat back on his head, he nodded. "Good night, Miss Bennett."

"Good night," Aimee answered briskly, but her heart sank and she felt oddly empty. Loretta had been wrong about this as well. Aimee couldn't compete with the memory of the woman Zack had left behind. Slowly she turned back to the Stuart wagon. She would have her work cut out for her in the days ahead as she tried to help Agnes and her children deal with their grief. As she walked, it seemed she carried a great weight on her shoulders

12

Three wagons had been lost, and the families doubled up with others, hoping they could buy extra wagons as well as supplies when they reached Fort Laramie. Some thought to buy the Stuart wagon once there, for they doubted Agnes and her children would continue. Manfully Wakefield took over the task of driving the team of oxen. Every morning, Aimee went to help him lift the heavy yokes over the great shoulders of the lumbering beasts.

The train wove its way past the rock formations that had been dubbed Courthouse Rock, giving new heart to the weary travelers. Although it was only late June and the days remained warm, the nights had grown chilly as they climbed higher through the foothills of the Laramie Mountains. Fourteen miles beyond Courthouse was Chimney Rock, a stone spiral that rose majestically against the azure sky. The emigrants paused at its base, marveling at its height. Another day's travel and they reached Scotts Bluff. If there were no further mishaps, Fort Laramie lay only two days' journey away.

There was a festive air in the camp that night, and much good-natured whispering among the women. Aimee paid it scant attention as she hurried through her chores. Since her husband's death, Agnes had become even more helpless and more demanding.

"That woman's fairly runnin' you to death," Biddy said, setting a pot of stew over the coals.

"Shh, she'll hear you," Aimee whispered.

"Might do her some good if'n she did. Her husband may be dead, but her kids still need her," Biddy answered, and nodded toward the pot. "Ah brung you some stew for them young 'uns. My family weren't so hungry tonight."

Aimee smiled. "We're much obliged, Biddy. I don't know what we'd do without you."

"You'd survive, girl. You're smarter an' tougher'n you give yourself credit for." Biddy looked at the girl's tired face. "Hurry with yo'r chores and spruce yourself up a bit for the socializin' tonight. I 'spect there'll be some dancin' after the weddin'."

"Wedding?" Aimee asked with a smile. It always amazed her how resilient the travelers were. In the face of all the danger and hardships, and in spite of the recent tragedy, someone had decided to marry. It would be a bright spot after all their grief. "Who's getting married?"

Biddy looked at her in surprise. "Why, I thought you'd know about it, seein' as it's your friend what's about to get hitched."

"Loretta? Whom is she marrying? Billy?" Aimee's eyes mirrored joy. They'd worked out their problems after all.

"Why, no, she's marryin' up with Royce Sawyer," Biddy said.

"But he's just been widowed," Aimee said stupidly.

"I know, I know," Biddy answered. "And a pity it was, the way that poor woman had to die, but some thought it wasn't seemly for a young unmarried woman and a widower to be sharin' a wagon that way."

Aimee stood considering all that Biddy had said, dread building in her heart. She'd been devoting all her time to the Stuart family and hadn't seen Loretta much lately. Now guilt washed over her.

"Biddy, I have to go see Loretta," she said. "Would you dish up some stew for the children?"

"Why, shore," the big woman said generously, and Aimee hurried across the circle toward the Sawyer wagon. No one was in sight when she arrived. Hesitantly Aimee looked around.

"Loretta?" she called softly, and heard a scuffling in the wagon. The back flap was thrown back and Loretta looked out.

"What d' yo' want, Aimee?" the girl said, and Aimee was shocked at her appearance. Loretta's eyes were dark-circled, as if she hadn't been sleeping, and she looked thinner.

"I heard about the wedding, Loretta. They say you're going to marry Royce Sawyer." Aimee stood by the tailgate and peered up at her friend.

"Yes, Ah am," Loretta answered bleakly.

"What about Billy?"

"Billy and me are finished." Loretta's voice wavered, then steadied itself. "Royce has asked me to be his wife."

"But you don't love him."

"Yes, Ah do," Loretta answered steadily. "He's a good man and he treats me well."

"Oh, Loretta, is this really what you want to do?" Aimee asked.

"It's the best Ah can do, best for ever'body," Loretta said impatiently. "Now, don't talk to me no more about it, Aimee. This is life, not a dream, and Ah have to do what's necessary."

"Loretta, you don't have to do this if you don't want to. You don't have to marry an old man if you don't love him."

"If Ah want to stay on this train and go on to Oregon, Ah do. Ah got to git to Oregon. Ah can't go back. Can you?"

"What do you mean?"

"They're goin' t' leave all widows and orphans and all them without sponsors at Fort Laramie when we git there. They'll have to go back east on the supply train."

"They can't do that," Aimee cried.

"Ah tell you, they're going to, Aimee. Ah heard

'em talkin'. They're goin' t' leave you and the Stuarts there too."

Aimee pushed away her concern for herself and the Stuart children and looked at Loretta. "Is this why you're marrying Royce Sawyer?"

Loretta's face took on a closed look again. "Partly," she muttered.

"You don't have to marry him, Loretta. Talk to Billy."

"Ah have." Loretta's hands twisted in her lap. "He wishes me happiness." Loretta's voice broke on the word, but she raised her chin. "Ah have to finish dressin' now, Aimee," she said, and pulled the canvas cover closed. Aimee stood on the other side of the cover, listening for any sound of weeping from the wagon, but there was nothing. Aimee felt like weeping herself. With dragging steps she walked back to her campsite, mulling over all that Loretta had said. They were going to be left at Fort Laramie, she thought dully. She would never get to see Oregon. Then another thought struck her. She'd never see Zack again. A sudden chill seized her.

"Dearly beloved . . ." Ben Thompson intoned. ". . . to unite this man and woman in holy matrimony."

Loretta's face looked pale and drawn in the light of the campfires. Royce Sawyer looked solemn. The faces of the emigrants were happy and relaxed, their cares forgotten for a little while.

Zack's eyes met Aimee's and she read some dark message in them that made shivery tingles crawl along her stomach and breasts. Quickly she looked away. Across the circle she caught a glimpse of Billy Parson. His eyes were black as he watched the wedding.

"Do you, Loretta, take Royce Sawyer as your lawful wedded husband?" Ben Thompson droned out.

"Ah do," Loretta answered steadily, and never looked aside at the sound of a horse being galloped out of camp at breakneck speed.

"Whoee," one of the men shouted when the vows

had been completed, and before Royce could claim his kiss, his bride had been swung out of his arms and amid much laughter was passed around the circle, where men and women alike planted a kiss on her. A fiddle tuned up, and with much stamping and calling, the emigrants swung into a lively dance.

Aimee danced often, and sometimes it seemed the men might fight over the right to dance with her next. Graciously she smiled and danced with each of them, and all the while she was waiting for a tall, dark-haired man to step forward and claim her, but Zack never did.

Between dances, Aimee looked for him. Once she caught a glimpse of him standing back in the shadows watching her, and her heart beat faster. When she looked again, he was gone. She caught a glimpse of his dark head as he ambled away from the circle of wagons, a blanket tucked under his arms. He was leaving for the night, she thought in dismay, and quickly excused herself from her partner and left the circle of firelight. Let them think what they will, she thought, and hurried into the dark rocks where she'd last seen Zack. He was nowhere around, and she hesitated, suddenly fearful of the looming dark masses.

The moon shone down brightly and soon her eyes adjusted. She caught a movement higher up in the rocks and moved forward, groping her way up the steep path. Once the gravel beneath her feet gave way and she fell, scraping her hand and crying out before she could stop herself. She wished Zack would come back down the trail for her, but all was silent. She climbed on. The firelight and music were behind her now and she was aware of a quiet here in the mountains, different from that of the prairie. Suddenly she rounded a boulder and stopped, gasping in her breath. Zack stood on the path watching her. Even in the pale light of the moon she could see the anger and irritation in his stance.

"What are you doing up here, Aimee?" he demanded.
"I . . ." Now that she was here, she didn't know

what to answer. She hadn't thought of an excuse to come to him, she'd only followed her instincts.

"Well?"

"I came up here to talk to you," she answered defiantly.

"Couldn't it have waited until morning? It's dangerous to climb around in these rocks. You might start a rock slide or come upon a snake."

"Snakes?" Aimee yelped, and moved closer to him, her fingers clutching at his shirt.

"Come on, let's go up by the fire," Zack said, and led the way back to a ledge where he'd built a fire and made his bed under the rock overhang. It looked cozy and warm and secure. It reminded her of their first nights together after they'd left Webster. A coffeepot sat over the coals and Zack pointed her to a nearby rock and poured her a cup of coffee.

"This doesn't look so dangerous," she said, looking around.

"As a little girl, didn't you learn that appearances can be deceiving?"

"Umm. Why are you up here, then, if it's so dangerous?"

"Because I scouted this out before dark and I know what's around me."

"Well, I saw you come up, and I figured it was safe for me as well," Aimee answered saucily. She rose and moved to the edge to look down. From there she had a clear view of the circle of wagons and the terrain around it. The dancing figures leapt and twirled in the flickering light of the campfires.

"It's very beautiful up here," Aimee said. "I see why you chose to spend the night here."

"Actually, I'm one of the lookouts tonight," Zack answered, and threw another log on the fire.

"Are we in danger of Indian attacks?" Aimee asked in surprise.

"No, but it's best we keep a lookout. Advance warning is what saved so many lives back there at that stampede." His words reminded her of all that had occurred, and of the impact it was having on Loretta and herself. Silently she stood watching the firelight play over his face. There were so many things she wanted to say to him, and soon she wouldn't be able to. She'd be on her way back east.

Zack glanced up and caught her pensive look. "What is it, Aimee?" he asked quietly.

She dashed the last drops of coffee from her cup. "I don't know," she answered inanely. Restlessly she moved back to the ledge. The music drifted up to them, a quiet melancholy waltz. Figures wove to the strains in the flickering light of the dying campfire. The festivities were drawing to an end. Aimee saw Agnes Stuart shepherding her children back toward the wagon. She should go down and help, she thought, and stayed where she was. A cry went up from the other dancers and Aimee watched as Loretta walked beside Royce Sawyer back to their wagon. She was his wife now, and where was Billy? Aimee wondered. Somewhere out there on the prairie nursing his pride. Pride! What good was it, if it cost you the things you wanted most?

"Aimee?" Zack said softly, and she whirled to face him. "I'll take you back to your wagon. People will be wondering where you are."

"I'm staying here tonight," she said quietly, and saw a fire flare to life behind his eyes.

"You can't," he answered with an effort. He wanted to take her in his arms and kiss her. "You have to go back."

"Are you going to make me?" The challenge was issued in a soft, husky voice that caused him to shudder with the effort of staying on his side of the fire.

Her gaze held his as she slowly walked toward him. She paused with the fire between them. She could feel the heat of it. One slender hand moved to the buttons of her bodice, and one by one she undid them. The fire cast shadows over her face, accenting the hollows of her cheeks and throat. She pushed the gown over her shoulders and let it slither over her hips until it fell in a heap at her feet. She was ivory, warmed by the glow of the fire. The light flickered in her hair, gilded her chin and nose, and caught flame in her eyes. He couldn't tear his gaze from her. She was lovely, warm, and desirable.

"Don't make it harder than it has to be, Aimee," he pleaded hoarsely.

"It isn't hard when you know what you want, Zack," she murmured. Her eyelids lowered and she smiled up at him. Her glance was seductive, with all the wisdom of the ages in it. Her hand toyed with the ribbons holding her chemise gathered at the bodice. Slowly she loosened it, her eyes watching his, gauging the rise and fall of his chest, the flicker of his eyelids, the tightening of his lips. He wasn't thinking of Caroline now. His thoughts were on her alone. The ribbons were untied, the gathered lace falling loose on the curve of her breasts. Slowly she eased a strap over one shoulder and then the other.

"Aimee," he said helplessly. Smoke swirled between them. Bright orange sparks flew into the air, then fell to earth, spent. Aimee pushed the lacy chemise to her waist and over her hips, carrying her pantaloons with it, and straightened, her arms hanging loosely at her side.

"Tell me to go, Zack, and I will," she whispered.

"You're beautiful," he said huskily, his gaze devouring her. Slowly he moved around the fire, and she waited, breathless and wondering. He raised his hands to her hair and his fingers loosened the pins holding it in place. The rich chestnut strands tumbled to her shoulders and down her back.

"So beautiful," he crooned, and gathering a handful of hair, buried his face in its silken tresses. She could feel his breath, hot and urgent against her cheek. He turned his head and kissed her earlobe, her throat, and her cheek. His teeth nibbled on her soft, sweet skin, his hot tongue rasped across its smoothness, tasting her. He breathed deeply, taking in her special fragrance. Slowly one fingertip touched the smooth ivory of her shoulder, savoring the feel of her. Lightly it traced along the delicate collarbone to the soft hollow of her throat, then downward to touch the swell of her breast and the sweet, tumid nipple. At his touch, her eyelids grew heavy, her eyes closed, and she felt as if she had ceased breathing and would never need to again.

He looked at her face, flushed with passion, her lips full in a sensuous invitation, her lashes quivering in anticipation against the pale curve of her cheek, and he knew that if he took her now, tonight, there would be no turning back for either of them.

"Aimee, are you sure this is what you want?" he whispered fearfully. What if she said no? How could he let her go now? She stood on tiptoe, arching toward him, her slender arms wrapping around him in passionate supplication, and he could fight it no longer. With a groan he wrapped his arms around her tiny waist, his large hands spreading wide across her back and hips, pulling her tightly against him. His lips settled over hers, his tongue probed. She yielded and clung to him.

Zack swept her up in his arms and carried her to his bedroll. Gently he laid her down, then stood and with the fire behind him stripped away his shirt and trousers. She watched him, taking in every detail of his body, the ripple of muscles across his shoulders, the lean, hard middle, the sleek, slim hips, the hard, muscular thighs, and his manhood, turgid and ready. Looking at him aroused her further, and she held out her arms to him. His body was warm, smooth leather, hardened by his days in the saddle. His mouth was hungry, demanding. He'd wanted her for weeks, ever since that day in the hailstorm. With an effort, he slowed his racing pulse, remembering the swiftness of that first encounter. She'd come to him again. By some miracle, she still had some feeling for him. He wanted this night to be special for her.

Slowly he caressed her, exploring, seeking, finding every hidden place of her. Sometimes his demands startled her. Always they delighted her. He guided, she followed. He taught, she learned, and returned his pleasure with a sweet generosity that took his breath away. Timidly, then with more boldness, she practiced the movements of love. They spiraled into the air like a shooting spark, until at last they exploded in an orange-red shower and fell back to earth, spent.

The chill morning air touched her briefly, and Aimee rolled over, snuggling into the warmth left by another body. At first her sleepy mind didn't register that something was different; then slowly awareness returned. She opened her eyes and gazed up at the rocky overhang that had sheltered them for the night. Memory returned and with it lingering reminders of the passion she and Zack had shared. A sound drew her attention and she turned her head to watch as he bent to poke at the dead coals, searching for any sign of warmth. Patiently he blew on them to coax a flame, added twigs and finally dead limbs he'd hauled onto the ledge. He set the coffeepot to boil and straightened. His glance moved to the woman in his bedroll and Aimee smiled softly.

"Good morning," she sighed, her voice still husky with sleep.

"Good morning." His eyes reflected the uncertainties he felt. "Did you sleep well?"

"In the time that was left, yes," Aimee laughed, a tinkling sound on the early-dawn air. "Did you?" Her glance was teasing. He answered her smile in spite of himself. One bare shoulder showed itself as she propped her head on her hand.

"Yes," he answered, and turned away, ostensibly to add coffee to the boiling pot, but in reality to shut away the sight of her, warm and desirable in his bedroll.

"It's still very early," she said, and he heard the invitation in her voice. He had to steel himself not to crawl back under the covers with her.

"The wagons will be moving out soon," he said.

"You might want to dress and go back before the others know you're gone."

"I don't care if they do know about us," Aimee cried, and sat up, stretching her arms above her head. The covers barely covered her breasts. Her shoulders gleamed creamy and pale in the half-light. She shivered and snuggled the covers up under her chin, regarding him with a bright gaze.

"Do you mind if they find out about us?" she asked curiously.

"I'd rather they didn't. You're a lady and I don't want them to think ill of you."

"How could they, when we're going to be married?" Aimee asked. She lay back against the blankets, her arms arched above her head, her face dreamy.

"Married?" His voice was hoarse, uncertain.

"Yes," Aimee said, then turned back to him. "Don't you want to?"

"I wasn't sure you'd want to."

"What did you think last night was all about?" she asked.

"I wasn't sure."

"I was." Her tone was confident and firm and he felt his anxieties slip away. He'd known last night he was making this kind of commitment, but he hadn't been sure she felt the same. Last night could have been nothing more than a whim for her.

"Then we'll get married," he said quietly. She sensed the restraint in him and held out her arms.

"Come show me you want that as much as I do," she said in a small voice, and he crossed to the bedroll. His kiss left little doubt. His hands knotted in her shining red-gold curls and he breathed in the perfume of her.

"I love you, Aimee," he whispered.

"Mrs. Zachariah Crawford," she crowed. "Now no one can send me back to Missouri." Her slender arms tightened around his neck and she kissed him sweetly.

"What's this about?" Zack asked. "Who's sending you back to Missouri?"

"That's what Loretta said last night. The wagon master and his committee were going to leave the Stuarts and me at Fort Laramie so we could go back to Missouri with the next supply train. They would have done it to Loretta too, but she married Royce Sawyer."

"You mean she wouldn't have married him otherwise?" Zack asked flatly.

"She wants to get to Oregon. She'll do anything she has to. She said we have to pay for everything we want in life. I suppose she's right. Anyway, she'll be happy to know I'm going on to Oregon too." As she babbled on, Aimee didn't notice the dark frown that crossed Zack's face. Now he looked at her with hard eyes.

She was no different from Caroline after all, he thought bitterly. Women just seemed given to duplicity.

"Is that why you came up here last night, Aimee?" he asked quietly.

She looked at him sharply. "What do you mean?"

"I mean, did you come here because you needed some way to stay on the train?" Aimee's face paled.

"Is that what you think of me?" She read the answer in his eyes and anger flared through her. "Where are my clothes?" she asked, jerking the covers away. They were pinned beneath him. "Let me out of here."

"Why?" he demanded. "So you can run away from the truth of what you are?"

"What am I, Zack? I'm sure you'll be able to tell me. You've been doing that ever since I met you. What do you think I am now—scheming, devious, a liar? Is that what you think of me?"

"Not exactly," Zack answered. It sounded worse when she said it, and yet wasn't that what he'd really thought? Hadn't he measured her with the same yardstick as Caroline?

Aimee saw the doubt in his eyes, and it cut her to the quick. "I'd better go," she said, and rolled out of the bedroll, ignoring the cold air against her skin. The chill she felt in her heart was much worse. Quickly she drew on her clothes, wishing Zack would take her in his arms and tell her it was all a mistake, that he really didn't think so badly of her. She bit her lip to keep from crying. Her head was high as she headed toward the path.

"Aimee, I'm sorry," Zack said, and wondered that he was the one apologizing when it should have been her.

"I'm not," she answered defiantly, and he was reminded of another time when they had made love. Their words had been the same then, but the meaning was vastly different. Aimee scrambled down the rocky path and he sat where he was beside the fire. He should go after her, he thought, and cursed himself. He'd brought Caroline with him over all these miles, nursing her memory as a shield against the innocence and trust of a woman like Aimee. And now he'd turned all the bitterness and distrust he'd felt toward Caroline and his brother against Aimee. He remembered her the night before with the firelight shining in her hair. He remembered the sweet promise in her eyes. There had been no calculations, no devious purpose in her coming to him. He was sure of it. He thought of the day of the hailstorm and their coming together under the wagon. He hadn't treated Aimee well, he realized. He hadn't trusted her enough, when she'd trusted him too much.

Once again he cursed himself, then, jumping to his feet, ran to the edge of the rocky ledge and peered down. "Aimee," he called, but she was already out of hearing. Zack plunged down the slop after her. He could see her far ahead of him, weaving her way through the wagons. He hurried after her.

"Aimee," Loretta called to her friend, seeing the tear-dampened cheeks. "Is somethin' wrong?"

"Oh, Loretta," Aimee cried, going into her friend's arms and laying a head on her shoulder. "Sometimes life gets so complicated."

"Sometimes it does," Loretta agreed, and Aimee straightened and peered at her friend.

"I'm sorry to burden you with my problems when you have plenty of your own."

Loretta shrugged. "Ah don't have any problems," she said. "Ah'm a respectable married woman on her way to Oregon."

Her words reminded Aimee of the quarrel she'd had with Zack. "You don't know how lucky you are," she murmured.

Loretta glanced at her friend. "We have to figure out some way for yo' t' go on t' Oregon," she said. "Have yo' talked to Zack?"

"I don't want to discuss Zack Crawford," Aimee cried.

Coming upon them, Zack heard his name and paused.

"But if he can help yo' git t' Oregon—" Loretta persisted.

"He won't," Aimee said.

"Have yo' talked to him? Have yo' tried ever'thin' yo' can?"

Aimee laughed, a small bitter sound. "Yes," she said shortly. She didn't want to go into it with Loretta. She didn't want to admit what a fool she'd made of herself again over Zack. "I tried everything, but it just didn't work."

Zack heard her words and his heart turned cold with rage. So she had come to him for some other reason than the desire she'd pretended to feel. He gritted his teeth in anger, then strolled forward.

"Zack!" Loretta said in surprise. "We was jest talkin' 'bout yo'."

Aimee whirled to face him, her chin high, her eyes defiant.

"I've been thinking about our talk," Zack said to her. "It seems like a fair trade to me. I'll see you get to Oregon in exchange for the favors you give me."

Aimee gasped. Her hand flashed through the air, marking his lean brown cheek with the imprint of her hand.

"I wouldn't go anywhere with you, Zack Crawford," she cried, "not even if my life depended on it. I think you're despicable and mean and I'm sorry for ever having known you." The tears were running freely down her cheek and he might have been moved by her impassioned words, if not for the cold anger he felt.

"Then I wish you a safe trip back to Missouri," he said coolly, and turning on his heel, stalked away.

Loretta stared after him. "Ah woulda never thought Zack could be lak' thet," she said in surprise. She turned to face Aimee, whose face mirrored all the misery she felt.

"Oh, Loretta," she wept, "if I'd only known myself, but it's too late now. I love him. God help me, I love him." Sobbing, she put her head on Loretta's shoulder. Her friend stroked her hair, shushing her as a mother would a baby.

"We'll think of somethin'," Loretta promised over and over while she worried over all the possibilities. Suddenly she stiffened as a thought came to her. Why hadn't she thought of it sooner?

"Aimee," she cried in elation. "Yo' can come to Oregon with Royce and me."

Aimee raised her head to study her friend's beaming face, then looked away, unable to meet her eyes. "I can't do that, Loretta," she said stiffly.

"Why not? Agnes and her children will be staying on at Fort Laramie. You can join our wagon then." She stopped, studying Aimee's evasive expression. "It's because of what happened 'tween Royce and me, ain't it?" she asked.

"No." Aimee shook her head.

"Yes, it is, Aimee, don't tell me no fibbers, now." Loretta glared at her.

"All right," Aimee admitted listlessly. It seemed she'd been through a gamut of emotions this morning, and the sun wasn't even up yet. Its yellow banner was just streaking the eastern horizon. "I couldn't travel with Mr. Sawyer, not knowing what he did to you."

"Are yo' fearful he'd bother you?" Aimee shook her head and Loretta relaxed a little.

"I just can't help thinking that if it weren't for Royce and Helen Sawyer, you'd be with Billy now."

Loretta's face fell. "Billy's gone," she said. "It's

time Ah forgot 'bout him. Mr. Thompson already tol' us, Billy's ridin' ahead to join up with the first wagon train."

Aimee's shoulders slumped as she peered at her friend. "Are you just going to let this happen, Loretta? You and Billy love each other."

"Ah'm a married woman now," Loretta said, drawing her shoulders up proudly. "Ah love mah husband. Ah don't aim to do him no shame. He's a good man, Aimee. If'n yo' want t' join us, yo're welcome." The words that Loretta had uttered lay between the two girls and Aimee realized there was a self-conscious pride in them. Loretta had never been able to offer hospitality to anyone before. She'd always had to humbly accept other people's charity.

Aimee looked away, unable to change the way she felt. "I'm sorry, Loretta," she said. "I can't accept your offer."

"Then there's naught else t' say," Loretta answered stiffly, and Aimee knew she'd wounded her friend's pride. She turned away toward the Stuart wagon.

With a heavy heart she built up the fire and set the spider over the coals. Her shoulders sagged as she watched the sun rise. The day ahead seemed dismal and gloomy to her. Wiping away the tears that filled her eyes, she turned to making breakfast. All around her, people were moving.

"Aimee," Agnes Stuart's voice called from the wagon. It sounded faint and reedy. With an exasperated sigh, Aimee remained where she was. Wasn't it enough that she must do most of the chores around the campsite? Must she tote and carry for Agnes as well? Like as not, the woman meant to berate her for not coming back to the wagon last night. Well, she couldn't bear any more ugly accusations, not this morning. She ignored the call. The cry came again, anguished and frightened. Putting down her spoon, Aimee stood undecided, trying to gauge if this was more of Agnes' hysterics. A chill of alarm swept over her and she hastened to the back of the wagon.

"Aimee, thank God you're back," Agnes moaned. "I'm ill. Bring me a drink of water." One look at her feverish eyes and dried lips told Aimee that this time the woman spoke the truth. She hastened to the water bucket and brought a filled dipper to the sick woman. Weakly Agnes raised her head to drink, then fell back against her pillow.

"I'll get Biddy," Aimee said. "She'll have something that will make you better." She turned away, but Agnes' hand gripped her sleeve.

"Don't tell anyone I'm ill," she whispered.

"They can help you," Aimee cried.

"No, th-they won't believe I'm really ill this time," Agnes gasped. "I'll be better soon. If you tell, they might not let us go on."

"But they would," Aimee reassured her, loosening the woman's grip on her sleeve. Her hands were ice cold and Aimee rubbed them. "Fort Laramie is only two days away."

"Yes, Fort Laramie. Don't tell anyone until we get to Fort Laramie. Promise me, Aimee." In her anxiety, Agnes had nearly sat up, and the effort obviously cost her much of her strength.

"All right," Aimee said hesitantly. Gently pushing the sick woman back against the pillows, she smoothed her hair from her thin face. Startled by the hot, dry touch of her skin, Aimee wet a rag in the bucket of water and bathed her face.

"I'm really not that ill. It's just the baby, just the baby," Agnes muttered over and over. Aimee left a damp cloth on her forehead, hoping it might cool the fever some. As she turned away, Agnes opened her eyes and stared at Aimee.

"Take Tad out of the wagon," she said with her old firmness. "Don't let him come in the wagon today, no matter how much he cries." Her words caused a chill of apprehension to run down Aimee's spine.

"All right, I won't," she said, and turned away to prepare breakfast and break camp. All the time she hurried through her chores, she worried about what to do. What if Agnes were really in need of doctoring? Aimee had no idea of what to do and wished she could talk to Biddy or Loretta. For a bleak moment her thoughts turned to Zack and she wished she could go to him. She'd relied on his strength many times before. Well, she couldn't anymore. She must decide herself what was best for them.

"Aimee, Zack is going to ride on ahead to Fort Laramie. Can I go with him?" Wakefield asked. He'd already been down to the makeshift corral and listened to the men talking as they saddled their horses. Aimee stared at him, thinking of what he'd said. So Zack was going ahead to Fort Laramie. Trying to avoid her, no doubt. Hopefully Wakefield waited for her answer, and Aimee sighed, remembering Agnes.

"I'm sorry, Wakefield," she said wearily. "I can't spare you today. I wish I could." His lips tightened in anger and then he saw the dark circles under Aimee's eyes and remembered that since his father's death, he was the head of the family. Manfully he swallowed his disappointment.

"That's all right. It wasn't a good idea anyway," he said. "I'd better get the oxen hitched." Aimee watched him walk away. His young shoulders seemed to sag under the weight of his new responsibilities.

Aimee bathed Agnes' face often during the morning. The relentless sun heated the interior wagon to an uncomfortable level. The fever was growing worse. Aimee loosened the canvas and tied it up out of the way so whatever breeze there was could blow through.

"Leave it down," Agnes croaked, and reluctantly Aimee tied it back in place. As the morning wore on, Agnes grew worse, moaning incoherently. Aimee was torn between getting help and keeping her promise. At times it seemed the sick woman had sunk into a stupor, but before Aimee could go for help, she would rally and remind Aimee of her promise.

Tad sensed his mother was ill and cried to be let in the wagon. Aimee soothed him and carried him on her hip until her arms ached from his weight and her knees trembled with fatigue. By the time the wagon train had made its noon stop, she collapsed at the side of the road, too exhausted to see to feeding the children. Wordlessly Hannah dug out the pan bread and cold fatback left over from breakfast. Too tired to eat, Aimee staggered to her feet and wet a rag in the tepid water and bathed Agnes' forehead.

"What's the matter with her?" a voice demanded.

Startled, Aimee turned to see Gladys Brewer staring at Agnes. "The baby's giving her a bad time today," Aimee said, and pulled the canvas covering together.

"That didn't look like baby-sick to me," Gladys accused. "Has she got a fever?"

"A little," Aimee hedged.

"I'm goin' t' git Biddy."

"Don't do that. Biddy has enough to do with her family," Aimee cried, but the woman was already hurrying down the line toward Biddy's wagon. Aimee turned back to her patient.

"Water," Agnes croaked, and Aimee held the dipper to her mouth. Desperately Agnes gripped the cool wet dipper and drank, then turned her head aside to vomit. Helplessly Aimee watched. By the foul odor, she guessed Agnes had soiled herself as well. Grabbing more clean rags, Aimee stripped away the covers and began to clean Agnes.

"No," the sick woman protested weakly, and Aimee was reminded of the proud way Agnes had carried herself.

"It doesn't matter," she soothed. "You're ill. It couldn't be helped." Quickly she changed the soiled gown for a fresh one, trying to cover the shock she felt at seeing the wasted body with its protruding belly. Agnes must be farther along than she'd admitted. Aimee tucked fresh bedding around the sick woman and smoothed back her hair. Wanly Agnes looked at her.

"Don't tell," she whispered.

"I won't," Aimee reassured her, and wondered what it was that Agnes wanted hidden from the others—her sickness, the soiling of her bedclothes, or the fact that she was closer to delivery than anyone realized? And why was it necessary to hide any of it? Agnes lived by some rigid code that closed her away from the sharing of the human condition. For the first time since beginning the trip, Aimee felt a twinge of pity for the woman who'd lost so much on this westward trek. Pushing aside her thoughts, Aimee bent to rinse away the foulness that stained the sheets.

"There, I told you it was more than just morning sickness," Gladys Brewer cried. She'd brought Biddy and Ben Thompson with her. "They've got cholera here and they're trying to hide it."

Aimee stood silent, not sure of what to say, too stunned herself at hearing her worst fears voiced.

"Hello, Aimee," the wagon master said. "Have you got sickness here?"

Aimee's gaze shifted from Biddy to Thompson and back again. "Yes, sir," she answered. "Agnes is gravely ill."

"Let me take a look at her," Biddy said, going to the back of the wagon. "You should've called me right away."

"They're hidin' it, that's why she didn't call nobody," Gladys said with an irate glance at Aimee. "I demand you do something about this, Ben."

"Let's wait and see what we have here, before we panic, Missus Brewer," he said evenly.

"Panic! I'm not panicky, Mr. Thompson. I just want my family protected. We've had troubles enough on this trip. We don't need more." Her strident voice had aroused the attention of other emigrants and they gathered around.

Biddy climbed down from the wagon and shook her head. "It's cholera, all right," she said in a low voice to the wagon master. "She's already pretty far gone with it. Ain't nothing I can give her that'll help much now."

"Oh, no," Aimee moaned, and looked around for the Stuart children. They were playing a game of tag with the other youngsters. Even Tad was there, trying to participate, although his chubby legs couldn't keep up. Only Wakefield stood nearby, his eyes dark, his fists clenched. His thin face had gone pale, so the smattering of freckles stood out starkly. Aimee thought of going to him, of putting an arm around him and reassuring him, but knew he wouldn't welcome that. He leaned against the wagon where his mother lay dying and fought to hold back the tears.

"Ain't much question of what we got to do, Ben," William Brewer spoke up. "We can't stay here and take a risk of infecting the whole wagon train, and these folks can't travel on with us."

"We can't jest leave 'em here," Biddy Potts cried. "They's young 'uns here."

"And they may already be carrying the disease," Brody Hopkins said. "I don't want my own young 'uns gittin' it."

"Oh, my Lord," Gladys cried, and turned to the group of children who moved as if one across the prairie. "Marybeth, Willie," she called, and other mothers added their cries. Hannah looked up and saw the crowd at their wagon and with a troubled face walked toward them.

"I tell you, we ain't got much choice," William Brewer said, and others nodded in agreement. "It ain't lak' they was goin' on with us. They was droppin' out at Fort Laramie anyways."

"That's right," others called out.

Ben Thompson turned an apologetic face back to Aimee. "I'm sorry to do this to you all," he said. "You've had your share of troubles on this journey, but it is the custom to leave sick wagons behind."

"You can't," Aimee cried. Now she understood why Agnes hadn't wanted it known she was ill.

"It ain't all that bad," Thompson went on. "Another train'll be along in a few days and you're only two days' journey to Fort Laramie."

"You can't leave us out here in the middle of nowhere. It would be too inhumane."

"It's inhumane to expose the rest of the wagons," Thompson said gruffly, and from the way he failed to meet her eyes, she knew he hated his decision. "My responsibility is to the rest of these folks. Something like this can wipe out a whole train. I'm sorry. As soon as we get to Fort Laramie, I'll send someone back to fetch you." Aimee made no reply, knowing he was trying to placate her to ease his own conscience. Perhaps she was being unfair to him, but fear of being left here alone held her in its grip.

"Don't you worry none. We'll stay here with you, Harry and me. I'll help you nurse her along."

"Biddy!" Her husband's voice was harsh. She glanced up in surprise. She'd never been spoken to that way by Harry Potts. Now she looked at his face and saw anger and stark determination there.

"We won't be stayin'," he said. "We got a passel of young 'uns t' worry about. We ain't goin' to put 'em in danger."

"Harry?" Biddy said. "You don't mean that."

"Yes, old woman, Ah do. Ah seldom say yo' nay, but this time Ah must. We got young 'uns to look out for."

"It's all right, Biddy," Aimee said faintly. "You go ahead with your family." They were the hardest words she'd ever uttered, for she wanted to have the capable, bighearted woman with her. With Biddy beside her she wouldn't be as afraid.

"We'll take the young 'uns with us, then," Biddy said.

"It's best they stay here with their mama," Ben Thompson said gently. "They may already be infected with the disease."

"We can't jest leave 'em," Biddy cried. Numbly Aimee listened to the men arguing with her. Finally they wore her down. "Ah'm right sorry, Aimee," Biddy said, peering into her eyes. Her own were full of pity for the girl's plight, and shame that she was about to abandon someone in need. "When my old man gits lak' this, ain't much Ah can do to change him."

"He's right. You've got your own family to protect," Aimee said, and threw her arms around the broad, rounded shoulders. "Thank you, Biddy."

"Yo' take keer a yo'self and them young 'uns. Maybe we'll see each other again someday."

"Maybe so," Aimee answered, although neither one of them believed it would happen.

"Ah'll bring yo' some pepper sauce. Put it in yo'r drinking water and have the children drink it. It's s'pose to keep yo' from takin' cholera."

"Thank you, Biddy," Aimee said gratefully, although she had little faith in the home-cure remedies of some of the overlanders. Still, if there was a chance it might protect the children and herself, she would try it.

Biddy was as good as her word, sending along extra food rations as well. Grateful tears stung Aimee's eyes as she held the package.

"Turn out," Ben Thompson called, and the wagons in the front of the line rolled forward. Most of the overlanders were unaware of the tragedy occurring farther back on the train. Those at the tail end pulled their wagons around the stranded family. With averted eyes men whipped up their teams and hurried away, leaving the threat of death behind them. Dry-eyed and silent, Aimee and the Stuart children watched the wagons roll away. Loretta didn't know, Aimee thought dismally. After their misundersatnding of the morning she hadn't come to join Aimee at the nooning. Aimee felt like running after the wagons, if only to say goodbye to her friend. It was best this way after all, she thought, and bit her lips to keep from crying. She couldn't scare the children.

13

"Why ain't we goin' with 'em, Aimee?" Sally asked, and Aimee bent to give her a hug.

"Because I'm tired of all that traveling, aren't you? I just want to stay here a few days and rest. It'll help your mama feel better."

"Will she get well faster?"

"I hope so," Aimee hedged.

"Then I'm glad we stayed," Sally cried.

"Me too," Tad chirped up, and began to run around the wagon whooping and yelling the way he imagined an Indian might. Sally ran after him.

"Hannah," Aimee called to the girl, "I want you and Jamie to take the bedding out of the front of the wagon and lay it out to air in the sunshine. Take it over there near those rocks. Tonight, we're all going to camp out." The girl sprang to obey.

"Wakefield . . ." Aimee paused, seeing the boy's hollow face.

"What do you need me to do?" he asked.

"We need to keep the young ones away from the wagon. Can you make a fire over near those rocks? I need to boil the water."

"I'll take care of it, Aimee." He turned away.

"Wakefield . . ." He faced her again. "I'm sorry." He said nothing.

Aimee boiled the water and then all the cooking utensils, including the dipper Agnes had drunk from. She added pepper sauce to the water, although Jamie and Tad protested that it made the water taste bad. She set a big kettle over the fire and threw in some of the venison to make a stew, thickening it with some of the barley left in the barrels in the wagon. The food was probably already contaminated, she thought in despair, and hoped the long hours cooking over the hot flame would kill whatever infection it might carry.

She worked steadily, dividing her time between Agnes, who was growing worse, and the needs of the children, who had grown quiet and watchful.

"Is Mama going to be all right?" Sally asked time and again, and Tad cried himself to sleep. The hours ran together, day meshing into night before Aimee was aware of it. She could hear Hannah soothing the fears of the younger children at sleeping out in the open. Softly she sang to them until they grew drowsy and at last fell asleep. The prairie stretched away all around them, dark and menacing. It had never seemed that way within the perimeters of the corral, with the lights of the campfires filling the circle. Aimee had little time to ponder over it, for Agnes grew worse, and keeping her clean and comfortable became an impossible task. The night hours assumed nightmarish proportions as Aimee worked.

"Do you want me to spell you?" Wakefield asked, and gratefully Aimee made her way from the wagon to stand in the moonlight and contemplate what had brought her to this pass. Where was Zack now? she wondered. Was he looking at the same star-studded sky and thinking of her? Would he care that he'd never see her again? She thought of their night of lovemaking. Had it been only last night that he'd held her? She propped her chin on her bent knees while she thought of Zack. She needed him here beside her, needed his strength. But Zack was lost to her forever. She had to learn to live without him. Aimee lifted a tearstained face to the night sky. Give me strength, she prayed silently. Give me wisdom. Help me, help us all. It seemed that her silent cry echoed across the prairie and the mountains beyond. A sound of gagging came from the wagon, and she sprang to her feet.

"Aimee," Wakefield cried out, and she ran to the wagon. He was already tumbling out the back, his face pulled in a helpless grimace of revulsion and panic, his cheeks riddled with tears. He looked at Aimee, his mouth open to speak, but no words came. The sound of retching came from the wagon, and with a final wild glance over his shoulder, Wakefield clamped a hand to his mouth and ran off.

Aimee climbed into the wagon and bathed his mother's feverish face and washed away the green bile on her bloodless lips. Wearily she cleaned the foulness and wrung damp cloths for Agnes' feverish brow. Caught in the grip of the disease, the sick woman tossed about in pain, drawing her legs upward. Her eyes rolled wildly. Her slashing legs kicked aside the covers and Aimee went to straighten them as Agnes shook with chills.

A smear of red caught Aimee's attention, and inspecting more closely, she felt the same panic she'd seen on Wakefield's face rise inside her head. She wanted to scream and cry out. She wanted to run away into the prairie and never return to the agony of this wagon. Deliriously Agnes brought her knees up to her chest while a strangled cry escaped her dry throat. Aimee looked, and her worst fears were confirmed. Agnes was giving birth to her baby.

It couldn't be. It was too soon. Aimee's frantic mind tried to remember the things she'd heard. She'd need water, and there was so little. She'd need scissors, but she wasn't sure for what. Frantically she tried to comfort the woman, bathing her skin time and time again, kneeling in the wagon until her knees were numb and her back ached. The long night hours dragged on and the sun rose in the east, but Aimee took no time to notice. The children woke and came to stand outside the wagon; then, hearing the agonized screams of their mother, they ran away again to huddle together near the fire.

It seemed to Aimee that no woman could bear so much pain, and she began to pray that Agnes would die, though the baby was alive and struggling for freedom from his mother's womb. At last, late in the afternoon, Agnes delivered her baby. As though the agony and joy of that birthing had reached through the delirium of fever, Agnes opened her eyes and stared at Aimee.

"How is my baby?" she asked weakly, and Aimee was startled by her lucidness.

"He's alive," she answered, not adding that he was so weak he probably wouldn't make it through the night.

"Another boy," Agnes said, and her eyes lit up. "Has Ulcie seen him yet?" Her face was luminous, and briefly Aimee glimpsed beauty in the thin woman's face.

"Not yet," she whispered.

Agnes chuckled weakly. "He'll be so proud. I know he will." Her smile faded. "Papa just doesn't understand Ulcie. He thinks he's weak, but Ulcie has hidden strengths."

"Yes, he has," Aimee said softly, remembering how Ulcie had lost his life trying to save Helen Sawyer. Her answer pleased Agnes, for she smiled again.

"I remember when Ulcie came to ask Papa for my hand. Everybody was so surprised. They all thought I was going to be an old maid. At first everyone said he was only marrying me for Papa's money. He said he wasn't, and I believed him. Ulcie never lied to me." Agnes turned her head and looked at her new son. Her voice had grown weaker.

"Papa wanted to buy him off, but I cried and told him if he did, I'd never speak to him again. I'd live there in his house with him and never speak a word." One hand touched her son's tiny fingers. "Wait till Papa sees little Jamie. He'll take us back and help us. He'll give Ulcie a job and we'll be just fine, won't we, little Jamie?" Aimee bit her lips to keep from sobbing out loud at the sadness of this woman's life.

Suddenly Agnes gasped and retched, and Aimee hurried to take the baby from her and settle him in a pile of bedding to one side.

"I thought I'd be done with all this morning sickness once I had the baby," Agnes murmured, then shivered as chills racked her exhausted body.

"You'll feel better soon," Aimee soothed her, but she could see the eyes clouding with fever.

Valiantly she tried to help the dying woman and her child, dripping water onto the tiny lips, but the baby made no effort to open his mouth and take in nourishment. Agnes flailed on the pallet, then whimpered in pain from the chills that claimed her. Her exhausted body could offer little resistance now, and death came swiftly. Aimee took little time to tend the dead woman's final ablutions. She labored over the tiny son until it too had ceased breathing; then she placed it in its dead mother's arms and climbed out of the wagon.

Numbly she stared at the dark sky. It was night again, she thought in dismay. Then the horror of the last days and nights swept over her and she fell to her knees on the ground and began to sob. Her tears were not just for the dead woman and her baby, but for Aimee's father and for Loretta married to an old man she didn't love, and for Wakefield and the rest of the orphaned Stuart children. She cried for Zack and all his suspicions of her, and even for herself, for the life she'd lost and the things she'd endured. She sobbed out all the terror and helplessness she'd felt ever since the wagon train abandoned them. At last she raised her grief-ravaged face to the sky.

"Why?" she cried to some higher being; then anger shook her frame. "I swear," she said, her voice hoarse from her weeping, "I swear if I ever get out of this alive, I'll never depend on others again. I'll never let someone else hold sway over my life." Sobbing wretchedly, she fell facedown on the ground as fatigue claimed her, and she slept where she was. Around the fire, the children stirred uneasily in the bedrolls; then all was silent.

* * *

The howl of prairie wolves woke her. With a start Aimee raised her head and looked around. Why was she sleeping here on the ground? she wondered. Where were Hattie and Sam and Papa? The wolf howled again and reality returned, sharp and horrible. Aimee jerked up, crouching on her knees while she looked around trying to catch a glimpse of the wolves. Had the scent of death drawn them so quickly? Aimee thought about the bodies in the wagon. She'd have to do something, and quickly. They'd have to dig a grave and gather rocks to place over the top so the wolves couldn't get to them. She leapt to her feet.

"Wakefield," she cried, running to the campfire. Fear edged her voice and he sat up. The same fear reflected in his face.

"What is it?" he asked. "Is it Mama?" Aimee stopped in her headlong rush and looked around at the children. They were all awake now and their eyes were solemn and frightened as they looked at her. She had to tell them their mother was dead, Aimee realized, and there would be little time to deal with their grief.

"Is Mama dead?" Hannah asked, and Aimee shook her head.

"I'm sorry," she said softly. "I did everything I could." The children began to cry, all except Wakefield, who only stared at her. "She had the baby. It was a boy."

Wakefield glanced up at her. "He's dead too," he said flatly.

"Yes. He was too weak. He didn't have much chance." Wakefield made no answer. He was too self-contained, Aimee thought, hiding his grief and shock. She hated having to add more on his thin shoulders, but a wolf howled his grim warning.

"We have to dig a grave for them, Wakefield," she said. "There's not much time."

"Wolves!" he said excitedly as another howl was heard. Silently Aimee nodded. He threw aside the covers and grabbed the shovel. Choosing a spot where the ground was soft, halfway between the wagon and the rocks, he began to dig.

"Can we see Mama one last time?" Hannah asked, and after a moment Aimee nodded. Clasping hands, the children made their way to the wagon for a first and final glimpse of their new brother and to bid farewell to the aloof, enigmatic woman who'd nurtured them. Morosely they stared at the figures, wondering if Aimee was playing a game with them. It seemed to them their mother and the baby were only sleeping. Then Tad began to cry and hold out his arms. He'd never seen his mother hold anyone else but him, and he was jealous of this newcomer.

"Take him back," Aimee told Hannah. "Build up the fire."

"Yes, Aimee," Hannah said, and trudged back to the rocks, tugging the younger children along behind. They were still linked by their clasped hands.

Taking a deep breath to steel herself for a task more gruesome than she'd expected it to be, Aimee climbed into the wagon and spread out bedding for a shroud for the dead woman. Tugging and pulling, she worked Agnes' body into it and tied the ends of the quilts together. It would have to do. She was reminded of her father's coffin. Pitiful as it had been, at least it was something. Her teeth clenched. She'd had enough of burying people.

"Aimee," Wakefield called, his tone too quiet, too careful. It struck a spark of alarm along Aimee's nerves. Cautiously she looked out the back of the wagon. Wakefield stood in the shallow grave he'd dug, his shovel forgotten in his hands, his body rigid as he stared off at something on the prairie. Aimee followed his gaze and her heart lurched in fear. A prairie wolf, his scruffy brown coat almost blending with the rocks and ground, stood watching them, his tongue lolling as he panted. Wildly she looked around and picked out other brown bodies slinking closer. The children were at the fire. They hadn't seen the wolves yet.

"Wakefield, where are the rifles?" Aimee called.

"In the wagon."

"Walk over here slowly and help me get them," Aimee ordered, and watched the wolf's reaction as the boy did as he was told. Wakefield seemed to move in slow motion, so that Aimee wanted to scream at him to hurry. She restrained the urge. Their best chance was in not calling attention to themselves any more than necessary.

Wakefield was at the wagon now. His gaze was still glued to the wolf studying them. "The guns are along the side," he instructed Aimee quietly, "and the ammunition is in that bundle at the end." He stayed where he was outside the wagon, while she handed out the guns.

"We have to get back to the children," Aimee whispered. "The wagon would probably be safer for them, but I don't think there's enough time to get them here."

Wakefield glanced around. "We'll go up in them rocks over there. I can hold the wolves off with my gun. Come on out of the wagon now."

Aimee clambered down. Taking one of Ulcie Stuart's rifles, she made her way across the expanse separating them from the other children. If only the young ones didn't spot the wolves and make an outcry that would spur the wolves to attack before she and Wakefield got to them. The wolves were prowling restlessly, as if they'd studied the campsite and knew every weakness of it. They were ready to close in.

"They're coming," Wakefield cried, and they dashed the last few feet to the fire.

"Wolves," Jamie cried, and Hannah and Sally began to scream.

"The rocks," Aimee shouted as she ran. "Climb up in the rocks."

"Hannah, the rocks," Wakefield yelled. The girl looked around, then headed the children toward the ledge of rocks. A wolf had already veered toward them. Aimee and Wakefield were at the campfire now. Wakefield put his back to the wall and took aim.

A wolf yelped in pain and limped away. Aimee pushed the little ones up the slope and handed up a rifle. Hastily she scrambled up after the children, and picking up the rifle, took aim. She'd never held one before, but she'd watched Wakefield and some of the men handling them.

"Wakefield, climb up," she called, but he made no answer. "I'll hold them off till you climb up," she yelled down. Still no answer. Only the steady shooting of the gun let her know he was all right.

"Aimee, look, the wagon," Hannah cried, and Aimee saw a lanky brown body circling the wagon. Of course, she thought, this was what had drawn them in the first place. Wakefield's rifle spoke again, and one of the wolves fell and lay still. There were too many of them. They'd never be able to kill them all. She had to do something. She couldn't let the children watch while the wolves devoured their mother's remains. They huddled together on the rocky ledge, their bodies jerking with sobs.

Helplessly Aimee glanced back down the rocky slope, wondering if Wakefield had any ideas. Her eyes settled on the fire, still blazing. Hannah and the children had just piled the last of their dead branches on it. Aimee had an idea.

"Hannah, no matter what happens, you and the others stay here on this ledge. Do you understand?"

"Yes, Aimee, but what are you going to do?"

"Never mind," Aimee said. "Can you shoot a rifle?"

Tearfully the girl nodded. "Wakefield showed me."

"Good. If a wolf tries to climb up after you, shoot it."

"All right, Aimee," Hannah sniffed. Tears were running down her cheeks, but her hands were steady as she took hold of the gun. Aimee slid back down the rocky slope, ignoring the scrapes and scratches.

"Aimee, climb back up," Wakefield cried. The freckles stood out on his pale face and he looked scared. Still, he'd stayed here to try to protect them.

"We have to burn the wagon," Aimee said, "otherwise the wolves will get your mother and the baby."

His stricken face blanched further. "I'll do it," he said manfully.

Aimee's grip on his shoulder stopped him. "I'll do it," she said firmly. "There's no time for arguing. You can shoot, I can't. Climb up on that ledge and try to drive the wolves away from the wagon until I can fire it."

"You'll never make it," Wakefield cried.

"That's going to depend on you and how well you shoot," Aimee replied. It was a terrible responsibility to put on him, but she had little choice. "If I don't make it back, try to take the young ones farther up in the rocks."

"All right." He turned toward the rocks, then paused. "Aimee, thanks for all you did for my ma."

"Go on, climb up there," she urged, but his words made her feel better, stronger. She could do this, she thought, eyeing the distance to the wagon. Why had she put the children's camp so far from the wagon? She knew the answer. She'd done it to protect them as much as possible from the fever.

"I'm ready, Aimee," Wakefield called from above. She glanced at the circling, prowling wolves and took a deep breath.

"Aim for the ones between me and the wagon," she called, and heard the report of a rifle. One of the wolves yelped and fell to the ground. The others stopped their circling and backed away. Wakefield shot again, and another wolf yowled and ran away over the prairie. Aimee drew a glowing brand from the fire. Wakefield had continued shooting until the wolves were driven back. Restlessly they paced, reassessing the situation, their jaws slathering hungrily.

Aimee took another deep breath, then plunged across the rough ground toward the wagon. She could hear the wolves growl and snarl. One loped toward her, but Wakefield fired and the wolf darted back to its pack. She arrived at the wagon breathless and trembling. One hand gripped the wagon wheel. The heat of the morning was already warming the canvas-covered wagon. The stench of death and decay lay heavy on the air. She offered one quick, silent prayer that she was doing the right thing, then plunged the brand against the canvas top. It caught fire, the flames sweeping upward, and she moved to the other side to do the same. A quick glance showed her the wolves were still keeping their distance. Wakefield's marksmanship had ensured that.

Tossing the burning brand into the wagon, Aimee grabbed up her skirts and ran pell-mell back toward the rocks. Thwarted of their original prey, the wolves might come after them now. The quick succession of shots from Wakefield's rifle told her the wolves were already making their move.

"Run, Aimee," Hannah cried fearfully, and Aimee's legs churned in a mighty effort to reach the safety of the rocks. She could hear the wolves padding after her and felt the heat of their breath on her legs as she scrambled up the slope. Wakefield crouched on the edge, working frantically at something in his lap. The wolves were scrambling up the slope after her.

"Shoot, Wakefield," Aimee screamed.

"My gun jammed," he cried, and cursed.

Hannah opened her mouth to admonish him, then closed it again. What did it matter what he said? There was no one to object anymore. The canvas top had fallen into the wagon now and the whole thing was ablaze, the dry wood burning quickly in the hot flame.

"Jamie, hand me that gun," Aimee ordered, and the frightened boy brought the other rifle. Aimee knew nothing about using it, but she could hit something at this close range. She put the gun to her shoulder, sighted down its barrel, and pulled the trigger. The recoil nearly knocked her off her feet, but she straightened, ignoring the bruising pain in her shoulder, and fired again. One of the wolves tumbled end over end down the slope.

"Got it," Wakefield cried, and took aim. Aimee did the same and heard the hammer click down on an empty chamber. Another wolf had made its way to the top, its evil yellow eyes gleaming, its tongue dripping saliva. Aimee struck at it with the barrel of her gun. Wakefield turned and fired. The wolf fell dead at her feet. He fired again and nothing happened.

"It's jammed again," he cried in despair. They could hear the menacing growl of the rest of the pack as they scrambled for a foothold on the slope.

"Get back," Aimee yelled at the younger children. "Climb! Climb up into those rocks." Jamie and Sally scurried for the rocks behind them. Tad stood where he was, wailing at the top of his lungs. "Hannah, take Tad and climb," Aimee ordered.

"What about you and Wakefield?" the girl asked tearfully, her dark eyes darting from one of them to the other.

"Don't worry about us," Aimee cried, grabbing up Tad and handing him to the girl.

"Go on, Hannah," Wakefield yelled. "Don't talk back."

"I wasn't." Hannah began to cry. "I just don't want to leave you."

Aimee pushed her toward the path the other children had taken. "Take Tad to safety," she ordered. "Hannah, he's little and can't help himself. You'll have to help him. Now, go." She gave the weeping girl a push, and when she was sure Hannah was obeying her orders, turned back to the path. Wakefield was pelting the advancing wolves with rocks. Aimee ran to help. Suddenly shots rang out and from below a wolf yelped and tumbled down the slope, carrying one of the others with him. Shots rang out again and more wolves fell dead. The rest of the pack, sensing this new danger, scrambled back down the slope and raced off into the prairie.

"Look, Aimee, there's help," Wakefield cried, pointing to the approaching riders. Aimee sagged against the rocks, tears of relief dimming her vision. They were safe. Help had arrived. Her knees gave way beneath her and she slumped to the ground, burying her face in her hands. She could hear Wakefield and Hannah shouting in glee.

"Aimee," a familiar voice cried hoarsely, and she sat up.

"Zack?" she whispered, wiping at her grimy cheeks. "Zack?" She was on her feet and climbing, half-sliding down the rocky incline. He was off his horse before it had come to a complete stop. His strong arms lifted her down the rest of the way and she was pressed to his hard body. "Zack," she sobbed over and over.

"Thank God, you're alive," he whispered against her temple. He pressed quick, grateful kisses on her brow and eyes, his arms gripping her so tightly she might have felt pain if not for the relief at feeling his solid strength. "I should never have left you," he said hoarsely. "I let my temper get the best of me, and like some damn fool I rode off and left you out here."

"You didn't know," Aimee whispered.

"I shouldn't have left you," he repeated. She could hear the anguish in his voice. He just held her for a time, unable to believe he'd come so close to losing her. Aimee rested against his broad chest, her weight supported by him, while she cried tears of relief. They were safe, she and the children.

"The children!" she cried, thinking of the little ones climbing up into the rocks. What if they'd come upon a snake, or one of the wolves had circled around and got to them?

"They're safe," Zack reassured her, and Aimee could see a man carefully lowering Tad down to the waiting arms.

"How did you know?" she asked, turning back to Zack.

"Cholera hit the whole wagon train just one day out of Fort Laramie," Zack explained. "They sent some men on ahead to say they were in trouble. When I got there and found out you'd been left behind, I started out immediately."

"Thank God you did," Aimee said, and shuddered. "I don't know what would have happened if you hadn't arrived when you did." Zack said nothing. He had a very clear picture of what would have happened, and the thought haunted him.

"Where's Mrs. Stuart?" he asked instead, and saw a spasm pass over Aimee's face. She nodded toward the charred remains of the wagon.

"We had to burn the wagon to keep the wolves from them," she said.

"It's a good thing you did. It helped us find you."

"Excuse me, ma'am." A lean, rough-looking man with a bushy beard and uncombed long hair doffed his hat. "Jim Culby at your service. Anytime you and the little ones're ready, we'll head back to the fort."

"We're ready," Aimee said gratefully.

"We'll double up," the man said. "Each one of us'll take a young 'un up on his horse. Ah 'spect you'll be takin' the lady."

Zack nodded. "I'll take care of the lady," he said, and Aimee knew he was making a promise to her. She thought of the promise she'd made to herself the night before, but said nothing.

Even traveling double, they made better time on horseback than they would have with the wagon train. When they were halfway to their destination, they spied a lone wagon making its way toward them. They rode to meet it.

"Hello," the driver hailed long before they had reached each other, and Aimee recognized Loretta's voice. The two girls ran to greet each other.

"Oh, Ah thought yo' was dead," Loretta wept, hugging Aimee tightly.

"I thought we were too, some of the time," Aimee cried.

"Ah didn't know they'd left yo' till that night," Loretta explained. "Ah wouldn't 'ave gone off."

"I know. It's all right," Aimee reassured her.

"Ah tried t' make Royce come back fo' yo', but he was feelin' poorly hisself. He said wait till mornin' and he'd come back fo' yo', but when mornin' came he was too sick t' move."

Aimee was moved by Loretta's words. She'd never be able to like Royce Sawyer, but she was grateful that he'd been willing to come back for them. She'd never criticize Loretta's husband again. She peered toward the wagon. "Is he better now?" she asked, and was stunned when Loretta burst into fresh tears.

"He died this mornin'."

"Oh, Loretta, I'm sorry." Aimee hugged her friend.

"Seems lak' he jest went so fast," Loretta sobbed. "One minute he was talkin' t' me, tellin' me how grateful he was for all Ah done for 'im, and the next, he was gone."

"We'd better move on," Zack said gently. "We'll try to make the wagon train by tonight."

"It ain't much further," Loretta said. "Yo' may not want t' stay there. Folks're takin' sick and dyin' at a fierce rate."

"I recall seeing a stream just this side of their campsite. We'll camp there and see what we can do to help."

"We oughta put the childers in the wagon," Jim Culby said. "They's plumb tuckered out."

"Good idea." Zack waved the other men forward.

"I'll ride with Loretta too," Aimee said, aware of how drained she felt after all they'd been through. Loretta gave her a quick hug. With the children resettled, the group made its way along the trail and about nightfall reached the stream Zack had mentioned. In the distance they could see the white canvas-covered wagons huddled in a corral. There were gaps where wagons had been pulled out of the circle. They dotted the terrain around. The acrid smell of burnt wood came to the new arrivals and they guessed by the smoldering remains that some wagons had been burned in an attempt to halt the spread of the fever.

Bile rose in Aimee's throat. She couldn't go through it again. She'd had enough. She turned away and went to sit on the banks of the stream.

"Aimee, what is it?" Zack asked, coming to squat beside her.

She turned an anguished face to him. "Oh, Zack, take me away from here," she begged. "I can't bear any more."

"It'll be all right," he soothed, wrapping an arm around her shoulders. Trustingly she leaned against his knee. "You won't have to go up there. Stay here until we figure out what we want to do."

"I'm not a coward," she whispered, her eyes wide and anxious that he not condemn her for her feelings. Gently he touched her dirty cheek, saw the dark circles beneath her eyes. They were all caught up in a nightmare, but Aimee had been through much more than the rest of them.

"You've done your share, Aimee," he reassured her. "Clean up a little and I'll start a fire and make some supper."

"I'll help," she said, and tried to rise, but he pushed her down again.

"Rest," he said. Gratefully she lay back in the sparse grass and closed her eyes, letting the sound of the rushing stream lull her to rest. Sometime during the evening Zack brought her a plate of food, but he couldn't rouse her enough to eat it. Finally he gave up and brought blankets to cover her. With Loretta's help, he put the children to bed and finally made his way back to the stream for a few hours' sleep beside Aimee. He would never let her out of his sight again, he vowed, and held her close, listening to her deep, even breathing.

With the morning the nightmare hadn't ended. Aimee stayed where she was at the creek, ostensibly to watch the children. In truth, she couldn't bear the thought of facing such an awful death again. Loretta went up and brought down some of the children who were free of any signs of the fever. Aimee set about teaching them and telling them stories, anything that would keep their minds off what was happening to a father or mother or brother. The children who had once run so free-spiritedly over the prairie sat subdued and melancholy.

"Two of Biddy's young 'uns died yesterday," Loretta said.

"No," Aimee said, looking around at the huddle of children. Some of Biddy's young ones were there. Reluctantly Aimee counted heads, unable to accept this latest tragedy. Two were missing. "Which ones?" she asked.

"Sarah and Bennie," Loretta replied.

"Poor Biddy," Aimee said, remembering all the big woman's kindnesses. Pepper sauce, it seemed, hadn't helped Biddy's family.

Aimee wasn't sure how long Zack meant to stay there, but one day another wagon train hove into view. Some of the outriders went to meet them and warn them away. After a while they rode back, and the new train set up camp far downstream. Zack rode back to camp that evening with news for them.

"We can join this train if we want to," he said, looking at Aimee. She seemed on the point of breaking down. She'd been unusually quiet the last few days, but her eyes held a haunted look that disturbed him.

"Can we?" she cried, her eyes brightening

"We cain't jest go off and leave all our friends," Loretta objected.

"Why not?" Aimee cried. "They left us." Startled at her vehemence, Zack and Loretta glanced at each other. They could understand her bitterness.

"There's nothing we can do for people here anyway," Zack said finally. "We might as well go on." Reluctantly Loretta nodded. Aimee smiled.

"There's only one problem. This train is headed to California. It seems there's word of a gold strike out there."

"Gold?" Aimee said.

Zack nodded. "You can never be sure about rumors like this. The train's here and pulling out in the morning. If we wait, there's no guarantee the next one won't be heading to California as well."

"What if we stay?" Loretta asked.

"There won't be enough emigrants left to make a train. They'll have to wait and join up with another one. Ben Thompson died this morning."

Loretta and Aimee sat silent, taking in the knowledge that people they'd known only a few hours ago were now gone.

"I want to go," Aimee cried, putting her hands over her face. "I want to get away from here. I never want to see or smell death again."

Loretta put her arm around her friend. "I'll go," she said.

Aimee raised her head and stared at Loretta. "What about your dream of Oregon?" she said. "What about Billy? Maybe you can find him again."

"That ain't hardly likely," Loretta said sadly. "As for Oregon . . . it don't hold the promise for me it onc't did. California's just as good."

"Are you sure, Loretta?" Aimee asked, and when the girl shook her head, threw her arms around her.

"I guess it's settled, then," Zack said, and Aimee hugged him too.

"It will be better there. I know it will," she cried, and gripped Zack's hand so tightly he thought she meant never to let go.

"I'll tell Wakefield and the others," he said.

Wakefield was strangely resistant to the idea. "My pa and ma died tryin' to' git t' Oregon," he said. "I kinda figured the little ones and me would go on out there." They couldn't argue with his thinking or with the sad new maturity they saw in his eyes.

"I'll look for a place for you until a wagon train headed for Oregon comes along," Zack said, wondering who would want to take on five orphans.

Wakefield seemed to understand the problem. "Mr. Crawford?" he called. "Tell 'em I'm a hard worker and I know how t' handle a gun."

"I will, son," Zack said, and headed to the camp. It was said that the trail could make or break a man. He didn't think any man could have been made stronger than Wakefield Stuart.

It was Biddy who provided a solution. She came down to the stream camp that evening to tell them all good-bye. Now that the disease had taken its toll on her family, she was anxious to leave. Two small graves marked her sojourn here. Hannah and the other children ran to greet her. Aimee was shocked at the woman's appearance. She looked as if she'd aged ten years, and her big shoulders slumped.

"My old man's takin' us on into Fort Laramie," Biddy said as she sat by the campfire. "We'll rest up a few days and wait for the next wagon train for Oregon."

"Come to California with us, Biddy," Aimee urged, but the old woman shook her head.

"My man's got his heart set on Oregon," she said. "Fact is, so've Ah."

"That's how Wakefield feels," Aimee said, "One place seems as good as the other to me."

"What's goin' to happen to them young 'uns now?" Biddy asked, her eyes sharp.

"Zack's trying to find someone to take them," Aimee said, "They don't want to go to California with us."

"Ah'll take 'em."

Aimee stared at her in surprise. "Biddy, are you sure?"

Slowly the old woman nodded. "Ah lost two of mine. Ah feel lost. They need a mother and a daddy. You know I'd treat 'em right."

"I know. I'll call them and you can ask them." There was little doubt of their decision. When Biddy's offer was put to them, Hannah and the younger children threw themselves on the old woman, hugging her. The strain on their faces was eased somewhat for the first time in days. Even little Tad laughed. Wakefield stood to one side, his eyes watchful, a first glimmer of hope in his eyes.

"What about Harry?" Aimee asked, and everyone stopped smiling.

"Jamie, run up to my wagon and tell your new daddy to hitch up the team and pull the wagon down here. We'll spend tonight gettin' t' know our new family." The other children laughed, the sound a welcome relief after the past few days.

Harry Potts proved himself to be a man of compassion and flexibility. He did as his wife bade and never batted an eyelash when the Stuart children first called him Papa.

"Ah turned my back on 'em once," he said, "and the good Lord smote me for it. Ah won't be doin' it again. They're my young 'uns same as if they was blood." His stoicism in the face of such loss moved Aimee.

Biddy bedded the kids down in her wagon. Eagerly they crawled into the covers with their new brothers and sisters. They'd been through a great deal in the past weeks, losing both their father and mother, but if anyone could help them recover, Aimee knew it was Biddy and her family.

Zack and Harry Potts spent the evening talking around the campfire. The fact that their number had swelled to nine children didn't seem to bother the Pottses at all. They accepted what fate had handed them with equanimity. The evening passed in a facsimile of the companionable evenings they'd once spent around the campfire. By the time they were ready to retire, everyone felt better, more hopeful about what the morning would bring.

Aimee fell asleep in the warmth and safety of Zack's arms. The worst was behind her, she thought sleepily. Tomorrow her life would begin anew.

14

Fearful of the lingering taint of cholera, the new wagon train bypassed Fort Laramie. Some of the California-bound emigrants shunned the new arrivals until it was clear they'd brought no contagious fever with them. They climbed high into the Rockies, finding some reassurance that here, at least, the danger of cholera was behind them. Aimee soon discovered that the new wagon train was different in temperament from the old one. These travelers were not hardworking farmers who'd sold everything they owned to make their westward dream a reality. They could hardly be called emigrants. In fact they'd coined a name from Greek mythology—the argonauts—and they wore it proudly. The argonauts had no dream of building a new home in the west. They carried in their breast a greed for the yellow gold discovered in the California rivers and streams.

They were an adventuresome lot, young and boastful, their heads filled with impossible schemes. They talked more freely of where they'd been and of where they were going. Eagerly they speculated on what they'd find once they reached the California gold-fields. Much of the anxiety present on the first train was not in evidence here. Charlie Webster was their wagon master and he'd been over the trail many times. There were fewer women and children, and Aimee was glad Loretta had given up her plans to go to Oregon and joined them.

Likewise, the argonauts' wagons and supplies reflected their single-mindedness. No barrels of family china or heirloom clocks would be found among them. Their wagons were loaded with picks and shovels and any other paraphernalia they might need for panning gold. Wagons were gaily painted, their canvas coverings bearing the legend of their new dream. "California or Bust," they read, or sometimes, more simply, "Gold." Even their dress was different. Most wore slouch hats and high boots and knee-length coats that nearly covered their baggy canvas trousers.

They were a hardy bunch of men. Obstacles were overcome with hardly a second thought. The pace was quicker. All energy was directed to getting to the goldfields. Everyone was in a hurry to make his fortune. The promise of gold drew them as nothing else could. Whenever the wagon train stopped for a nooning or at night, men gathered to talk of gold.

Although they were now undertaking the hardest part of the trail, traveling had become easier for Aimee. There were no small children needing her time and attention, no heavy work. There were still plenty of chores to be done, but now they were shared with Loretta and Zack. No longer did Aimee gather wood or carry water. It was done for her, and she rode in Loretta's wagon so much that it became a relief to get out and walk. With the other men Zack hunted and fished the streams for mountain trout to supplement their diet.

With less work and more food, Aimee gained back weight and the hollows in her cheeks and ribs filled out. Zack was delighted with the change in her and showed her so in a thousand ways. Their nights were spent loving each other beneath a dark sky studded with stars so big and bright in the clear, cold mountain air that it seemed she could touch them. Aimee lay snuggled in Zack's arms, warmed by his body and his passion, and for a while forgot every hardship of the trail.

Zack always let Aimee sleep later, while he built the

fire and put on the coffee and bacon. During the warm afternoons, when she'd taken her turn at driving and Loretta held the reins, Aimee crawled into the back of the wagon for a nap. She'd never felt so pampered in all her life, yet knew she once had been. She no longer took such simple comforts for granted.

With more time on her hands, Aimee soon found herself caught up in the talk of gold. It seemed no one had much real information, except that the precious yellow metal had been discovered at a place called Sutter's Mill on the American River. Towns with strange-sounding names like San Francisco and Sacramento were mentioned often. Aimee marveled that western towns existed when they were journeying through such barren and unsettled wilderness.

One argonaut in particular, a shy young man named Bayard Louden, captured Aimee's attention. He'd been a schoolteacher back in Kentucky and wasn't used to the coarse ways of some of the gold seekers. He blushed whenever he was spoken to, so naturally the other men teased him whenever they got the chance. Aimee took pity on him and often sought him out. When he got over his shyness, he proved to be a lively and intelligent man with definite ideas about finding gold.

Aimee listened to him talk about glaciers, rock strata, and water flow, only half-understanding what he said. Sometimes in his excitement he would take up a stick and draw in the dirt a trellislike picture of a river and its tributaries. Other times, when they'd camped for the night, he'd invite her to join him for a walk and lead her to rocky formations or ledges where he would point out the layers of rock that formed the mountain. His brown eyes behind their wire-rimmed glasses were earnest as he explained how the freezing water caused the compressed rock to split and yield up its treasure of gold. He showed her a sluice box, a cradlelike affair set on rockers, and explained how the riffles caught the grains of gold, separating it from the sand as the water washed through. He told her about Long Toms and troughs and all the ways man had devised to get gold out of the ground. Aimee spent so much time with Bayard that Loretta grew alarmed and Zack grew jealous.

"I think we'd better talk," he said one night when she had kissed and teased him seductively. Aimee was startled by his aloofness. Zack was always quick to respond to her. The scowl on his face made her heart skip a beat. What had she done wrong? Had he changed his mind? Did he not love her anymore? It was a fear that haunted her. There had been too many losses in her young life, and Caroline still remained very much in her mind.

"What do you want to talk about?" she asked stiffly.

"This Bayard . . . Bayard . . ."

"Bayard Louden?"

"Yes," Zack said with some irritability. "You're spending a great deal of time with him."

"Yes, we talk about gold," she answered. What could be wrong with that?

"There can't be that much to say about gold!" Zack was nearly shouting as he whirled to glare at her. His anger confused and frightened her.

"There's a great deal," Aimee cried in amazement at his ignorance and his lack of interest. "Did you know there are different kinds of gold and you have to mine it differently? There are actually chunks of gold that you can just pick up with your hand, and then there's gold dust, for which you must pan. Sometimes you can find it in rocks. Bay says—"

"You see what I mean?" Zack shouted. "He's got you as crazed with gold fever as some of these other fools."

Aimee just stared at him, and slowly comprehension washed over her. "I suppose I am being silly to spend so much time on this," she agreed. "Mining for gold is really something only men can do. Certainly not women. That's why Mr. Louden left his wife at home."

"He's married?"

"Less than a year," Aimee replied sweetly. "Why,

if he's not talking about gold, he's talking about his bride. He misses her terribly."

"Umm, well he might," Zack said, mollified somewhat by Aimee's words. "He shouldn't have left her."

"That's what I told him, but he has this mistaken notion that dainty little women aren't capable of making such a hard trip."

Zack glanced at her innocent face and realized he was being teased. In one swoop she was in his arms and nestled against his chest.

"He's nearly as big a fool as me," he murmured against her lips. His kiss was passionate and demanding, and Aimee answered in kind, letting him see her own desire.

"I could never bear to lose you," Zack whispered hoarsely.

"Nor I you," Aimee whispered, remembering the panic she'd felt at his anger. She thought of that night on the prairie when Agnes and her baby died. She'd made a promise then that she wouldn't be dependent on anyone again, yet here she was cringing at the slightest frown from Zack. She mustn't care for him so much, she thought hazily as his hands skimmed down her waist and hips, caressing her body. Tomorrow! She'd begin tomorrow to make herself less dependent on him. For tonight she gave herself to the special pleasure of loving and being loved by Zack Crawford.

Yet later, as they lay exhausted and satiated, Zack was aware that she'd held back some small part of herself, and he thought again of Bay Louden. Zack had lost one woman he loved, but he'd never loved as much as this. He couldn't bear it if Aimee turned from him to another man. He wrapped his arm around her tightly, nestling her warm body against his. She mumbled sleepily, automatically raising her lips to his. His sweet responsive Aimee, he thought, and held her throughout the night.

The next night Aimee invited Bay to join them for supper. She saw Zack's frown, but ignored it, acting as if Bay were as much his guest as hers. It was easy to get Bay talking about his wife and later about searching for gold, his two great passions. Soon Loretta was also hanging on his every word, and finally even Zack had warmed to the young man. The hours passed and still the two men sat on talking. Delightedly Aimee excused herself and went off to bed. She'd have something else to tease Zack about, she thought gaily.

If the first wagon train had seemed plagued by bad luck, good fortune seemed to smile on the argonauts and their caravan. They were well into the mountains now. What had seemed like gentle green ascents proved to be dry sand and rock. Only a few stunted bushes and trees relieved the barren landscape. Poisonous springs and potholes dotted the arid fifty-mile stretch along the North Platte, but they made it in only two days. After a short rest at the Sweetwater River, they pushed deeper into the Rockies. Aimee was enthralled by the sweeping vista of sky and mountains. The argonauts were not. Using a windlass, they pulled the wagons up the mountainsides and set their brakes to ease them down the other side.

"It's as if we'd climbed to the top of the world," Aimee told Zack, who laughed and hugged her close. True, he'd once argued against her coming on this trip, but now he couldn't imagine being here without her. No longer overworked and underfed, her small body was possessed of an energy that amazed him. Still, the trip was not an easy one, nor without its hazards, and he guarded her zealously.

At Independence Rock, Aimee and Loretta wrote their names in charcoal on the famous stone that marked the halfway point. Other names were scrawled there, as well as messages for those who followed. Loretta stood for a long time reading the messages and Aimee knew she hoped there was something there from Billy. It made her feel guilty to be so happy with Zack when Loretta was so alone.

Though it was mid-July, the nights and mornings were cold as they crossed through the South Pass and beyond to the Ice Slough, where the argonauts chopped ice from the ground to fill their water casks. They were in the Wind River Mountains, Charlie Webster told them.

Two weeks later they left behind the Oregon trail and headed southwest toward the arid wasteland of the Great Basin. It seemed incredible to Aimee that only a few weeks before they'd shivered in the cold mountain air and now they struggled through a blistering heat that set false images shimmering on the horizon. The burning rays of the sun were reflected in the white sands of the Great Basin, so there was no escaping its bitter intensity. Nothing grew in the alkaline soil, nor was there any sign of animal life. The argonauts' wagon train moved ghostlike and silent, at last intimidated by the vastness of the salt desert through which they traveled. Bones of oxen and abandoned wagons lay bleaching in the sun.

"I hate this place," Aimee croaked through a dust-parched throat.

"Me too," Zack said bleakly, and she was not reassured as she'd hoped to be. Carefully they hoarded their supply of water. It took them two days to cross the waterless basin and finally reach the Humboldt River, a pitiful muddy thing that offered them little surcease from their terrible thirst. They followed its winding course until it disappeared altogether, losing itself in the thick white sands. Forty miles of desert lay between them and the Sierra Mountains. Aimee stood looking over the flat, hot sands and her shoulders sagged.

"I can't make it," she said, shaking her head slowly.

"Yes yo' can," Loretta said. She was huddled on the ground in the little patch of shade provided by the wagon. She was trying to get some sleep before they started out again. They would travel the great desert at night. Somehow that made the vast hot sands seem even more formidable. "At least our mules are still goin'," she answered lethargically.

"That's true," Aimee admitted. Many argonauts had been forced to walk, carrying their goods on their backs, for their teams had not been able to endure the punishment of the salt desert. "Of course, we were smart enough not to overtax our mules in the first place." Aimee stretched out beside Loretta. "One or the other of us has been walking across this whole desert."

"Ah don't expect our little bit of weight had much t' do with that," Loretta observed. "We've jest been lucky." Aimee lay thinking about what she'd said. They *had* been lucky on this leg of the trail. Much of that luck had come from Zack and his skills. She smiled and took a deep breath of the dry air. Most of the time she felt like she couldn't breathe at all.

"Do you ever think of Billy?" She could feel Loretta stiffen, but the girl's voice was casual as she answered.

"No, Ah don't. He's like a dream t' me. When yo' wake up and busy yo'rself with real life, yo' forget about the dream."

Aimee sat up, leaning her weight on her elbow as she peered at her friend. "You haven't really forgotten about him, have you?" she insisted.

"Jest 'bout," Loretta answered. "We bettah git some sleep or we'll be in bad shape tonight."

Aimee took the hint and remained silent, but her mind was going back to the early days of their trip, when Loretta was obviously so in love with Billy and he with her. How could feelings change like that? she wondered. Could it happen to Zack and her? There seemed to be a terrible kind of impermanence to all relationships. It was more important than ever that once she reached California she find some means to take care of herself. She didn't want to depend on Zack entirely. When the day came that he no longer wanted her, she would be ready.

The weary travelers filled every container they could find with water from the last stream. Some argonauts even filled their rubberized boots. As soon as the fierce rays of the sun had been diminished into long wispy streamers on the western horizon, they set out.

Whips cracked in the eerie light of dusk; men and beasts were silhouetted in the waning light. Darkness fell, the only sound the labored breathing of men struggling toward their dream of gold. In their wake they left the rotting carcasses of tired mules and the dried wooden bones of wagons too heavy to be pulled through the shifting sands of the desert.

Those whose teams were still going at the break of dawn turned a blind eye to their fellowman's misery. To offer too much help might bring death to oneself. The cohesive group that had set out so jauntily from Missouri, had bested treacherous rivers, cholera, and steep mountain passes, now succumbed to the relentless fury of the desert heat. They struggled forward individually, no man a part of another, except in their undiminished dream of gold.

The wagon train paused to rest in the heat of the day, man and beast alike struggling for any spot of shade that would protect them from the searing sun. Aimee and Loretta crawled under the wagon and collapsed in the sand. Zack unsaddled his horse and unhitched the team of mules and joined them.

"I want a bath," Aimee gasped, wiping at her neck with the bandanna she'd worn around her hair while they traveled. "I want to take a bath in a cool mountain stream, with ice still thawing and floating on its surface."

"Shut up, Aimee," Loretta croaked.

"The water's so cold," Aimee murmured. "I can feel a bit of ice touching my back. It's deliciously cold."

"I'm contemplating murder," Zack growled. Aimee shut up and soon they fell asleep. She awoke late in the afternoon and peered out. Heat waves shimmered on the horizon. But in the distance Aimee could make out a smudge of trees and mountains. Where there were trees and mountains, there were streams. She crawled from under the wagon.

"Zack! Loretta!" she called, but they slept on. Let them sleep, she thought. She'd go to the stream and take a bath, and when they woke up she would tease them about sleeping when they could be bathing in a cool mountain stream. She started out. Bay was busy trying to soothe his mules. They looked all done in. He had a discouraged look on his face.

"They need water," he said when he saw Aimee looking at him. "They're aren't going to make it."

"Then come with me and we'll get them some water," Aimee said with a smile.

"Where?" Bay's head came up in surprise.

"Right over there, see?" Aimee pointed to the clump of trees. "I'm going over to take a bath."

Bay eyed her measuringly. "Where's Zack?" he asked, licking his lips nervously.

"He's still sleeping." Aimee giggled. "Can you imagine sleeping when he could go to the stream with me? Do you want to go with me?"

"I can't, Aimee. I have to stay here and take care of my mules." He paused. "I don't think you ought to go off without Zack." But she had already walked away, heading out across the desert.

It seemed she walked a long way. She stumbled and fell in the hot sand. It burned her skin. She was so thirsty and hot. She'd left the bandanna back at the wagon. The sun beat down on her uncovered head. Aimee peered across the shimmering desert, searching for the trees and mountains. Yes, they were still there. She hadn't been mistaken. Pushing herself upright again, she trudged toward the cool mountain stream.

"Aimee," Zack's voice called to her. For a moment it penetrated her numbed mind and she contemplated stopping. But no, Zack was still sleeping and she wanted to take her bath before he woke. Head down, she staggered on.

"Aimee!" This time his voice was closer. Aimee wanted to stop and wait for him, but the trees and stream were closer now. She could smell the water. She could hear the splash as the water fell into a rocky basin. The pond would be cold and clear. She'd be able to see all the way to the bottom. She could feel the mountain air on her face. She smiled and walked on.

"Aimee, stop. It's a mirage," Zack shouted hoarsely. His voice frightened her. He wasn't going to let her go to the stream. He was angry because she'd found it first. She began to run. She had to get there ahead of him. She had to. She stumbled and fell, then scrambled up and ran on again.

"Aimee . . ." Zack's voice broke on the cry. "Stop running, Aimee. Wait for me." She paid him no heed and he was surprised that she could move so quickly across the clinging hot sands. Drawing in a breath of air so hot it seemed to burn his lungs, he ran after her. She could hear his feet plodding in the sand, feel his closeness; then his hand clamped over her shoulder and she tried to shrug away. He held on tight and the momentum of their effort carried them forward head over heels in the sand. His grip was broken. She was up again, her skirts pulled high, her legs churning. One long arm swept out, an iron hand closed around her ankle, and she went sprawling in the sand. Aimee screamed and kicked out at him with her free foot.

"Aimee, stop it," Zack cried, and crawled forward to pin her down with his body. His chest was heaving with the exertion of running in the hot sun.

"Let me go, Zack," Aimee cried piteously. "I want to get a drink of water and take a bath."

"There's no water, baby," Zack whispered. He cradled her face in his hands. "It's a mirage, Aimee, a hallucination. The heat causes it. There's no water."

"That's not true," she cried. "I saw it. It's there." She struggled in his grasp, straining for another glimpse of green trees and granite mountains and the silvery cascade of a waterfall. There was only desert. "No!" Aimee screamed. "What have you done with it? You've tricked me."

"Shhh, it's all right. We'll find water soon, Aimee," Zack soothed her.

"I don't believe you," she cried out. "Put it back. You took it away. I hate you. I hate you." Her shoulders heaved with sobs, and Zack lay in the sand with her, cradling her while she sobbed herself into exhaustion. Finally he got to his feet and pulled her up. Wrapping her arm around his neck, he turned back to the wagons, which looked tiny and forlorn in the distance. He half-dragged, half-carried her back, and Loretta was there running to meet him and help take the burden of Aimee's slight body onto her own shoulders. Bay Louden stood by anxiously as they dampened a cloth with some of their precious water supply and laid it across her brow. Loretta dribbled water on Aimee's lips until she opened her mouth and swallowed. They put her inside the wagon and took turns watching her.

Aimee woke and looked around. Darkness was falling, and from outside came the sounds of people readying themselves for the journey. She pushed aside the canvas and looked out.

"Aimee," Loretta said. Her voice held relief. "Zack, she's awake."

Zack turned from harnessing the team of mules. Aimee watched him walk toward her. She remembered everything in the desert. His expression was tentative.

"I'm sorry," she whispered, and saw the relief on his face.

"It's all right. It can happen to anyone. The desert plays strange tricks on you."

"I truly thought there was water out there." She glanced out at the expanse of sand. "Even now, part of me wants to believe it's there."

"Don't look out there so much," Zack advised her, "and try not to think about it."

"I won't," Aimee promised. "Thank you, Zack." He smiled, one large brown hand coming out to cup her cheek. "I have to go. Bay lost his team. They can't go on."

"What will he do?" Aimee asked in concern.

"Abandon his wagon and equipment and walk the rest of the way."

"He can't do that," she cried.

"He'll be able to make it," Zack said. "He can travel with us."

"But he can't leave his equipment behind," Aimee cried. "It's for mining gold."

"Aimee . . ." Zack's voice sounded exasperated. "We have to think about lives now, not gold."

"This is important to him, Zack," she insisted.

"So are lives."

"You don't understand."

"Apparently not." He swung around and headed back to the team. Aimee climbed out of the wagon. She paused, clinging to the tailgate, her head spinning.

"Are yo' all right?" Loretta asked, hurrying to offer help.

Aimee swayed and straightened, forcing the dizziness away. "I'm fine," she answered, "but, Loretta, we have to help Bay. His equipment can't be left behind."

"What kin we do, Aimee?" Loretta asked.

"We can take it in your wagon. Say yes, please."

"Ah don't mind if Zack don't," Loretta said.

"Thank you, Loretta," Aimee cried. "I'll tell Bay."

"Only thing is . . ." Loretta went on, puzzled, and Aimee waited impatiently. "Why should yo' care what happens to his equipment?"

Aimee stared at her in surprise. "I don't know," she said finally. "It's just that he knows how to find gold. I'm sure of it."

"That don't mean anything to us."

"No, it doesn't," Aimee admitted, "but it's exciting just to think someone will find gold." She turned away before Loretta could question her further about feelings she couldn't understand herself. She didn't love Bay Louden; of that she was sure. There would never be any other man for her but Zack, but she was drawn by the thought of gold. She hurried to Bay's wagon.

"You can take your equipment in our wagon," she said. "I've spoken to Loretta and it's all right."

"Are you sure? It might be too heavy for your team."

"We'll take the chance."

Bay peered at her from behind his glasses. "You're a most extraordinary woman," he said. Aimee didn't know how to answer him. She wondered if Zack had ever thought her extraordinary.

Zack was angered by the arrangement. He fumed and cursed, but he didn't forbid Bay to load his equipment. The wagon was heavier. The wheels sank into the deep sand and required all of them to push. As the hours passed and it seemed they were making little headway, Aimee began to doubt her offer. The night wore away, and once again they slept in the burning heat of the day. Aimee was careful not to look out over the searing dun-colored landscape.

Another night's journey brought them to the Carson River and the foothills of the Sierra Nevada Mountains. They camped under the dry, dusty branches of a cottonwood tree. It was the prettiest sight Aimee had seen in a long time. The two girls walked upstream, and stripping off their itchy, dust-laden clothes, plunged into the cold spring. It was everything Aimee had imagined, heavenly. That night, their thirst for water slaked, their bodies clean of the stinging, salty sand, Zack satisfied another hunger that had been building in them in spite of the hardship of desert travel. Gently, passionately, he made love to Aimee and at last she lay in his arms and slept. The worst was truly behind them. They had only to cross the mountain range of the Sierras and they'd be in California.

Although the new mountain range presented its own set of problems, they tackled them with a light heart and in four days' time had scaled the summit. After the harshness of the arid desert, the greenness of mountain pines, the gleam of snow on distant peaks, the icy spray of a waterfall, the wonder of leaves floating on the surface of a quiet reflecting pool, all delighted their tired spirits. They paused, captivated by the simple beauty of a green mountain pasture, and made love in the first flush of alpenglow.

They journeyed past the foothills and into Sacramento, the heart of the northern goldfields. The ragtag little town hugged the eastern shore of the Sacramento River near the fork where the American River flowed into it. San Francisco was only seventy miles away.

The pitiful little town might have looked dismal and forlorn against the majestic backdrop of fir trees, mountains, and wide blue skies if not for the exuberance of its inhabitants. Tents jauntily nestled beside hastily built plank shacks and log cabins. Colorful, crudely lettered signs named the purposes of some buildings, while others simply threw open their doors, letting their wares spill forth onto steps and porches.

Aimee looked at the canvas-roofed shanties, the muddy streets, and the rough-talking, swaggering men and thought she'd never seen such a wonderful place in her life. They were here, they'd made it through where many hadn't. Where were all the others on that first wagon train? she wondered. Had they made it to Oregon safe and sound? Standing in the shabby, raw little town of Sacramento, she hoped they had. Loretta stood looking around, and her thoughts were similar. Where was Billy, she wondered, and when would she stop looking for him in the face of every man she met?

"I'm much obliged to you for bringing my gear on your wagon," Bay said when they parted. "I won't forget your kindness." He held out his hand.

"We didn't mind," Aimee said. "We wish you luck."

"It's not a matter of luck," he replied. "I think I'll be able to find gold."

"That's what every man here thinks," Zack replied. He hated to disillusion the young man. He'd grown to like him during the long trip west, but he didn't want to offer encouragement for an enterprise that obviously held little guarantee.

Bay seemed unperturbed by Zack's skepticism. "Every man must have a dream before he can begin to make it come true," he answered, and the two shook hands. "I wish you the best with your dream, Mr. Crawford." With a final wave, Bayard Louden shouldered his heavy gear and turned toward the general store. By nightfall he planned to be well out along the river, searching for the best place to stake a claim.

"Where are the hotels?" Aimee asked as Zack headed the team and wagon down the center of town.

"There don't appear to be any," he grunted. "We may have to stay in the wagon for a while."

"Ah was lookin' fo'ward to a bed," Loretta groaned.

"And a proper bath," Aimee said.

"And a piece of steak about this thick," Zack said, holding up his thumb and forefinger. His words reminded Aimee and Loretta that they hadn't eaten for several hours. The thought that they wouldn't have to prepare their supper over a campfire held a great appeal to the two women. Eagerly they looked around for a restaurant. The best they saw were makeshift affairs with tables set up out-of-doors and a long line of men waiting patiently for their turn to eat.

"Let's find a place to leave the wagon and look for a general store," Zack suggested. They drove along a line of covered wagons where other emigrants were setting up housekeeping and found an empty spot under an oak.

"Looks like this'll be home for a while," Loretta said, and Aimee nodded. They walked along the line of makeshift stores, peering in doors; few of them had windows. All were filled with roughly dressed men buying gear for panning gold. If they were having much success, it surely wasn't reflected in their appearance, Aimee thought. Their hair was long and uncut, most had beards, and their clothes were dirty and shabby-looking. Loretta and Aimee picked out food supplies, gasping at the exorbitant prices, yet unable to resist paying for an egg apiece and real coffee, items they hadn't seen much of on the trail.

Zack stood talking to some men lounging against the counter. After a bit he joined Aimee.

"You and Loretta finish getting the things you need," he said, digging money out of his pocket. "Go back to camp without me. I've heard about a ship for sale and I'm going down to the harbor to take a look at it."

"A ship?" Aimee exclaimed. "What do you want with a ship?"

"Sailing ships is the way I make my living."

"I thought you were going to look for gold," Aimee said.

Zack shook his head. "I don't intend to be one of those besotted fools chasing after a pipe dream. I'll meet you back at camp." Without a backward glance he strode away, joining a tall thin man with a rolling walk.

Aimee looked at Loretta, her expression troubled. Zack hadn't asked her opinion about the sailing ship. He'd issued his orders to her and assumed she'd obey and that she'd accept any decision he made. She finished her shopping in tight-lipped resentment.

As they paid for their items, a woman came into the store, leading three small children. They were all shabbily dressed, although their clothes were clean and painstakingly patched. Their eyes were wide and scared-looking in their thin faces. Something about them caught Aimee's attention. The woman approached the storekeeper.

"Excuse me, sir," she said in a low, tentative voice. "We jest arrived on one of the wagon trains and I wondered if I could get some supplies."

"Sure thing," the storekeeper replied. "I sell anything to anyone who's got the money."

The woman twisted her work-hardened hands together. "I haven't got any money," she said in a low voice. "I was hopin' you'd allow me some credit until my husband makes a strike."

"We'd be out of business in no time atall if we give credit to ever' man who come out here expectin' to make a strike."

303

The woman seemed to shrivel a little at his words. Her eyes looked at her children's pinched faces. "Maybe I could do some work of you in exchange for a little food," she persisted. "I'm a hard worker."

"Ain't got no need for a worker," the storekeeper said, "leastways not one with extry baggage." He looked at the woman's children.

"The young 'uns won't get in the way. They'll stay outdoors. I'm a good worker. I'll work harder than any helper you ever had. Please, I need the food for my family." The storekeeper stood looking the woman over, his eyes lingering on her bosom, and Aimee saw the thread of color start to her cheeks. Still, she stood rigid under his inspection, the need to feed her children greater than her pride.

Finally the storekeeper shook his head. "Nah," he said. "I ain't got no need for a scrawny, half-starved woman and her brats. If you ain't got the money to buy, get on outta here."

Shoulders slumping, the woman turned and left the store. Silently the children followed after her. Aimee and Loretta looked at each other and with one accord moved forward. The woman was already walking down the street.

"Ma'am," Aimee called, and slogged through the mud after them. The woman waited, her expression bereft of hope.

"My friend and I couldn't help overhearing you in the store." The woman glanced away, her pride further diminished at the knowledge that someone had heard her beg.

"It was for my kids," she said dully. "We come down off the mountains without much food left. We ain't et in a couple of days."

"Come to our wagon," Loretta said. "We have extra food."

Hope flared in the woman's eyes. "I ain't expectin' charity," she said. "I'll be glad to do whatever work you need to pay you back."

Aimee nodded. "We'll figure out something," she said. "Come on."

Back at the campsite, the woman insisted on helping to build a fire and in no time at all they had a stew bubbling in a kettle. The rich aroma soon filled the campsite. The children sat around the fire, well out of the way, their round eyes fixed on the pot.

"This here is Johnny," the woman said, pointing to the eldest boy, who looked to be around seven years old. "That there is Nancy, and the baby's name is Bobby."

"Hello, Bobby," Aimee said, smiling at the little boy. "How old are you?" Fumbling to get the right number of fingers, he finally held up four chubby fingers.

"He's kind of shy," his mother said. "I guess I never did tell you my name. I'm Ruth Cooper."

Aimee introduced herself and Loretta. "Did you say your husband is out looking for gold?" she asked.

Ruth nodded. "He left this morning."

"But didn't he know you and the children didn't have any food?" Aimee asked, trying not to sound judgmental.

"I . . . I pretended there was plenty," Ruth said. "I made up a packet of the last of the food for him to take back in the hills with him. I figured there wouldn't be no place out there for him to get food. A man needs food on his stomach if he's to work all day long. I figure I can git me a job and earn enough for the kids and me." Ruth shrugged. "Dan wouldna ever gone off and left us if I'd told him the truth. We went through a lot to come out here. He's got to have his chance in the goldfields." Aimee and Loretta were silent, awed by the kind of sacrifice the woman was willing to make for her husband and children.

"Excuse me, ma'am," a voice called, and the women whirled to look at the miner standing at the edge of their campsite. His clothes were dirty and shabby and his face was bearded. "I was passing by and caught a whiff of that stew you're makin'. It kinda reminds me of what my wife used to make back home. I was wondering if you'd be willin' to sell me a bowl. I'd pay you a dollar, two dollars."

Aimee and Loretta looked at each other and then at Ruth. They'd made a large potful and there would be more than enough to give the man a bowl. Aimee nodded and Ruth went to dish it up. The man had his own pan, a wide flat affair.

"It's what I use to pan for gold," he explained, handing over a small sack of gold dust. It was the first gold Aimee had ever seen and she spilled it out into her hand and stood staring at it. It glittered in the sunlight. She pinched it between her fingers, feeling the coarse texture. So this was gold. She closed her finger over the mound of dust, liking the heavy feel of it.

Taking a spoon out of his back pocket, the miner sat down on a nearby rock and began to eat. Soon another miner stopped and talked to the first, then turned toward the campsite.

"Excuse me, ma'am," he said politely, his eyes wavering toward the pot over the fire. "My friend over there said you sold him a pan of that there stew. I was wondering . . ." His voice trailed off. Aimee looked at Loretta and saw the consternation she felt mirrored on her friend's face. Even as they stood undecided, another miner approached, his gold pan at the ready.

"What are we goin' t' do?" Loretta asked. "If we give them all the food, we'll have none left for ourselves."

"Are you plannin' to make another pot, ma'am?" the miner asked. "I'll wait if'n y' are."

Aimee was thinking hard. There were few restaurants, and clearly there was a need for more. She nodded at Loretta, who dipped out a pan of soup for the miner. He paid her in gold dust, as had the first one. While Loretta dipped up another bowl, and still other bowls for the line of men who waited, Aimee turned to Ruth.

"Get some stew for your children and yourself before it's gone," she ordered.

When Ruth had fed her children, she turned back to Aimee. "Do you want me to get you a bowl?" Aimee shook her head, too excited to eat.

"Did you mean it when you said you wanted to work?" she asked, and Ruth shook her head. "I have a plan," Aimee said, glancing at Loretta to be sure she was listening. "Let's cook up some more stew. It's obvious we can sell it. The miners are willing to pay for it. We'll start our own eating place."

"D 'yo' think we could?" Loretta asked doubtfully.

"Of course we could. You've helped your father in his tavern. You know how things are done. Ruth is a good cook. Look how quickly the miners found us."

"We don't have any money to buy a building or enough supplies to get started," Loretta said.

Ruth shrugged, disappointment evident on her face. "I have no money, either."

"I still have some of the ten-dollar gold pieces left," Aimee said. "We'll begin with what we have."

"What if it don't work?" Loretta cautioned. "Yo' won't have anything left."

"I'm willing to take that chance," Aimee cried, her eyes glowing.

"Excuse me, ma'am." A miner approached and the three woman grinned at each other.

"Ruth, you serve up the stew. Loretta and I will get some more supplies. We'll make another pot of stew and maybe some sourdough bread to go with it."

"See if you can get some leavening and I'll make up some real bread," Ruth cried, "and some dried apples for pies. Those ought to sell real well."

By the time Zack made his way back to camp, he had to shove his way through the crowd of miners standing and perched everywhere. Each one held a pan of food. The enticing aroma of apple pie rose on the air.

"Aimee, what's going on?" he demanded, looking around.

"Oh, Zack, isn't it wonderful? We've gone into business. We're opening a restaurant."

"A restaurant?" Zack stared at her as if she'd lost her senses. "You can't do that. I've just bought a ship."

Now it was Aimee's turn to stare. "You mean, just like that, you bought a ship? With what? A ship takes a lot of money."

"I had money. I brought it from back east for this purpose," Zack replied. "I thought we could sail north, up to Seattle. I understand a lot of shipping is going on up there."

"I see," Aimee said. "You're planning on going to Oregon territory after all." Her expression was tight and evasive.

"I'm planning on all of us going. Come on, get your things together. We can leave the wagon here, unless Loretta wants to sell it." He was talking hard and fast, not giving her much time to think it through, he knew, but he was anxious to be gone from the mud and decay man had left upon the land. He wanted the tang of salt air in his lungs. "Loretta . . ." he called.

"Zack," Aimee said, and his name cracked in the air. At her tone, he turned to face her again. She looked tired, he saw. Her gown was smudged, her hair loose in its coil, and her face was red from bending over the flames of the campfire.

"What is it?" he asked, not realizing that his impatience showed in his voice and in his eyes.

"I'll not be going with you," Aimee said in a rush of words. Her eyes snapped with defiance and purpose.

"Why not?" he demanded.

"I have no wish to go to the Oregon territory. I want to stay here."

"Now's a fine time to tell me," Zack exploded.

"If you'd taken the time to talk to me about this, I would have told you how I felt."

"Aimee, don't tell me you're caught up in this gold-fever madness. You can't go out and dig for gold."

"I have no intentions of doing so," she said. "As I mentioned earlier, I've started a business."

Zack laughed, then realized his error, but it was too late. Anger drove him on. "This isn't a business," he said. "It's three women cooking for a bunch of hungry men."

"And being paid for it," Aimee said, drawing herself up. She pulled out the bags of gold the miners had paid her. It was a considerable amount now. Zack looked at the bags and at her animated face.

"You've caught the gold fever," he said. "You may not be going out to pan for it, but you've got the sickness just the same."

"Well, what if I have?" Aimee cried. "What's wrong with wanting to have gold of my own? If Papa had had his own money, he could have paid back his creditors and not have been forced to kill himself. If I'd had gold, I wouldn't have been forced to work as a servant. If Loretta'd had gold she wouldn't have been forced to marry a man she didn't love. If Ruth had had gold she wouldn't have had to beg for food for her children. What's wrong with having gold?"

He couldn't answer her. He looked at her determined face, and fear etched its way into his heart. "Forget about the gold, Aimee," he coaxed. "I have enough money for us both. You'll never want for anything again. I promise you."

"What happens when you don't want me anymore?"

He was startled by her words. "That time will never come," he said. "How can you doubt my feelings for you?"

"I've learned one thing through all this," Aimee said slowly. "People change. You may think you know a person, but you don't. He can become someone else entirely."

"Aimee . . ." Zack grasped her shoulders. "I'm not your father."

"No, you're not," she said, and drew herself up. "I won't be sailing with you, Zack," she said. She saw the anguish in his eyes and she saw the steel of the

309

man. He'd not be changed from his plans by a mere girl.

"You're right, Aimee, when you say people change," he said slowly. "You've changed. You're not the same girl I met back in Webster."

"Thank you," Aimee answered, and he saw she'd taken the words as a compliment. That told him more than anything else. She had changed. The thought frightened and angered him. Clenching his fists, he swung around and headed back toward the harbor.

"Zack?" Aimee called after him. "Zack, don't go. Stay here. We can make our fortunes here." He made no answer and soon his tall figure disappeared from view. A wave of pain washed over Aimee and she clamped her lips together tightly.

"Excuse me, ma'am, is this where I can buy some apple pie?" a miner asked, and Aimee blinked back her tears and turned to face him with a smile.

"This is the right place," she said gaily, and led the way to the cooking fire.

15

She couldn't believe he was gone. She waited, sure he'd come back, but he didn't. At the end of the day she walked down to the harbor, sure she'd find him sulking. She didn't even know the name of the ship he'd bought. One of the idlers thought the *Sea Lady* had exchanged hands in the past few days, but it had headed back upriver to San Francisco that very afternoon. Aimee stood on the dock looking down the muddy, wide river, willing Zack to return. Finally she went back to the campsite. Lines were already forming for the evening meal and she was needed.

The only way she could bear the pain of Zack's departure was to work harder than the others so that by the end of day she fell into her bedroll too exhausted to think or even to cry. The response of the miners to their homey cooking continued, and in a few days they'd amassed enough extra gold to buy planks and saw-horses for tables and benches. They were able to seat thirty diners at a time and often had a line waiting for the second seating.

Loretta and Aimee took the canvas covering off the wagon and tied it off to trees and the wagon bow to form a canopy over the tables. The wagon bed became a storage area for their extra supplies, its tailgate a worktable. Ruth expanded their menu to include pan-fried steaks, johnnycake, and salted fried cakes as well as the stews and pots of beans. She learned a dish that the local Spanish peasants made, adding beans and hot

311

peppers to a pot a beef and serving it with a flat bread of ground corn. She couldn't keep up with the demand for apple pie.

They started out charging a dollar a meal, which seemed exorbitant, but were soon forced by escalating costs to raise their prices to two dollars and finally to five. Bear steak was an unheard-of two dollars and fifty cents a pound, while a lowly head of cabbage cost a dollar. Flour got to be twenty dollars a pound and eggs five dollars a dozen. But Ruth was a careful cook, never wasting anything. The miners paid and the women prospered. At the end of each day they had accumulated two or three hundred dollars in little bags of gold dust.

Even Ruth's children did their part for the burgeoning business, running errands and carrying around town signs printed with the day's menu. Often they ran to the general store to get extra supplies when Ruth ran out. Jackson, the storekeeper, got so used to seeing Aimee or one of the children come that he finally did the very thing he'd thought he never would. He set up a line of credit for the women. They were his best customers, he reasoned. It was also easier to add a few extra dollars to the items he sold them. They were going through such great quantities of supplies, they'd never notice anyway.

Four weeks had passed since Zack left, and they had accumulated several hundred dollars. One day Aimee walked along River Street until she'd found a building site large enough for what she had in mind. It was two blocks farther away from the riverbank and the ragged cluster of buildings that housed Sacramento's other businesses, but for that reason she hoped to get it cheaper. As it was, she paid three hundred dollars. Two weeks later it was worth twice that.

Fearing their reaction, Aimee told Loretta and Ruth of what she'd done. But they were excited at the prospect of being in a proper building and began to plan its layout. It would have a large serving room, a separate kitchen, and three sleeping rooms at the back. They had continued to sleep on the ground under the wagon bed. It would be nice to be in a real bed again. Gleefully they ordered the lumber shipped down from San Francisco and looked around for someone to build their restaurant. That was a harder task than earning the gold to pay for it. Everyone was in the hills searching for gold. One day Loretta came back to camp, her eyes shining, a raggedly dressed man in tow.

"Ah've found someone to do the building," she exclaimed.

Aimee and Ruth stopped what they were doing and looked at the strange, wild-looking man. His eyes were sunken in his thin face and his uncut, matted hair straggled to his shoulders. He looked as if he hadn't the strength to lift hammer and nails. The knuckles of his hands looked swollen and painful.

"This is Jake. He's a miner, but he's back for a spell."

Ruth stepped forward and peered at the man hopefully. "Did you happen to meet up with my husband?" she asked. "His name is Dan Cooper."

Jake shook his shaggy head. "I don't talk to other miners out there. I mind my business and they mind theirs. Less trouble when you strike a claim."

Aimee listened to his words and felt pity for the man. What a lonely existence he must live. Jake seemed to have lost all desire to be around other people. What good would a rich gold claim do him now? The hills had exacted their toll on him. Still, they couldn't afford to hire someone who couldn't do the job. "What we need, Jake," she said, "is someone who'll stay until the building is completed."

"Yep, that's me," he said solemnly.

"But if you're a prospector, you'll want to go back into the hills to hunt for gold."

"Yep, I will," he answered.

"Then why should I believe you'll stay and build our restaurant for us?"

The tall half-wild man focused his gaze on her. "Afore I come to the goldfields, I was a builder. I been in the hills for"—he paused, counting backward—

"nearly a year now," he reckoned. "I run outa supplies and I come back needin' a grubstake. I'll build your eatin' place so's I can buy me what I need to go back into the hills."

"I see," Aimee said, and understood that the man would leave the moment he had the supplies he needed to winter over. She'd have to tell Ruth and Loretta to keep all their extra supplies locked up. "I won't be paying for the job until it's done," she warned.

"As long as you pay me," the man said without a trace of humor.

"All right. We'll hire you. Can you start immediately?"

"Sooner I start, sooner I'll be done and back to prospecting."

"Good," Aimee said. "We'll be needing a big fireplace to cook in. Can you build a decent chimney?"

"Yas'm," Jake answered.

"I'll take you down and show you where we want it built." Aimee untied the apron wrapped around her middle. She still had doubts about the prospector's ability, but he soon dispelled them. His big rough hands knew unerringly how to handle the wood, so that at times it seemed the building was going up of its own accord.

One night as the women sat around one of the makeshift tables under the canvas covering talking, a man approached them.

"I'm sorry, we're already closed for the night," Aimee said, glancing up at the tall figure. A lantern hung in a tree nearby was the only illumination and Aimee caught her breath, hope flaring. The man shifted his weight from one foot to the other and now his face was in the light.

"I was wondering if you knew anything about my wife and young 'uns," he said. "Her name's—"

"Daniel, oh, Daniel," Ruth cried, leaping up and running to throw herself against the tall figure. He wrapped his arms around her waist and held her tightly, burying his face in her neck. Aimee and Loretta could hear Ruth's sobs of joy. "You've come back," she cried. "I've been so worried."

"I worried about you too," he said, "you and the young 'uns. How are they?"

"They're fine, just fine," Ruth cried, hugging him again. "They're sleepin' now. I just put 'em to bed."

"Don't wake 'em up. I'll see them in the morning." He reached out a hand and touched his wife's hair in a particularly gentle way that conveyed all his love for her. "Have you been makin' it all right?"

Ruth nodded happily. "We came to work for Miss Bennett and we've been doing just fine. There's plenty to eat and a place to sleep. What about you? There was so little food to send with you."

"I ran out two weeks ago," Daniel Cooper said. "I've been livin' on whatever wild game I could catch up in the hills. Finally I couldn't take it no more, not seeing you and the kids, not knowing if you was goin' hungry too."

"You shouldn't have worried about us." Ruth drew back and looked at him, running her hands over his shoulders and down his ribs to his waist. "You've lost weight. You must be hungry now. Come on and let me make you something to eat." She led the newcomer to the table where Loretta and Aimee sat.

"This is my husband, Daniel," she said needlessly. One work-reddened hand gripped the sleeve of his shirt and her thin face fairly glowed. With a start, Aimee realized that Ruth must once have been very pretty. Aimee and Loretta talked to Dan Cooper while Ruth rushed about the campfire, warming leftover stew and laying slabs of bear steak to sizzle in a pan of hot grease. Aimee thought she'd never seen a man eat so much food as Dan Cooper put away, and when at last he pushed himself away from the table, groaning and holding his stomach, Ruth pressed a piece of apple pie on him.

"Maybe later," he said, his gaze catching hers. Ruth colored and glanced away, and Aimee felt a surge of envy sweep through her. She would have given anything if the man seated at the table were Zack. A glance at Loretta's face told her she was having similar thoughts about Billy.

"Well, what are you planning to do now, Mr. Cooper?" she asked. She saw Ruth look at him sharply.

"I don't know," he said in a low voice. "I know there's gold up there. Other men are findin' it. At times I felt like it was right there, just within my grasp, if I only knew where to look."

"Are you planning to go back?" Aimee held her breath and waited.

"I ain't rightly sure," he said. "I got my wife and kids to think on. It might take me months, even years to find gold. I got to take care of my family. I just don't know." He raised his head and looked at his wife. "I got to thinkin' when I was out there, half-starved and half-crazed with worry, that maybe we ought to go on back home and take up farmin'. We ain't ever gonna git rich at it, but we sure wouldn't starve."

"Whatever you want to do is fine with me," Ruth answered, sitting beside her husband, her hand lying beside his on the table.

Aimee felt concern ripple through her. She'd just made arrangements for a real building for their restaurant. It was taking every penny they had. She was depending on Ruth's cooking to continue drawing the miners. She took a deep breath. "If you're concerned for your wife and children, don't be," she said. "With the restaurant, there's plenty of food. Your children won't be sleeping on the ground too many more nights."

"Do you want to go back to Maryland?" Daniel asked.

"I want to do what you want," Ruth answered steadfastly.

Daniel ran a weary hand through his hair. "It's harder than I figured, and I ain't a man to shirk hard work," he said. "I stand in water all day, bending over the streambed coaxing a few little specks of yellow gold out of the sand. My hands get numb from the cold water and at night they ache somethin' fierce." Ruth put her own hand over his as if to take away the pain. Aimee saw that the joints were swollen and red, much as Jake's had been.

"Don't go back," Ruth urged. "I don't need to be rich."

"But you might find gold the next time," Aimee exclaimed. "You can't give up so soon."

"It don't hardly make sense to go back. I didn't find enough gold to buy food to take with me."

"We can give you food," Aimee said. "We have plenty of supplies. Every week or two you could come down to see your family and stock up again."

"You'd do that?" Ruth asked in amazement. "You'd stake him until he found gold?"

Aimee shrugged. "Why not? I need you for my restaurant."

"Still, you don't have to do this," Ruth cried. "You've been so good to us already."

"Without you, I couldn't have opened a restaurant," Aimee said. "It's been a fair trade. Is it a deal then?"

Ruth and Daniel looked at each other. "I'd like to give it a try for a while longer," he said, and reluctantly Ruth nodded her agreement.

"Good," Aimee said, and yawned widely. "I guess it's time I went to bed," she said.

"Me too." Loretta picked up her cue. "Ah got up awfully early this morning." Ruth gave them a grateful glance. The two girls walked off to their beds under the wagon. The last glimpse they had of Dan and Ruth Cooper was of the couple making their way across the campsite to their own wagon, their arms around each other. Aimee bit her lips against a wave of loneliness for Zack and crawled under the covers. Where was he, she wondered, and was he ever coming back to her?

"That was a kind thing you did for Ruth's husband," Loretta said. "You have a tender heart, Aimee."

Although the words had been meant as a compliment, they angered Aimee. "Not really," she answered.

"I do need Ruth for the restaurant. I couldn't let them go back east. Who would cook for us?" She could hear Loretta's sigh.

"Why don't you want anyone to know how kind you are?" Loretta asked.

"Because I'm not. I'm going to make my fortune here, Loretta. I'm going to get so much gold that no one can ever tell me what to do again. I'm never going to need anyone again."

"You mean the way you don't need Ruth?" Loretta asked sarcastically. "What about Zack?"

"Especially not Zack."

"You mean you don't care that he's gone?"

"No." They both knew she lied. "Go to sleep now. Morning comes too early as it is."

Loretta said nothing more and soon her even breathing indicated she was sleeping. Aimee lay awake staring at the starlit sky, remembering the times Zack had made love to her beneath its canopy. "Oh, Zack," she whispered, "why did you go away?" Rolling over, she buried her face in the covers and willed herself to stop thinking about him, to stop needing him. Sleep was a long time in coming.

A few days later, another miner returned from the fields and he too had suffered bad luck. Bayard Louden was a different man from the one who had left a few short weeks earlier. He stumbled down the street, peering around as if he didn't know where he was.

"Bay!" Aimee cried, running to take his arm.

"Aimee?" he asked in bewilderment, squinting at her. His glasses were gone, his hair was long and unkempt, his clothes mud-spattered and rumpled, as though he'd slept in them every night since she'd last seen him. He wore his arm in a sling and his face bore the lingering traces of cuts and bruises.

"Bay, what happened to you?" Aimee asked.

He shrugged and let her lead him to a stump. "I found gold, Aimee," he said. His eyes were feverishly bright. "I found a rich claim."

"That's wonderful," Aimee cried in delight, then

searched his face. "What happened to you? Why are you bruised? You look as if you were beaten."

"I was," he answered. "Claim jumpers robbed me, beat me, and left me for dead. They didn't know how tough they grow 'em back in Kentucky."

"You're lucky to be alive."

"Yes, I am," Bay said cheerfully. "They wrecked my cradle, but I rebuilt it. I've got it hidden out there. I just came back for more food."

"Come back to my wagon," Aimee invited.

He shook his head. "I can't. I have to get my gear and go back out there." His eyes looked spooked in his pinched face.

"We've got a pot of hot stew," Aimee urged.

"Stew, hot stew?" he mumbled, and she sensed he was ready to collapse in the middle of the road.

"It's not far." Gently she tugged at him, and to her relief, he followed.

"Bayard," Loretta cried with delight when Aimee led him into camp.

" 'Lo, Retta," he slurred, and slumped down on the bench at one of the tables.

"Ruth, quick, bring some coffee and a bowl of that soup," Aimee ordered. She feared he would pass out before they'd had a chance to feed him something. She was alarmed at his condition. With Loretta's help Aimee managed to get some coffee down him and he seemed to rally enough to spoon some of the stew down before he began to weave in his seat again.

"Let's get him to a bed," Aimee said. Each girl took a side and half-dragged, half-carried him to one of their bedrolls. They were appalled at how wasted he was. Obviously he'd hardly eaten since leaving them.

"Poor man," Loretta said, smoothing his dark matted hair off his forehead. She went back to the fire for a pan of warm water and gently bathed his face and hair. He slept late into the afternoon, waking only when the children called to each other around the campfire. With a start he sat up and looked around.

"Feeling better?" Aimee asked, handing him a cup of coffee.

He swallowed down the hot liquid and nodded. "I think I'll make it now," he said, and got to his feet, gathering up his floppy hat. "I'd best be on my way."

"Where are you going?" Aimee asked.

"I've got to get back out to the goldfields. I don't want anyone to jump my claim."

"Bay, must you? You've already been robbed and beaten. What will happen if you go back?"

"I'll get me a gun. Next time I'll be ready for them."

"What about your gear and your equipment? They've taken everything."

"I'll get credit from Jackson, just until I can mine my claim."

"He won't give credit, Bay."

"He has to. You don't understand, Aimee, I found gold. I held it right in my hands, the richest claim you ever saw."

"But if they took over your claim—" Aimee began.

"They only claimed the end of the run. I know where it begins. I may have found the mother lode."

"Mother lode?" It was what every miner dreamed about. They talked of little else around the tables of Aimee's restaurant.

"It must be a rich vein, Aimee. I'll be rich. I'm going back. If Jackson won't give me supplies, I'll go back without them." He jumped to his feet.

"Stay here, Bay, at least for a little while, until your arm has healed," Aimee urged.

"There's no time. You don't understand. I'm close, so close. I know I'll find the source my next trip out. I have to get back before someone else finds it." He paced anxiously, then whirled. "I have to go," he cried restlessly.

"Wait, Bay," Aimee said. "You can't go out there without food and supplies. I have no money left. We've started building a real restaurant and it's taken all our gold, but I have this." She took the brooch off her dress and handed it to him. It was the same brooch she'd once given to Abner Horn to bury her father, the one Zack had returned that fateful night she left Webster. It was the last thing she had left of that old life, but Bay was her friend. He'd die of exposure and starvation if he went back out in the hills without proper gear.

"I can't take this, Aimee," he said.

"I insist you do," she said. "When you strike it rich, you can buy me a new one." He stood looking down at the gold and precious stones. She hadn't said "if," she'd said "when." She had faith in him. It was one of the few acts of kindness he'd received since leaving his bride and home.

"You've helped me once," he said, eyes lowered. "I won't take your pin unless you agree to a partnership between us. You take half of whatever I find."

Aimee gasped. "I couldn't. You're the one who must do the searching and digging."

"Without your brooch, I couldn't buy the food that will enable me to keep looking."

"All right," Aimee said finally. Chances were he wouldn't find the gold he sought. Too many men were coming back empty-handed. At least he could eat decently.

"Thank you, Aimee," he said. "You'll not be sorry for your actions this day." Before she could say more, he was gone, hurrying down the path toward Jackson's general store. Aimee sighed, thinking that if anyone had the gold fever, Bayard Louden was a perfect example of it. Was that the way Zack saw her? He'd accused her of the same thing. No, Aimee thought, shaking her head. She wasn't chasing pipe dreams. She was a businesswoman, and there was nothing wrong with wanting your business to succeed. She turned back to the campsite and the line of miners waiting to be served.

"I've been thinking," Aimee said, stirring the kettle of stew that was a part of their daily menu. The miners never seemed to get enough of it. "If we used a little less meat and thickened this with a little more flour, we could save some money."

Ruth glanced up. "I'm already watering the stew as you requested. If we put in any less meat and vegetables it won't fill 'em up enough."

"We'll just give them bigger portions of bread," Aimee said.

"We could just make stone soup," Loretta said, "and then look at the money we'd save. We wouldn't even have to buy meat and vegetables."

Aimee glanced at her sharply and Loretta looked away. It seemed they disagreed more and more on how to run things.

"We have to cut costs where we can," Aimee said. "We'll be moving into our new building soon and we'll want new tables and better dishes, maybe even tablecloths."

"Out here in the goldfields?" Loretta asked.

"Why not? The miners are willing to pay for the comforts of home. Some of them are getting mighty homesick now."

"Doesn't it bother you to play on that homesickness?" Loretta asked, her head cocked to one side.

"No," Aimee answered shortly. "We're giving them something they want and need."

"Do they need whiskey and the likes?" Loretta demanded. Aimee looked up in surprise. "Ah heard you telling Jackson to order in whiskey."

"Some men like a drink with their supper," Aimee answered, "and I see no reason why we can't supply it to them instead of having them eat supper with us, then bolt off to spend the evening in one of the saloons."

"So what we're really opening is a saloon?" Loretta demanded.

"Oh, my," Ruth declared. "I had no idea. I'm not sure Dan would want the children living behind a tavern. I know he wouldn't want me working in one."

"It's not a tavern, Ruth," Aimee defended herself. "One half of the building will be a restaurant and the

322

other half will serve drinks. You won't even have to go into the other side if you don't want to."

"It would still be a tavern—" Ruth began.

Aimee whirled to face her, eyes blazing angrily. "Do you think I'm asking you to do something that's wrong? I'm a banker's daughter. Don't you think my father would be appalled if he knew? But these are different times, it's a different place from the one we grew up in. We have to be different in order to survive and get ahead here."

"I'm just not sure if I can go against my teaching," Ruth said bleakly.

Aimee sighed in exasperation. "If you feel so strongly about not working there, then I won't hold it against you," she said. "I release you from any obligation you might feel toward me for feeding you and your family."

"Aimee," Loretta cried, appalled at her words.

Ruth hung her head and turned away. "I couldn't do that to you," she murmured. "You've been kinder to us than anyone since we left home. I'll keep on working for you, Aimee. Maybe it won't be so bad."

"It won't, Ruth, you'll see," Aimee coaxed her. "You can stay in the restaurant side. You don't even have to go by the saloon. You'll see, Ruth. In the end, we'll be happy we did this."

Ruth turned back to her cooking and there was only Loretta, her gaze direct and accusing. "That wasn't real nice of yo', Aimee," she said quietly. Although Loretta now spoke like a lady and with few mistakes most of the time, Aimee noticed she lapsed back into her country brogue when upset. Now Loretta was upset, her eyes snapping, her cheeks bright with color.

Aimee sighed. "I didn't force Ruth to continue with us."

"Yo' shamed her to it, which is worse."

"That's not true," Aimee flared. "She can leave anytime she wants. I'm sure I can find others willing to cook for me."

"Can yo' find another partner?" Loretta snapped.

Aimee stared at her in consternation. Loretta didn't mean it. She was just trying to scare Aimee.

"Don't tell me it goes against your teachings to work in a tavern." Aimee sneered angrily. She saw the shock and hurt on Loretta's face and wished she could recall the words.

"Ah just thought partners talked before they did something," Loretta answered carefully. "You never even asked me what Ah wanted to do."

"I'm sorry," Aimee said meekly; then anger flared again. "If I had talked to you, you would have said no. You always fight with me about every decision."

"That's true," Loretta conceded. "There's a passel of things we don't see eye to eye on. You've changed since you got to California. Sometimes it seems like Ah hardly know you anymore."

"I just want to get my share like everyone else around here," Aimee said sullenly.

"What is your share?" Loretta asked, and went quietly away.

Aimee sat thinking; then defiance spiraled through her and she sprang to her feet. "As much as I can get," she yelled after Loretta's departing figure.

It seemed Loretta avoided her after that. Even gentle Ruth's gaze seemed censorious. Aimee ignored them both. The restaurant was making money. The day to move into the new building arrived and in the excitement old hurts were forgotten. Eagerly the children ran in and out of the room they would share with their mother. Ruth admonished them sharply when they entered the long bare room that would be the saloon. By nightfall they had things in order and served their first meal in the new dining room. The old makeshift tables had been set up until the new ones arrived from San Francisco. By the next evening, Aimee had the rough plank bar set up in the other room.

"Who's going to tend it for you?" Loretta asked, standing in the doorway, hands on hips.

"I haven't found anyone yet," Aimee admitted. She didn't trust the idlers that hung around the wharves.

They'd soon drink up her profit. "I figured I could do it until we found someone reliable."

"Do you know how?" Loretta persisted.

"It can't be that hard," Aimee said. "I'll make out."

"Ah swear Ah never saw anyone with so much pride," Loretta snapped. "Can't you ever ask for help?"

"Would you help me in here?" Aimee asked in dismay.

Loretta nodded and grinned. "We're partners, ain't . . . aren't we?"

"I thought you were against the saloon," Aimee persisted.

"It's not the saloon," Loretta said, sauntering over to lean against the bar. "It's the fear that Ah might end up back where Ah started."

"That can't happen for either of us, even if we wanted it to," Aimee said softly.

"Are you sorry?"

Aimee considered her question, thinking back over all they'd been through. "No, I'm glad I'm here," she said finally, and Loretta smiled.

"Me too," she said. "Ah got to thinking: if a banker's daughter can work in a saloon and still be a lady, then Ah can too."

"Thank you, Loretta," Aimee cried, clasping her hand across the plank bar. She was glad their misunderstanding was over.

"It's just till we find someone to do the job for us."

"Agreed," Aimee said. "We'll take turns serving food and tending bar. You don't believe me yet, Loretta, but we're going to be rich ladies, and soon."

"It's the 'lady' part I want the most," Loretta said.

Aimee laughed. "Sometimes yo' fairly simple, Loretta," she mocked gaily. "Don't yo' know yo' cain't be one without t'other?" Their laughter mingled.

"What're we going to call this place?" Loretta asked, looking around proudly.

Aimee smiled. She'd known Loretta would come

around. "What do you think about the Golden Promise?"

"The Golden Promise Saloon and Café," Loretta tested it. "Ah like it."

"Here's to the Golden Promise," Aimee said, pouring two glasses of whiskey. She'd never drunk any before. The girls clicked their glasses and swallowed the fiery contents. Aimee gasped and began to cough. Loretta slapped her on the back.

"Are you all right?" she asked anxiously. Aimee met her gaze and they began to laugh like old times.

"Excuse me, ma'am." A man stood in the doorway, his hat in his hand. "Is this here saloon open for business?"

"Yes, it is," Aimee called. "Welcome to the Golden Promise. Step right up to the bar."

In the weeks that followed, the Golden Promise was a bigger success than even Aimee had anticipated. Their income doubled and then some. They were forced to scour the town for help, hiring weary-faced emigrant women to help serve in the restaurant, and for the bar, disillusioned gold miners waiting to return home. "Gobackers," the other miners called them, and they seldom lasted long, leaving as soon as they had earned passage on a ship east.

The tables and chairs came in on one of the ships that plied the muddy Sacramento River, carrying supplies from San Francisco to the riverport towns. Aimee had long since given up going down to the docks to look for the *Sea Lady*. Zack had said he was going to the Oregon coast. He wouldn't be back. At times she sat mulling over his abandonment of her, picking at a wound that refused to heal. How easily he'd left. Nearly three months had passed and the pain was as fresh as if it were yesterday. In spite of his vows, it was obvious he'd simply grown tired of her. He was probably happy she'd chosen to stay in Sacramento. Where was he now? Was there another woman somewhere, loving him and believing in him as she had done?

Aimee threw herself into the business of earning as much gold as she could. More lumber was ordered, this time for a two-story addition to the restaurant. She was going to have a hotel. Her plans moved along so rapidly that Loretta could barely get her breath.

"Why do we have to build a hotel?" Loretta asked. "The town already has one." They were in Aimee's room. Loretta glanced around. She'd never been in this room when it wasn't meticulously neat. She wasn't sure how Aimee managed to do it all. Even as they talked, she was bent over a small table that served as a desk. Quickly she totted up a column of figures and entered the amount in the right-hand column, relishing the neat little zeros that added up to a six-figure income. They now had over fifty thousand dollars in gold dust. Clear profit.

"The town needs another one," she answered, rubbing at her eyes wearily. She'd labored over the books all morning. She'd soon discovered that Jackson was padding their bill, and only by her diligent efforts had she been able to keep this thievery to a minimum. She longed to buy her supplies from someone else, but he seemed to have a monopoly on all the goods that came in. Aimee sighed. Opening a hotel now, so soon after arriving in Sacramento, was a daring step for them. She wasn't sure they had the money for it. Still, a hotel would bring in double the profit the Golden Promise made now. It was worth the risk.

"What's this?" Loretta picked up a pouch with several small bags inside. "It's heavy," she said, balancing the bag in her hands.

Aimee glanced up. "It's gold dust some of the miners asked me to keep until they come back to town. They have some sort of superstition that it's bad luck to take gold back to the mines with them. I'd better lock it away." She rose and crossed to the loose floorboard near the foot of her bed. Taking out a set of keys she unlocked the metal box hidden in the recess and placed the gold inside.

"Aren't you afraid you'll be robbed some night?" Loretta asked.

"I've thought about it. That's why I keep a gun beneath my pillow."

"So that's why you had Daniel Cooper teach you to shoot the last time he was home."

"That's right." Aimee replaced the board. A thought came to her. "Isn't it about time for Dan to come visit his family again?"

"Ah believe so," Loretta said. "Ruth's been humming a lot the past few days."

"Dan's been searching for gold some time now, hasn't he?" Aimee mused.

"He hasn't had much luck," Loretta sighed. "Poor Ruth. She misses him something terrible."

"She'd probably like to have him around all the time, wouldn't she?" Aimee asked.

"Ah expect so," Loretta answered, then glanced at Aimee. "What've you got in mind," she asked suspiciously.

"We need someone reliable to tend the bar," Aimee mused. "If Daniel were to take over the job, he could be with his family more."

"Ah don't think he would," Loretta said doubtfully. "Remember what a fuss Ruth made when you first opened the saloon."

"Yes, and I also remember how she changed her mind," Aimee said thoughtfully.

"Ah remember how you went about changing her mind." Loretta glared at Aimee. "You're not planning anything like that again, are you?"

"Trust me, Loretta." Aimee stood up and brushed the dust from her dark skirt. In the past few weeks she'd ordered new gowns for them all from San Francisco. Though not as elegant as the gowns she'd once worn, the plain dimity was stylish and feminine. She crossed to the small mirror hanging above her chest and tucked an errant strand into the simple bun she wore.

328

"Is Ruth unhappy with us?" she asked, and saw Loretta shake her head slowly.

" 'Course not," Loretta said. "Ah just don't want to do anything to make her unhappy."

"Neither do I," Aimee said, and with a swish of her skirts headed to the door. It seemed liké she couldn't sit still for very long, Loretta thought, and followed, her expression troubled.

Things continued to go well for them. By staying open extra hours and cutting cost every place possible, Aimee had the money to pay for the lumber for the hotel by the time it arrived at the river dock.

Johnny Cooper came running with the news. "The man says you're to come down and tell him where you want it delivered," the boy said breathlessly.

"I'm too busy, Johnny," Aimee said distractedly. Jackson had sent them bad meat and she'd spent the morning down at the general store arguing with him over it. Then she'd returned to a chimney that wouldn't draw properly. She knelt before the offending fire-place and with a broom handle reached up to dislodge whatever was causing the problems. Soot spilled down the chimney and out onto the floor, covering Aimee's face and arms and gown. Taking a breath to calm her frustration, she glanced at the boy, who tried hard to stifle his giggles at her appearance. His merry eyes made Aimee smile at herself.

"Go down to the boat and tell the captain I said you're to show them."

"That's what I told him," Johnny said disgustedly, "but he said he had to see the owner."

"All right," Aimee sighed, and shaking out her skirt, hurried to wash away the grime. "While I'm down at the docks, I'll look for someone to come clean the chimney," she called to Ruth. She hurried down the dusty street after Johnny. Lately it seemed no one could do anything without her there to lead him by the hand. Crossly she wiped at the perspiration forming on her brow. The days were long and hot now, reminding her of the awful trek across the desert. It seemed a lifetime ago. The hills were a green shimmer in the distance.

Like most young boys his age, Johnny was fascinated by the ships that docked at the wharf and could name every one of them and their captain on sight. This ship was a new one to him, although he thought he'd met its captain once. Unerringly he led the way along the line of sailing sloops and cargo vessels to the trim sailing ship sitting near the end. Aimee followed, her eyes automatically picking out the names of the vessels they passed. When they paused before the trim white ship, she read the gold scroll along its bow and glanced away. Then her mind registered the fact of what she'd read and she looked again. It was the *Sea Lady,* Zack's ship.

"Ahoy," Johnny called. He was proud of the nautical terms he'd picked up around the wharf.

"Ahoy, mate," a familiar voice called out, and Aimee put up an arm to shield her eyes from the sun. She could make out a tall, lean figure standing in the rigging. Heart pounding, she watched as he climbed down and slid over the side of the ship to the dock.

"Hello, Aimee," he said, studying her face as if comparing it with his memories. He seemed taller than she remembered, and his dark hair waved across his forehead in an achingly familiar way.

"Hello, Zack," Aimee whispered, one hand at her throat. How often she'd dreamed of this, his return. How often she'd thought of the things she would say to him, and now she stood silent, mesmerized by his dark glance.

He wanted to pull her into his arms and take her here on the docks. The sweetness of her had lingered with him every moment he'd been gone. He'd known when he sailed away that he would return. She'd wooed him back as surely as a siren of some mythical tale. For months he'd carried cargo from one port to another, and in each one he'd searched for a woman to make him forget her. None would do. None could compare with her beauty and spirit.

He looked at her flushed face, at the smear of soot across one cheek, the gray eyes glowing with some inner light, the glorious hair, twisted into a knot with golden tendrils clinging to her temples. The smattering of freckles across her nose was fading now and her skin was the color of ivory once more. There was a certain natural elegance to her in spite of the calico gown she wore. Its sleeves were rolled up to the elbow, exposing her slim arms.

"How are you?" he asked. The husky intimacy of his voice and the caring she read in his eyes were nearly her undoing. She'd vowed when he returned she would be aloof, restrained, untouched by his charms. Yet here she stood silent and blushing before him. He smiled, his teeth flashing white against his tanned face. His glance held all the magic it always had. Before she knew what she was about to do, she drew back her hand and slapped him. She saw the surprise on his face before she whirled and stalked across the dock.

"Why did you do that?" he yelled after her.

"You went away and left me. You promised you'd never do it again and you did," Aimee yelled back. Her arms were akimbo on her hips, her eyes flashing.

"You could have come with me," Zack exclaimed.

"I wanted to stay."

"And I wanted to go." His words struck a chord of fear in her heart. He took a step forward, his hands out as if to beseech her to understand. "I told you, I'm a sailor, Aimee. It's what I grew up with, what I've always done, all I've ever wanted to do. I can't change what I am and what I want from life. I traveled across this country trying to find out who I am, but I can't get the feel of the sea out of my head."

"So you chose sailing over me," Aimee said bitterly.

"I wish I could make such a simple choice," Zack said, and she heard some of the torment in his voice. "I'm caught between the two of you. I can't leave the sea and do something else, and yet the memory of you won't let me go."

"Is this how it will always be with us?" she asked.

"I hope not. I came back to you because I couldn't bear never to see you again." He walked toward her until he was scant inches away. She could feel his breath on her face. His eyes were dark and warm as they looked into hers.

"I came back to ask you to marry me, Aimee," he said softly. She stared at him, while all around swirled the noise and movement of the busy dock. Men cursed and shouted to one another as they heaved barrels of supplies on their shoulders. Mules neighed in protest at the loads they were expected to pull. Bails and crates of foodstuffs, and even Aimee's lumber, were dumped on the plank wharf with jarring thumps.

"I'm sorry," Zack said. "This wasn't the way I'd planned it. I had in mind something more romantic."

"This is romantic enough," she said, and he could see the glowing lovelights in her eyes.

"Aimee," he groaned, and took her in his arms. Eagerly she raised her mouth for his kiss, while the roustabouts and sailors whistled and called to them. "I love you, Aimee," Zack whispered hoarsely.

"I love you, Zack." Her face was alight, her eyes shining as she drew back. Taking his hand, she pulled him along the dock. "Come with me," she urged gaily. "I have something to show you." He'd moved her by his need for the sea, but she had needs too, and she had to show him what held her here. Perhaps when he saw all she'd accomplished, he'd forget about sailing. They could make their fortune here. She led him through the streets to her restaurant and stood waiting while he looked at the big hand-painted sign bearing the name.

"Golden Promise," he read. "Is this yours?" He looked at her in amazement.

Aimee nodded happily. "Mine and Loretta's. What do you think about it?"

"How did you manage to do all this?"

Aimee laughed delightedly. He was as astonished as she'd wanted him to be. "It's the gold dust, Zack. The miners are so hungry for decent food and a place to have a drink and relax and talk about their gold that they'll pay almost any amount. Come inside. I want to show you everything. Loretta will be so surprised to see you." In her enthusiasm, she didn't notice the scowl on his face.

"Zack," Loretta cried when she spied him, and ran from behind the bar to throw herself into his arms. Amid much laughter and talk, Zack hugged her.

"What do you think about it?" Loretta asked, sweeping her arm around to include the long narrow room with the bar at one end.

"You two are amazing. You've done more than many men could have."

"Only because the men are too busy digging for gold to want to stay here and cook and serve," Aimee said modestly.

"Aimee did most of it," Loretta spoke up. "She's like a whirlwind, never happy with the way things are. Before Ah can get used to something, she's off with another idea. Now we're going to build a hotel."

Zack glanced at Aimee. "That's what all the lumber is for?" She nodded. He glanced away, and for the first time she was aware of his reserve. Oh, he'd said all the right things, but there was a restraint about him.

"Zack?" she said tentatively. His smile dispelled her unease. He was pleased by what they'd accomplished, she told herself. His strong brown hand closed over hers.

"Show me the rest," he urged, and she did, although her pride was diminished somewhat. Aimee introduced him to Ruth and the Cooper children, showed him the dining room and kitchen. He peered up the chimney she had been poking in earlier and withdrew, his head and faced dusted with soot. Laughing, Aimee wiped away the blackness and their laughter ended in a kiss that created an urgency in them both.

Shyly she led him to her room, closing and locking the door behind them. Once, long ago, when she was

333

a different person, he'd come to her bedroom. He'd been a stranger to her then; he wasn't now. Eagerly she went into his arms.

"Aimee," he gasped against her cheek. Hungrily his lips claimed hers. "I missed you. I couldn't get you out of my mind. No matter what I was doing, you were there, pulling me back to you."

"Every day I went down to the dock, searching for you." His teeth skimmed across the softness of her chin and up to one delicate earlobe. Shivers ran through her. "I couldn't believe you'd really gone away and left me."

"I was a fool," he cried.

"It doesn't matter now, you're back."

"Aimee . . ." He drew away from her. "I'm not back to stay." His dark eyes met hers and Aimee felt a chill run through her at the message she saw there.

"You came back because you love me. You said you couldn't stay away."

"I couldn't," Zack said hoarsely, his hands gripping her arms. "I love you more than I thought it possible to love someone."

"Then stay with me, Zack. Stay, and together we'll have more gold than either of us ever dreamed about."

"It's not the gold I want, Aimee. It's you and my ship."

"I see." Aimee shrugged herself out of his embrace. "You choose your ship over me."

"Didn't you hear any of the things I said on the dock? I choose that way of living over this one," Zack said patiently. "I can't stay here in these gold-mining towns and be part of the madness."

"Madness?" Aimee exclaimed.

"Don't you see, Aimee? This greed for gold distorts men, it changes them. These people are grasping for a dream that will never come true for most of them, and in the meantime, lives are lost. Men shoot other men just for wrong glances or in hopes of stealing claims or for any number of other reasons that don't make sense. I don't want to stay here and become a part of it."

"You don't have to. You can help me with the tavern and the new hotel. I need a man I can trust to oversee things. You wouldn't have to be a part of the gold mining."

"Don't you see, Aimee? If you stay here around the gold camps, you *are* a part of it. You depend on the poor devils who come to town lonely and in need of a good time. Your little empire is built on the promise that an ever-increasing amount of gold will be taken out of the ground. One day, when the gold is gone, your empire will crumble."

"Perhaps," Aimee said coldly, his words striking fear in her, "but in the meantime, I'm not afraid to build an empire and I'm not a hypocrite. You and your ship are just as dependent on the goldfields. You bring the supplies the miners need. It's inescapable. Our lives are touched by the gold whether we're out there in the hills digging for it or selling our services for it."

Zack sighed wearily. "I won't be staying," he said. "I won't ask you to go with me this time. I wish you well, Aimee." His hand was on the doorknob and then he was gone. She could hear his boots against the plank floor.

"Zack," she whispered, then bit hard on her lip to keep from calling out again. She could taste the blood, and sobs shook her slender body, but she stayed where she was. Pride, stubborn pride. That's all it was. He couldn't bend for her. She must give up everything for him. Well, she wouldn't. She thought of the last few months, when she'd worked longer and harder than anyone else to make the restaurant a success. She wouldn't quit now. She wouldn't.

That night, as she moved from the restaurant to the saloon and back again, serving meals, pouring drinks, joking with the customers, and dealing with anything else that needed her attention, she kept her mind deliberately numb. It wasn't until a lull after supper that Loretta unknowingly undid her rigid control.

"It was nice to see Zack again," she said. "Where is he?"

"I don't know," Aimee said, busying herself behind the bar. At her strained tone, Loretta glanced up.

"Did you have a fight?" she asked softly.

Miserably Aimee nodded. "He's so stubborn and bullheaded and—"

"Ah know. You've told me so before."

"He won't stay here."

"Ah didn't expect he would," Loretta said.

"I offered to let him oversee the new hotel and to help us run things, but he refused."

"Zack's not the kind of man to live off a woman's earnings."

"He wouldn't be. I really need him," Aimee exclaimed.

"He couldn't be an errand boy for you, Aimee. It'd go against his nature. You wouldn't want him to be. Zack's a strong-willed man."

"And I'm a strong-willed woman," Aimee flared.

"Yes, you are. That's why you and Zack clash as much as you do."

Aimee's shoulders slumped. "So what's the answer, Loretta?"

"Well, a ship's captain ain't . . . isn't always around. Seems like his lady'd have to do something while he's gone. In the meantime you ought to remind him of all the reasons why you love him, so's he'll know you'll be waiting when he comes home again."

"Oh, he's too stubborn to see that," Aimee declared petulantly.

"Ah expect you could persuade him, if anyone could." Loretta grinned. "The *Sea Lady* doesn't sail until tomorrow morning."

Relief flooded through Aimee as she considered everything Loretta had said. With a grin, she yanked off the apron covering her gown. "Don't wait up for me," she cried gaily. "I'll be gone the rest of the night."

"Ah kind of figured that," Loretta said wistfully,

and Aimee thought of Billy. Would there ever come a time when Loretta forgot about him? Could Aimee forget about Zack? Never, she realized, and gave not another thought to Loretta and Billy. She hurried through the noisy streets. She'd never been out in them at night, and she was surprised at the brawling, drunken men who moved restlessly from one saloon to another. In the sedate atmosphere of the Golden Promise, the miners had behaved like gentlemen. When they hadn't, she'd had them ousted by Simon, a 'gobacker.'

She passed the doors of the Mother Lode, one of the noisier saloons. Wilson Lundy owned it, and Aimee had heard rumors of his underhanded dealings. Most people steered clear of him and the hard-eyed men in his hire. Still, his saloon was busy, and out of curiosity, Aimee glanced in.

Women danced on the bars, their petticoats held high as they wildly kicked out their legs. Clusters of boisterous men grabbed for their ankles, and when they succeeded in catching one, yanked the dancer down into their arms. The girls seemed not to mind. With much laughter they submitted to the miners' sloppy kisses. Other men sat at tables gambling, and at one end of the smoky room a roulette wheel whirled while men leaned drunkenly to watch the twirling ball.

Aimee hurried on and soon came to the wharf. Ships' masts stood tall and ghostlike in the pale moonlight, their halyards creaking with the lazy movement of the river current. Aimee made her way to the place where Zack's ship was docked. What if he were not there? From one of the other ships came the sound of a woman's squeal, ending in laughter. What if Zack had a woman on board? Aimee thought in panic. She couldn't bear the humiliation of it. She paused at the gangplank, shivering in the dampness while she considered turning back to the Golden Promise. Then she saw him, a darker silhouette against the dusky sky.

"Zack?" she called softly, and saw the figure stiffen.

"Aimee?" Zack exclaimed in surprise. "My God,

337

what are you doing down here at this time of night?"
He ran down the plank to clasp her hand.

"I love you," she whispered. "I don't want to lose
you again."

"Aimee!" His cry was joyous. He swept her into his
arms, holding her high against his chest while he covered her face with kisses that left her shaken.

"I thought you wouldn't come with me—" he began, and she placed her hand across his mouth.

"Shh, don't talk now," she urged. "Take me to your
cabin. Make love to me." She sensed the tension
mounting in him as he peered down at her in the
darkness. Without another word he scooped her up
and strode up the gangplank. Aimee clung to the
strength of him, her lips sliding across the strong brown
column of his throat. She'd make him stay. Somehow
she'd make him stay. She couldn't be without him. He
fumbled at the latch to his cabin door, while her own
fingers went to the buttons of his shirt, pushing aside
the cloth that covered his smooth, muscular shoulders.
Her mouth claimed his, her teeth gently nipping at his
lower lip. His breath came in gasps and she knew it
had nothing at all to do with carrying her.

He kicked the door closed, his mouth demanding
and fervent. He released his hold on her knees, his
arms holding her tightly, molding her to him. Sensuously
she slid down the length of him, feeling the hard flat
muscles of his middle and the hard bulge of his need.
An answering need flared inside her. Swiftly she pushed
his shirt aside, her hands skimming over his sun-bronzed
skin, down to the fastening of his breeches. The ardor
of his kisses left her breathless. Her knees were
trembling and she swooned backward onto the floor,
cradled by his strong arms. The touch of his mouth on
hers was constant, unrelenting. Swiftly he pulled aside
the flounces and petticoats. Her desire consumed her
and she welcomed him with urgent words of love and
the heat of her passion.

Later they lay on the floor, spent, Zack's long muscular body sprawled across hers. He was heavy, but

she uttered no complaint. How many nights had she cried herself to sleep longing for the feel of him? She sighed contentedly. Zack chuckled.

"What is it?" she asked. He raised himself on his elbows, his large brown hands framing her face lovingly.

"I thought we were finally going to make love in a real bed. We didn't quite make it," he teased.

Aimee peered across the cabin at the wooden cot, then gazed deeply into his eyes. "I guess you'll have to do it all over again," she whispered huskily.

Passion flared in his eyes. "I always try to please a lady," he said, and in one swoop gathered her up and carried her to the bed.

They slept afterward, limbs tangled comfortingly. When the sky beyond the porthole lightened with the promise of dawn, they woke and loved again, then lay drowsing, her head cushioned on his shoulder.

"You won't be sorry for coming with me, Aimee," Zack murmured against her hair.

Her body stiffened in his arms. "I won't be going with you, Zack," she said softly.

He grew still. It seemed even his breathing had stopped. "I thought you said last night that—"

"That I didn't want to lose you."

"I don't understand," he said stiffly. His muscles had hardened to stone beneath her. She prayed he'd be amenable to what she was about to say.

"I'll be here waiting for you whenever you come to port."

"Damm it, Aimee, that's not what I want." Zack slid out of bed. Wrapping a cover around his lean waist, he stalked to the porthole to stare out pensively. She waited until he turned back to her. "I want us to be together all the time," he ground out, "not part-time, whenever I happen to have cargo to bring upriver."

"Zack, there are always ships bringing cargo up to Sacramento. Can't you make this one of your regular runs? There's a need for more ships to bring in the miners and then bring them supplies. You could do that just as well."

"I don't want to, Aimee. I don't want to be scuttling up and down a narrow muddy river. I'm a seaman. I love the wide-open spaces of the ocean. The river makes me feel hemmed-in."

"You're the man that I love. Can't you do this for me, so we can be together? Please, Zack."

"You never planned to leave, did you?" he asked, and she felt fear sweep through her.

"I can't," she said appealingly. "People depend on me. There's Ruth and her children and Loretta and Simon and Daniel Cooper. I've hired some of the emigrant women when they come to town with their husbands, and when the hotel is built, I'll hire more."

"That's not the reason you want to stay," he said hoarsely, and Aimee nodded.

"You're right. I want to stay here for me, for all the things I've built up in just a few months. Me, helpless, pampered Aimee Bennett, whose only choice is to marry a man who'll take care of her. Well, I've taken care of a lot of people myself since I left Webster. I found out I can do a lot of things I never thought I could. I'm proud of what I've done."

Zack looked at her sitting in his bunk, the coverlet crumpled across her lap, her small, perfect breasts bared, the chestnut hair lying in fiery strands across her shoulders. Her eyes were earnest as she gazed up at him. He had an urge to tease her for her seriousness as one would a petted child who refused to cooperate. Then he remembered the trek across the Oregon trail, the way she'd kept the Stuart family together after Ulcie died, the sight of her swinging a rifle at a wolf. She looked like a dainty child sitting there, but she was already a woman of substance. She'd used her intelligence and hard work to make a better way for herself and those depending on her. What right had he to ask her to give it all up? Once he'd scoffed at her and now he saw how much his words had affected her.

He thought of the sea and the sails of his ship

billowing in the wind and he saw how unimportant it was, if it meant losing Aimee. As much as he loved the sea, he loved her more. He crossed the cabin and sat on the edge of the bed. "I'll do it your way," he said softly. "I'll sail along the coast and inland."

"Oh, Zack," she cried, and clasped her hands in front of her while tears shimmered on her lashes. For the first time he realized how much his decision meant to her.

"I'm proud of the way you've done things," he said, and she threw her arms around his neck, pressing her face against his shoulder.

"I'll make you prouder of me, just you wait and see," she cried. "I'm going to have a lot of gold, Zack, enough for all of us."

He cradled her in his arms, troubled by her preoccupation with the gold metal that had already wrecked so many lives. His only hope was that this fever that afflicted her would burn itself out before she was seriously hurt by it. His arms tightened around her. He'd protect her. She might think she was self-reliant, but she still needed him. The thought gave him some comfort as he contemplated the months ahead, hugging the coast, sailing the muddy Sacramento, and plying the river trade.

16

"A little higher. Yes, yes, that will do." Aimee stood in the dust of the street, the sun beating down on her, her eyes shielded from its rays as she studied the sign over the two-story building. "Golden Promise Hotel," it read in bold red lettering. Jake and his partner took hammer and nail and began fastening the sign permanently. Aimee sighed. She'd done it. The hotel was completed, its rooms smelling of new wood and fresh paint. And none too soon. All up and down the street, buildings were going up overnight, stretching eastward away from the riverbank. Jake hadn't gone back to the goldfields after all. His fortune lay in building a town. Some evenings he helped Simon in the saloon. He still enjoyed hearing the other miners talk about their search for the elusive yellow metal.

Aimee stood watching Jake, going over a mental list of all that must be done. Each guestroom sported a new bed and chest, and the lobby was decorated with rich burgundy carpets and crystal chandeliers, all of it brought up from San Francisco on the *Sea Lady*.

The thought of the *Sea Lady* reminded her of Zack. He should be returning soon, she thought, and wondered what he'd think of the things she'd accomplished in his absence. The hotel had taken on an elegance even she had not anticipated, and the miners were already clamoring for rooms. Aimee frowned as she glanced at the saloon. It seemed shabby in comparison. She'd have to tell Jake to give it a whitewash.

The buildings opened onto each other, so hotel guests could walk through the lobby and enter the restaurant and beyond to the saloon, if they wished. Perhaps the hotel would help increase business for the bar. Of all her enterprises, that was the one least profitable, which surprised her. Down the street, Wilson Lundy's saloon was already filling up, in spite of the early hour, and it would remain so until late into the night. She thought of the night when she'd passed Lundy's saloon on her way to Zack's ship. It had been packed that night as well. What made his saloon so popular? Aimee had given it some thought, and sent for a different kind of cargo on the *River Queen*. Instinctively she'd known Zack would object to what she was about to do. She glanced back at the two men on the porch roof.

"Lower the right corner just a bit," she called, and when it was done, walked into the hotel lobby.

"Aimee, come look at the bathhouse," Loretta invited, and she hurried across the lobby to a door that led onto a back porch.

"Ah'm still not so sure this is goin' to work out," Loretta said, leading the way along the porch to the small single rooms facing the courtyard. Aimee had had them built on a whim. A large wooden tub sat in the center of each room, cept one, which was slightly bigger and held washtubs. In the center of the courtyard was an outdoor fireplace where huge kettles of water were kept heating for baths and laundry facilities. Even now, two women labored over scrub boards, recruited from the scores of emigrants who came down off the mountains broke and desperately in need of money. Aimee paid them in gold dust, closing her mind to the fact that they were vastly underpaid for what they were required to do. At least she provided them with some means of feeding their families.

"Put in stools, clean towels, and soap," she said, inspecting each bathhouse. "We want each guest to know we've thought of his every need. He won't have to leave the hotel for anything."

"That's right smart of yo', Aimee," Loretta said,

but she didn't look happy. She'd become quieter and more withdrawn since they'd come to Sacramento. She said all the right things, but somehow her heart didn't seem in it. Aimee missed the old spirited Loretta, who had seen the black and white of things with a clear vision. She'd come to depend on that. Aimee shook her head. She wasn't depending on anyone anymore, not even Loretta. She glanced at the women bent over the washtubs. Ruth had come out of the restaurant and now stood chatting with them, her face animated as she talked.

Aimee's eyes narrowed. "The next time Dan comes to visit Ruth, tell him to come by my office," she said, and Loretta glanced at her sharply.

"What've yo' got in mind?" she asked.

"I want to offer him a job again," Aimee said, but her gaze didn't quite meet Loretta's. "Maybe this time he'll take me up on my offer. He's geen going into the hills to search for gold for months now and we've grubstaked him. It's time he takes a real job to support his family properly instead of leaving it on someone else's shoulders."

"Ruth has earned her own way," Loretta said fiercely.

"Yes, she has," Aimee said agreeably. "My goodness, Loretta, I don't know why you're acting so suspicious. I only want to offer the man a proper job."

"The Coopers have a mighty amount of pride," Loretta commented.

"Pride!" Aimee scoffed. "Seems to me everyone's overly concerned about pride."

"Ain't yo'?" Loretta said calmly. "Ain't that what all this is about?" Her arm made a sweeping motion to take in all the buildings. Aimee glanced at her wordlessly, but before she could think of a proper retort, Loretta had turned and walked away, her shoulders seeming unaccountably thin beneath the rich fabric of her gown.

What was wrong with Loretta lately? Aimee fumed. She always acted as if the things Aimee planned and did for them were wrong, as if it were wrong to make money and be successful. With an impatient swish of her skirts, Aimee went back to the hotel. She had hundreds of things to do; she couldn't spend all day worrying about Loretta's feelings. She'd come around. She always did.

That night when Aimee was poring over the books, Dan Cooper knocked at her door. He entered on Aimee's command, his hat in his hand, his eyes shy as they met hers.

"Howdy, Miss Bennett," he said, and shifted his weight uneasily.

"Hello, Dan," she said. "Thank you for coming by. Have a seat. I'll just be a few minutes more." She bent over the books again, deliberately taking her time while Dan creased and recreased his hat and fidgeted, trying to find a place to put his big awkward hands. His eyes took in the dark grained desk and thick carpeting on the floor. Since the hotel's completion, Aimee had claimed one of the upstairs rooms for herself and converted her bedroom into an office. With great care she'd furnished it in an opulent manner that clearly stated her prosperity. Now a large safe stood in the corner where her bed had once been. It was more for show than anything, for she still kept the hiding place below the loose floorboard. At last she set aside her books and smiled at Daniel.

"How is the digging going?" she asked, keeping her tone friendly.

Daniel squirmed and looked away. "Not as well as I'd hoped." He twirled his hat and cleared his throat.

"That's too bad," Aimee said sympathetically. "It must get very discouraging in the goldfields."

"Yes, ma'am, it does."

"And lonesome."

"Yes, ma'am." Daniel nodded.

"We've staked you for a long time, Dan," Aimee said tentatively, and let the words hang in the air between them.

"Yes, ma'am, you have," Daniel said in a low voice, "and I'm mighty grateful. I'm right sorry I haven't had a strike so I could start paying you back."

"Don't worry about that," Aimee reassured him. "I'm sure we can work something out. In fact, I may have hit upon a solution." He glanced up at her, his face open and hopeful. "I need someone here to help me out, a man I can trust. I don't know anyone I'd trust more than you, and you'd be close to Ruth and the kids. You'd like that, wouldn't you?"

"Yes, ma'am, I would," Daniel said, and frowned. He knew what was coming.

"I need a bartender, someone to oversee things and keep order. I expect to make some changes soon and there'll be more customers. As a woman I can't keep them in line, and Simon will be leaving soon."

"Like I said before, I don't rightly think I could do that, Miss Bennett," Daniel said, shaking his head. "It goes against my teachin' to be sellin' spirits to another man."

"I see," Aimee said, feigning disappointment. "I just thought you might want to be here near Ruth during her time of confinement."

"Confinement?" Daniel looked at her blankly.

"Surely she's told you she's expecting another baby."

"No, ma'am, she hasn't," Daniel said. His face was flushed with pleasure and the old battered hat was crushed between his big hands.

"I'm sorry I gave away her secret, then," Aimee said. "It could be she's not planning to tell you, for fear you won't go back to panning for gold."

"Yes, ma'am. Ruth'd do that." Daniel nodded. He twisted the hat between his hands. "Still, I don't think it would make her happy to see me workin' in the saloon."

"Then don't do it, if it goes against your nature," Aimee said gently. "And don't worry about Ruth. I'll take care of her and the children until she has the baby, just as I've always done." She watched as the flush crept up from his neck onto his face. His lips tightened and he shifted in the chair.

"I don't hardly think I can let you do that, Miss Bennett," he said finally. "You been doin' too much for us as it is. I reckon I'll be takin' care of my own family, the way a man ought. If you still want me for the job, I'd be much obliged to take it."

"The offer's still open," Aimee said quietly, and refrained from smiling.

Ruth wasn't happy with the way things happened. It was evident in the stiff back she presented to Aimee as she went quietly about her chores. Daniel started work behind the bar and after a few nights seemed to settle into the routine easily enough. Loretta was unnaturally quiet. She said nothing to Aimee, but her eyes were accusing and sad. Aimee ignored them all. She'd done what was best for everyone, and eventually they'd see it and get over their anger.

A week later, Johnny Cooper came running from the docks to tell her her cargo was in. At first Aimee's heart leapt with pleasure until she remembered this was the *River Queen*. Zack would be gone several more days. He'd sailed to the Isthmus of Panama to bring back a shipload of miners who'd made their way by sea. Quickly Jake and Daniel were dispatched with a wagon and the hired buggy. Nervously Aimee paced the lobby, waiting for their return. How would Loretta and the rest of them take to this new idea of hers? she wondered. It seemed to take ages before they returned. She could tell by the scowl on Daniel's face that he wasn't happy with this new development. He stopped the wagon in front of the saloon and began to unload it, while Jake pulled the hired buggy to a stop near the hotel.

"Here's the rest of yo'r cargo," Jake called as the women in the buggy climbed out and stood on the hotel porch looking around. There were four of them. Their gowns were garish and suggestive, their faces heavily painted. There was little doubt as to what they were. Aimee stood where she was, her face calm, her eyes unsmiling. Inside she was shivering with uncertainty, but the four women who faced her had no way of knowing that. Their laughter died away as they studied the slender girl.

"We've come to see A. Bennett. Tell him we're here, please," one of them said, fluffing the ratty-looking fur piece draped over her arm.

"I am A. Bennett," Aimee said, drawing her slender shoulders back.

"You?" The girls squealed a protest. "I thought I was workin' for Mr. A. Bennett."

"My name is Aimee Bennett and you'll be working for me."

"I'm not sure I want to work for a woman," the first girl said haughtily.

"My driver will take you back to the *River Queen*. Your passage will be paid back to San Francisco," Aimee replied firmly. The woman's mouth settled into a pout and she thought about protesting this treatment, but the look on Aimee's face precluded any argument. Sulkily she climbed back into the buggy. "Is there anyone else who wants to go back?" Aimee asked.

"I'm willin' t' give it a try if you are," one of the women spoke up. She was older than the other girls and the wrinkles were beginning to show around her eyes and throat. Aimee considered sending her back as well, but there was a sparkle of humor in her eyes that made her appealing. "My name's Val, this sassy one's Molly, and that's Bonnie. Sally's the one leaving."

"Welcome, ladies," Aimee said, and tried not to smile at the title. "Won't you come in?"

"Just a moment, please?" Another woman stepped out of the hired carriage. Aimee stared at her in amazement. Her hair was a soft golden color and was wound into a swirl of curls and waves, on the top of which perched a saucy little hat that made Aimee long for one herself. She thought of the squashed straw bonnet she usually wore in the streets and felt incredibly dowdy. The woman was so obviously of a different cut than the other dance-hall girls that Aimee wondered what circumstances had brought her to this low pass. As if reading her thoughts, the woman nodded and smiled.

"I'm not here looking for . . . employment," she said with an arch of her eyebrow. She glanced at the other women and smiled patronizingly. Obviously she didn't want to be associated with the dance-hall girls in any way. One of them sneered and made a comment and the rest laughed derisively. Aimee sent a warning glance to her new employees and the laughter died.

"Your man was kind enough to give me a ride from the harbor," the woman continued unperturbed. Her voice was low and musical and she spoke with an assurance that said she was used to people paying attention to her and her needs. Once I was like that, Aimee thought, then pushed the memory away. It was some other lifetime and had nothing to do with her now.

"I wonder if you could tell me where I might find a Mr. Zack Crawford?" she asked.

Something uneasy stirred in Aimee's breast. "Mr. Crawford is on his way back from Panama right now," she answered pleasantly. "He won't be back for several days."

"I see." The disappointment was evident on her face. "Is there a Wilson Lundy in town?"

"Mr. Lundy owns the Mother Lode," Aimee said, and noted the puzzlement on the woman's face. "It's a saloon down on River Street."

"A saloon?" the woman exclaimed, then sighed wearily. "I might have known." She glanced around. "Is this the best hotel available?"

"Yes, it is. We've just opened," Aimee said proudly.

"I suppose it will have to do." The woman barely refrained from wrinkling her nose in distaste. "Do you work here?" Her manner was haughty. The other women grinned.

Aimee frowned. "I own this establishment," she said coolly, beginning to dislike the newcomer. "I didn't catch your name."

"Caroline," the woman said. "Caroline Crawford. Have someone see to my trunks." She swept past Aimee and into the hotel. Aimee watched her go,

349

willing the cold knot of fear to recede before she turned back to the other women.

"She's a fancy piece," Molly said, placing her hands on her hips and sashaying a bit.

"She's a lahdee," Bonnie said in a mincing tone.

"She didn't act like a lady with the captain on the *River Queen*," Val said, and Aimee longed to ask what she meant, but she couldn't stand here on the porch discussing the woman Zack had once loved—and might still, for all Aimee knew.

"Mrs. Crawford is a guest at this hotel," she snapped, "and you must remember that guests are to be treated courteously at all times, no matter what."

"Yes, ma'am," Molly sassed back, but under the heat of Aimee's gaze her defiance melted.

"If you'll come with me, I'll show you around. If we get the tables set up in time, you'll begin work tonight." Aimee led the girls along the porch to the saloon. "Your rooms are at the back of the saloon. You'll have no reason to go into the hotel. I expect this rule to be obeyed at all times."

"What's the matter? Ain't we good enough?" Molly asked belligerently.

Aimee turned to face them. "You are hired help and you may not mix with the customers. You're here to do a job. Do it and you'll be well paid. Fail to do as you're told and you'll be dismissed. Understood?"

Sullenly the two younger women shook their heads. Val, the older woman, studied Aimee but said nothing.

Dan and Jake were already setting up the special tables and installing the wheels. Tables for three-card monte, vingt-et-un, lansquenet, faro, and craps were set up at one side. Everything was nearly finished when Loretta arrived. Mouth hanging open, she walked around the room and turned to Aimee, her eyes sparkling with anger.

"Did Ah forget yo' tellin' me about this?" she demanded.

"I didn't talk to you about it, Loretta, because I wanted it to be a surprise," Aimee said reasonably.

"Ah'm surprised. Are there any other surprises for me?"

"I have some dancers to help work the tables and put on little shows for the miners."

"Dance-hall girls?" Loretta asked incredulously. Aimee could see Daniel's troubled, disapproving face. Ruth had come to see what was going on and her face was pale with shock.

"Let's not discuss this in front of the help. Come back to my office," Aimee said. Loretta looked stunned, then embarrassed as she glanced at the Coopers. Quietly she followed Aimee.

"How could yo' say that about them?" she asked furiously. "The Coopers ain't help, they're our friends."

"Don't be sentimental," Aimee said impatiently. "Of course they're our friends, but they also work for us and they have no say in the decisions we make for our business."

"Apparently Ah don't either," Loretta said. "What would yo' call me, one of the hired hands?"

"Loretta, don't be difficult. I have too many other things on my mind."

"Are yo' thinkin' of some other great plan to help us get rich?"

"Yes, I am," Aimee snapped. "God knows you aren't coming up with anything. You seem to know only one way to make money." She paused. The cruel words were out before she could call them back. Loretta's face was pale, her eyes bleak with pain.

"Loretta, I didn't mean that."

"Yes, yo' did," Loretta said quietly. "Yo' been thinkin' it, else it wouldn'ta come out."

"I never meant to hurt you," Aimee cried.

"Once Ah woulda believed that," Loretta said, "but now Ah'm not so sure. Yo've changed, Aimee. Yo'r not the same girl as the one who started out for Oregon." Her words cut through Aimee and she whirled to pace across the room.

"You're right, I'm not," she cried. "I don't want to be. That girl was a victim. We both were. Look at what happened to you. I don't ever want to be dependent on someone again. I don't want to need anyone to take care of me."

"Does that include your friends?" Loretta asked, and Aimee stared at her wordlessly. "Ah'll be leavin' here then."

"Loretta, you can't. We're partners."

"Not really. This was all yo'r ideas."

"But you've worked just as hard at it as I have."

"Then pay me the same as you do the other hired hands," Loretta said quietly, and left the office without a backward glance. Aimee stood looking after her, too stunned to call out. Loretta wouldn't leave. She was just angry over the gambling tables and the dancehall girls. She'd get over it. She always did. Aimee pushed aside her longing to run after Loretta and make up. It would be comforting to tell her of Caroline Crawford's arrival, but she no longer had need of any reassurance. Let Loretta and Zack do as they wished. They couldn't hurt her.

Aimee made her way to her room to dress for the evening. She'd learned to wear more flamboyant clothes, to pile her hair on top of her head in an intricate design, and to apply rouge and powder. In lieu of the jewels she'd once worn, she'd had jet beads sewn over the low-cut bodices of her evening gowns and on matching ribbons which she wore around her throat. She'd also taken to wearing long gloves and carrying a fan to match her gown. It lent a touch of elegance that the miners appreciated, and set her apart from other saloon women.

She was the proprietor of a large and increasingly successful establishment here in Sacramento. Local businessmen were beginning to sit up and take notice of what she did. Well, after tonight, they'd have even more reason to concern themselves, for she intended to draw the miners away from their saloons and into the Golden Promise. Aimee added a black plume to her elaborate coiffure, and taking up her fan, turned toward the door, her head held high. She didn't need

Loretta, she thought, and Caroline Crawford's appearance wasn't a threat. Zack loved Aimee.

The night was a bigger success than she'd dreamed possible. The men who came to eat their supper as had been their custom since Aimee opened, now poured into the saloon to see her new gambling tables. There was an added incentive for staying at the Golden Promise. Aimee had always dealt with them fair and square. That was the reason they'd continued to bank their gold with her, and they were certain of an honest wheel.

Word spread and other miners stumbled in off the street, eager to try a new place. There hardly seemed room for another body to press into the building by the time the music started and the three women pranced out on the stage. Their short skirts and bright petticoats were held high to display their shapely legs as they swung into a high-stepping dance. Miners pressed against the door, straining to catch a glimpse of the new women. Good-naturedly, men passed mugs of beer and whiskey glasses to those who couldn't get to the bar. Regally Aimee walked among the customers, greeting those she knew and introducing herself to those she didn't. One and all nodded and doffed their hats, aware they were dealing with a lady.

The evening wore on and Aimee looked for Loretta, hoping she had changed her mind and come to join the festivities, but there was no sign of her. Grimly Dan Cooper worked behind the bar, pouring drinks and collecting money while Jake tried to keep up with washing glasses.

"We don't have to go to San Francisco now. We got our own place right here in Sacramento," the miners congratulated themselves and her. They seemed to have forgotten the Mother Lode. When the show was over, the girls went back to dealing. The wheel spun away the hours and it seemed to Aimee they might never close their doors. The walls seemed to bulge with the noise and smoke of the miners. Sometime late in the evening, Wilson Lundy made an appearance.

"Hello, Lundy," Aimee greeted him. "Can I buy you a drink?" Without waiting for his answer, she signaled to Jake, who brought her a bottle and a glass. She poured a liberal amount and left the bottle sitting at his elbow.

"You're not joining me?" Lundy asked, studying her through the haze of his cigar smoke.

"I've never developed a taste for it," she replied graciously.

Lundy tossed down the contents of the glass and poured another. Once again his pale eyes slid over her figure, lingering too long on the swell of breasts exposed by her low-cut bodice. "You surprise me, Aimee," he said, his voice assuming an intimate huskiness she found offensive.

"In what way, Mr. Lundy?" she asked, more out of politeness than curiosity.

"Gambling, women—you're more grown-up than I thought." His leering gaze slid back to her bodice and she knew he wasn't talking about her saloon at all. She restrained the urge to toss his glass of whiskey into his face and got to her feet.

"It was kind of you to come by, Mr. Lundy," she said stiffly. "Now, if you'll excuse me, I must see to my customers."

"By all means, do that, Miss Bennett. They were my customers only last night and they will be again." His pale eyes issued the challenge.

"I'm sure there's more than enough gold flowing through these streets for the two of us," she answered, suddenly fearful of having him for an enemy.

"There's never enough gold." He smiled, a thin contraction of the muscles around his mouth that had nothing to do with the rest of his face. It frightened Aimee more than any threat he could have uttered.

Dan called to her and gratefully she turned away. One of the more prudent miners wanted her to keep his gold dust.

"If it ain't in my pocket, I can't spend it," he said cheerfully. "I got me enough here to have a week's worth of good times." Aimee took the gold and headed toward her office, then remembered Caroline Crawford and her inquiries about Wilson Lundy. She'd forgotten to mention it to him. He was probably gone already. Involuntarily her eyes darted to the table where she'd left him. He was still there and his gaze was fixed on the heavy bags of gold she held in her hand. The greed she saw in his eyes was a tangible thing. Aimee gripped the bags tighter and hurried from the saloon, suddenly eager to be away from the noisy, boisterous crowd. She didn't feel safe until the gold was locked away beneath her floorboards.

Sinking into the chair at her desk, she sat thinking of Wilson Lundy and his unspoken threat and of Caroline Crawford. Was she an even greater threat? How did Caroline know Lundy? Another thought came to her, perhaps this Caroline Crawford had nothing at all to do with Zack. In her heart, Aimee knew it wasn't so. Caroline Crawford had asked for Zack. That was too much of a coincidence. How would Zack feel when he saw his brother's wife?

All the fears she'd been trying to ignore came hurtling in on her and she sat with her face buried in her hands. Well, she'd always known this moment would come. She'd prepared for it the best she could. If Zack left her, she'd go on with her life the same as before, but in her heart she knew if she lost Zack, nothing would ever be the same again.

By morning Loretta was gone, her room so devoid of any trace of her that Aimee felt like weeping. Then anger took hold and carried her through the day. Caroline Crawford descended the steps about midmorning, her golden curls gleaming, the lace and flounces of her gown fresh and impeccable in spite of the heat. Aimee felt the moisture on her forehead and the middle of her back and wished for a leisurely bath. Instead she bent her head over the hotel register and pretended to be terribly engrossed.

"Excuse me, sir?" Caroline said, her tone sweet and beguiling.

"Yes, ma'am," Sam Barnes answered eagerly. He was an elderly man who'd decided he was too old for the rigors of the gold camps and had settled for an easy job as hotel clerk. He straightened his string tie self-consciously and smiled at the beautiful woman addressing him.

"Could you tell me where I might hire a carriage and a driver?" Caroline asked, fluttering her eyelashes the tiniest bit before lowering them modestly.

Sam's face reddened all the way to his thinning hair and he cleared his throat. "You'd have to go over to the stable, ma'am," he stuttered. "W—would you like me to send a boy to tell Luke to bring one over here for you?"

"Would you? I'd be most grateful. Thank you, sir." Caroline smiled prettily.

"I . . . I'll do it right now," he said, and nearly stumbled in his haste to get to the back courtyard to send for Johnny. Caroline glanced at Aimee and her smile died.

"Where's the Mother Lode?" she asked abruptly, drawing on her gloves. Aimee met her arrogant gaze with a pleasant smile, stifling the desire to glare back at her.

"You'll find it down the street a few blocks," she said instead, then forced herself to smile. "However, if you're looking for a saloon, we have one here."

"I'm not," Caroline replied shortly.

"That's right," Aimee tried again. "You were looking for Wilson Lundy."

Caroline glanced at her with an amused air. She was all too aware Aimee was trying to find out more about her. "How do you know Zack Crawford?" Caroline asked the question that Aimee had wanted to. The woman's eyes were watchful as she waited for Aimee's answer.

Aimee raised her chin and smiled. "Zack and I are . . . friends," she answered softly, leaving no doubt as to how friendly they were.

Caroline smiled again, her gaze sweeping over the

serviceable plain gown Aimee wore during the day when working around the hotel and restaurant.

"How lovely for Zack that he found someone to occupy his time. I was afraid he would grow into a bitter, lovelorn hermit."

"Hardly," Aimee said wryly. "You must be his brother's wife."

"His brother's widow," Caroline corrected. There was an air of satisfaction about her words. Aimee felt the shock hit her and wanted to ask more, but Sam was hurrying in the door.

"Your carriage and driver are here, Mrs. Crawford," he said breathlessly. "I saw to it personally, myself."

"You are so kind," Caroline said, and with much bowing, Sam escorted her out of the hotel and into her carriage. Aimee stood looking after the slim golden-haired woman, and more than ever longed for Loretta to be there to advise her and for Zack to be there to reassure her and hold her in his arms.

When Caroline returned, Aimee was in her office, down on her knees beside the hiding place under the floorboards. A knock sounded and before Aimee could answer, the door was swung open and Caroline Crawford entered. Quickly Aimee drew the corner of the carpet back in place.

"Am I interrupting?" Caroline asked, her eyes bright as she studied Aimee.

"No, I . . . I've managed to drop my . . . my pen," Aimee said, sweeping her hand across the carpet as if searching. "It must have rolled under something."

"Is this it?" Caroline asked, crossing to the desk to pick up the writing instrument.

Aimee flushed at being caught in a lie and got to her feet. "I must have overlooked it," she said, and straightened her shoulders. "What can I do for you, Mrs. Crawford?"

"We didn't have a chance to finish our talk," Caroline said. Her gaze was direct and full of candor. Her lips curved in an open smile. "I'd hoped we could become friends. After all, we have a lot in common."

Aimee was thrown off-guard by the woman's offer of friendship. Slowly she walked to her desk, stalling for time to adjust her thinking about Caroline. The offer might be made out of the purest motives. Although Sacramento teemed with miners, there were few women. Life could be lonely here without the friendship and support of other women.

"I'm not sure I understand just what we do have in common," Aimee answered.

Caroline laughed, a delightful tinkling sound. "I'm talking about Zack, of course."

"Ah, yes, Zack." Aimee turned to face Caroline and knew immediately that this woman was her worst adversary. An absent Caroline had been formidable enough. How much worse to have her here in the flesh. "What are your plans here in Sacramento?"

Caroline shrugged. "That depends on Zack." She said his name softly, possessively.

Aimee took a breath, wondering how to deal with this beautiful woman who was stating her claim on Zack very clearly. Well, Aimee had some claims too. She raised her head proudly. She wouldn't give up without a fight. "I'm sure Zack will offer you whatever help you need," she said stiffly. "He never turns away a person in need."

"I remember." Caroline's smile was soft with special knowledge and remembrances of Zack. She made Aimee feel an outsider. "When did you say he would be returning?"

"Not for several days," Aimee answered, hoping to discourage the other woman from staying, but her hopes were dashed with Caroline's next words.

"Such a long time to wait." She pouted. "I shall grow bored."

"Some of the ladies have formed serving guilds," Aimee began, and wasn't surprised when Caroline laughed derisively and got to her feet.

"I'll find something to occupy myself until Zack's return," she said, and crossed to the door. Aimee got to her feet.

358

"Did you say you own this hotel?" Caroline asked, glancing back over her shoulder.

"My partner and I do." Aimee nodded. "We also own the restaurant and the saloon."

Caroline nodded as if in approval. "Then you aren't depending on Zack."

"No. I take care of myself," Aimee snapped.

"Good. That makes things so much easier." The door closed softly behind Caroline, leaving Aimee to contemplate the challenge that echoed around the room. All her fears were being realized. Caroline Crawford had come to Sacramento to claim Zack for her own.

The next few days were busy ones, filled with anxiety. Now Aimee had to perform Loretta's duties as well as her own. She was surprised at just how many of the daily problems Loretta had handled. Loretta had sent her word of where she was staying and Aimee had thought of going there to beg her old friend to return, but pride held her back. Instead she sent Dan with a large portion of the profit they were realizing on the Golden Promise, along with word that more would be forthcoming each month.

In the midst of all her problems, another tragedy struck. Word came that Bayard Louden had caught pneumonia and died. A miner brought Aimee a letter and a pouch of papers from Bay. Inside were a deed for his claim, naming Aimee as partner, and instructions for finding the gold he'd already mined. Aimee dispatched Dan to claim the gold. She was surprised when the bags were laid before her. Obviously Bay had hit a rich claim. The gold, the deed to the mine, and a letter telling of Bay's death were sent back east to a young bride who patiently waited for a husband who would never return to her.

"Aren't you going to take your share?" Daniel asked, and Aimee shook her head.

"This isn't gold I earned," she said. "It belongs to Bay's widow."

Daniel looked at her closely, then turned away, but that night he told Ruth about Aimee's generosity.

"Sometimes, when she forgets about herself, she's a real generous-hearted girl," Ruth sighed.

"She's done right by us," Daniel replied. "Least-wise I feel better about working for her now."

Ruth smiled and hugged her husband to her. Maybe what Aimee had done enticing her husband back here to work in a saloon wasn't so bad after all.

Aimee was unaware of their speculations concerning her. She hired Chinese laborers to continue mining Bay's claim and made arrangements for all gold to be shipped back to Kentucky. Bay's widow would be a rich woman.

Now her time was taken up with one crisis after another. One night a drunken miner shot up the saloon, and during the commotion most of the whiskey bottles were broken. It had taken two days to clean up the mess and two more days before another supply of whiskey arrived from San Francisco. A Peeping Tom was caught spying on a lady as she bathed in one of the bathhouses at the back of the hotel. Thereafter tubs and pails of water were lugged up the stairs for the lady's use. Her irate husband threatened to shoot up the hotel.

A fire mysteriously started in back of the storage shed, but Johnny Cooper discovered it and put out the flames before the food was destroyed. Miners began to grumble about a crooked wheel, and business fell off, until Aimee ordered the wheel dismantled under the miners' watchful eyes and reassembled. Satisfied they weren't being cheated, the miners flocked back. Someone was trying to put her out of business. Aimee thought of Wilson Lundy's threat.

One day Jackson delivered a load of tainted meat. Exasperated beyond all reason, Aimee sent Daniel to deal with the wily storekeeper. Because of his price padding, she had long since begun to order her supplies directly from San Francisco, buying only those things from Jackson that she had to. While Daniel was gone, Aimee worked behind the bar, using the time between customers for inventory.

"Excuse me, ma'am," a soft Tennessee drawl sounded at one end of the bar. Aimee glanced up. Billy Parson stood at the end of the bar, his hands braced on the planks, his face alight with a lopsided grin.

"Billy," she shouted, and hurried along the bar toward him.

Billy snatched his hat off his bright curls. "Ah thought that was yo', Aimee," he cried, and held out his hand. "How've yo' been doin'?"

"I'm fine, just fine," Aimee said, taking his hand. "I can't believe you're here. I thought you were headed for Oregon."

He glanced away. "Ah did go on to Oregon," he said, "but seemed lak' onc't Ah got there, wasn't nothing worth workin' for." His eyes met Aimee's and he forced a grin. "Ah heard about the gold strike and figured Ah'd come on down and see what it was all about."

"Loretta will be so happy to see you," Aimee said gleefully.

Billy's head jerked around. "Yo' mean she's here?" he asked incredulously.

"She is," Aimee cried, then remembered that Loretta was no longer with her. "Well, she's not here anymore." Billy's face fell. "She's here in town, though."

"Is she . . . is she happy? Is Mr. Sawyer good to her?"

"Mr. Sawyer died from cholera out on the trail," Aimee said gently.

"You mean she's all alone?" Billy asked as if he couldn't believe the turn of events. Aimee nodded, smiling at the young man's shock. "Do you reckon he'd want to see me?" he asked tentatively.

"I'm sure of it," Aimee said warmly.

"Ah acted such a fool," Billy said. "Ah shoulda been more understandin'."

"Yes, you should have," Aimee said, remembering the pain of her friend out on the trail. "She would never have married Royce Sawyer if you'd asked her not to."

Billy flinched. "Would yo' tell me where to find her?" he asked hopefully.

Aimee did so, and as he whirled away from the bar, she called after him, "Billy, tell her I'm . . ." Aimee paused. "Tell her I'm happy for her."

"Ah will," Billy said, touching his hat brim in farewell. Aimee watched him go, thinking of the joyful reunion they'd soon share and wishing Zack were back with her. How wonderful it would be if the four of them were together again, she thought happily; then her shoulders sagged as she remembered Caroline Crawford and the animosity between Loretta and her.

One day Wilson Lundy arrived at the hotel, a stout cloth bag clutched in his hand. Dan ushered him into Aimee's office.

"Mr. Lundy wants to store some of his gold in your safe," Dan explained.

Lundy smiled, but it never reached his pale eyes. They remained cold and assessing.

"Won't you come in, Mr. Lundy," Aimee said, laying aside her pen.

Lundy placed the bag on her desk and sauntered around the room, assessing the furnishings. "Quite a setup you've got here," he said.

"Thank you," Aimee answered, feeling uneasy to have him here in her office. "Is this the gold you wanted me to keep?"

"That's right." Lundy ambled across the room to the safe. "Any guarantees it'll be safe here?"

Aimee picked up the bag of gold and weighed it on the scales kept handy on the corner of her desk. There was hardly enough to warrant a safe.

"You have my personal guarantee," she answered. "The safe is too big to be carried out of here easily and only I know the combination."

"Reckon someone could blow it up," Lundy suggested, running his hand around the edge of the door.

"Someone might," she answered, "but I don't think that's much to worry about."

Lundy studied her confident smile, trying to deter

mine the reason for it. "Do you mind?" he asked, reaching for a cigar. He stepped away from the safe toward the desk, and the floorboard creaked beneath him.

Aimee's lashes flickered; then she smiled and nodded graciously. "Not at all," she answered, and Lundy took out a small knife and cut away the tip of his cigar before placing it in his mouth. He lit it and shuffled his feet, watching her face again through the haze of smoke.

"I assure you, Mr. Lundy, that if you want to leave your gold with me, it"—the board beneath his feet creaked as he rocked his weight back and forth—"will be safe."

"I'm sure it will be, Miss Bennett," he said slowly. "I'm quite sure it will be." He exhaled, his eyes glittering as they met hers. Aimee glanced away first.

She waited for some time after he was gone before she opened the floor safe and placed his gold with the rest. The safe was becoming so full she had little room left. She would ask Zack to take some of her gold back to San Francisco and sell it.

It seemed she thought of little else but Zack's return lately. The time for his arrival came and passed, and still there was no sign of the *Sea Lady* floating up the river. Johnny Cooper had been permanently stationed at the docks to watch for the ship. Aimee wanted to know the moment Zack arrived.

Even with all those precautions, she was caught unawares. She was lazing in a tub of warm water in one of the bathrooms at the back of the hotel. It had been a particularly difficult morning and she lay with her head back, her eyes closed, enjoying the soothing comfort of the warm water. The door opened and closed. Believing it to be Zelma come to bring her another bucket of warm water, she remained as she was. Suddenly a bare foot nudged her legs to one side.

With a startled exclamation Aimee opened her eyes. Zack stood before her, his clothes thrown to one side, his lean brown body towering over her, his dark eyes filled with laughter and some other emotion that made her blush. She couldn't glance away from him; she'd been hungry for the sight of him for too long, and now he stood boldy inviting her gaze, while his own dark eyes swooped over her face and the tops of her breasts, barely covered by the sudsy water. No word had been spoken between them. None was needed. Aimee held out her arms to him and he lowered himself into the water, catching her to him, covering her mouth with his in a demanding, satisfying kiss.

"Aimee—"

"Shhh, don't talk, kiss me," she commanded. He did. "I missed you so much. You can't ever go away so long again. Never."

"Shhh, don't talk," he whispered, covering her face with kisses. His hands glided over her wet skin. His strong arms pulled her against his hard body. They floated in a large wooden tub bracing their feet against its sides, turning in the warm water, mindless of the way it sloshed over the edge of the tub. Their mating was tumultuous, impatient, glorious, and when at last they left the bathhouse, there was more water on the floor than in the tub.

17

Aimee's joy in Zack's homecoming was short-lived. From the bathhouse they went to her room, where they made love again. Afterward they lay drowsing in each other's arms.

"I'm amazed at what you and Loretta have accomplished since I left," Zack murmured sleepily. "The hotel looks bigger and better than I'd expected."

"Umm, we've been busy too." Aimee yawned. "The rooms are filled nearly every night. With the hotel and the saloon, we've tripled our income . . . which reminds me. Would you take some of my gold back to San Francisco on your next trip?"

"Send it over to the ship. Of course, there's always a risk the *Sea Lady* will sink."

"Not with you at the helm. Besides, it will only be for a little while. I may open a real bank soon." She felt Zack stiffen beside her.

"I'm happy for your success," he said, and Aimee knew he wanted to be supportive of her endeavors, but with each success, she was more firmly entrenched here inland in Sacramento, while he longed for the open sea.

"Tell me about your trip," she said, and was happy to feel him relax again. "What took you so long?"

"It went well," he said enthusiastically. "After Panama I took some cargo up to Oregon. It's pretty country up there, Aimee."

"Was it a profitable trip?" she asked.

Zack sighed and nodded. She sensed her question had displeased him. "We made a good profit from our cargo."

"As good as you make hauling goods from San Francisco to the mining camps?" she asked, and immediately wished she hadn't.

Zack sighed. "Not as good as that," he admitted, and changed the subject. "I saw the Pottses."

"Biddy Potts?" Aimee cried, and sat up to look at him, her eyes bright with joyful laughter. He hadn't seen her look like that in a long time, he thought. It seemed she always wore a scowl or a frown, with her nose buried in her books.

"How are they? Are they well? Did they get a farm? How were Wakefield and Hannah and Jamie and the others? Did they ask about me?"

"Whoa! Slow down," Zack laughed, "and I'll tell you everything. Let's see, now, which question shall I answer first?" He paused, trying to decide, and Aimee tickled his ear, his neck, and finally his ribs, until he caught her against him and lay looking into her merry face.

"The Pottses are all fine, and so are the Stuart children. They all asked about you and sent their love, especially Hannah, who said to tell you she misses you most of all."

Tears filled Aimee's eyes. It seemed as if the Oregon trail had happened to someone else. Now, hearing about the Pottses and their generous outpouring of love made Aimee view the trail and its hardships with a more forgiving eye than she had heretofore.

Zack told her about their farm and the wild Oregon coastline with the small towns perched among the rocks, and of the seals and sea lions that played on its vast beaches.

"In spite of all the people who've come and the ones yet to come, there are still hundreds of miles of unsettled lands," he said in wonder.

"There's no gold there," Aimee reminded him.

"There's no need for gold," Zack said, and they fell silent, each unable to reach the other on this issue.

"I've also met someone from the old wagon train," Aimee said softly, trying to mend the rift between them.

"Is Bay back?" Zack guessed, and Aimee's smile wavered.

"Bay's dead," she told him. "He got pneumonia and died out at his campsite."

"Damn," Zack cried. "He was so young. He had his whole life ahead of him and he threw it away in his search for gold."

"He found it, Zack," Aimee exclaimed. "He found a rich vein that will make his wife wealthy."

"Do you think she really cares, if it cost her husband his life?"

"No." Aimee glanced away. "I only meant his search wasn't in vain."

"Wasn't it? He lost something more valuable than any gold he might have found."

Aimee swallowed. It seemed all their discussions came to this disagreement over gold. She sensed Zack's disappointment in her. "Billy's here," she said.

"Billy Parson?" Zack's voice was full of delight. "Where is he?"

"He's with Loretta at the Sacramento Hotel."

"Why is she there?" His dark eyes regarded her and he saw what he'd missed in the first passion of their reunion. There was a sadness in Aimee's eyes and tight little lines around her mouth, as if she were hiding even from herself something that caused her pain. "You've had a falling-out?" he asked gently, and suddenly she was burrowing her face in his shoulder, letting the tears flow while she forgot her resolution not to need anyone.

Zack let her cry it out, his large hand smoothing her hair, patting her shoulder in comforting little strokes. At last her sobs stilled and she told him all that had transpired, even her own failure to consult Loretta and that final insult that had cut too deeply for their rift ever to be mended. Zack listened and made no judgments against her, for which she was heartily grateful. Afterward he held her protectively, reassuring her that it would all be forgotten and Loretta would come back. Aimee doubted it, but allowed his words to ease some of the tension she'd felt. There was only one other problem to be dealt with, and she felt too drained to broach it now.

"I have to dress and check on the supper menu," she sighed, rising and drawing on her clothes.

Zack sat up on the edge of the bed and looked at her. "Business first, eh?" he said with mock anger, but the laugh lines radiating from his eyes gave him away.

"Some business," Aimee sassed back, her eyes taking in the rumpled bed. His teasing lightened her mood considerably. She fastened her hair back into the smooth knot she wore during the day and turned back to him. The laughter was gone from her eyes, although she contrived to keep her tone light.

"Mr. Crawford," she said with a quick curtsy, "Miss Bennett, the proprietor of this fine establishment, wishes to extend her personal invitation for you to dine at her special table tonight at eight."

"I'll have to check my schedule, Miss Bennett," Zack replied, buttoning his shirt, "but I assure you that whatever is on my agenda, I'll cancel it for the privilege of dining with so beautiful a lady." His words were intended to make her smile. Instead she winced and looked away.

"Don't be late," she said, and was gone, closing the door behind her. Zack was left staring after her in perplexity. He sensed an unease in Aimee. For all the gold she was accruing, she wasn't happy.

Aimee descended to the hotel lobby, where she wrote out a message on the fancy stationery she'd had sent up from San Francisco and left it at the desk for Caroline Crawford. She'd been too cowardly to tell Zack herself that Caroline was here, but she knew a meeting between them was inevitable. The best she could do was make sure that meeting occurred in a neutral, very public place where it would be more difficult for Caroline to practice her wiles on Zack. Aimee had little doubt that was just what the new widow had in mind. Caroline was out, as she was most of the afternoons, but Sam was instructed to give the message to her as soon as she returned.

Aimee busied herself for the rest of the afternoon seeing to the menu and a thousand other details in preparation for the evening. Packaging up the gold she'd accumulated since the Golden Promise opened, she sent Dan down to the *Sea Lady* with it, then turned to arbitrating an argument among the dance-hall girls.

"She's gettin' too fat to dance with us," Molly said coldheartedly, and Val, the oldest of the girls and the one about whom Molly complained, scowled.

"What's the matter, Molly? Can't you take a little competition? You're just jealous because the men like a woman with meat on her bones."

"Meat? Ha! More like lard," Molly snapped. "You can't do the new routines."

Aimee listened to them squawking with half an ear. "Val, I overheard you singing the other day," she said finally. "Why don't you forgo the dancing and concentrate on singing more?" The suggestion seemed to mollify all of them. They went away discussing the new changes in their show.

Aimee dressed carefully for her supper engagement, choosing a new gown of a pale green that reminded her of the prairie grasses when they'd first started out on the Oregon trail. She tied a matching ribbon around her neck and wove another one in and out of the golden brown curls piled high on her head, then stood back to study the effect. The color of the gown made her gray eyes appear green and mysteriously deep. She liked the effect. Zack had never seen her so attired. She wondered how he'd like the change in her. Remembering his earlier remarks and his passionate lovemaking, she felt sure of herself. Caroline wouldn't have a chance.

Zack's eyes lit up when he saw her; then he scowled as he noticed the low-cut bodice. Aimee smiled, delighting in the show of jealousy. Hadn't she been feeling the same emotions these past weeks? They ordered champagne and sat toasting each other and the success of their ventures, their love, the reunion of Loretta and Billy, and each one of the Potts family, until they were quite giddy. The clock hand crept around until nearly an hour had passed and still Caroline had not put in an appearance. Aimee had begun to suspect she wasn't coming at all, when she felt Zack stiffen beside her.

"Caroline," he exclaimed, his eyes riveted on the beautiful woman who posed in the entrance waiting until all eyes were trained on her. She was even more dazzling than usual and Aimee's spirits sank. Caroline had chosen a gown of pale blue, trimmed at its demure collar with wide ruffles of French lace. Her eyes seemed even more blue. Her golden hair was piled high on her head and a beautiful diamond necklace glittered at her throat. Regally she moved toward them. Zack shifted beside Aimee. He still cared for Caroline, Aimee thought numbly. There had been too much emotion in his voice for her to believe anything else.

"Did you know she was here?" he demanded, his voice low and furious.

Aimee nodded, biting her lower lip.

"Why in God's name didn't you tell me?" His dark eyes bored into hers accusingly.

"I didn't think she was important to you anymore," she whispered.

He took her hand, squeezing it tightly. "She isn't," he muttered thickly. There was no time to say more. Caroline had arrived at their table. Hastily he got to his feet.

"Good evening, Aimee," Caroline greeted, perfectly at ease. "It was so kind of you to invite me to join you." She turned to Zack and her smile changed, becoming intimate and seductive, yet retaining its air of innocence.

"Hello, Zack. We meet again." Her voice was husky. It trembled as if she were barely able to contain her emotions.

"Caroline," Zack said stiffly. "How are you?"

"I'm fine . . . now," she answered breathlessly, then threw herself into his arms. "Oh, Zack," she wept, "it's all been a terrible nightmare." She drew back, fumbling for a handkerchief. Zack gave her his. Helplessly Caroline glanced up at him. "Could we go somewhere private and talk?" she asked piteously. "I know Aimee meant well to have us meet here, but . . ." She turned her face into the hollow of his neck as if to hide her tears. Zack glanced at Aimee, and all the time, his arm was around Caroline, his hand patting her gently on the back as he had Aimee just that afternoon.

"You can use my office," Aimee said stiffly, and led the way. When she glanced over her shoulder, she saw Caroline clinging to Zack's coat, her head still on his shoulder, her slim body pressed the length of his so he could hardly walk. Awkwardly they followed Aimee to her office.

"Stay with us, Aimee," Zack commanded when he'd lowered Caroline into a chair. Aimee caught a look of displeasure on Caroline's face, quickly replaced by an insincere smile.

"Oh, do stay, Aimee," she echoed.

Zack paced across the office and turned to look at her. "Suppose you start at the beginning and tell me what's wrong?"

"You didn't get my letter?" Caroline asked sadly. "No, of course not, or you would have returned immediately, as I requested. I sent a letter to Independence in the hope of catching you before you started west. Eli took sick. You know how he had a way of not taking care of himself. He grew worse . . ." She paused, as if gathering her courage. "Zack, Eli's dead." Her words ended in sobs and she held the handkerchief to her eyes. Only another woman would have noticed how contrived her movements were.

But it was Zack that drew Aimee's attention. His face turned pale, his lips thinned, and his eyes were black with grief. He turned away from the two women, but Aimee saw the strong shoulders shudder beneath the worsted suit coat, and his head slumped into his shoulders. Quickly she crossed the room, lightly touching his sleeve to let him know she was there. She didn't want to intrude on his grief. She remembered the pain of it all too well. Behind them, Caroline's weeping grew louder.

"Zack," she cried, and crossed to stand in front of him, raising her tearstained face so he could see her grief. "Zack . . ." She repeated his name helplessly and leaned against him so he could do nothing else but put his arms around her. They stood together, with Aimee alone and apart from them. Her heart grew tight in her chest. How well Caroline played her part. She hadn't been so grief-stricken while waiting for Zack's return. Feeling defeated, Aimee left the office, her last image that of Caroline in Zack's arms. Deliberately she busied herself with the restaurant and saloon, driving herself to do more than she needed to and yet unable to stop hoping that Zack would come looking for her, that he would tell her Caroline meant nothing to him. Late in the evening she went back to her office, but it was empty. She'd known it would be.

"Have you seen Mr. Crawford?" she asked Sam. She'd come on a pretense and couldn't keep herself from asking.

"Yes, ma'am. I saw him escortin' Mrs. Crawford upstairs. The poor lady was nearly faintin'. He ordered some whiskey."

"Has he come back down yet?" Aimee asked, willing her heart to stop its erratic beating.

"No, ma'am, I ain't see 'im," Sam said, and glanced aside at the sick misery he saw in Aimee's eyes. She went back to the saloon, where she ordered a glass of whiskey and drank it down without taking a breath.

The men clinging to the bar laughingly encouraged her, then slapped her on the back when she coughed. Aimee ordered another glass and then another. Each one was easier to drink down than the one before. The crowd around her grew noisier, more boisterous, and she never realized she was the noisiest of the lot. She laughed often and loudly, slapping the bar at a ribald joke, then ordering drinks all around.

She never noticed Daniel's disapproving looks. Nor did she see him signal over the heads of the crowd. She picked up another glass of whiskey, lifted it high, and taking a deep breath, drank it down. Her eyes saw the bar and her brain told her to put the glass back there, but the two seemed unconnected. Her knees buckled, but before she slid to the floor Zack was there, his strong arms lifting her high against his chest.

"You little fool," he said, and she turned to grin at him.

"Hello, Zhack," she mumbled. "Where's the n-neooow widow? Caroline's a widow now, a poor liddle w-widow—black widow. Be careful, Zhack, be . . ." Her head lolled against his shoulder. His bleak expression turned gentle as he looked at her. In spite of her avowals of independence, she still needed him to watch out for her. He carried her to her room and settled her on the bed, gently loosening the gown and restraining undergarments beneath. Then with her tucked under the covers, he pulled a chair around and settled himself into it. He needed to do some thinking and he didn't need the distraction of Aimee's body next to his.

Her head hurt. She'd been run over by a herd of buffalo. Her mouth was dry. She needed water. Surely they'd find water soon. She tried to open her eyes, but the sun burned too brightly, bringing pain with her slightest effort. She had to get up and move. Agnes Stuart was about to be sick on her. She could see her face. Aimee moaned and rolled away, her hand flopping over the edge of the bed.

"Aimee?" Zack was there. She raised her head and

looked at him, her eyes rolling wildly, and quickly he brought the chamber pot and held her head as her body rejected all the whiskey she'd forced down the night before. Spasms shook her body and at last she lay back exhausted and drained. Zack set the chamber pot to one side and dampened a cloth for her forehead. Blearily she looked at him, all the events of the night before coming back to her.

"Where's Caroline?" she blurted out.

Zack's lips tightened in annoyance, but he smiled. "In her room, I would imagine," he answered evenly.

"I'm surprised you're not still with her," Aimee said dully, "the grieving widow and all that."

"She is my brother's widow," Zack admonished her. "It hit her pretty hard last night, the realization that he's really dead." Zack glanced aside as he said the words. He still couldn't get used to the thought that Eli was gone.

"Do you still love her?" Aimee asked, and knew she shouldn't have, but fear was gnawing at her insides.

"You shouldn't have to ask that," Zack said, feeling angry with her. Didn't she realize what an effort it was for him to turn his ship away from the sea he loved so much and travel up the sluggish, muddy river to Sacramento? Only the fact that she was here brought him back to the madness of the gold-mining town. Restlessly he got to his feet and crossed to the window. He didn't want to quarrel with Aimee this morning. He needed time to think, to remember all the good times with Eli, and to put away his guilt for not being there when his brother needed him.

"I'm going back to the ship," he said. "I have some work to do."

"Zack, I'm sorry for what I said," Aimee cried, her eyes wide and uncertain. If he left now, she feared he might never come back. "Don't go yet. Let's talk."

"We'll talk later," he said wearily, and without another glance, left the room.

Aimee sat on the bed feeling miserable. Was she losing Zack? She couldn't bear it if he left. He was tired, she reassured herself. He needed to rest. He was grief-stricken over his brother. His aloofness had nothing to do with Caroline Crawford. She didn't believe any of it. In spite of a throbbing head, she sprang out of bed and washed and dressed in a simple day gown, thinking of the beautiful clothes Caroline always wore. She had nothing to do but look beautiful, Aimee thought resentfully. She didn't run three businesses. Deliberately she pulled the heavy honey-brown strands of hair into a severe knot, securing it with long pins and combs. It made her look older, more capable, she thought, studying the effect. She wasn't aware how it revealed the delicate prettiness of her nape.

She descended to the lobby and a myriad of problems, the first of which brought her immense pain. Shoulder to shoulder, Ruth and Dan Cooper approached her as she stood at the registry desk.

"We appreciate all you done for us," Ruth said in her gentle voice, "but we'll be leaving you."

"Where will you go?" Aimee asked, trying to dissuade them and knowing she couldn't. The Coopers hadn't been happy at the Golden Promise. "You've tried gold mining and failed to find anything. How will you feed your family? Ruth is due to have her baby in a few more months."

"We've been saving our earnings," Dan said proudly. "We figure we have enough to get a start on a farm up in Oregon."

"Oregon?" Aimee repeated blankly. "Why would you want to go there?"

"It's where we want to raise our kids," Ruth said. "We aren't cut out for this kind of life, living in a hotel, eating our meals in a café, working in a saloon."

"Then I'll move Dan. He can work in the hotel and I'll put Sam behind the bar."

Dan shook his head. "We want a regular home for our young 'uns. We want to be like a family again." He shuffled his feet. "I should have known when I come here that I'm better suited to digging fenceposts and plowing fields than I am at digging gold."

"We're much obliged for all you did for us," Ruth said, taking Aimee's hand and smiling gently. "You helped me and my little ones when we were about to go hungry. I can't ever forget that." She paused, then hurried on. "You're a good woman, Aimee, but maybe you ought to consider leaving this place too."

"You don't seem very happy for all you've done," Dan chimed in, "and I know for a fact that Mr. Crawford don't like it here. He talks about it all the time. You're the onliest reason he's still coming here."

"My place is here," Aimee said, turning away. "I can't leave all I've worked so hard to build."

"You've made some right smart choices," Dan conceded. "I've never seen a town build so fast as this one has. We wish you well."

"Dan, Ruth, wait. Won't you reconsider?"

They shook their heads in unison. "We got a different kind of dream," they said, and she knew there was no dissuading them.

"We'll stay a few more days until you get someone to take our place."

Aimee nodded in agreement and stood mulling over what they'd said. A sound on the stairs caused her to glance up. Zack was just coming down. His gaze met Aimee's and he paused, his face coloring. Obviously he'd spent the morning with Caroline Crawford. Aimee whirled and walked away from him. She could hear his footsteps bounding after her.

"Aimee, wait, let me explain," he cried, catching hold of her shoulder when she would have retreated into the kitchen. She turned to face him, her eyes flashing, her expression closed and cold.

"There's nothing to explain," she said with mock sweetness. "You couldn't stay with me because you had to rush off to your brother's widow."

"Caroline opened the door as I went past. She asked me to come in and talk." His words inflamed Aimee more.

"As I recall, I asked you to stay and talk this morning, but you just weren't able to."

"I'm sorry. Please try to understand. Caroline and I share the sorrow of losing Eli."

"Sorrow isn't all you've shared with Caroline, is it, Zack?" Aimee demanded.

"That's damnable of you to say at this time," Zack raged. His eyes were dark with fury. She'd pushed him too far, Aimee realized, and watched him stalk away, his shoulders rigid.

Her words hounded him all the way back to the ship. All the old guilts washed over him. He'd treated Eli badly, first in making love to his wife, then in leaving Eli to believe he'd driven Zack away by marrying his woman, and last, by abandoning Eli to handle a business that overwhelmed him. Eli had always been his little brother and Zack had always assumed responsibility for him; then in anger he'd walked away from him, ignoring the plea in his eyes, ignoring the signs of ill health. He should have been there with him instead of striking out cross-country. Now Caroline was here and it was Eli's request that Zack take care of his widow. Zack had failed Eli once, he wouldn't do so again.

Aimee chewed on the inside of her lips to keep from crying. Every time she felt the sting of tears behind her lids, she bit down on the tender skin until she tasted blood. She would not shed tears over Zack Crawford, she thought fiercely, and busied herself with finding a replacement for Ruth and Dan.

Zack didn't come back to the hotel the rest of the day or that evening. In the afternoon, Caroline descended the stairs, her gown and hair impeccable as usual, and with a gay little nod left the hotel, heading in the direction of the harbor. No doubt she was going to meet Zack, Aimee thought morosely, and wished fervently the *Sea Lady* might sink with both of them on it. In spite of herself she watched for Caroline's return, and when the evening shadows claimed the last light of the setting sun and she still hadn't returned, her anger turned to melancholy.

Aimee worked late over the books, until a sound at

the window spooked her and she put everything away and went up to bed. She tossed restlessly throughout the night, waking often from dreams of Zack and Caroline in each other's arms. When the first light of dawn shone in her window, she rose and dressed. She'd get a head start on the day's chores, she thought without enthusiasm.

At the top of the stairs she paused, staring down into the lobby at the lady who was quietly letting herself in. Glancing around surreptitiously, Caroline Crawford tiptoed across the entrance to the stairs. At the bottom, she looked up, startled to find Aimee glaring down at her. With a little shrug she gathered her skirts and started up. When she was level with Aimee, she smiled. Her eyes were smudged-looking from lack of sleep, and her hair, usually so perfect, was straggling around her ears. Her lips were full and bruised-looking, as if they'd been kissed often. It was obvious she'd spent the night making love. Once again she smiled and shrugged, a self-deprecating gesture that said she was, after all, a woman and couldn't help herself.

"I've been found out," she said lightly, her eyes dancing with knowing, secretive lights. "Zack and I have been in love for a long time."

"I don't believe you," Aimee blurted. "If he loves you, why doesn't he tell me so?"

"You know how men are. He doesn't want to hurt you any more. Be kind to him, Aimee. Let him go. He feels guilty enough as it is about you."

"He needn't," Aimee said stiffly.

"But he does. Zack's an honorable man. I always find honorable men so . . . interesting," Caroline mused. Her light laugh followed her down the hall to her room. Aimee thought of all she'd said; then, as the full import of the words hit her, she clasped a hand to her mouth, holding back her sobs until she was in her room again. Zack with Caroline. All her nightmares had become a reality.

Aimee spent the day in her room, not even answering when someone came to ask her about how to handle something in the hotel or saloon. Nor did she answer when Sam brought her a message from Zack. He shoved the note beneath her door and it lay there on the floor mockingly. She couldn't find the courage to open it and read the words Zack had sent her. She already knew the worst. She lay there all day and all night. Memories of the times she'd spent with Zack came back to her in all their sweet poignancy. She saw how he'd become so much a part of her life. How could she live without him? She never once thought of how she didn't need him.

When the morning came, she rose and changed her gown and went downstairs. As she moved through the rooms that comprised her empire, she thought of all she'd lost in the year since she'd first heard the shot that ended her father's life. Everyone she'd ever loved or depended on had left her, even Zack, but this building with its hotel and restaurant and gambling rooms, this was still here, something solid to depend on. It wouldn't walk away from her. She would devote all her time and energy to making the business bigger and better. Her establishment would be the best on the west coast, better than anything even San Francisco offered.

Late in the morning Johnny Cooper mentioned that the *Sea Lady* had set sail for San Francisco and Aimee never missed a count in her figures. She was getting over Zack Crawford already.

The spectacular success of the first weeks of business in her saloon slacked off as the fickle, restless miners moved on to new places opening further east along the main street. The town was growing, but Aimee no longer felt a part of the excitement and energy. Halfheartedly she went about her business, supervising new shows, hiring new dance-hall girls, bringing in new gaming tables. The miners continued to use her as their banker. Aimee Bennett might only be a woman, but she was someone to be trusted.

One morning, as Aimee worked behind the bar,

washing up glasses in preparation for the evening trade, the door opened and a woman entered.

"We're not open for business yet," Aimee called without looking up.

"Ah know," a familiar voice said, and Aimee glanced up.

"Loretta!" A mixture of emotions ran through Aimee. She straightened and dried her hands.

"How've you been?" Loretta asked softly, her bright eyes studying Aimee's face.

"I'm fine," Aimee answered. "I don't need to ask about you. You look wonderful." There was a glow about Loretta that had been missing for months. Aimee knew Billy's return had something to do with it. "Are you and Billy happy?"

Loretta nodded. "We're going to be married as soon as he gets back," she said joyfully. "He's off in the hills somewhere looking for gold. Ah couldn't help thinkin' how we used to talk about getting married and all. Ah was wondering if you want to be my bridesmaid."

"Oh, Loretta," Aimee said, and her eyes filled with tears. Suddenly she was around the bar and the two girls were hugging each other. "Oh, Loretta, I've been so sorry for the hateful thing I said to you. I didn't mean it. You've been the dearest and best friend anyone could ever have."

"It's all right, Aimee," Loretta reassured her. "Ah knew you didn't really mean it. It just seemed like Ah was so sad about everything, and hearing those words reminded me that underneath the fine talk and pretty gowns, Ah was still the same."

"Thank God, you are," Aimee cried. "You don't need to change anything about yourself. You're one of the greatest ladies I've ever known. Oh, Loretta, I've missed you so much. I've missed your humor and your common sense. Can you stay for a while? I've so much to tell you."

Loretta nodded. "Ah'm all alone right now, with Billy gone."

"Is he having much luck?" The two girls settled themselves in Aimee's offices.

"Some," Loretta said. "He ain't findin' it as fast as he'd like. Ah reckon no one is. We're talking about going to Oregon. Billy says it's pretty up there." Aimee felt her heart squeeze. Loretta was leaving. Soon she'd be all alone here in Sacramento.

"Ruth and Dan are going to Oregon too. They've given notice."

"Ah'm sorry they're leaving you," Loretta said sympathetically.

"I'm not. It's what they want. I wish them the best."

Loretta glanced at her sharply. "You seem different," she said slowly.

Aimee looked away. "Yes, so you told me before."

"No, Ah mean different from how you got to be. You seem more like the old Aimee."

"Not really." Aimee shrugged. "I don't want to be that person anymore. She suffered through too much."

"We all did, Aimee," Loretta reminded her. "It made us stronger."

"Perhaps you're right." Aimee stood up and paced around the room. She'd been plagued by a terrible restlessness the past few weeks.

"How's Zack?" Loretta asked, and saw how Aimee's shoulders stiffened beneath the dark silk of her gown.

"I don't know," Aimee answered flatly. "I haven't seen him for several weeks." She turned to look at Loretta, and suddenly all the misery she'd kept bottled up burst forth and she rushed to kneel beside Loretta's chair and bury her head against her friend's knee. "Caroline's here," she whispered, and Loretta guessed at her fear by the quiet desperation in her voice.

They talked late into the day. Ruth brought lunch for them and stayed to chat for a while, catching up on all the news and exchanging information about Oregon. Aimee felt oddly left out. Try as she might, she couldn't persuade Loretta to move back to the hotel.

"Billy and me have a little house down by the docks,

and that suits me just fine," Loretta said gently. "Ah'll come and visit you as often as Ah can."

"You promise?" Aimee insisted. "I'll be looking for you every day." Taking Loretta's hand, she gripped it tightly, as if she meant never to let her go. "Thank you for coming back today."

"Be careful, Aimee." Loretta clasped her hand back. "Billy stopped in at the Mother Lode one night and he heard Lundy and his men talking. They seemed pretty upset that you've taken some of their business. Lundy said he was going to teach you a lesson."

"I'll be careful," Aimee reassured her, and walked her to the door.

"Who's that woman?" Loretta asked as they crossed the lobby.

Aimee looked at the slim figure standing at the counter talking with Sam and quickly looked away. "That's Caroline Crawford," she whispered.

"She can't be," Loretta said, still studying the golden-haired woman. Aimee nodded.

Loretta looked perplexed. "That's puzzling," she said. "She's the same woman that visits Wilson Lundy in his back rooms at the Mother Lode."

"Are you sure?" Aimee asked, startled.

"Ah'm positive," Loretta said firmly. "Our window looks out over the back entrance to the Mother Lode." A slow smile spread over her face. "Maybe it's not over yet, when Zack finds out the kind of woman she is."

"It won't change anything at all," Aimee sighed. "Zack and I are finished. He chose Caroline over me and that can't be changed."

"He didn't say that. Caroline did, and she doesn't look like the kind of woman to trust over something as important as this." Loretta waved farewell and disappeared down the street.

Thoughtfully Aimee made her way up to her room to dress for the evening crowd. Everything Loretta said was true. She'd just been going on what Caroline had said the morning Aimee caught her sneaking back into the hotel. The woman had never actually said she'd spent the night with Zack. She'd only implied it, and Aimee had jumped to her own conclusion. But Caroline had said Zack loved her, not Aimee. She'd said Zack didn't want to hurt Aimee's feelings. Had she been lying? Aimee wondered, her heart beating wildly.

But there was Zack's note. She'd never read it, assuming it said those things that Caroline had already told her. What if it hadn't? What if it had? She couldn't bear to hope and be hurt all over again. She took out the note and propped it front of her mirror. Zack had been gone for nearly two weeks now, and they had been weeks of pain and humiliation for Aimee. She dressed, her glance straying time and again to the note. At last she took it up and with trembling fingers opened it.

"Sweet Aimee," he had written. "I'm sorry for not staying to talk this morning. Let's try again. Come to me tonight aboard the *Sea Lady*. I love you. Zack."

He loved her, not Caroline. Aimee pressed her lips to the boldly scrawled words. Come to me, he'd urged her, and out of anger and pride she'd stayed behind, suffering a thousand deaths. Soon . . . soon he'd be back. He had to return. She'd ask him about Caroline and she'd listen to everything he had to say. Hurry back, my darling, she whispered, and it was like a prayer gliding through the night, pulling him back to her.

Aimee went down to work that night with a lighter heart. Even Caroline's insinuations didn't daunt her spirits.

"Mrs. Crawford," Aimee said pleasantly, "I've been meaning to talk to you about your bill. It has become quite large."

"Zack will take care of it when he returns," Caroline said, her eyes glittering with amusement. "He's handling all my personal business now."

"Then I shan't worry. Zack Crawford has unlimited credit with me."

Caroline raised an eyebrow. "I won't be staying here at the hotel much longer," she said. "Zack will be back soon and we'll be making other arrangements."

"Will Mr. Lundy be included in those plans?" Aimee asked smoothly, and was pleased to see the ugly flush that stained Caroline's cheeks.

"I'd be very careful what I say to Zack if I were you," she snapped. "He won't believe any vicious gossip you may have heard about me."

Aimee raised her chin, meeting the other woman's glare unflinchingly. "If what I'm hearing is just vicious gossip, then you have nothing to worry about, have you?" she said.

With a snap of her parasol, Caroline stalked away. But Aimee noticed that she did not go out as she'd originally planned. She climbed the stairs back to her room and later in the evening ordered a tray of food to be brought up to her.

"You're looking bright-eyed tonight," Ruth observed when Aimee stopped in the kitchen for a quick bite of supper.

"Things are looking up, Ruth," Aimee said gaily.

"Having Loretta back for a while made me feel better too," Ruth said. "It seemed like old times again."

"Old times," Aimee echoed, but her thoughts were not on Loretta. They were on a dark-haired man whose skin was burned brown by the wind and sun and whose dark eyes held all the tenderness and love a woman could ever want.

Business was brisk in the days that followed. Aimee could barely handle it all. She'd hired a new woman to take over the cooking, and Ruth was showing her the way things were done in so large a restaurant. Companionably the women talked and exchanged recipes. Dan was working with Jake behind the bar, but it seemed a hopeless cause. She'd have to find someone else to take over when Dan left. Caroline Crawford was seldom seen in the days that followed Aimee's conversation with her, and Loretta reported her absence from the Mother Lode. Aimee looked forward to each day, hopeful it would be the day the *Sea Lady* came sailing up the river again.

Aimee's nights were restless. She lay in the lonely dark hours remembering the feel of Zack's hands on her, the taste of his kisses, and wondering why she was here alone instead of out there somewhere with him. If she'd sailed away with him when he first asked her, perhaps Caroline never would have found them. Yet she knew that was wishful thinking. If it were true that Zack still loved her, they had to resolve this issue of Caroline. Aimee couldn't live with the threat of an old love clouding her future.

There were other things to worry about as well. Even if Zack loved her rather than Caroline, what was she to do about the Golden Promise? She'd worked long and hard and in one short year had built up more than most men had. She was proud of the hotel and saloon, but could she go on living apart from Zack as she had? He was a seaman and there would always be separations, but they wouldn't be as long if she weren't tied down here in Sacramento with her own business. Was the Golden Promise worth the sacrifices she'd made?

Still, her old fears made her cling to the security the Golden Promise offered. She was wealthier now than even her father had been. Wasn't that enough? Yet, remembering how quickly that other world had been wrenched away from her, she yearned for more riches.

Her decision was made for her one dark night when the heat of the summer day had given way to a sultry, clinging dampness that crept up from the river and shrouded the streets in fog. Lamplight spilling from the windows was blurred and then lost altogether in the gray mist. Miners, given to superstition, hurried uneasily from one building to another, where they swallowed down whiskey in great quantities or settled themselves at tables, content not to go out again until the saloons closed. A group of sailors came into the saloon and ordered whiskey.

"Where you fellas been?" Dan asked, filling their glasses.

"Just come in on the *Sea Lady*," one of them said. "Thought we'd never make it. The fog was so thick we couldn't hardly see our hands in front of our faces."

"I'm surprised you sailed on a night like this. Why didn't you just pull over to the riverbank and wait it out?"

"We was all for it, but the captain, he says no, he's anxious to get here."

"We figure he's got hisself a woman," another man said, and they all laughed. Aimee listened to them talking and her heart leapt with joy. Zack had returned. Nervously she wiped her palms against the folds of her gown.

"I'll be gone for the rest of the evening," she told Ruth, wrapping a shawl over her head and shoulders.

"You can't go out in this weather," Ruth protested.

"I'll be all right."

"Where are you going, in case we need to reach you?"

"I can't be reached," Aimee answered, then relented and smiled at the gentle woman. "I'll be at the *Sea Lady*," she said softly, and Ruth smiled and nodded her approval.

"I don't expect we'll be needin' you the rest of the night," she said, and for a moment Aimee thought she'd winked. The last sight she had of Ruth was of her standing in the middle of the restaurant, one hand curving protectively around her protruding stomach, the other massaging the small of her back.

Aimee made her way through the streets of Sacramento, her heart beating rapidly against the wall of her chest, and she thought of another time she'd gone to Zack after one of their quarrels. She prayed this time they would be able to resolve their differences as well. She almost ran past the *Sea Lady*, so thick was the fog. This time there was so sign of Zack on the deck. He must be below in his quarters, she thought, and swallowed hard, wondering what she would say to him. She crept aboard the ship and timidly knocked at the door of his cabin. There was no answer. He'd gone

386

out. Perhaps he'd only gone for a drink and would soon return, she thought, and paced the deck, wondering what to do.

It had taken a great deal of courage to come here tonight. She couldn't go back until she'd talked to him. She'd wait all night if she had to, she decided, and settled herself into a corner against some bales of cargo. The fog was thicker down by the river, and she couldn't see beyond the ship's railing. The rigging creaked and the river current moved the water against the hull in a soothing rhythm. Aimee laid her head back and sat thinking of Zack. This was his world, she thought. Could this be her world too? She yawned and shifted her weight. She could be happy anywhere as long as Zack was there with her.

A shout woke her. She raised her head and looked around, startled at her surroundings, then surprised that she'd slept. The sky to the east was light gray already, tinged with the fiery red of a sunrise. It was going to be another hot day. She jerked upright as she saw the orange-red glow on the horizon. Black smoke billowed in the sky. Something was on fire. Alarms rang in her head. Fires could quickly spread along the line of wooden frame buildings. The Golden Promise could be endangered. They had to wet down the building so the flames would pass over it. She made her way down the gangplank and ran down the street toward the fire. A wind sprang up, sweeping the smoke back toward the river. It filled her lungs. Coughing, she ran on. The fire was close to the Golden Promise, she thought frantically, and then she reached the end of the street and halted. It was no use going on. The Golden Promise was ablaze, the hot orange flames licking greedily at the roof and balconies. The sign they'd so proudly hung smoldered, the painted words glowing red hot before bursting into flames. Men worked frantically, filling buckets from the well and flinging them against the blazing building, to little avail.

"Nothing we can do now," one man called to another. "Let's wet down those buildings over there so they don't catch fire."

"No, you can't give up," Aimee wanted to cry out, but knew it was hopeless. Then she thought of something else. Where were Ruth and Dan and their children? What about the hotel guests? Had they made it to safety? Frantically she pushed through the crowd, calling to Ruth.

"Aimee, they're over here," Loretta called from across the street, and Aimee hurried to them. Ruth sat on the plank porch of the general store, her arms cradling her unborn baby, her hands held stiffly in front of her.

"Ruth, are you all right?" Aimee cried. Silently Ruth nodded and continued rocking back and forth.

"She burned her hands getting the children out," Loretta said, tearing strips off her petticoat.

"The children," Aimee cried. "My God, Ruth, are they safe?"

"They're all right," Loretta said. "Val and the girls took them to safety. Dan's helping with the fire. Everyone got out safely."

"Thank God," Aimee sighed in relief, leaning her cheek against Ruth's. "Did they get all the guests out of the hotel?"

"Zack and Dan are working on that right now," Loretta said, and bringing a can of lard from the general store, smeared it on Ruth's hands and wrapped them in the cotton strips.

"Zack?" Aimee jumped to her feet. She could see his tall figure leading Sam from the hotel. Burning timbers were falling, and with a loud crash and a shower of sparks, the top floor caved in. "Zack!" Aimee screamed, and started toward him, but Ruth's bandaged hand clutched hers.

"The baby's coming," Ruth cried, her fingers biting into Aimee's arm in a painful grip.

"It can't be. It's too early," Aimee said soothingly.

Ruth shook her head, gasping against her pain. "It's coming now," she insisted.

Aimee glanced at Loretta, remembering another woman and her baby struggling for life out on the prairie. I can't go through this again, Aimee thought, and wanted to run away, but Ruth was curling over in a paroxysm of pain.

Aimee cast a last frantic look over her shoulder, the need to go to Zack strong within her. She glimpsed his broad shoulders outlined against the fiery flames of the Golden Promise. The crowd shifted and now she could see Caroline cradled against his chest. Her hair was in disarray and her face streaked with soot. Even as Aimee watched, she tilted her head for Zack's kiss. He pressed his lips against her forehead and broke away. Caroline clung to his arm, sobbing, and once again Zack pulled her to him. Ruth moaned and Aimee turned to help.

"What're we goin' t' do?" Loretta asked frantically, and Aimee glanced at her in surprise. For all her other skills, Loretta had never helped at a birthing. Aimee remembered how wretchedly she'd received her own experience.

"Let's lay her down on the porch," she said. "And we're going to need more rags. Get someone to look for the doctor." Automatically she reeled off a list of things to be done. She had little hope the doctor would arrive in time. He'd be busy attending those injured in the fire. Ruth cried out in pain, and Aimee moved to smooth back her hair from her forehead. "Get a bucket of water from the well," she ordered, and Loretta flitted away. She was back in no time with the water. Both girls shed their petticoats and Loretta set to ripping them in strips while Aimee bathed Ruth's forehead and crooned words of encouragement.

The hours seemed to last interminably. The fire spread to another building and raced on to a third. A heavy pall of smoke hung in the air, obscuring the bright morning sun. The doctor stopped by to examine Ruth and instructed them to continue as they were. A woman came to offer her home, but it was already too late to move the laboring patient. Sheets were tied to the porch posts to afford her some privacy, and late in the morning, as the firefighters slowly brought the blaze under control, Ruth gave birth to a beautiful daughter. Wearily she raised her head to peer at the tiny being and with uncharacteristic whimsy named her Flame. By the time Dan came to check on his wife and children, mother and child were fast asleep in spite of the hardness of their plank bed and the commotion outside their makeshift room.

"She's beautiful," Dan said softly, and Aimee wasn't sure if he meant mother or new daughter.

He glanced at Aimee. "The fire's out," he said. "We weren't able to save much."

"You did your best," Aimee said. "Do they know what started it?"

"Someone burned you out, Aimee," he said. "I'm right sorry." He went away then, somehow feeling guilty that he hadn't been able to prevent the whole thing. She'd worked hard for the Golden Promise. She didn't deserve to be burned out like that.

Numbly Aimee wandered across the street to the smoldering ruins of what had once been the Golden Promise. The large metal safe stood nearly unscathed in the charred timbers. She'd have to put Jake to guard it until it could be opened. As she stood before the ashes, a shadow loomed nearby and she turned to look into the angry face of Zack Crawford.

18

"Where the devil have you been?" he growled, and before she could gather her wits and answer, he stepped forward and grabbed her shoulders, shaking her briefly. "Answer me. Where were you all night?"

"Where was *I*?" she demanded, her fatigue forgotten as she glared at him. "Where were *you*?"

"Don't play games with me, Aimee. I was sick with worry over you. You weren't here at the hotel. Just tell me where you were all night." His face was grim, long lines radiating down his lean brown cheeks. He was covered with soot and smelled of smoke, and one side of his hair was singed. Her anger melted at seeing him so weary, but pride kept her from admitting where she'd spent the night.

"I was helping Ruth. She's had her baby," she hedged.

"That was this morning. Where were you last night?" he insisted.

"I . . . I prefer not to say," she answered.

"Never mind," Zack said flatly. "I already know. I just wanted to see if for once you'd tell me the truth."

"What do you mean?" Aimee asked in alarm.

"I know you spent the night with Lundy. You've been with him before."

"Lundy?" Aimee cried, amazed that he could be so mistaken. "And how have you come to this knowledge, pray tell? Let me guess. Caroline told you." Zack looked at her in surprise. She wasn't denying it.

Aimee rushed on in anger. "Caroline is so helpful about these things. She also informed me that the two of you spent the night together before you left for San Francisco."

"I haven't. We didn't," Zack stuttered, wondering how he'd become the accused.

"I was so frightened . . . afraid you still loved her," Aimee whispered, her anger forgotten at his quick denial. "We have to talk." Her eyes were unwavering as they met his. "Just tell me one thing. Do you honestly believe I would choose Wilson Lundy over you?"

"Well, you didn't come to the boat as I asked you to the last night I was in port, and Caroline said she caught you sneaking into the hotel before anyone was up." Aimee waited, her gaze unwavering. "You seemed more interested in staying here in Sacramento than in being with me," Zack continued, and the evidence seemed feeble even to his own ears.

"Do you believe all that?" she asked again, and he read the truth in her eyes.

"No, I don't," he admitted, and cursed himself for the jealous fool he'd been. Still, he wondered where she'd spent the night.

"I was on the ship waiting for you," she admitted, realizing it was important for him to know. Caroline could defeat them only if they allowed misunderstandings to exist. Once on a mountain ledge Aimee had understood that pride could cost her the one thing she wanted most. Now she saw the truth of it again.

"Aimee . . ." Zack caught her up in his arms and she closed her eyes against a surge of joy.

"You came to the *Sea Lady*, even after what Caroline told you?" he asked, his large hands cupping her face, his dark eyes filled with love as they gazed into hers.

"I wanted to ask you—to beg you—not to leave me."

"I promised I would never leave you again."

"I didn't want to hold you to a promise if you loved Caroline."

"I love you." Zack crushed her lips beneath his.
I'm sorry about the Golden Promise."

"It doesn't matter as long as you're here," she said.
he was in Zack's arms again. Nothing else mattered.

"I have the money for your gold. It's on the *Sea
Lady*. You can rebuild the Golden Promise. If you
n't have enough money, I'll help you." His offer
as sweet and Aimee hugged him for it.

"I don't want to think about it now." She kissed
m again, just glad to have him near. "We're to-
ther once more. I'll never let anyone come between
again."

"I hope you can forgive Caroline," Zack said softly.
he's all alone now and she's not used to it. She
esn't have your strength. She's afraid you'll resent
presence."

"I do," Aimee said honestly.

"You don't have to fear anything from Caroline,
mee. I love only you. I couldn't be with another
man now, especially not Caroline. I told her that
fore I left for San Francisco."

"You told her?" Aimee asked breathlessly.

"I told her I was going to marry you as soon as you
reed to it."

"Oh, Zack." She rested her head against his chest.
was her mainstay. She couldn't live without him.
r gaze settled on the ashes of the Golden Promise.
l her dreams ended in the fire—except one. She
htened her arms around Zack's waist. This dream
would never let go. "Let's get married right away,"
said.

"Do you mean it?" Zack asked, holding her away
m him so he could peer into her eyes.

"Let's go now, this very minute. We won't even
e time to change our clothes."

"Whoa!" Zack's laughter was strong and deep. "The
vn's still in an uproar about this fire. Let's clean up
it and make arrangements for a wedding tonight.
ce there's no church, we can have it at the Mother
de. It'll take everyone's mind off what's happened."

Reluctantly Aimee agreed. Zack called out the news to the men still standing around in the street discussing the fire. "Everyone's invited." Their dirty faces brightened considerably.

Caroline came along the walk, her eyes inquisitive.

"Caroline, there's going to be a wedding," Zack called, ready to forgive her for her lies, since he had Aimee back.

The woman stood silent and still for a moment, struggling with the news Zack had given her. With an effort she smiled at them. "Congratulations, Aimee," she said simply. Her tone said: You've won. "I wish you both the best."

"Thank you," Aimee answered.

"I'm sorry if I caused trouble for you and Zack," Caroline continued. "I do hope you can find it in your hearts to forgive me." She looked at Zack appealingly.

"It's all right," he said gruffly. "We understand."

"I was just so afraid of being abandoned by you. I've lost Eli. I couldn't bear to lose you too. I never really meant to come between you and Aimee. You do believe me, don't you?" She looked at Aimee with guileless eyes.

Aimee nodded. "Let's forget about it."

Zack smiled in relief, glad there would be no feuding between the two women. Other men came to congratulate him. Someone passed around a bottle of whiskey. Eagerly the men drank, washing away the acrid taste of smoke.

Caroline turned back to Aimee. "You've been so kind, Aimee," she said softly. "I—"

The rest of what she was about to say was interrupted by Loretta flinging her arms around Aimee. "At last, Aimee Bennett, yo're showin' a little bit a sense." Loretta laughed, and Aimee hugged her back.

"I want you to be my maid of honor, Loretta."

"Ah'd be honored," Loretta exclaimed. "There's not much time to plan for your wedding."

Aimee looked at her in dismay. "I have nothing to wear. All my gowns were burned in the fire."

"I'll give you one of mine. It'll be a little big, but we can pin it," Loretta offered.

"Excuse me." Caroline stepped forward. "I'm closer to your size, Aimee, and I have the perfect gown for you. Let me give it to you as a wedding present to show you how sorry I am for everything that's happened."

"I . . . I . . ." Aimee glanced at Loretta helplessly. The last thing she wanted was to be married in Caroline's gown, but the offer had been made so humbly that to turn it down would seem ungracious.

"That's right generous of you," Loretta was saying, so Aimee had little choice.

"Thank you," Aimee said.

"Thank you for letting me atone for my mistakes," Caroline said piously.

A thought came to Aimee. "How is it your gowns didn't burn in the fire?"

Caroline smiled, a sad, deprecating smile. "I was so ashamed of my behavior that I'd made arrangements to move out of the Golden Promise. Last night I had Sam take my trunks to the Mother Lode until I could find another room."

"I see," Aimee replied. Caroline's explanation sounded plausible, but something about her actions bothered Aimee.

"Why don't you come to the Mother Lode with me now?" Caroline suggested. "Mr. Lundy has been kind enough to offer me a room there."

Warily Aimee agreed. After making arrangements to meet Loretta at her house, where she would bathe and dress for the wedding, she followed Caroline along the boardwalk to the Mother Lode. It seemed incredible to her that she was now being befriended by the very woman who'd done her best to take Zack from her.

"Zack is a special kind of man, Aimee," Caroline was saying. "I hope you know how lucky you are."

"I believe I do," Aimee answered stiffly.

"I truly do wish him happiness," Caroline sighed.

"If it can't be with me, then I'm glad it's you he loves."

"Thank you," Aimee said, and realized they'd been extremely polite during the past hour, but there had been little friendship. They arrived at the Mother Lode and Caroline led the way to her room. It was far more elaborate than Aimee had expected and she guessed that Wilson Lundy had once occupied the room, and indeed still might. Caroline crossed to a chest and opened its ornate lid, digging through the assorted gowns.

She's probably looking for the ugliest gown she owns, Aimee thought, and vowed she wouldn't wear it. To her surprise, Caroline pulled forth a frock of pale silk, its draped skirt festooned with lace and matching silk flowers.

"It's beautiful," Aimee exclaimed in surprise. "Are you sure you want to lend it to me?"

"It's a gift," Caroline said. "It's never been worn. It was one of the last gowns Eli had shipped from Paris for me and of course after his death, I simply couldn't wear it." Her fingers smoothed the silk in a wistful gesture that made Aimee feel ashamed of her earlier thoughts. Perhaps she'd judged Caroline too harshly.

She hurried back to Loretta's to prepare for the wedding. Loretta helped her with her hair and gown, telling her all the news since the fire. Ruth and the new baby had been moved to the doctor's house. His wife would take care of them for a few days. Dan was sleeping down at the stables; the Cooper children had been taken in by the same kindhearted woman who'd offered a bed to Ruth during her labor. Others who had once worked at the Golden Promise had found places for themselves, and everyone was anticipating the wedding. Some of the town ladies were preparing dishes of food to serve. There was even going to be dancing.

"They're impressed that after losin' everything you can just up and get married," Loretta said proudly.

"They must not have come over the Oregon trail," Aimee said. "It teaches you a few lessons about living."

The gown fit her perfectly. The tight waist flared into a full skirt draped into a demure bustle at the back. Aimee coaxed her hair into curls at the back of her neck and ears, much as she'd worn her hair back in Webster.

"You make a beautiful bride," Loretta sighed, and the two girls hugged each other out of sheer happiness.

"Oh, Loretta, I wish Billy were here so we could have a double ceremony," Aimee murmured.

"Me too," Loretta said wistfully.

At the appointed hour, they walked across the yard to the Mother Lode. The bar had been converted for the festivities into a table holding numerous dishes of food. One end of the room had been festooned with bright streamers of cloth and lanterns. The preacher stood stiff and ready in his good suit, his gun strapped to his hip, a worn Bible clutched in his hands. Nervously he wiped his boots against the backs of his pant legs. A bouquet of wildflowers, already wilting in the heat, stood in a glass nearby.

Caroline Crawford stood to one side wearing a simple gown of blue faille. The piano player pounded out a somber rendition of the bridal march. The room was crowded with guests, but Aimee had eyes for none of them.

Zack stood beside the preacher, wearing a dark suit with a white shirt. She hadn't seen him so formally attired since they'd started out on the Missouri riverboat. He looked rugged and virile and incredibly handsome. Not a few of the women present sighed over him. Loretta pressed a bouquet of flowers into Aimee's hand as she stepped forward to join Zack. His dark eyes captured hers, glowing with love. His lean hand took hold of hers in a strong, sure grip. Together they turned to face the preacher. He cleared his throat.

"We are gathered here tonight to—"

"I want to talk to the little lady about my gold," a belligerent voice called from the door.

"You can't come in now, there's a wedding going on."

"Ain't nobody gettin' married here until we find out about our gold," another man called.

The preacher paused while everyone turned to the men standing in the door. McCabe, one of the miners who banked with Aimee, shouldered his way in.

"What's the meaning of this?" Zack demanded.

"That's what we'd like to know." McCabe sneered. "We heard there was a fire at the Golden Promise, so we come down here to find out about the gold we banked with Miss Bennett. When we get here, we find out she's getting married and leaving Sacramento."

"I've made no plans to leave Sacramento," Aimee said.

"Are you planning to rebuild the Golden Promise?" someone called.

"Yes, I suppose I am," Aimee answered, and was startled at the look of anger on Zack's face.

"That ain't what we heard," McCabe called. "We heard you're planning to leave town with all our gold."

"I assure you I've made no such plans," Aimee said, looking around the room. Some of the men relaxed. She'd always been trustworthy with them; there was no reason to doubt her now. But others were not so mollified.

"I'll just take my gold now," one of them shouted. "That way I know its safe."

"Me too," others chimed in.

"I'm afraid that's impossible right now," Aimee said, and at the angry mutterings hastened to explain further. "The safe is still too hot to be opened. Your gold is safe, though. It may have melted a bit, but it's all there."

"I'll take a look now," McCabe said. He seemed to have assumed the role of spokesman for the others. "Who else wants to go?" Several men hurried to join him.

"Zack." Aimee turned to him in alarm. "I only have Jake guarding the safe." Quickly he grabbed a gun from the preacher's holster and headed for the back door. Aimee followed close behind. Other miners and their wives were streaming into the street. Aimee caught a glimpse of Caroline and Wilson Lundy. Something about the two of them made her feel uneasy.

By the time they arrived, the miners had already reached the blackened remains of the Golden Promise. Aimee saw Jake arguing with them; then someone grabbed his rifle and shoved him aside. Ropes were thrown around the safe and several men ran to grab the ends and haul it out of the hot ashes. One of the miners greedily reached out to touch the iron box.

"Hot damn!" He let out a yell and did a quickstep away from the safe, nursing his hand against his chest. "Watch it, she's hot," someone shouted. "Bring some water." Other men ran to fill pails and pour them over the metal box. Steam rose in the air and water sizzled and danced across the hot metal.

"You're goin' to crack it wide open if you keep that up," Jake yelled. He'd picked himself up and drawn closer to see what the men were doing.

"That's what we're aimin' t' do," one of the miners yelled, and tossed his bucket of water on the steaming safe.

Zack stepped forward. "This safe belongs to Miss Bennett. You have no right to break into it."

"We want our gold now, Crawford," the men yelled.

"Miss Bennett has told you she'll give you the gold as soon as the safe cools enough to be opened."

"It's cool enough now," McCabe yelled. "We want it open, otherwise we'll open it ourselves. Simon, head over to the general store and get some dynamite." A man loped across the street to the store.

"What's it going to be, Miss Bennett? Do we blow it up or are you going to open it?"

"That's enough," Zack commanded. "Get away from the safe."

"You can't stop us, Crawford." McCabe sneered.

Zack pulled back the hammer of his gun and leveled it at him. "I may not be able to stop all of you," he said evenly, "but some of you will never live to see what's in the safe." The miners backed away.

"Grab him, men," McCabe yelled, and Zack jumped to one side, but he was too late. Two burly miners grabbed him from behind, while a third disarmed him. Zack struggled in their grip. McCabe stepped forward and slammed his meaty fist into Zack's middle. He bent double from the pain, but the two miners pulled him upright as McCabe slugged him again.

"Let him go," Aimee cried. "I'll open the safe."

"Now you're cooperating," McCabe said approvingly. "Give the little lady some room. Come right on over here." The miners made a path for her.

Aimee crossed to the safe and worked the dial. "I can open the safe, but your gold's not in there."

"Where is it?" the miners howled menacingly. Their faces were harsh and brutal-looking in the flickering light of the lamps.

"I can't tell you," Aimee said, and flinched back as McCabe came closer and grabbed her shoulder. "If I do, the gold will be gone before daylight."

"Tell us where it is or your bridegroom will be dead before morning."

"No," Aimee cried, looking at Zack. The two miners still held him, but now one of them had a gun to his head. "Please don't," she implored. "I'll tell you where I've hidden it. It's . . . it's in a metal box under the floorboards near where you found the safe."

"It's a lie. She's just stalling," a miner shouted angrily. "Why would she put the gold under the floorboards when she's got the safe?"

"What about that, Miss Bennett?" McCabe demanded.

Aimee looked around the circle of faces. Even Zack was waiting for her answer. She took a deep breath. "My . . . my father was a banker and he used to always say the safest place to keep money was outside the safe. A robber always goes to the safe first thing."

The miners mumbled among themselves, some agreeing with her father's reasoning.

"The safe was a decoy!" they exclaimed. Zack grinned at her illogical solution.

"I still don't believe it," McCabe growled. "Show us." He shoved her toward the smoking ashes.

"Don't be a fool, man. She can't go in there," Zack cried out. "There are still live coals."

"Simon, Whitey, get some men and pour water over this part of the ashes," McCabe snapped. The men sprang to do as he ordered.

"Now, Miss Bennett," McCabe said, glaring down at her. "Suppose you show us where our gold's hidden." Taking her arm, he propelled her through the black rubble to the area where the safe had stood. The floorboards were scorched but intact. Aimee looked around, gauging where the floor safe had been.

"Look in this area here," she instructed, and the miners pushed forward with shovels and picks to clear away the fallen timbers and charred wood. The burned carpet crumbled at the touch. When the men had cleared a spot, Aimee pointed to the loose planks and two men leapt forward to pry them up.

"There's nothing here," they cried, looking around the circle of onlookers. "She's lied to us."

"No, I haven't," Aimee protested. "It must be there." She pressed forward to see better, then dropped to her hands and knees in the ashes and reached into the empty space. The gold was gone. But who could have taken it? Her suspicious gaze went to the faces of the men who'd worked for her—Sam, Dan, and Jake. But they hadn't known about the hiding place.

"You'd better do some explaining," McCabe said.

"Search the *Sea Lady*," someone called out. "She's probably hidden it there."

"Yeah, the fire was just a ruse to cover the theft."

"Any man who puts one foot on the *Sea Lady* will die," Zack called. His face was bloody and bruised from McCabe's punches, but his eyes were dark and deadly as he studied each man as if remembering his face. The miners eased back.

"We don't aim to harm the ship," one of them said.

"We just want to get our gold back. We worked hard to find it, dug it out of the ground, and toted it down here to the Golden Promise for safekeeping. We ain't gonna let someone steal what's ours."

Aimee stepped forward. "I'm not stealing your gold. Please believe me," she appealed to them. "I took your gold for safekeeping and I am responsible for it. I'll pay you sixteen dollars an ounce for the gold left with me. That's what they're paying in San Francisco." The miners glanced at each other.

"That seems fair enough to me," McCabe said. "What d' you think, boys?"

"Yeah, it's fine with me," the other men muttered.

"Good." Aimee squared her shoulders and looked around the crowd. "If you gentlemen will be kind enough to release Mr. Crawford, he can return to his ship and bring my money back here." Quickly the men dropped his arms. Zack studied Aimee.

"Will you be all right until I get back?" he asked, and she nodded. He hurried away from the knot of men.

"We will also need a table and chair." A man hurried away.

Caroline Crawford and Wilson Lundy exchanged glances, then turned back to the Mother Lode. Caroline's hand was tucked beneath Lundy's elbow.

Wearily Aimee made her way out of the remnants of the burned building and stood in the street looking down at the beautiful dress that was to have been her wedding gown. It was blackened at the hem. There was no time to think of that now. A table and chair were set up in the middle of the street, a lamp was brought. The safe was opened and the stiffly curling remains of her account books spread before her.

Zack returned with the money and the men lined up before the table. One by one they stepped forward. Aimee called the men by name and they told her the amount of gold they'd left with her. Without consulting her account books, Aimee paid the sums. Only two men named higher amounts than they were enti tled to. Both times, Aimee's direct gaze caused them to shuffle their feet and glance away while they mumbled the correct amount. When it was all done, Aimee's money was gone.

Zack paid off the last two miners with his own money. Aimee sat alone in the middle of the street, the blackened remains of the Golden Promise behind her, the charred books before her, each account marked paid. Zack waved good-bye to the last miner and crossed the street to her. "That was a brave and honorable thing you did," he said softly.

With an air of finality, Aimee closed the books. "I had to do it," she answered, thinking of her father. "I had to."

"You're tired. Come back to the *Sea Lady* with me and rest," Zack urged, but Aimee only shook her head.

"I have nothing left," she said, resting her head in her hands.

"You have me," Zack said softly. He squatted before her, his eyes warm and filled with love, his smile gentle.

"Don't try to placate me, Zack," she cried. "Everything I worked so hard for has been destroyed."

"I have plenty for both of us. What's mine is yours. Come with me now to the *Sea Lady*. We'll leave in the morning and you can put all this behind you."

"I can't leave now," Aimee cried. "Don't you understand? Someone stole the gold and burned the Golden Promise to cover up the crime. I can't leave until I get that gold back. It's all I have left."

"Aimee, tonight you could have lost your life, and all for the sake of gold. Is gold so important to you that you can turn your back on the people who love you?"

"I have to find my gold, Zack," Aimee cried. "I have to. I was penniless once. I won't be again."

Zack studied her streaked face and his expression grew stubborn. "Tomorrow morning the *Sea Lady* sails out of this port and it won't be coming back.

Make up your mind once and for all, Aimee, what it is you want, the gold or me."

"Zack!" she called, watching his tall figure stride away down the street. He didn't look back. He'll come back; he has before, she thought. She had to find out who had taken her gold. Everything she had was gone. Suddenly the events of the day seemed to overwhelm her and she laid her head on the table.

"Aimee?" Loretta was there. "Come home with me. It will be all right. You'll see. Things always look better in the morning."

"Zack doesn't understand," Aimee said dully. Meekly she got to her feet and followed Loretta.

"He'll see things different in the mornin'," Loretta said. She tucked Aimee's books under one arm and lent support with the other. Together they made their way down the street to Loretta's little house.

Loretta lit the lamp and placed the books on the table. She was worried about Aimee. She was too quiet, too calm. "Ah'll get you some water to wash up with," she said, looking at Aimee's bedraggled gown and grimy face. A smudge of soot streaked one cheek, and the hem of her skirt was permanently stained.

While she waited, Aimee stood at the table, her hands smoothing the curling blackened edges of one of the account books. Everything was gone, she mused. Everything it had taken her nearly a year to build had been destroyed in one night. The Golden Promise was no more. She opened the book and looked at all the neat columns of names and figures, all the men whose gold she'd banked. A name leapt out at her and Aimee stiffened. Loretta walked into the room and saw her gaze riveted to the book.

"What is it, Aimee?" she asked in alarm.

Aimee turned to her, eyes wide and triumphant. "I know who took the gold and set the fire," she said.

"You know? Are you sure?"

Aimee nodded. "Every man who left his gold with me came to be paid off, every man except one." Her finger jabbed at a name on the page. "Wilson Lundy."

"Lundy from the Mother Lode?" Loretta asked doubtfully.

"Yes, don't you see?" Aimee said. "He didn't come because he had his gold. No one except you knew about the hiding place beneath the floorboards."

"Ah never told him," Loretta cried.

"I know you didn't," Aimee said quickly. "One day when I was putting something in the hiding place, Caroline Crawford walked in and later Wilson Lundy brought his gold to be stored with me. He'd never done it before. While he was there, he seemed to be searching for something. He looked all around and he stood over the hiding place. He knew it was there. I'm sure of it. Caroline must have been part of it."

"There's something else," Loretta said. "Ah saw Caroline talking to McCabe tonight before the wedding."

"She must have told him about the missing gold, otherwise why would he have come at just that moment to demand it be returned?" Aimee glanced down at her gown. "No wonder Caroline was so nice to me. She planned right to the end to stop the wedding." Anger at the way Caroline had schemed drove Aimee to the door.

"What are you going to do?" Loretta asked in alarm.

"I'm going to confront them both and demand they return the gold."

"Maybe you ought to wait till morning so Zack or somebody can help you."

"Zack is sailing back to San Francisco in the morning," Aimee said. "I can't wait. I can take care of this myself." Without waiting for Loretta's reply, Aimee hurried out, closing the door firmly behind her. She was already across the square and at the door of the Mother Lode by the time Loretta got to the door. Undecided, Loretta stood watching her disappear into the saloon while she chewed on her bottom lip. Her innards told her Aimee needed help. Grabbing up a shawl, Loretta hurried away in the direction of the *Sea Lady*.

"Hello, Aimee. It's rather late to come calling, isn't it?" Caroline said, tying the satin sash of her robe.

"I'm sorry if I've interrupted your sleep," Aimee said. "You must need it after last night."

Uneasily Caroline glanced at Wilson Lundy. "Yes, it was a difficult night for us all. We're sorry for your losses."

"I appreciate your sentiment," Aimee replied, and turned to Lundy. "I'd like to thank you as well for not demanding repayment of your gold." Lundy looked at her, startled. "Had you forgotten you'd stored a small bag of gold dust with me?"

"N-no," Lundy stammered. His eyes darted sideways to Caroline. "It was such a small amount, and in view of your losses, I decided to forget about it."

"That's very generous of you," Aimee said sweetly, "and totally out of character. Are you sure you didn't manage to recover your gold when you took all the rest?"

Once again Lundy darted a glance at Caroline. "Aimee!" she cried in outrage. "Mr. Lundy is being most generous to you, and you accuse him of this heinous deed."

"I do. What's more, I'm accusing you as well." Aimee swung to face the woman whom Zack had loved. "You told him about my hidden safe."

"How would I have known about it?"

"You walked in on me one day and you became curious. You went back and searched my office and then you told Lundy about it. Lundy didn't come to claim his gold tonight because he knew it wasn't there, but you didn't want me marrying Zack, so you told McCabe about the missing gold so he'd come and stop the wedding." Caroline's face was white with shock and guilt.

Lundy jerked around to confront her. "You fool," he shouted, and his hand slashed out to slap her. "You couldn't give up your old love even when he no longer wanted you."

"You're the fool," Caroline cried. "We could have

brazened this out if you hadn't given way to your jealousy. Now she knows everything."

Lundy glanced at Aimee and his eyes narrowed. "It won't do her any good," he said. "I'll take care of her."

"What are you going to do?" Aimee demanded, fear sweeping over her. She should have heeded Loretta's advice.

"We can't have you repeating this little story to anyone," Lundy said, buckling a gun holster at his wasit. "I'll take her up in the hills someplace and get rid of her." Carefully Aimee began backing toward the door. Before she could escape, Lundy was there, twisting her arm behind her. Aimee cried out in pain.

"Lundy, no," Caroline shouted, and her voice shook with fear. "You can't kill her. I won't be a part of a murder."

"You already are." Lundy sneered. "If I get caught, I'll tell the whole town you helped me set the fire at the Golden Promise and steal the gold. You're to keep silent, understand?"

Whimpering, Caroline shook her head in agreement.

Lundy took out his gun and pressed it to Aimee's throat. The cold metal bit into the soft skin, causing her to flinch. "We're going down to the stable now," Lundy growled, "and if you scream, it will be the last sound you make."

"I won't," Aimee whispered, her eyes wide with fear. She had little doubt Lundy meant what he said. She'd cooperate for now, and when he relaxed his guard, perhaps then she'd have a chance to get away from him. No such opportunity presented itself on the walk to the stable, and once there, Caroline held the gun on her while Lundy saddled the horse. The gun wavered in Caroline's hands and she looked as if she were about to weep again.

"Caroline," Aimee whispered urgently, "help me. I'll tell them you helped me escape. I'll tell them you had nothing to do with the fire and taking the gold."

Caroline shook her head and tried to steady the gun

with both hands. "I can't help you," she said. "Lundy won't let me."

"Why are you involved with this man?" Aimee tried again. "Zack told me about your husband's business. He must have left you with a great deal of money."

"He lost it," Caroline said bitterly. "Zack turned the whole business over to him and in less than a year it was in ruins. Eli was a fool for any story that came along. He made some bad investments. He left me penniless. I almost think he did it on purpose. At the end, he hated me."

"Zack will help you," Aimee said, and was surprised at the shift of emotions on Caroline's face.

"Zack . . . Of course," she mused. "With you out of the way, he'll come back to me." Her eyes shifted to Lundy's back where he stood tightening the cinch. "I could have the gold and everything," Caroline whispered. The barrel of the gun swung around, and without blinking an eye, Caroline fired. Lundy grunted and half-turned, his face mirroring his surprise before he sank to the floor and lay still. One of the horses broke away and ran out into the street. Relief flooded through Aimee until she saw Caroline bring the gun up again and aim it at her.

"Caroline, you can't."

"Can't I? I'll tell them Lundy was trying to kidnap you. I overheard you talking and followed you down here to the stable, where I shot it out with him. In the confusion you were shot accidentally. I'll hide the gold. So sorry, Aimee." Her finger tightened on the trigger. The sound of a shot rang out, but Aimee felt no pain. Instead Caroline slumped against the stall. The gun dropped from her nerveless fingers and she slid to the floor. Lundy still lay on the floor, a small derringer clutched in his hand. He leveled the gun at Aimee and she drew back.

"Don't move," he ordered, and painfully got to his feet. The shoulder of his jacket was drenched in blood. He hobbled to Caroline's body and snatched the gun from her outstretched hand. Aimee sidled along the edge of the stall, but Lundy aimed the gun at her. "Get on the horse," he ordered. Aimee hesitated and he pulled back the hammer of his gun. "I can leave two dead women as well as one," he snarled. "The only reason to keep you alive is that you may be useful as a hostage." Aimee turned toward the horse and pulled herself into the saddle. Lundy slung his saddlebags, heavy with gold, over the rump of the horse and tied them in place, then mounted behind her.

"What's goin' on in here?" Luke, the stableboy, muttered sleepily. "I thought I heard a shot." Lundy brought his gun up and fired and the boy slumped against the stable door. Aimee screamed. Lundy kicked at his horse and they galloped out of the stable and down the street toward the foothills of the Sierra Nevada.

"It was Lundy," Luke gasped. "He had Miss Bennett with him. She looked awful scared. Aigh—" His words ended in a cry of pain as the doctor dug for the bullet embedded in his side.

"Was she all right?" Zack asked. The boy nodded, white-lipped.

The doctor poured some antiseptic in the hole and stood up. "You'll live," he grunted. "You were luckier than the woman." The men glanced at the blanket-covered figure lying in the straw. A muscle jumped in Zack's jaw. He began saddling a horse.

"You won't be able to track him in the dark," the doctor said. "Wait till morning and some of the men'll go with you."

"I'm leaving now," Zack answered. "They can catch up." He checked the barrel of his gun and stepped up into the saddle. "Tell them I've headed northeast." He rode out of the stable and down the street toward the foothills. It was the only way Lundy could have gone. Zack kicked his horse to a gallop.

They rode through the night. Lundy seemed to know the trail surprisingly well. By the time the sun rose over the mountain peaks, they had left the foothills behind and were picking their way along rocky ledges past dense canyons. The lush greenness of the valley had given way to the sturdy gnarled pines which stubbornly clung to the sparse soil. The morning air was sparkling. A bird trilled from a nearby tree. If not for her grim captor, Aimee might have found joy in the mountainous trail.

They rode with Lundy slumped against her back. At times Aimee thought he might have lost consciousness, but when she turned her head to peer over her shoulder, his eyes were open and fixed grimly on the trail. They were angling north, and once Aimee thought she heard someone shouting. They must be near a mine, she thought, and considered calling out, but Lundy's hold tightened on her, warning her to silence.

At midmorning they stopped beside a stream at the bottom of a waterfall. Lundy tied her wrists, then looped the rope around a tree. After washing himself in the cold water, he wet his bandanna and pressed it to his wound. His eyes constantly studied the terrain around them.

"Why don't you let me go?" Aimee reasoned. "You could ride faster with just you on the horse." He ignored her. "The horse can't last much longer with two people and that gold on the back."

Lundy's pale eyes came back to study her. "I may need you to barter for my freedom," he said, and his tone was so menacing that Aimee fell silent. He lay down on the rocky ledge and pillowed his head on his arm and soon feel asleep. Aimee lay waiting until his breathing was deep and even, then tore frantically at the knots that bound her wrists. No matter how she tugged and strained, she couldn't loosen them. By the time Lundy woke, she was exhausted and defeated. He untied her, grinning nastily when he saw the raw skin on her wrists, and motioned her onto the horse.

They climbed higher into the mountains and Aimee wondered where Lundy was going. On the other side of the mountains, just a five-day journey away, wa.

the great desert, and beyond that the Great Basin. She'd crossed those once. She had no desire to do so again. Late in the afternoon they halted again. Aimee was exhausted, thirsty, and hungry, but they had no food. Lundy sat nursing his shoulder, his gun cradled in his lap, at the ready in case she tried to escape. The heat made her drowsy, so she leaned her head back against a rock and closed her eyes. A horse snorted nearby. Lundy's mount whinnied and raised his head. Lundy jerked upright. They listened. All was silent, save for the wind blowing down the side of the mountain.

Cautiously Lundy got to his feet, his gaze darting around the rocks and scrubby trees. With his gun he motioned Aimee to the horse. She mounted and kicked the horse's sides, but Lundy held the reins. He lashed out at her with his gun. The barrel raked along her thigh, leaving behind a tearing pain. Quickly he climbed up behind her and set the horse to scrambling up the trail. They could hear the hoofbeats of another horse behind them. They climbed steadily, and all the time, the rider behind seemed to draw closer. He was not riding double as they were.

They came to a steep wall and Lundy jumped off the horse, pulling Aimee after him. "Go on, get up in those rocks," he ordered, while his fingers worked at loosening the saddlebags. Aimee did as he'd ordered, climbing swiftly in the hope of getting away from him, but he was right behind her. He was breathing heavily from the exertion of carrying the bags of gold slung across his shoulders. He was at her heels now, urging her on with harsh words. Aimee could hear the rattle of stones behind them.

"Lundy," a voice called out. It was Zack. Aimee's heart leapt with relief. He hadn't left her after all. "Leave the woman, Lundy," Zack called. "You can have the gold."

Lundy wasted no breath on an answer. They reached the top of the ledge now and Lundy grasped her arm tightly, pulling her after him across the ledge in a headlong run.

"Aigh!" Aimee screamed as they came to a sheer drop. Loose rock skittered over the edge to the river below. Frantically Lundy looked for a way off the ledge. There was none. He'd come to a dead end. Zack's head appeared at the far edge of the shelf and Lundy pulled out his gun and aimed. With a cry Aimee threw herself against him and the shot went wild. Before he could aim again, Zack was there, his long arms knocking aside the gun. It slid across the rocks and disappeared over the edge.

Lundy slashed at Zack with the heavy bags of gold, the momentum carrying him near the edge as Zack ducked. Zack was on him, his fists swinging against Lundy's jaw. The bags flew out of his hands and bounced across the rocks after the gun. Heart pounding in her throat, Aimee crawled across the rocks and reached for the bags teetering on the edge. The slightest brush would send them careening down that long drop to the river. Her fingers closed around the leather pouches and she struggled to pull them back up the rocks to safety. They were too heavy. Aimee teetered there on the edge.

Zack and Lundy struggled above her. Zack's blows had left Lundy's face battered. In spite of his shoulder, the wounded man would not give up. Zack landed a blow that sent Lundy sprawling against some boulders. He picked up a rock and swung it at Zack's head. Another blow sent Lundy sprawling on his back on the ledge.

"That's enough, Lundy," Zack gasped. "It's all over." Lundy lay gasping in air and slowly nodded. Zack turned back to Aimee, crouched near the edge his glance going over her face and shoulders.

"Are you all right?" he gasped. Aimee nodded and he bent to help her to her feet. A shadow loomed above them.

"Zack, look out," Aimee screamed as Lundy charged at him. The two men rolled over and over, each time moving closer to the edge. Lundy bore him back toward the drop. Zack's head and shoulders hung over the edge. Lundy strained forward, slowly forcing him over. Zack twisted and Lundy lunged forward into empty air, his grip on Zack's shirt pulling them both over the edge. Lundy's scream was high-pitched and long, fading into nothingness as he made the long drop to the river.

"Zack," Aimee screamed, and the sound echoed from the mountain walls.

"Aimee," he gasped, and she dug her toes into a rocky crevice and strained forward. Zack dangled from the ledge, his hands gripping the stunted, wiry trunk of a small tree. His toes scraped against the rocky wall, seeking a toehold where there was none. "Aimee, give me a hand," he called, and she reached for him. The bags of gold hung like a deadweight in her other hand, pulling her away from him.

"Hold on, Zack," she cried, stretching out her arm until her muscles ached. Zack reached for her, but couldn't touch.

"Let go of the gold," he shouted. Numbly she shook her head, once more straining to touch him. The tough roots of the little tree loosened their hold on the mountainside and Zack swung out over the precipice. "Aimee, drop the bags. Give me a hand." His dark eyes met hers and she read fear in them, the fear that she would let him fall to his death in order to save the gold. Aimee relaxed her hold on the bags and they slid away from her down the slope, arcing out into space. She heard the distant sound of a splash as the gold fell back into the river that had given it up.

A weight had lifted off her shoulders. She lunged across the slope, her hands touching Zack's. She could feel his strong fingers gripping hers and she dug in her toes, feeling the weight of him pulling against her arms as he worked his way up the slope and back on the edge.

"Zack," she cried, throwing herself into his arms. He gathered her close, holding her tightly against his pounding heart. Aimee sobbed against his chest, her hands skimming over his shoulders and arms as if to assure herself that he was safe.

"It's all right," he murmured, patting her back. "We'll get some more gold for you, Aimee."

She stopped crying and sat up, staring into his eyes. Her gray eyes were bright with tears and something else. "I don't care about the gold," she said.

"Then why are you crying?" Zack asked.

"Because I'm so happy. Because you came in time. Because I was so scared. Because the gold is gone and for the first time in a long time I don't care."

"Aimee," Zack said tenderly, his hand going to wipe away the tears on her cheeks. "I love you."

"I love you, Zack," she whispered, and he saw there were no reserves now. Gently he pulled her into his arms and she came willingly.

They made their way down the mountain slowly, each savoring the nearness of the other. How close they'd come to losing each other again. There wouldn't be another time. They'd see to that. Halfway down the mountain, Zack told her about Caroline.

"I'm sorry," Aimee said, and decided she wouldn't tell him about Caroline's part in all of it, not yet anyway.

"I am too," Zack sighed. "She wasn't a happy woman and she didn't make the people around her happy. Poor Eli. It must have been hell being married to her." He looked at Aimee, and grabbing the reins, drew her horse to a stop. "Do you suppose we could do a better job of it?" he asked.

"I'm sure we could," Aimee said.

"Will you marry me?" he asked, and she nodded. "As soon as we get back?" Again she nodded.

"I'm still wearing my wedding gown," she said, looking down at the grimy, tattered dress Caroline had given her.

"Aimee, I'll stay in Sacramento with you from now on. I'll hire a man to captain my ship. We'll build a new Golden Promise. I'll help you."